THE

SAINTED

TRILOGY

Revelations

BOOK TWO

by

MICHAEL MEDICO

© 2016 Harbour Point Publishing
Harbour Point Publishing, LLC
Northport, New York 1168
thesaintedtrilogy@gmail.net
www.thesaintedtrilogy.net

Printed in the United States by Harbour Point Publishers, Northport, NY

The Sainted Trilogy, Harbour Point Publishers.

Library of Congress Cataloging-in-Publication Data
Revelations, Book Two of The Sainted Trilogy
(Formerly titled The Sainted)
Medico, Michael p. cm.

Fiction—General 2. Fiction—Thriller 3. Fiction—Horror Fiction, I. Title.

Paperback ISBN: 978-1-0879-9390-4
Ebook ISBN: 978-1-0879-9395-9

Second Edition Printing

DEDICATION

To the men and women who selflessly serve
In the name of God the Father,
Of The Son and
Of The Holy Spirit.

"All the darkness in the world
cannot extinguish the light of a single candle."
—St. Francis

His face was like the sun shining in all its brilliance
When I saw Him, I fell at His feet as though dead
Then He placed his right hand on me and said,
"Do not be afraid"
I am the first and the last. I am the living one; I was dead,
and behold I am alive for ever and ever!
And I hold the keys of death and Hades.
—Revelation 1:12-18

"So that the saints may enjoy their
Beatitude and the grace of God more abundantly
They are permitted to see the punishment of
The damned in hell."
—St. Thomas Aquinas

PREFACE

His screams shake the very foundations of hell itself.

    Even the torture and torments of the souls of the damned cannot quell the rage and hatred he feels. He should be exalted above all, but he has been condemned and it shall be this way for eternity. He tries to take comfort in the knowledge that God holds no power in his domain, but he has to concede that it is God whose judgment imprisons him here.

It is happening to him now…when the fury becomes uncontrollable his entire figure grows and grows in magnitude. He is now the size of what the pitiful minions call a mountain. He looks down in anger and smashes his limbs into the swarm of evil spirits and the condemned souls cowering below. The hoards scream in terror begging for mercy but he is merciless…you would think they would know this by now.

He now screams again, "I AM LUCIFER! I AM ETERNAL!"

God has condemned him to this fate. "He sent Michael to vanquish me. Michael, my brother angel, how could this be?" God has condemned a full third of the heavenly host of angels to the lake of fire for eternity. The demon recalls how he could not understand what has happened, after all, is he not like God Himself? He remembers that he would not beg for forgiveness, after all, there is nothing to forgive. It was long ago, in the beginning of times and he vows that he would seek vengeance. He would make it his eternal mission to destroy the souls of the pitiful creatures that God has placed on earth. Lucifer's sneers become full faced and clear as he thinks of how easy it is to take advantage of the free will God has given these creatures. He knows what temptations best suit men; pride, envy, lust, depravity, heresy, hatred and so much more. There are many weapons in his arsenal and Lucifer will use them all.

He knows the minds and hearts of men are weak and many can easily be led to temptation. These temptations lead to transgressions and those transgressions lead to corruption and it is corruption that leads to a sinful existence and the fall from grace. Many have found this out too late and all the damned in the hellish realm he rules, are a testament to the weakness of men and the fate of their souls.

He would have his revenge against God, revenge against His Son and revenge against the cursed Sainted, especially his brother Michael. Yes, he would have his revenge. His rage continues to grow as he thinks of the encounter with the man and woman in the pit. He thinks to himself, how could he have not seen how powerfully they protect Christopher? How could he not have seen the power of the cursed Sainted, and how their meddlesome interference would deny him the one soul he now vows to possess? How could he have not seen the strength of the forces of good? He has failed to be victorious in his battle against God, His Son, the Heavenly Host and the Sainted, but there must be a way to see that victory could be his…but how?

The demon Lucifer continues to ponder these questions, but he is so enraged that it blinds him to any answers he may find. He hates that God has condemned him to this fate, he hates humanity and now he must wreak havoc on the earth so the souls of so many pitifully weak humans will be his. It is the only way to overcome the goodness of God and redress this greatest of injustices done to him.

This is his dream, his one overwhelming desire, but how will it be made manifest? It is then that a thought comes to him and it is the first time in a long time the Lucifer smiles. God may have the Sainted, but he has something far more powerful.

From the burning lakes of fire and the molten pits that surround Satan hellish realm they come…he merely thinks it and they assemble. He commands the princes of hell, the first hierarchy of demons to appear before him, and they always do exactly what he commands. Satan looks over the unholy Seraphim *at his feet and he begins to feel better. He has been cheated of his rightful place in time without end. A cruel twist of fate has forced him to make many errors and miscalculations, but that is in the past and that will change. Now the way is clear, now all his longings, all the desires he could only have hoped for will become manifest. These dark angels will assure that redemption will be his, that the forces that align against him will fail, and ultimately the souls of men will, at long last, suffer at his hand.*

One by one the hellish demon masters assemble in front of him, loyal soldiers before their leader waiting to follow his command. Lucifer gazes at the devilish legion that stands at hand and as he looks at each one, it gives him pause to delight.

First there is the ever-constant Beelzebub who, with him, was among the first three angels to fall from grace. Beelzebub is able to tempt men with pride and that would be a great asset in the battle to come. Pride, Lucifer knows the sin of pride, but it is not the time to dwell on this, he will have his revenge and his so-called sin of pride will become his redemption, his victory over God Himself!

Standing next to Beelzebub there is Leviathan, an unholy prince of the Seraphim as well, who can tempt even the strongest souls into heresy. His special skills will be needed for the confrontation with the bastard faithful. For the first time those dedicated to the Son of Man will know doubt, know fear and they will know the true power of evil. Men and women will suddenly realize they are doomed and they will turn their backs on Heaven and curse their beliefs. They will come to this realization as they kneel to worship the supreme master of Hell itself, albeit too late. As these pitiful creatures confront the inevitable, then Leviathan will be triumphant and this will help assure his ultimate victory.

Lucifer's gaze moves toward Asmodeus, the third prince, with his burning desire to tempt men into depravity. Ever devoted Asmodeus; he would have prevailed in the battle of the pit if it were not for that bitch, Agnes. Satan assures Asmodeus that he will have his chance at retribution for the humiliation he has endured. The dragon Asmodeus sits upon breathes flames as all three heads on the demon Asmodeus roar in anticipation and bow in appreciation.

This time it will be different, this time victory will be his and it will be Lucifer they will fear.

Standing behind the first three is Pesado, the keeper of chaos. It will be Pesado that shows humans the true meaning of fear. This will occur as all goodness and honor are corrupted. It will come to pass when every one of these creatures abandons all loyalties in the vain attempt to protect themselves. Following behind Pesado is Berith, a prince of the Cherubim, who tempts men to commit homicide. Murder has always held a special place in the hearts of men and Berith will have a special role given the chaos that is to follow.

To the left of Berith there is Astaroth, the prince of Thrones, who tempts men to be lazy. Lucifer's smile becomes wider as he thinks that Astaroth has the easiest of tasks. When vigilance withers, laziness becomes the powerful force that takes over the mindset of men and women. Lucifer has great understanding of laziness and he knows it is the easiest way to lead humanity to sinfulness.

Next to Astaroth stands Verrine, another of the prince of Thrones, whose special skill tempts men to impatience. Lucifer knows that impatience can lead to so much more. Lucifer's smile continues to grow as he stares and sees Gressil, the third prince of Thrones. Gressil, who tempts men with impurity, has already captured so many of the souls that now litter the very foundation of hell itself.

Finally, there is the ever-dependable Sonneillon, the fourth prince of Thrones. He tempts men to hate and he is a particular favorite of Lucifer. He recalls how Beelzebub and Sonneillon inspired the temptation of Judas Iscariot to betray the cursed Son of God and seal His fate on the cross. Even now the screams and torment of Judas ring in terror as his punishment is mete out in each and every measure of time immemorial.

How many souls have Sonneillon and the others sent to him? There are too many to count, especially in the last 100 years! Lucifer and Sonneillon take special pleasure in tormenting and afflicting horrendous pain and suffering on the most-vile of men including the likes of Stalin, Mao, Pol Pot and new arrivals like Osama bin Laden. The demons take special delight and their enjoyment is boundless, especially when inflicting the cruelest of punishments for the likes of mass killers such as Hitler. Lucifer and his demons look forward, with relish, to the torture they are inflicting on Hitler and so many more souls that are damned for eternity.

Lucifer yells "Sieg Heil!", and he bursts into laughter.

Nine in all! These are his princes, his weapons to strike at mankind and reap revenge on the self-righteous bastard Sainted of holiness. He is ready to reveal his plan, but he needs to have his first hierarchy prepare for the inevitable battle and with that he speaks,

"It is time. The forces of heaven must not prevail, and it is through you they will fail and the souls of mankind will be doomed and they will be mine. Go and assemble the 66 rulers and the 666 legions of 6,666 demons each and let them be ready to receive my command."

The dark angels look up at Lucifer and as he looks upon their hideousness, he knows they are ready. If the battle is to be won these demons and their hoards are all that he will need. The epic confrontation between good and evil is inevitable. Dark versus light, hell versus heaven and the ultimately victory of evil over good is the plan he devises, and it will be the path to his glorious victory. These devils, demons of the first order would, at last, overwhelm the forces of heaven and then there will be nothing to stop the horror that mankind will confront.

This would be his reward, his dream come true and the reason he exists. Lucifer, once ensconced over the souls of the damned, would derive such immense pleasure from the anguish and horror he would inflict that he will finally know true pleasure for the first time in his eternal rule.

From the time he had been cast into the lake of fire, Satan has tried many times to incite God and His faithful to conflict, but it has never come to pass. He knows his strength and that of the demon hoard. He knows his plan is perfect, but he also knows it will not be easy. The heavenly host has powers too, and they will not be readily brought to battle.

The plan is all-encompassing, but there will need to be a catalyst for the impending conflict. The means to an end and it will all begin with a messenger, a conduit, and he will prepare the way. It will all start with the greatest of blasphemies, and end with the victory of Hell itself. Satan would then have his revenge and this time the Sainted and their visions will not be able to save Christopher Pella and all of humanity.

CHAPTER 1

"Isn't it nice being here, just the two of us?"

It is more a statement than a question, but the answer is the same. "E 'meraviglioso" I reply.

Beth smiles and kisses me.

It is a cold and blustery winter's night as we sit by the fireplace in the living room of Beth's home. We each have a glass of wine and sip it as we gaze into the flames. This time the heat from both the fire and the wine warms our bodies and our spirits and the comfort we take in each other's arms is better than either of us could hope for. My relationship with Beth, and our feelings for each other, has grown beyond anything I could hope for or imagine.

I often think of St. Valentine and the vision I was fortunate enough to experience. In my vision I remember the note, the relic that he gave me. It read "Ex tua Valentine", "From your Valentine" with his guidance to give it to anyone I choose to love unconditionally and, with that, he smiled at me and disappeared into the light. I believe St. Valentine knew I would give it to Beth because he knew that in my heart, she is my true love.

Beth and I are closer than ever and our love for each other seems to get stronger each and every day. The Christmas and New Year holidays are here and we're excited to celebrate with each other along with family and friends, for now though, on Christmas Eve, we are able to spend some time together, alone. The horror of the events we lived through just a few months ago seem to fade from memory, more for Beth then me. However, even I am able to relax a bit more as time passes.

My visions of The Sainted continue to come and the latest one came to me the evening I sat with Beth in her home the day before Christmas. Beth and all the surroundings freeze in time and as in the past; I am transported to the special place that The Sainted want me to go. This time I find myself in Myra, a city on the southern Mediterranean seacoast in the 4th Century AD. I am standing outside a miserably small hovel. Inside there is a man sitting on one of the few sticks of furniture that is there.

The poor man sits in the corner of the dark, tiny two room hut he calls home. The man is distraught and weeps for his children as he sits by the fire burning in the small hearth. The poor man cherishes his daughters and they are of an age where each should be married and have families of their own. But he is too poor to afford the ample dowries that provide support to the type of men who will take care of his daughters and be good husbands and fathers to their children.

He quietly cries saying to himself, "My children, my loves, what am I to do?"

Through his tears he imagines his daughters, his beautiful girls, sold into servitude, just to stay alive all because they have no dowries. The poor man knows that without dowries the situation is hopeless. His despair is so overwhelming that he collapses in a heap on the dirt floor of the hut while his daughters are asleep in the next room. Eventually, though his grief is all consuming, the man falls asleep on the cold dirt floor.

The night is cold and calm as a figure approaches in the dark. He is cloaked in the garb of a priest, but not just any priest; this man appears to be an important figure dressed in the cloak of a bishop. In the moonlight it can be seen as the face and figure of a man. He is large and rotund with a wonderfully long white beard. The man reaches the window and looks in. He sees the father of the girls lying on the floor and knows of the poor man's agony. In the next few moments, he does something truly extraordinary as he reaches into the pocket of his cloak.

The bishop takes out three bags filled with gold coins and tosses them through the window. The bags seem to float in the air as they hover over the mantle of the fireplace where there are three pairs of his daughters' stockings that had been washed and hung by the fire to dry.

In the next moment each of the bags of coins drops into each of young girl's stockings. The father, now fast asleep, remains unaware but when he wakens, he will become conscious of this gift and for him, this miracle.

I see the bishop smile and even hear a little chuckle as he steps out of his body and stands by my side.

"I do so very much enjoy this. Sometimes I even feel guilty at the pleasure I get but I know it is God's will and I know He will forgive me this slightly impious delight." With that St. Nicholas begins to laugh out loud.

I smile at his funny ways and say, "So the legends are true. You do visit homes in the still of the night and bring gifts to good little girls and boys and even good little adults."

He smiles at me, "Well when I was alive, I did not have the means or a way to give the people all they wanted or even all they needed, but the Lord did call on me to help provide for the poor and sick and, as I was able, I helped when I could. It is for all a blessing from God to His people."

I am enjoying this encounter immensely. To meet this legendary saint and historical figure is a genuine treat for me and I ask him, "St. Nicholas, can I call you St. Nick?"

He thinks for a moment, "You are the very first to call me that to my face" but he smiles and says, "Of course you can."

"St Nick, I suppose that you know what they've done to you and your legend. You're now referred to as Santa Claus and you come every Christmas and make sure the economies of the world survive until next Christmas." It is my attempt at explaining an often-repeated observation on the commercialization of Christmas.

This time St. Nicholas laughs out loud. He laughs so hard that tears appear in his eyes. One thing you can believe is that St. Nick's laugh sounds nothing like a "Ho, Ho, Ho!"

He pats me on the shoulder and says, "Glad to help. Actually, I do get embarrassed a bit by all this fuss. Those silly elves in funny costumes and all those tales of flying reindeers and so many of the gifts that have little meaning beyond the day they are given. It is distressing to me that it takes something away from the holy season of Christ's birth. But still, I know there are many who celebrate the day in His name and the prayers of the faithful continue to sustain me and all The Sainted."

I understand what St. Nick is talking about, but I want to know something of the poor man so I ask him, "What happened to the man and his daughters back at the hut, the one you gave all that gold to?"

St. Nicholas looks back at the small shelter and tells me, "His daughters will be wed. I will preside over their marriages and they and their families will live with the dwell with the Holy Spirit and the blessings of God the Father and His Son."

I smile back at St. Nick "That is so much more than anything they could ever hope for."

Then this wonderful saint, a man who did so much in his lifetime asks me a question that I am not expecting. "Well Christopher, now that we are together, what is your wish? What can St. Nick give you?"

His kindness and genuine affection for me is apparent and the answer comes easy to me. "Are you kidding? I have everything that I could ever want. I am blessed to know you and so many of the Sainted; I have Beth and Uncle Al and all my family and friends, all those special people in my life that love me. What more can any man want?"

St. Nick looks questioningly at me and says, "Well if not for you, then who?"

For a brief moment I think about how I would answer his question and I say, "Well there is my girlfriend; actually, she is so much more. She is all I have ever wanted; I guess you can call her my true love and, if there is anyone that I would want you to give a gift to it's her. God has blessed her and her family and she has so much already so I think it would have to be something special, not in terms of money, just special. Am I making sense?"

St. Nick smiles at me, "Yes you are." As he considers my request he reaches into his cloak and pulls out a necklace. It is a beautiful gold necklace and hanging from the chain is a round pendant set with an early 4th century Roman gold solidus, probably the same kind of coin that he gave the poor man's daughters. He holds up the necklace and seems to examine it before he hands it to me.

I am astonished as I stare at the necklace and when I look back up at him, I say, "It is so beautiful. This is far too precious for me to give, St. Nick. I can't accept this."

"Christopher, when someone gives you a gift it is because they want to. This gift of gold is but trash without the love and devotion of someone and that of the person they give it to. When she holds this necklace in her hands, she will know that you are her true love. So, take this gift and give it to the one you love, it is only then that it becomes precious."

I stare at the beautiful gold necklace as I look back at St. Nicholas. I am dumbfounded, but all I can say to him is "Thank you so very much."

He smiles as he says "You're welcome" and with that he waves to me and the form of St. Nicholas becomes transparent. He walks into the familiar bright lights of heaven and as he does, the sainted vision disappears.

I return to the present as if nothing happened and I find myself back at Beth's side, on the couch, with her in my arms. She looks up at me with her beautiful hazel brown eyes and says, "Chris, I need to tell you something."

"What?"

"I love you."

I smile back and say, "I love you too."

Now Beth jumps up from her seat on the couch and hurriedly rattles off, "Well if you love me you have to accept one of my family's long standing Christmas traditions."

I start to laugh and say, "Oh yeah, well what is one of your family's long standing Christmas traditions?"

"We get to open *one* present on Christmas Eve, *before* we go to Midnight Mass. What do you say?"

I'd left all the presents that I bought Beth for Christmas at home because I didn't plan to give them to her until Christmas day. Then I thought St. Nick probably knew all the time what Beth was going to say so I tell her, "That works for me."

Beth jumps off the couch and runs to her wonderfully decorated Christmas tree. The tree is 9 feet tall, but it easily fits into her living room because of the vaulted ceiling. The Fraser Fir tree is perfectly shaped and decorated with gold colored garland, long strings of sparkling lights, multi-colored blown glass Christmas ornaments and handmade decorations of past Christmas' that she and her siblings made as children. Beth reaches underneath the tree and picks up a beautifully wrapped present and rushes to bring it over to me. She places it on my lap and as she does Beth eagerly exclaims,

"Your turn, you open your gift first!"

I smile at her "OK!" and I rapidly tear off the special wrapping and bows and rip open the box that contains my gift. When I do, I can't believe my eyes. With my mouth wide open, I stare up at Beth, but all I could say is,

"It's St. Nicholas. How...?"

"Yeah, it is! I got it from an antique dealer who runs a shop in Huntington Village. He said that it came from a monastery somewhere near Turkey that was originally a place called Myra. Anyway, the statue is over one thousand years old!"

I sit there nearly speechless and stammer, "I, Beth, I uh, I can't believe you got this for me."

"I know! I'm the best thing that ever happened to you and you better not forget it. In any case, I went into the shop thinking the antique dealer is going to show me one of his treasures and then try to rip me off, but something very strange happened when I came in. He just looks at me and tells me to wait there while he walks into the storage room in the back. When he comes out, he has this statue of St. Nicholas in his arms and he smiles and hands it over to me. As I hold it in my hands, he tells me that he's had this statue of St. Nicholas for many years. The statue was in his inventory since his dad opened the shop more than 60 years ago, imagine that!" Beth's face is glowing, she is always beautiful, but I never saw her more beautiful than when she gives me this gift.

She becomes even more animated as she continues telling me her story, "I look at it and I'm no expert, but even I know that these antique statues are very expensive and I am waiting for him to give me sticker shock. I told him it is a present for you and I ask him how much it is and here's the weird part."

I am now getting very curious, "What did he say?"

"Well, he tells me that this statue is only meant to be possessed by a certain person. No one else can understand this work of art other than that one person it is destined for."

I am amazed, "He really said that?"

"Yes, he did and he told me that I am meant to have this statue of St. Nicholas to give to you. You know what else is weird and wonderful about this Chris?"

"You mean other than this whole experience? No, what's weird and wonderful?"

"The weirdest part of all is that when he hands me the statue, he tells me it's mine for free. Can you believe it, free! When I tell him I want to pay, the antique dealer says he wouldn't accept any money and refuses to take it when I offer it to him. He told me that if I wanted to, I could make a donation for the Christmas collection at our church and that's what I'll do, but he wouldn't take a dime from me. The dealer, his name is Jeffrey, seemed very happy that I came in and that he could give the statue of St. Nicholas to me and that I could give it to you. The minute I saw this statue of St. Nicholas I fell in love with it because I knew it was meant for you, that's the wonderful part!"

I am staring at the statue of St. Nick and looking back at Beth, I tell her, "Beth, you will never know how much this statue of St. Nicholas means to me and how much I love it and how much I love you."

Beth smiles and kisses me, but then she jumps up on the couch, sitting on her legs and says, "I got you some other stuff, but it's just a sweater, shirts and sox. Okay buster, now where's mine."

I start doing my traditional Christmas mumbling and muttering when I can't think of what to say. "Well, Beth, I 'um…now here's the thing…I uh…I didn't…"

"Oh, you probably didn't bring a gift. I know that it's a silly tradition to open a gift on Christmas Eve. Don't worry, I can wait until tomorrow." She says this, but I know she is disappointed.

"No, I actually did bring you a gift, but it is something I got at the last minute and I didn't have a chance to wrap it for you." Immediately Beth's eye light up with excitement and anticipation. I keep thinking that Christmas' must have been something at her house when she was growing up.

"Oh Chris, please let me see it! I don't care if it's unwrapped. It's from you and that's all that matters." I must seem reluctant because I see an immediate change in her. She slowly crawls over to me on the couch and she looks straight through me, into my heart, with those sexy dark hazel brown eyes. Beth puts her arms around my shoulders and I feel her hot breath as she starts to kiss my neck and cheek. She then whispers in my ear, "Come on big boy and give me what I want."

So, what's a man to do? "Listen Beth, I hope you like my present, it is kind of a last-minute thing, but I need to give it to you because you are the most special person in my life and I love you." I continue to mumble as I reach into my pocket and my hand closes around the necklace. I take out my hand holding the necklace and as I do the pendant falls and dangles from the chain that's looped around my fingers. At first Beth looks like she doesn't understand what I'm holding, but then she looks up at me and there are tears in her eyes.

Now I'm getting upset and I want to know, "Why are you crying Beth? Don't you like the necklace? Please don't get upset, I can get you something else."

Beth reaches for the necklace and she can't seem to stop staring at it. "NO, NO…I, I love it. It's the most beautiful necklace I've ever seen."

"Then why are you crying?"

"I don't know? It's…it's…just that there is something so special about this necklace and this coin. I don't know why I'm crying, but it just seems like the right thing to do."

She looks up at me and all I can see is how much she loves me. I reach for Beth and hold her in my arms. She hugs me tightly and looks up into my eyes.

"Chris, thank you so much I have never had such a wonderful gift in my life and I love you for giving it to me."

I smile and tell her, "You are my life."

CHAPTER 2

Well, the holidays were great, but now they are over and it's back to work. I have my usual daily routine; I get up to shower, shave and make myself breakfast. I particularly enjoy making breakfast because if I have the time I like to experiment.

This morning I rummage through the refrigerator to find whatever leftovers I have to see if they can combine to make an interesting and hopefully tasty frittata or omelet. I take out some plastic containers that I had in the back of the refrigerator. I open them to smell the food inside to see if they are still good and some containers seem fine and others appear to be lab experiments that have gone horribly wrong. As I look through the containers, I realize that I need to clean out my refrigerator more often.

When I identify the containers that look most interesting, I say to myself, "Hmmmm, how about a leftover Moo Shu Pork, sautéed eggplant and salsa omelet with a two-day old brioche." I'll zap the brioche in the microwave but even I had to nix the salsa idea, so I substitute low fat Asiago cheese for the salsa and make the omelet anyway.

I prepare the omelet with my customary panache and only wish that Beth was here to witness this culinary marvel in the making. Next, I zap a two-day old brioche, make some coffee and in about 15 minutes I'm sitting down to a meal that looks and smells pretty good and something I am anxious to taste. After the first bite I have to acknowledge that this combination might be best served to someone with more exotic taste buds; someone who can fully appreciate my culinary feat and marvel at my imaginative use of ingredients. In the end though, I think my distinctive breakfast is fine and I eat it all.

The January day is cold and even though the ride to my shop is only ten minutes, I need to fortify myself for the journey. An extra layer of clothing is the order of the day so I bundle up and head for the car. I drive down the familiar streets of Huntington past boutiques, medical offices, fitness clubs, auto repair stations and restaurants and I arrive at my shop a few minutes later.

As I sit down at my desk behind the counter, I am happily aware that I have to be thankful that all is going well at my little business, St. Aloysius Gonzaga Coins and Currency. I had a great Christmas season as a number of people in town came in to buy gifts for their loved ones. I am especially happy to see that a number of parents came in to buy coins, starter collecting kits, albums and other items for their children that are just beginning to get into the hobby.

The online part of my business is also doing very well. I do some online advertising and social media during the holidays and that's generated over 2,000 unique visits a day with the conversions of visitors to sales growing nicely. I'm now looking to expand what I do online to a full-service coin collector site with greatly expanded information, detailed photos of all that I offer and a forum where collectors can talk to each other about their collections, ask questions and help each other enjoy their leisure pursuit. I'm even starting to write a blog. Anyway, I'm excited about things and always grateful to the Lord for my good fortune.

While I'm sitting at my desk, I lift my head up to look out the window. I see that it is beginning to snow and every time it snows, I think of what my Aunt Trixie used to day when I was a kid. It is something she called the "Snow Rule" and I think about the first time I heard her tell me and my cousins.

It was at the time when I was a little and growing up in the Bronx. My mother invited company to our house so we could celebrate my dad's birthday. We always invite our entire family and some close friends to the feast and the whole house smells wonderful with the aromas of the special meal my mother has prepared. She makes her special antipasto with roasted peppers, tomatoes, Italian cheeses, olives, cured meats and so much more. Mom also prepares my dad's favorite pasta course; lasagna, plus a leg of lamb for the second course. All my relatives acknowledge that my mom is a great cook and they are looking forward to the meal and the company of family and friends.

My cousins and I are forced to take a break from making loud noises and annoying all the adults and we are admonished to go the next room and be quiet or play something that doesn't involve screaming. In order to comply with the edict from our parents we begin telling stupid knock-knock jokes sitting on the floor by the front window. We sit there laughing until we notice that it's snowing, you know the kind of snowflakes that are big and heavy. Well, all of us kids get very excited and we start screaming and jumping up and down at the prospect of not having to go to school the next day.

Enthusiastically we begin listing all the fabulous things we would do; build snowman and snow forts, start a snowball fight, go sledding down dead man's hill…the joys of winter seem endless as we imagine all the pleasures of a day full of fun and free of school!

Now, Aunt Trixie hears all this commotion and she comes over to find out why we are making such a racket. "What's going on guys?" she questions us secretly knowing what we are so excited about.

I pipe up "Look at the size of those snowflakes! We're gonna have ten feet of snow tomorrow. No school, no teachers!" My cousins wholeheartedly concur with my weather forecast and we just sit there with shit eating grins on our adorable little faces.

Aunt Trixie looks at us with that look adults get when they know something we don't know and she says "I wouldn't be too sure about that."

My cousins and I immediately become quiet and we look up at her. My cousin John is the first to ask, "What do you mean?"

"Well, I grew up in upstate New York and I have seen a lot of snowfalls since I was a little girl and there is one thing I've seen happen, over and over again, I call it my snow rule."

All the kids start to get worried and it is my cousin Margaret who asks, "What do you mean, Aunt Trixie? What's the snow rule?"

"Well, here's the rule, are you listening?"

"Yes?" we all say at once.

Aunt Trixie looks around to make sure that she has our undivided attention and says, "Big snowflakes, little snowfall, little snowflakes, big snowfall. Got it?"

"Huh?" we answer in unison.

"That's right, "Big snowflakes, little snowfall, little snowflakes, big snowfall. So don't get your hopes up."

We are silent as we look at each other, half of us turning pale at the thought of school not being cancelled and the other half wanting to lock Aunt Trixie in the hallway closet at the prospect of her being right.

"I am sorry for having to tell you this; I really didn't like it much when I was a little girl either, but I don't think that you should count on getting the day off." My aunt looks at each of us, feeling slightly remorseful that she has to pass on such sad news to us children. I'm sure she felt a tinge of regret knowing we needed to confront the inevitable, but she looks lovingly down at us and walks back to the adult table for dessert.

From that moment on knock-knock jokes didn't seem so funny.

These memories of my childhood and family come in waves and always make me feel better no matter what mood I am in. As I prepare to return to do the work that has piled up over the holidays, the world once again stands still, the shop fades from view and a vision comes to life.

The fields near the shore of the lake are in close proximity to Silena. The fields are littered with the bodies of men. Armies sent to battle the monster have been slain, slaughtered would be more accurate, in the most hideous of ways. The villagers try to quell the savagery, but it seems that the beast knows the people are powerless against its wicked and evil ways. Each day two sheep are sacrificed to the dragon, but soon all the sheep have been butchered.

Fearful for their lives, pagans from all the surrounding towns assemble to confront the reality of what they must do. They have little choice; they must continue to sacrifice or forfeit their lives. If armies cannot kill the beast how could poor farmers, shepherds and shopkeepers hope to survive. It has been decided by the villagers that young maidens are to be sacrificed; as substitute for sheep in desperate hope that this would appease the monstrous creature…at least for a while.

The men and women gather for a ghastly ritual where lots are to be drawn. While all this is taking place no one seems to notice the man, a soldier, who sits astride a white stallion as he gazes over the lake. The soldier is clad in armor and he holds a lance and shield. The dragon appears to be asleep, but the rider knows better. It is twilight and the villagers come to the shoreline and walk until they are knee deep in the water. The first to be sacrificed is a young maiden, a princess actually, and she takes her place in the front of the multitude. Even from far away the soldier could see both abject fear and hopeless resignation on the face of the maiden. She is fully aware in knowing what is to become of her…she is to be eaten alive.

In silence, the people all watch and wait for the inevitable.

Slowly the dragon opens its eyes. Its monstrous form rises with great deliberation from a shallow part of the lake. The monster seems to delight in the terror of the people standing by the shore and it wants them to gape and cower at the majesty of its size. The monster's large green scales glitter from the water that clings to its form and many of those present begin to step back out of the lake in dread of the dragon.

The princess sees the monster and begins to scream, this to the delight of the dragon. Step by step the hideous beast comes closer and the princess stares in horror as she sees that the beast seems to be smiling. Now the last few of the people standing in the shallow waters slowly begin to move onto the shore for fear of their lives, leaving the maiden alone to face the terror before her.

The beast is taking its time approaching the sacrificial maiden as it takes delight in the terror it is creating. The soldier-rider slowly guides his steed down the slope toward the shore of the lake and nearer to the dragon. As all attention is focused on the horror taking place no one seems to notice the rider, not even the monster. Quietly he comes closer to the beast and once he comes very near the shore the rider lets out a battle cry and charges toward the dragon.

The villagers, the maiden princess, even the dragon stops and all turn in the direction of the soldier-rider. His horse races at full gallop and comes charging toward the scaly creature. The soldier is holding a long iron tipped spear and he has a sword at his side. It all happens so fast that there is no time for anyone to react as all present seem frozen in place.

Momentarily, the dragon appears stunned, surprised as any of the people that have gathered on the shore of the lake. But before the dragon has a chance to react, the soldier drives his spear directly into the flesh of the beast and through its heart. The dragon looks up at the rider and down at the wound and the monster falls dead in the waters of the lake.

I stand in the shadows, stunned and amazed by what I have witnessed and it is then that St. George steps out of his earthly body and comes towards me.

The Sainted asks, "I suppose you know of this beast, this evil abomination."

I answer, "I do."

"He can take many forms, but he is always Lucifer."

We both turn back to the vision of St. George who is speaking to the people of Silena and the surrounding towns.

"You are witness to the power of God to defeat the greatest of evils. All the armies of Rome could not defeat the beast, but it is only through faith, through his humble servant, that God Almighty is victorious over wickedness. God is eternal, He is all powerful and by placing your faith in Him, His Son and all the forces of Heaven, you will overcome fear and you will know true peace and the love God has for all His children."

St. George then continues to speak of all that he believes, all he knows and all that sustains him. The crowds of onlookers are mesmerized with the passion of his words. Once the soldier-rider finishes, all in the crowd sense the power of his words and his faith and they are immediately converted. Even the king of Silena is overwhelmed by what he has witnessed and he himself is converted. The king then gives St. George a large treasure, but the soldier knows the will of God. He immediately begins to give away the riches bestowed by the king, to all the people who assemble there. St. George then rides off back to Rome to join his legion.

I turn back to face the Sainted before me and ask him, "What does this mean? Why have you come and shown me this vision?"

"I am here to warn you that you must always be vigilant. There is no time ever that evil will rest from what it must do. Sometimes evil will appear in a form that will leave no doubt of its intent. Sometimes it will appear in a form that will beguile or it will try to endear itself. It is then that you must be even more vigilant for that is when you are at your weakest. Knowing this you will know the truth."

I stare at one of the bravest men I will ever know and as I do the vision of St. George fades from view and he disappears into the glow of his heavenly reward.

I've had visions like this before, visions that are a warning of events to come, but I have no idea of when or where they might happen. The Sainted are often cryptic in our encounters, but after so many visions I guess, I'd better get used to it.

CHAPTER 3

I gaze into nothingness as I try to understand this most recent vision and the words of St. George. I am alone in my thoughts when the phone rings, I pick up the receiver and say, "St. Aloysius Gonzaga Coins and Currency, can I help you?"

"Hi Chris, how are you doing?" It's my Uncle Al who tries to call me every day. He's Chief of Detective for the Suffolk County Police Department and kind of a surrogate father since my dad died.

"Oh hi, I'm good, just getting caught up on some of the work here at the shop. How are you?"

"I'm okay I guess, I just called to hear a friendly voice and to see how you're doing?"

He sounds a little strange so I ask, "Are you okay?"

"Sure, what are you up to?"

I tell him, "I'm looking outside the shop window at the snow coming down and reminiscing about Aunt Trixie."

"Oh, what about?"

"Guess…"

"Oh, yeah…big snowflakes, little snow falls yadda, yadda, yadda."

It has already stopped snowing when I say to Uncle Al, "Correct you are. Anyway, you've got to admit she has it right most of the time. How is she by the way?"

"Oh, she's doing fine; she and Gene are enjoying their retirement. They still travel a lot and with all the grandchildren they have, they keep pretty busy all the time."

"That's good, by the way how's it going with you and Eileen? Hey, I guess I get to call you Romeo now!" It was one day after work that my uncle, a life-long bachelor, had met Eileen Silverman, a widow and school-teacher, while examining the available inventory of supermarket rotisserie chickens. They appear to hit it off immediately and now, after a few dates they are a couple.

"Great, she really is a terrific person and we get along very well. I told you that I met her kids and they are very nice to me and a real source of pride to her. We're taking it slow for now, but I enjoy the time we're together very much." He tells me this over the phone, but I can almost see his face and I am sure he is smiling.

"That's fantastic. When you introduced me to her, I saw how much she likes you just by the way she looks at you. I also see how you can make her laugh at your stale, stupid jokes." I love to try and get him pissed off.

Uncle Al pretends to be insulted, "Stale? Stupid? I'll have you know that my jokes have withstood the test of time. I like to think of them as classics."

"Well, I've heard them a few thousand times and they don't get funnier with age." Thinking that I have kidded him too much I say, "Come on, just kidding big guy! I'm really happy you have someone in your life other than me. Now that I come to think of it, if I weren't around who would wake you up at 3AM and nearly get you killed by a dope peddling pimp. You are one lucky guy to have me as your nephew."

Uncle Al laughs and says, "Listen buddy boy, I am lucky to have you in my life except if you wake me up at 3AM again I'm gonna strangle you. Comprendere?"

"Si ho Comprendere."

There is a lull in the conversation. I thought that I had detected a bit of worry in Uncle Al's voice when he first called. We don't hide anything from each other so I ask him again,

"Hey, Unc, when we first spoke, I noticed you sounded sort of down. Are you okay?"

"My, my we are spending too much time together, aren't we?"

"Come on stop bullshitting and tell me what's wrong."

He sighs and says, "I don't know Chris, the burglars, murderers, perverts and other assorted scum seem to be taking their dirty deeds to the next level. Their crimes even exceed what is the traditional normal post-Christmas pandemonium. The criminals and their crimes are getting more and more violent and I just can't shake this feeling that something very bad is going to happen."

I know he is serious, but I try to make a joke, "Listen, these lowlifes took time off during the holidays so I guess they're playing catch up after enjoying a well-deserved rest. You should just do what comes natural to you…ridding the earth of these scumbags. When it's all over we both know that you'll be totally fulfilled continuing to happily arresting and convicting the increased numbers of garden variety of murderers, kidnappers and thieves more in keeping with the routine you are used to!"

Al laughs a little but says, "You are such a wise ass. I haven't been sleeping well lately so I guess I'm on edge a little."

It's my turn to be serious and I ask, "Uncle Al, now I'm worried about you, maybe you should see a doctor?

He sighs again, "Don't be concerned I'm fine…it's, well it's just that I can't seem to shake the feeling that something is going to happen, you know, something very bad. It's bigger than anything that I can even imagine. I can't put my finger on it and I have nothing to go on except a cop's intuition."

My radar goes up when Uncle Al says this because his intuition is usually spot on so I ask, "Got any idea of what it might be?"

He sighs a third time, "No. I haven't a clue nor have I anything concrete to go on. Maybe it's just a case of an over-active imagination, who knows; anyway, I'm sure it'll pass, at least I hope it will."

Now I am really getting worried, "This is totally unlike you, you have no imagination and you usually are spot on when it comes to your intuition. You aren't thinking about the events on Pit Island, are you?"

The horror of that night and the fear and anxiety it creates could not be forgotten even if we try.

"No, no…nothing like that. God forbid nothing like that. Listen, I'm gonna try to cheer up and I don't want you to think about this anymore. Okay?"

I didn't want to add more sleepless nights so I say, "Okay, but promise you'll let me know if you need anything and let me know if something happens, I mean something bad happens."

"I will. Hey, I'm going to call Aiden today to see if he wants to have lunch on Friday. I'll pick someplace in town, want to come along?"

"Sure, sounds great."

Uncle Al speaks and this time he doesn't sigh, "Good, I'll call you and let you know when and where. Listen to me Chris, I know you are worried, but don't be, I'm sure it's just my over-active imagination. Anyway, I'll let you and you can let The Sainted know if I need any help."

"Well, I can't guarantee The Sainted will be available when you need them, but I can guarantee I'll be there."

I'm sure he is smiling as he says, "That's good enough for me. I love you."

"I love you too" and the phone connection goes silent.

CHAPTER 4

The bedroom of his home is warm even though a cold wind is blowing outside. He reaches out to touch the woman beside him. She is completely naked and lying there with her eyes closed, but he doubts she is asleep. They have just had sex and it was amazing. He thought that he had performed really well and took some kind of perverse pride in it all.

He had just met her this afternoon at, of all places, the bank. He was there to make a small deposit of $562.66. It's a surprise for him in that he just received a check from the IRS that indicated it was for an overpayment. He reaches for his mobile phone as he thought of calling his accountant with the good news. They would both have a laugh over this, but before he could dial, she walks up to him. She is beautiful, more beautiful than any woman he has ever seen. Her long blond hair seems to shine under the bank's harsh lights, but it doesn't matter because her hair glows.

She is looking directly at him. At first, he assumes she has mistaken him for someone else, actually he isn't all that attractive so it must be a mistake, but it wasn't. She walks right up to him and smiles. He is at a loss; he doesn't know what to say…what to do; but; that problem is solved.

"Hi, I saw you standing there and I wanted to meet you." Her smile is radiant.

"Hello, I'm Harold but call me…" she puts her finger over his lips before he has a chance to tell her that his nickname is Hal.

"Don't tell me your name, I don't want to know. Take me for a drink."

Now it's his turn to smile. "Sure. I know a place that's not too far from here. It's small and quiet where we can talk."

She touches his arm and laughs, "You really want to talk?"

They drive separately and arrive about 15 minutes later and it's early so the place is nearly empty. It's a rather ordinary place with dim lighting, wooden chairs and tables made to look shabby from too many spilled drinks and cigarette butts. There is a couple at one table and three men drinking at the bar when they walk in. The men turn and you can see them eyeing her and Hal put his hand around her waist so there is no mistaking that she's here with him.

The corner booth is empty so they sit down and wait to be served. The waitress comes over and even she is taken with his new friend's beauty. On some level Hal wonders why this woman would be with such an ordinary guy. He even believes the waitress is asking herself the same question.

"What will you have?"

"I'll have a champagne cocktail." Hal figures her for a martini girl, but who cares.

"I'll have bourbon on the rocks with a club chaser." He hopes that it will impress her by ordering a real man's drink.

While they sit back and wait for their drinks he asks, "Why don't you want to tell me your name?"

She answers, "Is it really that important?"

"I guess not, but it is kind of strange, you know meeting at the bank and not knowing each other. Now we are here having a drink. This kind of stuff never happens to me."

"Well, it's happening now." Her entire body oozes such a sensual aura that he finds himself getting aroused just talking to her.

The drinks come to their table and Hal raises his glass, "Well, what shall we drink to?"

She looks him straight in the eye and says, "Let's drink to you getting laid." She continues to stare right at him and raises her glass to take a sip.

Hal now has an erection so hard he can't stand up for fear of being embarrassed.

"What do you say we go to your place and have another drink…in private?"
Her voice and body have a hypnotic effect on Hal and all he can think of is
getting her into bed. "Sure" he answers. It's not even lunch time and his wife
is at work and his kids are still at school. They won't be home for at least 4 or
5 hours and he figures that's enough time to do what he wants to do.

"Before we go, I should let you know one thing." Hal figures he'd get it
out on the table. She touches his hand and smiles, "You're married, right? You
figure that I should know before we leave. I think that's very noble of you Hal,
but that's the reason I didn't want to know your name, I like the impersonal
touch." He smiles back at her, gulps down his drink and they leave. Hal gets
in his car and she follows him in hers. They park their cars about one block
away from his home because he figures that being careful is a good idea against
his nosy neighbors.

He walks ahead and goes to the rear entrance to his house. Hal decides that
she will follow and knock on the front door and all seems to be going according
to plan. As she enters the foyer of Hal's home she looks around. The house is
exactly what she thinks Hal's home would look like. An expanded Cape Cod
style with brick veneer and landscaping that doesn't quite work. The home is
decorated in a combination of furniture he and his wife bought when they first
got married and some that was passed down from relatives. The accessories are
a combination of cheap lamps, mismatched porcelain figurines, crystal bowls,
and wall hangings that were bought on sale or given as gifts to him and his
wife over the years. As part of the décor there are family photos of his twin
daughters and some other close family members scattered about.

She looks around as she asks, "How about that drink?"

At first it seems he doesn't understand, but then he recovers, "Sure, what
will you have?"

"Some white wine preferably chilled."

Hal goes to the refrigerator and finds an open bottle of white wine. Usually,
his wife likes to drink a variety of cheap white wines, but this is one time he
wishes she had splurged. Hal considers that he has no other options so he pours
of them both a glass.

Hal smiles at her, "Here you go. It's not the best of wines, but at least it's chilled." He hopes she gets the joke and hands her the glass and she takes a sip without comment.

"How about a tour of your home?" She asks as she continues to look around.

Hal gets up off the couch and takes her through the first floor, "It's a small house, but it suits us. We're in the living room and here's the dining area. Through that doorway is my home office." As he walks through the house, he realizes how small his home is and how small his world really is.

"This is the kitchen." Hal won't look her in the eye as he lies, "We are going to be remodeling it soon."

Now she turns to him and smiles, "Where are the bedrooms, I'd like to see them." Hal's heart starts to beat even more rapidly than before and his face becomes flush with anticipation of what he believes will come next. He thinks first the sex will come and so will I.

They walk upstairs where the expanded Cape has two large bedrooms; one for his twin girls and the other is the master bedroom.

She looks around and turns to Hal placing herself very near to him, "Very nice."

He doesn't know how to react, what to do next, but it's not necessary. She reaches for him and presses her body close to his. They embrace and he kisses her. He feels her warm body as she puts her tongue into his mouth. Hal has never felt like this before, ever, and he feels his cock getting harder as she probes his mouth with her tongue.

Hal reaches for her blouse, but she stops him.

"I want to make this last. Lay down on the bed." He does as he's told and lies down. She crawls over the other side of the bed and never takes her eyes off him. Her hands run up and down his leg and he closes his eyes in hopes this feeling will last forever.

"Look at me Hal." And Hal opens his eyes.

She slowly unbuttons her blouse to reveal he smooth flawless alabaster skin. She undoes her bra and exposes her perfectly formed breasts. Now she stands up and removes her skirt and undergarments and they fall to the floor. She is completely naked and Hal can't believe how beautifully perfect she is.

The woman crawls back on the bed and kneels next to Hal. "Stay there and let me do my best." With that she unzips Hal's pants and grabs hold of his cock. It is very hard and he groans at her touch.

It all seems to happen in a flash, but when he looks at the clock more than an hour has passed since they went into the bedroom. He rests his head on his elbow and looks over at the beauty beside him. "Wow!" he whispers to himself, satisfied he has performed well…very well.

She opens her eyes and smiles at him. "Nice job and now I need to go."

She jumps out of bed and starts' getting dressed, but Hal doesn't want her to go. "Can't you stay a little longer?"

She looks at him and smiles, the kind of smile you might give a child that wants something he cannot have. "No, I need to be going."

"Will I ever see you again?" Hal said this, almost pleadingly.

"You never know."

"Please, I want to see you again."

"We'll see." She says this knowing that she would see Hal again.

"Can't you at least tell me your name?"

She thinks about it and whispers her name in his ear. He smiles because he likes the name. It fits her and he whispers the name back to her as he lies in bed.

After she finishes dressing, she picks up her small attaché case and purse and turns to leave the bedroom. "Wait, let me walk you downstairs."

"No, just lie there, you must be exhausted. I'll show myself out." He starts to protest, but he's beginning to feel tired so he doesn't argue with her. He thinks a short rest before his wife and kids come home would do him good as his eyes become heavy and in a few short minutes he is asleep.

Hal doesn't often dream, but this time he does. His dream is a dark and disturbing patchwork and, in his mind, he tries to move to a brighter place, but there is no light he can see. Shadowy images swirl around, images that could be frightening, but he can't quite tell what they are or if he should be terrified. Hal doesn't realize that is thrashing about the covers of his bed. Sweat pours out of his body and he begins to burn with a fever that has no cause or cure. Then, in an instant, she comes into his nightmare…still beautiful, but somehow different. He tries to touch her, but she is always out of reach. Her eyes are like deep pools of sparkling blue water and he becomes lost in them.

"What troubles you, Hal?" He's waiting for her to speak and now that she does, he answers,

"Help me, help me. I can't seem to wake up from this nightmare." Hal screams these words both aloud and in his dream.

"Do you like me, Hal?" This seems an odd question to Hal. He is scared beyond wits end; however, he can't help but say, "I love you."

"You love me? How can this be, we've just met and you say you love me?"

"I do, I do love you. I don't know why I just love you. Please help me." Hal is feeling a bit better now and his fears abate now that she is with him.

"I want to help you Hal, but actually you are able to help yourself." She looks at him and he sees a single tear fall from her eye.

"Me? Help myself? How can I help myself?" Hal's confusion is apparent and he reaches out for her again, but this time she falls into his arms. She is now smiling at him as he holds her in his arms and as she looks at him, he is powerless to turn away. Hal is helplessly and hopelessly in love. "How can I help myself? This is a dream, what can I do in a dream?"

His words echo in his mind and she reaches for him. He feels himself getting aroused again and, in his dream, she takes his cock in her hands and puts him inside her once more. Hal comes almost immediately, this time in his dreams, and it sends him writhing on top of the sweat-soaked and wrinkled covers of his bed.

When it is over and he lays there exhausted. Hal doesn't know what to do next.

"You can help yourself Hal and I am here to show you the way."

"I will do anything for you." He says this as he looks up from the bed in his dreams.

She moves away and turns her back to him and speaks, "What you will have to do will require great sacrifice."

"What do you mean? Great sacrifice?" His dreams seem to get darker as all disappears and he is left alone. He cries out in the darkness, but no one is there to answer. He gets off the bed and begins to walk feeling his way around, but there is nothing to hold onto, nothing there. In his dreams he sees a dull glow in the distance and he starts to walk towards it, but he's not really walking, he's running.

He stops at the point where he is surrounded by the dreary light and he hears a familiar voice. "Welcome Hal, I am so happy you are here."

"Where are you?" Hal calls out her name.

"I'm here Hal, I'm right here. Can you guess where you are?"

"No."

"Would you like to know?"

"Yes! Where am I, where are you?"

"You are one of the few still living who have been honored to be here, you are in the kingdom of God...you are in Heaven."

"Heaven? How can I be in heaven? Don't I need to be dead?" His mind is numb as he asks these questions.

"No Hal, you are not dead because you are being celebrated. You have been given a very special honor and I am here to proclaim this to you."

"Please, can I see you?" There is a weak desperation in his voice as tries to fathom the overwhelming emotions that bombard his senses.

"God is watching you, Hal. God is looking down on you and He has a special plan for you and when it is done, we can be happy together, forever."

Hal is mesmerized by her voice and by this place in his dreams. "Together forever, is it true, can we really be together?"

"Yes Hal, we can."

"How, how can this happen? How is it possible?" He hears his own words and they are slurred as they come out.

"With God all things are possible."

Hal thinks for a second and he seems to get an understanding of what is happening. God has called on him for a special honor; imagine being called by God for a special honor.

"Why am I being chosen?"

"You are chosen because you are one among God's children and He has selected you above all."

Hal's mind is reeling as he thinks, God has chosen me above all...the reality of these words now strikes him and he is overcome by the situation he finds himself in.

"What must I do? I will do anything for the Lord our God."

There is a long pause and Hal becomes fearful. "Are you there? Please speak to me. I need to know that you are there."

"I'm here with you Hal. I'm near and I was chosen to deliver God's message and His reward for you. As He sacrificed His only Son, you must give your family in the same sacrifice, a sacrifice of the innocent. In this way you will help redeem the world from the sins of man and reap the rewards that God will give to you."

Hal stands there numb in his dream and numb in the real world.

"Once you have made this sacrifice you will have saved the world and you and I will live forever in ecstasy."

Hal begins to shiver from a chill that emanates inside his body. He now finds the words he couldn't speak before, "I must kill my family? How can God want me to do this? How can He ask me to do this?"

"God would never ask you to do something that He would not do Himself. He asks you to make the supreme sacrifice just as He made the supreme sacrifice of His Son, the innocent, the Lamb of God to take away the sins of the world and now you are commanded to do the same to your lambs."

Hal's mind turns numb again. He is trying to fathom what he is being asked to do and what it all means, but he refuses to recognize the madness that is overcoming his entire reality.

Her voice is soothing, comforting and he needs to hear it. "Your lambs will be with God in heaven. Your sacrifice of their earthly lives will allow them to live in His domain, happy, fulfilled and eternal."

Hal can stand it no longer. The screams of anguish come from deep inside him and they can only be heard in his dream. He is thrashing on the covers of his bed and the sweat is pouring out of his body in wet hot patches soaking the sheets. She begins to speak to him, he does not want to listen, but it is futile because she appears in front of him. Hal is now in a stupor at what he sees appearing in front of him. The woman he has just made love to, the woman who he now loves is enveloped in light. She is, as an angel would be, dressed in robes of bright white linen that covers her exquisitely formed body. Her long blond locks drape over her shoulders and his eyes go wide as he sees her wings unfold.

"What? Who…" Hal's voice trails off as she comes close to him?

"I am the messenger of God and you are commanded to do His will."

In an instant Hal forgets his heartbreak, forgets his anguish, forgets his humanity and pleadingly says, "…and then we will be together?"

"Forever"

As Hal lies in bed a key turns the lock to the front door. He thinks she's home as he hears the front door slam and rustle of packages being placed on the kitchen counter. He hears the refrigerator open and he hears his wife singing a tune. What's the name of that tune she's singing he asks himself? It didn't really matter though; she never had good taste in music or a good voice for that matter.

Hal leaves his bed and grabs a robe to cover his naked body as he walks to the door of their bedroom. Her voice can be heard louder as he stands at the top of the stairs leading to the ground floor. For the first time he realizes that he is holding something in his right hand and when he looks down, he sees a long blade. It is an old knife; a very old knife and he touches the tip with his finger and it cuts through the skin. "Ow!" he whispers but starts to wonder, "How did this knife get in my hand?"

Hal speculates that he must still be dreaming, but he knows he's not. "Lambs of God" Hal whispers as he starts to walk down the stairs. At the third step from the bottom, the wood creaks at the strain of Hal's weight and the singing stops.

"Who's there?" She is nervous as she calls from the kitchen. "Hal, is that you?"

"Yes."

She drops what she is doing and walks toward the stairs. "What are you doing home so early? Are you sick or something?"

"I'm or something."

"What? What are you talking about?" She is questioning him as she rounds the corner and comes face to face with Hal.

"Hal you're in your bathrobe, are you okay? You look awful, what's wrong with you? Tell me are you sick?"

"No, I'm not sick."

"Here, come upstairs let me take your temperature. You don't look well at all and I…" His wife's voice trails off as she sees the knife at his side.

"Why are you carrying that knife?"

Hal smiles, "I am the hand of God."

"What…Hal, you're scaring me. Put down that knife, please Hal, you're scaring me." She takes a step backward, but Hal stays close.

"There is no need to be scared for you are the Lamb of God." Hal's eyes are vacant except for the madness hiding behind them.

"You're not making sense Hal. You're sick and you need help. Please, please put down that knife I'm begging you. The girls will be home soon Hal, please for their sake please put down the knife."

"It is for their sake, Helen, you all are the Lambs of God and you will be with Him for eternity."

Helen is petrified and in panic she turns to run, but Hal grabs her by the hair. She screams, but Hal is deaf to her screams as he pulls her toward himself. Her throat is exposed, open to the long blade, as he slices through the skin and cuts through her vocal cord and the jugular. The screams now die and all that can be heard is the gurgling sound of blood coming from her mouth. The blood continues to spurt out of the open wound in a wide spray as the long blade is sharp and cuts through his wife's throat.

Helen is dead, but Hal considers cutting off her head to make sure.

He rethinks this as the twins will be home soon. Hal drags the body of his dead wife to the kitchen and puts her on the floor.

He wants to try and clean up the mess in the hallway before his kids' school bus pulls up in front of his home and his daughters get off.

They are laughing and smiling as they open the front door and daddy is there to greet them.

"Hi daddy, you are home early." They both say in unison.

"Yes, I am and how are my little lambs."

"Good. Where's Mommy?" But they are distracted by the sticking mess that is all over the floor.

"Daddy, what is all this stuff on the floor? It's real yucky!"

"Oh, I made a mess and I didn't have a chance to clean it up before Mommy gets home. Hey, do you guys want a surprise?!"

The twins look at each other and smile up at their father, "Yes daddy, please! Faith and me want a surprise, please daddy!"

"Well, I got a big surprise for you. Now go up to your room and I will follow."

Hal's daughters run up the stairs to their room with Hal following closely behind. They stand in the middle of the floor and look around, but they don't see a surprise.

"Daddy, there is not surprise here. Where is our surprise?"

Hal smiles at them, "You are my little lambs, aren't you?"

"You never called us your little lambs before daddy."

"Well, you are my little lambs and I want to give you your surprise, but you need to close your eyes and no peeking. If you peek you won't get the surprise, okay?"

"Okay daddy." With that the twins close their eyes.

Hal smiles down at his daughters, the lights of his life, his little lambs as he takes the knife and slits both of their throats. He hangs their bodies upside down and nails their bodies to the wall of their bedroom. Hal is covered in blood, but he is happy. He is the hand of God that sacrifices the lambs just like he is commanded.

Hal sits on one of the beds in the kid's bedroom and stares into space. His thoughts turn to the events of the day and he realizes that she is not here. Where is she? Didn't she say they would be together forever?

Hal hears a voice coming from behind him, "We will be together forever Hal."

Hal doesn't turn to face her; he just smiles and says, "You're here, just like you promised. You're here."

"I'm here Hal."

As he turns to face her, Juliana reveals herself as Leviathan, the dreadful demon. In an instance Hal realizes what has happened and what he has done. He is so horrified by the hideousness before him that his heart literally explodes in his chest.

CHAPTER 5

The cavernous arena is filled to overflowing.

They have all come to hear him. He is considered one of the greatest thinkers of the 21st century. The youthful, dynamic and extremely handsome man now heads the largest, most prestigious think tank in the world, "ACTELECT" with 20 offices throughout the United States and another 27 offices in various countries around the globe. Recent national polls taken by news organizations and political groups have given him an overall approval rating of 60% and growing. Over the years he's become immensely powerful and influential and he's also become feared by those who are opposed to his radical populist brand of political thought and policy. From poverty to privilege and wealth, from public school to Harvard and Yale, he has been chosen and groomed for exactly this moment and with that Dr. Thomas Houston, PhD takes the stage to thunderous applause.

As he walks onto the stage at the Nassau Coliseum, he is greeted by roaring cheers from the 17,000 adoring acolytes assembled there. He waves to the crowd and tries to thank them so he could proceed with his speech, but the applause and cheers are deafening. He looks around and secretly wishes he didn't have to do these things, however he knows it is necessary to his ultimate goal and, after all, it is the price of fame. He looks over the massive crowd in attendance taking satisfaction at all the banners waving in his face; "Atheists are Americans!", "The Anti-Capitalist Coalition",

"Income Equality NOW!" Every sympathetic coalition is there from abortion rights and right-to-die advocates to anti-law enforcement groups and the open border alliances; they are all there and they are rabidly vocal. The radical leftwing environmentalists, the "Legalize all Drugs" groups and the extremist animal rights factions are also represented in great numbers. Even the get out of GITMO crowd and the Pro-Hamas/Anti-Israeli groups are in the arena and their enthusiasm is palpable. These factions, and many more, are all present in eager anticipation to see him and he is pleased to see them in such large numbers.

His much-heralded theories on the meaning of the universe, the false premise of a supreme being and the neutrality of man's existence catapults him into stardom. At first these views were only common among the fringe groups but now they have become accepted into the mainstream of American popular culture. Given his leftist roots he is able to get a forum for his deep-seated philosophical thoughts and ideas on every major mainstream news outlet in the country.

Dr. Thomas Houston is tall, slim and very handsome and his sympathizers in the media love to have him on their shows. From his podium on the nightly news and progressive political talk shows, he is able to expand on radical theories relating to the economics of socialist redistribution and income inequity without appearing to be vitriolic. Thomas Houston preaches what he believes is the underlying fascism of America's conservative tradition, the misleading notion of criminality and the need to coalesce all power under one central authority for the good of all. His message is clear and it is resonating with more and more people every day.

"Thank you!" Dr. Houston tries to scream above the applause, but he knows that the adulation needs to subside when it subsides, so he waits patiently. After five minutes the crowd finally settles down to a dull roar and Tom Houston begins to speak reading from a teleprompter set up on either side of the podium.

"Thank you! Thank you so very much for that totally underserved, but much appreciated welcome." His opening line is a signal to the crowd to wildly cheer the speaker before them; their leader and teacher.

"I am here for one reason and for one reason only, to bring you the message of hope. The message that there are reasons that people are hungry in our great country, that people need free healthcare for all, that people need to be free of student loans, and that people need something they can believe in. So many Americans know that the rich exploit the poor and I am here to tell you this will change! The poor will know justice, the great center of our country, the great middle class will at last see their fortunes change, and they will change for the better."

The crowd is in euphoria. The cheers are wild and the adulation of the audience is as apparent as it is overwhelming. The multitude will not open their minds to anything else because, for them, there is nothing else.

Thomas Houston continues, "Now, my good friends on the other side of the table like to point to the strength of America. They tell us that America is the economic wonder of the world. America is the leader in manufacturing, in scientific research, in development of advanced technologies, but at what cost!"

Now there are loud boos coming from the crowd gathered before him in the arena.

"Ladies and gentlemen, I will tell you at what cost! It is at the cost of the happiness and contentment in the lives of the great number of hardworking decent people that live and labor in this great country of ours. The poor, the downtrodden, the working class and the great numbers of those men and women who spend their days making others rich and who ultimately become fodder for the cannons of Capitalism!"

Now his passion is on display for all to see. His voice is rising, his arms are outstretched, his gestures are animated and when he looks over the arena, he seems to be looking directly at each person there. The crowd basks in the light of his presence and they love every minute.

"It is only when the poor and working class are confronted with the reality of their situation, of what's been done to them, that they abandon all hope. Many of these poor, wretched souls are forced into a life they never chose, a life where they are required to commit acts of crime just to stay alive. I ask you now; look into your hearts for an answer. Should they be forced to pay for these transgressions just to stay alive? Should they be forced to spend their days imprisoned by a society that doesn't care? I say NO…I say let them GO…I say free their bodies and free their spirits NOW!"

The crowd shouts in unison, "NOW…NOW…NOW!"

"Are they responsible for their lot in life?"

The crowd shouts even louder, "NO!"

"Are they responsible to a society that will not listen to them?"

"NO!"

"Ladies and gentlemen, you can see the answers are simple, why can't the so-called ruling class see them?"

Thomas Houston continues on his idealistic rant, "And what of the law enforcement, what is their roll?"

This time the jeers and shouts of derision echo through the chamber in a deafening crescendo.

"How many of our fellow citizens have been stopped and searched because of some imagined suspicion? How many of our citizens have been handcuffed and dragged to jail for some imagined crime? How many of our fellow citizens have committed suicide at the hands of the authorities? How many more must die before we say STOP?!"

Dr. Houston can sense the fury that is rising among the people listening to him speak these words. He knows what they want to hear and he will not stop until it is all said.

"When you confront my friends on the other side with the facts, they protest, 'it's not true' they say. How can we live in a society where people are allowed to commit crimes even if it means feeding their children? How can we live in a society with no order, no discipline and no police even if it serves the cause of justice? How can we all be responsible to feed and clothe all the poor people even if it means they will die? How can you think that we can keep all of them down? How can we have so much power and control?" Question after question rolled off Dr. Houston's tongue, but he has the answers and the crowd knows it.

He continues, "They tell us, there are so few of us, how can we be so powerful? This is America and we live in a democracy! This power you say we have does not come from us. That kind of power can only come from the people themselves through a higher authority and then they point to God as that higher authority. Imagine how many people have been kept down in the name of God! Blown up in the name of God! Been made to starve or languish in prisons in the name of God! Imagine how many people have DIED in the name of GOD!"

The audience is now in complete and utter rapture, they don't need God; they have Dr. Thomas Houston.

"Why does the other side always tell us to turn to God when we are in need? Well, I'll tell you why. They always tell us to turn to God because if they didn't, they would all be punished for what they have done to us!" Now the crowd is in an ecstatic stupor.

He continues, "They, the rich and powerful, make up a god that we are supposed to worship and then hide behind him to control our lives. Ladies and gentlemen, we cannot allow this to continue. We cannot allow the abomination of the rich, the right and the religious to control our lives anymore. We can make a change, we can get all that we want for ourselves, for our families and for this great country we love!"

The crowd is in complete ecstasy and as they cheer, they join together as one body, one massive pulsating rhythm and in one raucously thunderous voice. The surroundings of the arena become surreal, sort of hallowed ground where the multitude can worship their leader, their chosen one, their savior.

Dr. Tom Houston basks in the adulation. He knows what must be done and he knows his moment is now.

"I did not come here tonight to proselytize. I don't need to do that because I am confident in my beliefs and all of you here need to be confident in yours. I look at the vastness of the universe and I see many wondrous things. I look up to see stars, planets, galaxies and the reality of physics that manifests itself each time we contemplate the universe. All of these wonders prove many things to me, but unfortunately they do not prove the existence of a god."

Now the roar of the crowd starts to rise. Thomas Houston is now in his personal sphere; a world that he fashions through sheer force of will and one in which he is the supreme leader. It is just him and everyone else as he looks out at the huge numbers of those who believe in him.

He continues, "Now, don't get me wrong. If you believe in a god, it is your right, no matter what any of us believe, but when you use a god to commit crimes against humanity in his name that is true BLASPHEMTY that is true HERESY, THAT IS THE TRUE EVIL WE MUST FIGHT!"

This is what the crowd wants to hear, this is why they came. It is their communion; this is the body and blood they would feast on.

Dr. Thomas Houston continues this speech for more than an hour and it is as good a rallying cry as he has ever performed. The people in the arena can't get enough of him and for this he is thankful. He needs them all, he needs their commitment, he needs their time and he needs their loyalty and most of all he needs their love.

It is now time for the closing statement. He and his aides have worked on this speech for weeks and it would be the most important in his career, maybe even his life. Dr. Thomas Houston, PhD takes a final glimpse at the teleprompter and takes a deep breath.

"My dear friends, and I consider all of you to be my friends, I have a special announcement and I want you to be the first to hear it."

Now the entire arena becomes silent.

"I am a Long Islander, born in Valley Stream, raised in Hempstead and now living in Garden City and Southampton. It is to my fellow citizens of Long Island, my home that I want to share this news with first. I want to make it known that I am forming an exploratory committee in preparation for announcing as the Socialist Liberation Party candidate for the Presidency of the United States of America!"

For a moment all those on the floor of the Coliseum are silent, disbelieving; but as the impact of his words are realized the walls of the arena shake from the deafening cheers that follow.

CHAPTER 6

Father Aiden Langford loves to walk the grounds of Immaculate Conception Seminary. The seminary is located in a beautiful area of Huntington that borders Lloyd Harbor with waters that lead to Long Island Sound. The priests, instructors and seminarians can wander the lawns and winding paths that meander through the 200 wooded acres that make up the entire grounds. On his daily walk, Father Aiden takes full advantage of its beauty, even in winter.

Construction on the seminary began in 1928 and Immaculate Conception opened for the first seminarians in 1930 with a class of 85 candidates. The buildings that accommodate classrooms and house students and instructors have wonderful architectural details. The structures have stucco walls and beautiful slate tile roofs and are surrounded by tranquil gardens which, when in season, come alive with plantings and colorful flowers.

The chapel at the Immaculate Conception Seminary is a special place of peace and prayer and the library has over 50,000 monographs and bound periodicals as well as a special collection of nearly 4,000 old and rare books. All in all, Immaculate Conception is a special place to reflect, to learn and to experience the serenity that can come from meditation. Fr. Aiden became familiar with all the special aspects of ICS and he supposes that's why he enjoys his position here. Fr. Aiden Langford is a lecturer and instructor in historical and biblical teachings to seminarians that are enrolled in masters' degree programs for theology and pastoral studies. He is a particular favorite among many of the seminarians who consider him a mentor.

It is a beautifully sunny, but cold day in late January and as usual Fr. Aiden likes to start the day with a long walk around the compound before his classes begin. The priest walks the same paths nearly every day and he always wind up sitting on a bench along the sand beach that is located on the seminary's property.

Father Aiden Langford was born near the seaside town of St. Ives in Cornwall and was raised as an Anglican by his parents. Over the years he came to know Catholicism and was intrigued by its particular focus on Christianity and the rituals and traditions of its teachings. He converted later in life, when his parents had passed and became a religious scholar with renowned academic standing among his peers. Fr. Aiden is still a youthful looking man, who tries to keep fit, but the priest ponders his health and, at 67 years, he often thinks of his mortality. He suffered what the doctor's call a "mild heart attack" and accepted the change it brought via his daily regimen of medication as well as diet and exercise. As a priest, Father Langford studies many of the teachings relating to the afterlife, of heaven and hell and of the unknown that waits to be revealed. He does not fear death, but rather tries to contemplate its mystery as it all seems very natural to him.

The sun is bright and the air is calm on this cold winter day. It is high tide as the water laps close to where he is sitting on the shores of Lloyd Harbor. The surrounding sound of the small waves is so soothing that Fr. Aiden feels himself nodding off. Just as he is contemplating the nap he would take; his cell phone rings. It plays his favorite ring tone, the AC/DC classic "Highway to Hell" and Brian Johnson's gravely vocals always make him smile.

"Hello, Aiden Langford speaking."

"Good morning, Father."

"Well, well! Spartaco! To what do I owe this wonderful surprise? Do you need me to lend you my Bible or some money?" Father Aiden starts to laugh and always enjoys teasing his good friend.

Al smiles when he hears the priest say his name, "You know you're the only one who can call me Spartaco." This is true, the only people who Uncle Al would let call him Spartaco were his mother and father, but now that they're gone Father Aiden Langford holds the enviable position of being the last remaining person alive to use that name and not walk away with a black eye.

"No thank you, I don't need your money and I've got my own bible. How are you feeling Aiden?" Uncle Al considers the priest one of his closest friends, sort of a counselor and confidant and he is genuinely interested. It was about a year ago that Fr. Aiden's heart problems required him to take treatment including consistent medical monitoring, medications and low-impact exercise and somewhat limit the stress of his academic activities.

"You are always concerned for me Spartaco and for that I am truly grateful. I am feeling fine and in good spirits, thank you for asking. As a matter of fact, I am taking my usual constitutional around ICS and enjoying the cold weather from the shore overlooking this beautiful place."

"Nice to be rich, huh?"

"Yes, it is. As a matter of fact, I am able to promote a tidy sum that amounts to a cool $48.19 and I, being in a most generous mood, would like to invite you to lunch at the renowned suburban culinary establishment I am sure you have heard of; Rosa's Pizza! It appears they only attract the best clientele and I understand that their eggplant parmigiana pizza is simply the best in the world! What say you, Spartaco?"

"I'd love to, but I'm paying. Anyway, I'm calling to invite you to lunch; I need to speak with you."

"Ah will wonders never cease! At last, you are finally going to make confession. This is truly a momentous occasion and if that is the case I insist, as a matter-of-fact God insists that I pay for lunch!"

"No such luck Aiden…my sins are going to the grave with me. God and I will sort it out. Besides, you're writing a book and the last thing I want is to be immortalized in Chapter 666. Anyway, I would like to discuss something with you, can we meet on Friday?"

Father Aiden detects seriousness in Uncle Al's voice and he asks, "Spartaco is something wrong? Are you well?"

Al smiles again, knowing his friend's concern, "Now you sound like Chris, no I'm fine. I just need to talk and you're always a friendly ear. So how about it, are we on for lunch on Friday?"

"Of course, we are. I am looking forward to seeing you again, it has been a while."

"So am I. Would you mind if Chris joins us? His shop is in the village and I know he would enjoy seeing you again."

"Of course, I would love to have Christopher join us, the dear lad! It has been ages since I've seen him." Fr. Langford loves to lay his thick British accent on Al as he knows it will make him smile.

Uncle Al chuckles, "Always the Englishmen aren't you Aiden?"

"Ah! Alas, there will always be an England and there will always be an Aiden to remind us all. Let us say 12:30P at Rosa's. Does that time suit you?"

"That works for me and thanks for taking time on your day off."

"For friends, there are no days off, only days on. See you for lunch on Friday my dear Spartaco. Fare thee well, pip, pip and Cheerio!" Fr. Langford laughs and hits disconnect. He continues to stare out from the water's edge, but he no longer is contemplating the beauty; he is concerned for his friend. In his heart, the priest knows there is something wrong with Spartaco and Aiden only hopes that he can help.

The priest inhales the fresh salt air and picks himself off the bench. As he turns to walk back to his quarters, a frigid wind blows off the water and cuts through him like a knife.

CHAPTER 7

"Come follow me."

Those are the only words that are spoken to John by the Son, and it is from that moment on he vows to serve Jesus; his Savior and Son of Man, for the rest of his days.

He thinks of these things as he waits in the cold, dark prison cell he now occupies. John recalls kneeling at the foot of the cross as the passion of the Christ is taking place. He weeps for his brother Apostles who have forsaken God's Son at His hour of greatest need. John remembers the weak and dying Jesus, nailed, by the feet and the hands, to a cross of wood looking down at His disciple and calling him "Beloved."

John will never forget the anguish the Lord has to bear as he looks up at the man hanging from the cross and begs Christ to reveal how he can help. What could John do to ease His Lord's pain and suffering? John is beyond consolation and continues to weep for the dying man until he hears a thin, weak voice speak to him,

"You are my beloved disciple. You are the loyal one among all and it is for you I have a most special undertaking."

John stares at Christ, not understanding the meaning of this request. "What can I do oh Lord? Command me anything and I will obey."

Christ looks down at his disciple, his dear friend and says,

"You are to take charge of caring for my mother, Mary. I trust you above all. She is strong and much loved by many, but she will need your help and service in her time of need and it is for this singular task you are charged."

"My lord and savior, I will not fail you. I will be her guardian. I will remain by her side in whatever may come until the day she and I are reunited with You in the Holy Kingdom of Heaven."

Jesus looks down at His loyal Apostle John, His Boanerge, His son of thunder, as Christ calls him, and smiles at him through tears of pain.

For all the time she has left on earth, John is sure to take special care of the Blessed Mother of Christ. He builds her a small home made of stone in the mountains near Ephesus. St. John preaches in the region near the Blessed Mother's home and visits her whenever he can. The Apostle John loves Mary and when she dies, he weeps for her and resolves that his promise of duty to the Lord has been fulfilled. He now awaits his own death and to be reunited with the Son and all those he's loved in life.

John goes over these thoughts again and again in his mind as he sits in the dark confines of the prison cell. He reflects on how much he misses his time with Christ and the brother apostles who followed the Lord. John remembers his time in the messianic communities in Asia Minor and the Middle Eastern regions of the Roman Empire. It is these lands John travels and visits the churches that have been established and where he will write epistles to the faithful. As word of his mission spread John recalls how his ministry has become reviled by the Roman authorities who see him as a threat to their rule. A short time later John views the soldiers approaching and it is then that he is arrested and sent to Rome for the punishment he will face for the crime of sedition.

From a cage atop the large wooden wagon, John watches the soldiers mounted on horses that pull the cart. The Apostle stares across the varied landscapes of all the places he passes on his way to Rome. He is taken there under guard and thrown to the prison where he is to be confined by the Emperor Domitian for his faith. Staring into the dark corners of his cell, he tries to recall, but he cannot remember how long he has been held captive. In the end it matters little to him because John accepts that he will die at the hands of Domitian and today would be the day of his death.

The door to his dark prison chamber opens and six Roman guards enter. They bind his feet, tie his hands behind his back and drag him from the cell. John is surrounded by the Roman Guards that escort him to the Latin Gate located near the emperor's palace. There he would be put into a large vat of boiling oil in full view of the citizens of Rome who have gathered there since early in the day. John thinks of the pain he will endure, how it would feel as his flesh would cook in the scalding oil. He is sad, but not fearful, because he knows that he has the strength of the Lord to see him through this, his final journey on earth.

The soldiers march him up the stairs into the light of day. At first John has to shut his eyes for the sun is bright and he has been in the darkness of his cell for many days. The guards continue to drag him through the streets until they reach the place where he is to die. The crowd continues to assemble and there is an uneasy quiet that settles over the public square. The cauldron stands at the center of the open area where there is a great fire burning beneath the large vessel filled with oil. The smell of boiling oil permeates the air as the Roman guards lead John before the Emperor.

The emperor stands and looks over the mass of people that have gathered to watch the execution. Domitian thinks to himself of how the followers of Christ seem to be growing more and more in influence each day and he will have none of this. This Christian needs to be set as an example of what happens to those who defy the powers of Rome and his powers, the powers of the emperor. Now John is standing in front of him, this Apostle of Jesus the Jew and Domitian vows that all of this arrogance and treason against Rome will stop…it must stop.

The crowd becomes quiet as the emperor begins to speak. "People of Rome; standing before you is the man I have condemned to death. This man John defies Rome, defies its laws, speaks falsehoods and preaches treachery and sedition. He conjures wicked visions to bring harm against citizens of the Empire. John, this disciple of the Jew named Jesus has committed subversion against Rome and for this he forfeits his life."

The crowd roars approval of the emperor, but John stands passively by as he listens to the emperor Domitian speak these untruths.

"Let this be the lesson learned to all who would defy the laws of the great Empire of Rome and its Emperor. Subversion of any kind will be punished in the severest possible manner, death to those who are guilty of defying the emperor." Domitian then looks down on the soldiers guarding John and gives the signal to cast him into the caldron of boiling oil. The soldiers lift the man above their heads and thrust him into the pot. There is a loud gasp of the crowd as the body falls into the boiling liquid and disappears.

The emperor sits back on his throne, relieved for the first time in a long while. He has been told by his spies of the impact John and the other Apostles are having on the peoples of Judea and the far reaches of the Empire. Domitian worries that the emperor's powers, his powers, to control the people would diminish over time if this apostate is allowed to persist. Now, that the apostle's demise is apparent, the emperor, at last, could feel at ease.

The crowd is now silent, still staring at the boiling oil, when something astonishing happens. John stands up; in the center of the boiling caldron, the apostle of Jesus the Jew stands up.

The emperor is thunderstruck. How can this happen? What evil has been unleashed to save this man from certain death? On seeing what has taken place, the crowd of people who came to witness an execution now recoils in fear. The soldiers appear to be as fearful as the rest of the crowd and they do not know what to do. The armed guards look up to the emperor for guidance, but Domitian has nothing to say as he stands there in stunned silence.

Domitian, ghastly pale, turns to his trusted advisor, *"Julianus, what am I to make of this evil? The citizens will expect me to take charge, but how can I? What am I to do?"*

Julianus is still staring at John, but turns to whisper in the emperor's ear, *"What has happened here is very dangerous my lord. If the people are allowed to hear from this man, they may consider that he speaks a malevolent truth no one can understand. As the leader of the Roman Empire, you cannot let this continue, this sorcery must stop."*

"Tell me what to do." The emperor seems to be in the state of panic.

"Tell the soldiers to disband the crowd immediately. Have the guards take this man back to prison while we think of what to do next."

The Emperor Domitian gives the command to the soldiers who order the crowd to disperse. But as they stand there, the murmur of low voices could be heard, questioning by what wonders have made the man named John survive. The people are told he is a sorcerer with evil powers, but evil or not, they question if his powers are greater than that of the emperor?

How could this be?

It is then John turns to the crowd and says, "I have been saved by the mercy and goodness of the one true God and His Son Jesus Christ. There is nothing to fear for those who believe."

Julianus now roars the command to the soldiers. "Disperse this crowd NOW!" and the soldiers do as the emperor commands. Domitian sees how the crowd looks at the Apostle and for the first time the emperor becomes truly terrified. It is then that the entire throngs, all whom have seen the miracle, go to their knees and are immediately converted by John. This man of a God, who is more powerful than the Emperor of the Roman Empire, now baptizes all those before him.

Julianus turns to see the emperor in a state of total desperation and thinks to himself, something will need to be done with this apostle named John and it must be done quickly.

CHAPTER 8

Chief Detective Al Barese hangs up the phone. He had hoped that speaking with Aiden and Chris would make him feel better, but it doesn't. He continues to hold onto this nagging fear that the rise in extreme violence has to do with something more than a series of unrelated incidents. The chief thinks back to his high school English Lit class and of the line from Shakespeare's Macbeth, "Something wicked this way comes", but he imagines the 'something' he fears is far worse than anything he has ever had to confront or even could envision and it frightens him.

For years the chief has counted on his intuition to understand the criminal mind so he could solve crimes, even to stay alive, so he can't ignore these feelings now. He remembers his oath as a young police officer; "To protect and serve the residents of Suffolk County", but his fears seem far beyond the normal boundaries of police work. It is nothing specific, just a nameless dread, but how do you prepare for a nameless dread.

It is an undeniable fact that the numbers of violent crimes seem to be mounting after the Christmas holidays, but that doesn't fit the past patterns. Criminals and the crimes they commit will always be a problem to one degree or another and these miscreants always fall into specific categories; drugs, muggings, theft, prostitution, armed robbery even murder are inevitable, but they are also predictable. However, this time it seems different. The crimes being committed are beyond what anyone would consider as having pattern; they are unprecedented in their execution, effect and violence. As he tries to make sense of what is happening, all he can think of is that something very bad is going to happen…something wicked. Chief Barese turns back to staring at his computer screen for some clue, some direction. He navigates his way through the Suffolk County PD site to see what is going on and to his surprise there is nothing major to report. Is this a sign of a return to some normalcy or is it a momentary lapse? The criminal activity in the past few weeks seems to be so violent and of such ferocity that Al feels a sense of powerlessness and a nagging suspicion that just won't go away.

As he sits in his office, alone with these thoughts, there is a knock on his door and he answers, "Come in."

"Hi Chief, we have some very bad news and we need to talk." It is Detective Dan Orello, the most senior member of Chief Barese's team and his closest confidant.

Al's heart sinks as his hope for a momentary lull in crime seems to evaporate, but he needs to maintain some control over his composure so he tells Dan to take a seat,

Al is almost afraid to ask, "What's up Dan?"

Dan continues standing at the Chief's desk and speaks, "Well you know that gnawing feeling you've been having about how things are bad and getting worse and that something very bad is bound to happen?"

"Yeah?" The chief immediately sits up straight and waits for Dan to continue.

"Well today we seem to have hit the jackpot. It's only 11AM and most of our patrols are handling crimes that are so weird, so unlike most of the things we've ever seen, so bizarre that there is no explanation, nothing. It's like the world has just gone mad and we…" Dan's voice just trails off and there is a sadness that overwhelms him as he tries to comprehend the reasons behind the crimes.

The chief knows what Dan is trying to say, but there are no words that could fully express the depth of his feelings. "Go on Dan, what happened?"

"Chief, here is the file on five incidents that are currently being investigated." Dan hands Chief Barese the files and continues to debrief him.

"Each one is more weird and violent than the next. I prepped this summary report for you to look over." Dan then hands Al the summary report and he finally sits down, but the look on his face makes Al very anxious so he prepares himself for the worst.

"Dan, I have the feeling that you have something to tell me, so go ahead and tell me."

Dan gulps before he speaks, "Chief, we just got a call from a patrol investigating what seems to be an ordinary break-in at a house on Rydal Street in Kings Park. They receive a call from neighbors who are concerned that there's been no activity from the house for two days and the lights in the home are on all day and night. A patrol car was sent to the address and when one of the officers enters the home to investigate, he finds the front door unlocked. He opens the door and he finds the floor in the hallway covered with blood. The officer walks through the first floor into the kitchen and that's where he finds the body of a woman lying on the floor. At first it seemed to the officers at the scene that it was a break-in and the woman accidentally discovered the thief. That's what the officers initially thought, but after looking over the scene they see that the wife was murdered in such a violent way, that they begin having second thoughts."

The chief sighs, "I understand that the officers may think this is out of the ordinary but this seems pretty cut and dry to me; woman comes home, confronts a burglar and she is murdered. I admit that her death sounds particularly violent, but this still is nothing new. We've encountered this type of crime a number of times before so why are you at a loss for words in this instance?"

"Well, that's not all they found at the house." Dan says this with such seriousness that Al feels that he might have spoken too soon. "Go on."

Dan continues to speak, but his voice starts to crack and betrays a crushing sense of sadness. "When the patrolmen called us, we told them to cordon off the entire area and we immediately sent detectives to the crime scene. We also called the coroner's office and they also sent a team to the scene. While one of the patrolmen is cordoning off the area outside the residence, his partner, an officer Burton, is inside the residence looking from room to room to see what else may be there. The neighbors had mentioned that the couple has twin girls, 6 years old, so he goes through the house looking for them." As Dan says this he begins to choke up and needs to wait before he speaks again.

"Take your time Dan. What did officer Burton find?" Al now fears he just might find the name behind a nameless dread.

Detective Orello tries to regain his composure and continues, "The officer went from room to room and when he enters the daughters' room, he discovers the corpses' of the twin girls'."

"Dead? They found the twins dead?" Chief Barese says this trying to make some sense out of the senseless.

Dan stares at his boss, his friend, and says, "Chief, that's not all."

Chill races down the chief's spine, "What else happened?"

"The girls were nailed, upside down, onto the wall. Their throats were cut and their blood was collected in large bowls under their heads. Someone then took the blood and wrote the words, 'Lambs of God' on the wall."

The chief just stares at Dan in stunned amazement. He questions Dan, "What about the father, does anyone know what happened to the father?"

"The officer also found the father in the kids' room, lying on his back on one of the kids' beds, dead with a knife at his side. The knife was covered in blood and it seems 99% sure that the father killed his wife and kids." Dan doesn't know what else to say, "I'm going to the crime scene now, Chief and I'll keep you posted if there are any other aspects of the murders you might need to know."

There are no words he can say, all the chief could do was to stare at Dan. Al knows his squad can handle the investigation, but it is a major crime and he needs to be at the scene with the team investigating the crime. He grabs the side of his chair and gets to his feet, "I'm coming with you."

Both Chief Al Barese and Detective Dan Orello leave the office and head down the corridor that leads to the parking garage. They walk down the hallway when they are stopped by another member of the team, Detective Christina Shannon. She has a very worried look on her face and says,

"Chief, got a minute?"

"Sorry, we're on our way to investigate a homicide in King's Park so I'm kind of in a hurry. What's wrong?"

"I don't mean to hold you up, Chief, but you know how you've been thinking that something bad is going to happen?"

When he hears her tell him this, all Al could think of is the nameless dread, but he swallows and says, "Yes, I remember, what happened?"

"We just got a call from a patrol working in Deer Park. They cover the precinct that includes the big mall; you know the one I'm talking about?"

"Yeah, the Stores of the World Mall on Selden Lane."

"That's the one. Anyway, the officers on patrol are called by mall security because of a disturbance that is occurring inside on the main promenade. There's like a piano player there and he's playing on a grand piano. There are lots of seats surrounding the piano for the tired shoppers to rest. Well, it seems that crowd is listening to the music being played; a young woman walks to the seating area in the center section. When she gets there, she sits down next to this poor old guy that's resting, actually sleeping, while his wife is shopping."

Now Al is starting to get a headache, but he has no aspirin so he has to keep listening as his head begins to throb.

"The woman is quiet for a while, she just sits there, but then, out of the blue, she proceeds to take off her clothes and completely disrobes. Now the piano player stops and the people in the audience turn around to see a naked woman standing there. As word gets out a large crowd starts gathering around, but she doesn't seem to notice according to eyewitnesses. The woman seems to be in some kind of trance-like state and unresponsive to some people in the crowd who are making jokes, whistling you know that sort of behavior. Just when everyone assumes that the woman is just a harmless, crazy weirdo she bends down and begins to rummage through a small shopping bag that she is carrying. She then pulls out a knife, but not just any knife, it's a very old knife, looks like it could be used in battle; you know like the one used by the Roman soldiers, complete with a twelve-inch blade. So, this woman is standing there, buck-naked, with this knife in her hand and she calmly walks over to the guy sleeping on the seat. But before anyone realizes what's happening, she slits the poor man's throat from ear to ear and screams at the top of her lungs. This is tough for me to even say, but next she puts her hand on the dead guy's bleeding throat and smears it on the floor and she writes the words, "Lamb of God."

The two men can't believe what they are hearing, "You've got to be shitting us, Christina."

"I only wish I was and to make it even worse, the poor guy's wife was just returning from doing her shopping and she witnesses the whole thing."

"Holy shit, that poor woman." Now Al is sure the headache he has will explode through his skull.

"Yeah, holy shit is right, but I'm not done. The crazy woman starts to scream 'Lamb of God, Lamb of God' while flashing the knife at anybody that is stupid enough to be close to her. By this time the security force at the mall has called the police and the patrol arrives just minutes after the murder has taken place. The two officers run to the area by the piano as the people in the mall are screaming and trying to get away. The officers draw their weapons, yell for the crowd to disperse, and order the woman to put down the knife and get on the floor, you know the drill. Well, she's screaming "Lamb of God' and starts cursing at them and won't drop the knife. They point their weapons at her, but she still won't stop. This goes on for a short time until she lifts the knife and throws it directly at one of the officers."

Dan is the first to say, "Please don't tell me that she hit one of the men?"

"She did, square in the chest. The other officer then fires his weapon at the woman and kills her on the spot."

Dan and Al become very concerned and AL says, "How is the wounded officer? What's his name? Will he be alright?"

Det. Shannon's look changes and she appears very worried. "His name is Nick Josephs. He was taken to the Huntington Hospital where's he's being treated for what doctors have characterized as a very serious wound. He's now in the ICU where the doctor's say that his condition is extremely critical and they won't know for another day or two if he will survive his wounds."

"My God! Listen Christina, I have to go with Dan, but keep me posted on the wounded officer's condition and get me a copy of the incident report as soon as possible."

"Sure Chief, will do." Det. Shannon then turns and walks away while Al continues towards the garage. As he is about to open the door leading to the garage, he hears someone call to him.

"Hey Chief, wait up for a second!" Al turns to see another member of his team, Detective Christian Oliver, coming to where he and Dan are standing. Det. Oliver is almost breathless as he catches up to his boss.

Al is painfully aware that his headache is becoming worse, but he knows he needs to hear what Christian has to say. "Well, what is it." The chief is expecting the worst and he is impatient to hear what he expects is more bad news.

"Chief, I was in the communications room and you're not going to believe this. We are getting communiqués from precincts all over the country about the strangest and most violent murders and they all have one thing in common." Detective Oliver needs time to catch his breath.

Al has lost all patience, "Well, spit it out, Christian!"

"Lamb of God, that's what they have in common. All the murders have Lamb of God in common. At each of the crime scenes 'Lamb of God' is what was screamed out by the perps or written in blood at the time the murders were committed. Chief, we've even received reports from Interpol that criminal acts including murder are being committed in Europe, South America and in the Far East, all with the similar MOs and all ending with Lamb of God. Even in the Middle-East, which is mostly Muslim, there are similar horrific occurrences and all with the same message, Lamb of God."

Al looks at Dan and then back at Christian, but he can't think of a single thing to say. His look betrays an overwhelmingly depression and sadness and he needs a moment to just reflect on what is happening. How can this be? What can possibly be causing these horrendous crimes? How can this be happening all over the country…all over the world?

He tries to find the answers based on his experience as a police officer, but he has no answers. Chief of Detectives Spartaco "Al" Barese has only one persistent, distressing thought that runs over and over in his mind… something wicked this way comes.

CHAPTER 9

Iam anxious to get to my condo so I close up at 5PM exactly and rush
home to change. I had made a date with Beth for dinner and we are
going to meet at a local pub for burgers and a beer, or two. She has been
working long hours due to some short staffing issues at the hospital and
I am looking forward to having some down time with the woman I love.

I'm always excited to see Beth, just being with her makes me happy,
but I can't shake my feeling of concern for Uncle Al. He's definitely not a
worrier so for him to be this consumed by the prospect of something bad
happening is totally out of character. In his position as Chief of Detectives
there is little in the way of crimes or criminals that he hasn't been exposed
to before. As much as I try to dismiss it, the only thing I can think of is
that his is an evil beyond what humans could execute; the type of evil I
had confronted in my battles with Julian. I start to consider the possibility of something rooted in the powers of hell, the all-consuming darkness
that will swallow the light wherever it shines.

All thoughts about forces of evil somehow being involved are going
through my mind; I try to shake off this dark mood. I start mumbling to
myself, "Why are you even considering this as something possible? Are
you some kind of self-anointed prophet? You've got a date with the most
beautiful woman in the world and you are thinking like an idiot! Uncle
Al is about the savviest guy on the planet, he'll figure it out without any

of your meddling? This is the kind of stuff you should leave to the Sainted anyway, they are far better than you at knowing when the shit would hit the fan." I guess I am trying self-deprecation to talk myself out of obsessing over what is bothering my uncle. In the end I vow not to let these things distract me. Besides, when he called and invited me to lunch with Fr. Aiden on Friday, I see that as a sign that maybe Uncle Al is getting back to his normal tough, 'know it all' nature…I could only hope.

I get out of the shower, shave and dress for my date with Beth. The pub in town is just a short ride away and we agree to meet there about 7PM. This should give Beth enough time to go home and get ready. I get to the Huntington Pub about 15 minutes early and settle into a booth with thoughts of a tall, cold Guinness draft. The pub is a warm, comfortable place with old wooden booths, beer signs, stained glass windows and lots of prints and photos of 19th century, early 20th century Huntington. I like dark beer which the pub serves in frosted steins, so the server takes my order and walks to the bar. While I'm waiting, I take a menu and start to look it over. That's when the world stops once more and the vision appears.

The streets of Rome are filled to overflowing. It is the Lenten season and those assembled in the square surrounding the church are waiting to hear the great and holy man. His powerful voice, commanding presence and above all his piety and holiness are legendary and the multitude gathered are waiting for a chance to see him and to hear him preach.

The Holy See understands that the faithful need to hear and understand the lessons that are being taught during the holy season of Lent and who better than the preacher before them. The pontiff speaks, "The blessings of the Lord are with you."

The priest answers, "And also with you your Holiness. It is with humility and gratitude that I am here in your presence."

"I have summoned you to Rome as I have a task for you. It is a mission that will be a lesson of the love of God and His Son to the many who have come together here at this, the holiest time of year."

"Your Holiness, I will do the best as I am able and ask for the guidance of the Lord so that I may be worthy to deliver His word."

The Pope blesses the priest with a sign of the cross and says, "Go in peace so that you may love and serve the Lord."

With that the preacher leaves the presence of the Holy See and walks down the long corridor that leads to the steps of the church. Before he goes out to greet the throngs who are congregated there, he stands in the vestibule for a moment to say a prayer,

"Dear Lord, it is through you that I am here at this time. It is by Your divine mercy that I am able to let Your words of love, Your words of joy, the passion of Your crucifixion and the fulfillment of God's promise with Your Resurrection resound to all. I ask for blessings on this day for all who are here in Your name, Amen."

With that the priest steps onto the landing above the square to the cheers and delight of the crowd. He is renowned for his marvelous gifts and the sanctity with which he leads his life. There are so many who come to Rome from distant lands. Peoples from France and Italy for sure, but there are many from all over the known world including Northern countries, from the Middle East regions and most of those present speak and know only their native language. The priest holds his outstretched arms over the throng and the crowd immediately becomes silent.

"Let us pray."

He leads all that are assembled in prayer. He quotes from the scriptures and his knowledge of theology keeps the masses of the faithful clinging to every one of the holy man's words. He is eloquent; a presence that commands respect and his splendid delivery keeps the attention of the audience for his entire time before them.

When he finishes, each and every person in the crowd knows of what he speaks, each and every person in the crowd understands the meaning and each and every person in the crowd knows of the miracle they are allowed to be part of.

St. Anthony of Padua steps out of his earthly body and stands before me. I am anxious to ask him the obvious. "How is it that you are able to speak to all those different people from different lands in the crowd and they are all able to understand you? How did this happen?"

St. Anthony of Padua answers, "I am blessed with the gift of tongues. It is the same as was given to the Apostles of our Lord after Pentecost and the Resurrection of Christ."

"Why have you shown me this vision?" I am at a loss to know a reason, but St. Anthony would only provide an overarching answer

St. Anthony seems to stare off beyond where we are standing as he speaks to me, "There are many who long for the word of God. They want to hear what they know in their hearts to be true, but often they cannot seem to find the courage to embrace this truth. There is always a choice between hearing what is being told and accepting or hearing what is being told and rejecting."

St. Anthony turns away from me and we are transported to Le-Puy. The priest is delivering a sermon to the congregation who is captivated by the words of the holy man. Without warning, a messenger suddenly appears in their midst and calls out to a poor old woman in the rear of the church,

"I bring news of great sadness; your son has died! Your son has been murdered by his bitter enemies. Oh, why has God done this to you? He has left you without a son."

The woman hearing of the news becomes distraught. She does not know what is to become of her without her beloved son.

The messenger now speaks to the crowd trying to turn the congregants away from the preacher and the word of God. "What has the woman's son done to deserve such a fate? Why has God forsaken her?" He shouts his words so that he will be heard above that of the priest.

St. Anthony ceases to preach and stares intently at the messenger and at once the priest knows who he is. Through his teachings and sermons, the holy man has become familiar with the evil one who is now before him. "You are to be silent in the house of the Lord! You have nothing to speak but lies and deceit, and it is the Lord who commands you to leave this holy place at once."

The messenger stares at the priest and his fear becomes evident. The messenger then turns into a demon that is cloaked in the form of a man and, with a hideous shriek, leaves the gathering.

St. Anthony now turns to the poor woman who is grieving for the son she believes has died. He places his arms around the poor frightened mother to console her and tells the woman, "Your son is very much alive and in good health. He is on his way to see you as we speak. It is the evil one that hopes to sow the seeds of fear with lies among those who gather here. It is

Lucifer that intrudes on the word of God and it is Lucifer who seeks to capture the souls of men and women. It begins when the faithful lose their understanding of the lessons that come from His words. The demon takes many forms and he will do all in his power to appeal, tempt and blind you to the goodness of God. You must be ever vigilant for you will not know from where or when the beast will come, but he will come again. Know this and always remember for he seeks your soul and he will not relent."

When St. Anthony turns to me again, he seems to recognize that I understand the lesson of the vision.

"I know the demon that tried to kill me can always come back. Is there any protection, any way I can recognize him before it is too late?"

St. Anthony of Padua speaks, "The woman who was told of her son's death believed it to be true. She did not want to believe it, but regrettably assumed that it was true. To all gathered here in the house of God it seemed unthinkable that anyone would lie about such a tragedy. However, it is Lucifer who will do all he can to cause violence, inflict fear and hatred… anything to attain what he wants, but he can also beguile, tempt and lure men and women to sin. What he yearns for is to have all turn away from the word of God so he may take possession of their souls. You will not recognize him when he comes, but you have your faith and that is your strongest weapon."

St. Anthony of Padua goes silent, folds his hands to pray and the light envelops the Sainted and he is gone.

I am back in the pub still sitting in the booth, but I have no time to contemplate the meaning of the vision as the door to the pub opens and in walks Beth. She looks around and sees me and flashes me her gorgeous smile as she navigates through the tables and walks to the booth. I immediately get up and give her my gentlemanly "in public hug and kiss" and we both take our seats.

She immediately starts talking even before she is seated, "You should have seen the day I've had. First Katie was out sick so I have to take over her duties. Then the patient in 411 has a fit about the lunch menu. Then the hospital administrator comes over to the desk and tells me we are behind in updating the files to our new online system. Then Laura loses her wedding band and we have to scour the floor to find it, thank God we did. Then Celia drops the afternoon medications all over…" Beth is rapidly firing off the events of her day, but I interrupt her,

"Hello Elizabeth! How are you? I sincerely hope you are well. I trust you will not let the unpleasantness of your day at work interfere with our time together as I am thrilled to see you. I am so glad we could meet for dinner; I thoroughly enjoy your company and hope we will have a mutually enjoyable evening." I say this with my patented quiz show announcer voice and a plastered on 'politician seeking voters' smile.

Not to be outdone, Beth responds, "Your point is well taken Christopher. I do apologize for my less than gentile outburst. How are you? I trust you are well. I've missed you and I am delighted that we could spend the evening convivially. I do treasure these moments."

Beth just looks at me and then she starts to laugh hysterically and I join in, gratefully knowing that she has a terrific sense of humor.

I reach over and hold her hand, "Sembra che lei ha avuto una giornata per i libri record."

Beth squeezes mine, "You said it and this day is really one for the record books. It isn't any one thing; it is just a number of small problems that seem to mount as the day went on. I am totally exhausted and hey, are you gonna buy me a drink or what?"

In life, timing is everything and just as Beth asks for a drink the waitress walks over to our booth with my drink. Beth looks at the cold Guinness and she tells the server that she will have the same. "Anyway, sorry for dumping my sorrows onto your lap, but that's what girlfriends do. Now it's your turn, how was your day?"

I feel happy every time she refers to herself as my girlfriend, even though we are much closer than that and for this I consider myself one lucky bastard. "Well, my day wasn't nearly as eventful as yours" but then I thought of Uncle Al and his fears, "I did speak with Uncle Al and he seems to be very unnerved about something." After I finish saying this, I immediately thought of the conversation I had with myself and the promise not to put a shadow over our date.

"I really shouldn't have said anything Beth. It's just that I am worried about him."

Beth looks at me, concerned herself and says, "What is it, Chris? Do you know what's bothering him?"

"I only wish I did, but even he can't put his finger on it. It is just some nameless fear that will cause something very bad to happen."

Beth looks puzzled, "Something bad?"

I take a sip of my beer. In my mind I go over what Uncle Al and I had discussed on the call and tell Beth, "Yeah, something bad…maybe even very bad and what's weird is that I've never really heard him speak like this before. He's a cop and he's seen it all and his gut is telling him that something's going to happen and it won't be good. I try to make light of it to him, but I'm worried, he's sounds troubled. He told me that there are some very serious violent crimes being committed after the Christmas Holidays, so much so that it borders on the worst kind imaginable."

Beth looks surprised, "You would think that violent crimes are something he would get used to because it's his job, but you say he thinks this seems beyond anything that even comes close to normal?"

"Yeah, it is his job, but he's not seeing it that way. He thinks it's just the beginning, kind of a prelude to a much bigger storm that's coming and according to him it's going to be something like the storm of the century. He doesn't know what to name the storm or when or where the storm will hit and that's what's got him very concerned."

Beth and I sit in silence for a short time and I want to change the subject so I tell her, "On a happier note, things seem to be going really well with him and Eileen and I know that she makes him happy." Beth perks up a bit and smiles, "I'm glad he's happy, I really like Eileen and they do make a nice couple."

"You mean like you and me?" I said with mock questioning.

"What! Listen kiddo, we better be a lot more than just a nice couple or you may go home with another black eye…even worse than the one you had when we first met." I know she's just kidding but I don't want to take any chances, "Vi prego di scusare il mio povero tentativo di umorismo."

"Okay, your poor attempt at humor has been duly noted." Now Beth smiles at me and I acknowledge to myself that I am out-of-control in love with her.

The waitress comes back to take our order. The burgers at the Huntington Pub are terrific so Beth orders a Swiss and mushroom burger and I order the special burger of the day, a hamburger with sautéed onions and peppers, tomatoes, cheddar cheese, bacon, guacamole and jalapeños on a whole grain bun. I also tell the waitress to bring me a large order of steak fries. Beth just looks at me and says, "I can't believe that you eat that kind of food and don't gain any weight. You know if you get fat, I'm outta here."

In mock indignation I tell her, "Oh so you're only after my body huh. I'll have you know that in some countries fat men are considered gods. Or is it fat women, I forget."

"I think its fat heads and you certainly qualify on some level." Beth is too quick so I just suck in my stomach and she starts to laugh.

Beth and I make small talk for a while until the food arrives and then we dig into our burgers with enthusiasm. We continue to talk between bites and I tell Beth that I am having lunch with Uncle Al and one of his closest friends, Fr. Aiden Langford, an instructor at Immaculate Conception Seminary on Friday. I explain that he is a scholar and a genuinely brilliant mind on the subject of theology and biblical studies.

Beth's family has a home in Lloyd Harbor and I'm sure they pass the entrance to the seminary every day. "You've mentioned Fr. Langford before. I would really enjoy meeting him one of these days. My mom and dad are big supporters of the seminary and I think they know him."

I ask her, "Would you like to join us on Friday? I know Al and Aiden won't mind at all."

"Oh no, I wouldn't want to spoil your lunch with the boys, besides I'm on duty Friday, but if ever the time comes, and he's willing, I'd like to meet him. He sounds like a fascinating man and it would be a very interesting experience." Beth's curiosity is genuine and I know that Fr. Aiden would love to meet her.

"Okay, it's a date. I'll set it up when I see him Friday."

"Sound's great."

Mounted on the wall of the pub there are a number of flat screen TV's, all with closed caption, and most are turned to sports networks, but one is turned to ACN News. I normally don't like the distraction of TVs in restaurants because I just want to enjoy the people I'm with, but for some reason Beth and I turn to the screen and see the photo of this very handsome man with his name superimposed on the screen.

"Hey Beth, have you ever heard of this Dr. Thomas Houston?"

"Of course, I have. What a hunk!" She continues to stare at the screen, but she knows I'm looking at her with my mouth wide open.

"A hunk? You call him a hunk? What is he, 6-foot, 6 foot 1? Wavy dark hair, 180 maybe 182 pounds, chiseled features, clear complexion, distinct body odor, a genius on some level, a wealthy player, wears suits that, if sold, could cover the deficits of most third world countries. I don't know Beth; I used to trust your choice of men." I added 'distinct body odor' to throw her off.

Now she looks at me in mock surprise, "Why Christopher, are you jealous?"

"Who me? Jealous? Don't be absurd, I am just pointing out some obvious flaws in the man." As we both turn back to the screen, the closed captioning crawling along the bottom announces that there will be a special interview with Dr. Thomas Houston, PHD on Newsmakers Now with Barbara Ellen Comstock to air Thursday evening at 8PM.

"Are you going to watch the interview?" I ask, knowing the answer.

"Of course, I am. He may become our next President. Don't you want to know what he has to say about all the issues that we will confront as a nation? I for one would like to know more about the hunk, 'er I mean the man!" She says this with a twinkle in her eye.

"Well, I for one won't be watching. I've heard a few things about this guy. He's an atheist and he has some pretty radical leftwing social and economic ideas that don't sync with mine. He attracts some real kooks to his rallies and, most importantly, I don't like looking at men that are better looking than me which happens to be the main reason I've stopped going to the movies."

Beth is now having too much fun and she decides that my torment should continue as she explains, "Oh Chris, he is not *that* much better looking than you. He does have, how shall I put it, an abundance of physical and material attributes that certain female members of our species find especially attractive. This doesn't necessarily make him *that* much more superior or *that* much better looking than you, so don't give it another thought." At this moment Beth is surpassing the urge to laugh.

"Is that so? Well, I'll have you know that my prospects are getting better each and every day. I will have the mortgage on my condo fully paid within the next decade or two, I am now driving a car that is *only* 5 years old, I expect my business to more than triple over the next 35 years and, as if that were not enough, I have purchased a Power Ball Lottery ticket that could be worth a cool $315 Million Dollars!" I fold my arms and look over at Beth, nose in the air, exhibiting my patented feigned indignation.

Beth slides out of her side of the booth and walks over to my side. She says "move over" and I do as she commands. She sits right up against my side and looks intently at me. She wraps her arm around my neck and places her other hand on my leg while her lips cross my cheek. I try to keep my cool and calm composure as I take a sip of Guinness. Beth begins to nibble on my earlobe and I can feel her hot breath on my neck as she continues to rub my leg. At this point I am getting very excited, but she stops her manipulations to look into my eyes and says seductively, "Mmmmmm, $315 Million Dollars, and a 5-year-old Mustang, huh."

At this point I turn and spit out the beer across the booth and I cave in laughter and there are tears rolling out of my eyes and Beth is just staring at me with the biggest shit eating grin I have ever seen on her face.

That's my girl, totally cool, totally hot and totally mine.

CHAPTER 10

The make-up artist is giving him a final touch up before his nationally televised interview. She applies his make-up with care, making sure to accentuate his strong, masculine features, especially his eyes. She is nearly hypnotized as she looks into those eyes.

This is to be the first interview after his announcement for the presidency and he knows that it is of paramount importance as many of the viewers will be seeing and hearing him for the first time. The interview is with Barbara Ellen Comstock of the ACN Broadcasting Network. Tom Houston has cherry-picked Comstock for the interview. She is attractive, popular and a fellow traveler, so to speak, and he knows where her sympathies lie.

For this appearance he chooses one of his hand-tailored, dark blue, micro texture Canali suits that he has specially made to measure. He wears a custom slim-fit Roma Poplin shirt designed by Stefano Ricci and for a tie he chooses a heavy silk Faubourg from Hermes, in red with light blue accents. Wrist watches and dress shoes are his passion, so he wears a new pair of black oxfords from John Lobb. To complete the ensemble, he ceremonially opens the special presentation case to his "Grand Lange 1" platinum, limited edition created by A. Lange & Sohne and places it on his wrist. When he finishes dressing, he stares into the mirror to admire his fit and trim stature and his striking good-looks.

The make-up artist finishes and she removes the towel from around his neck. She takes her time doing it as she looks at the man who just might be our next president, but she isn't so interested in that. He is so handsome and she is fantasizing what it would be like to make love to this man. He seems to notice the slowness with which she completes the task and he looks up at her and smiles. She smiles back knowing she will go home and watch his interview while she masturbates.

He gets up from the seat and puts on his suit jacket and in an instant his bodyguard rises and opens the door that leads to the hallway. The bodyguard knows where to go and as his boss and a small entourage stroll down the hall to the studio; most of the employees of ACN News stand to the side against the wall and applaud as he walks by. Dr. Thomas Houston smiles and shakes hands as he thinks it will be good practice for when he hits the campaign trail.

He enters the studio as a man with a purpose, a man that projects the strength and resolve of one who could inspire, one who could lead. A member of the crew shows him to his seat on the specially designed set and wires him up with a carefully hidden microphone. The set has been made to look like the surroundings of an important person; a leader even a president. Barbara Ellen Comstock, 'Barbara Ellen' as she likes to be called, is over to the side speaking to one of the producers when she turns and spots Dr. Thomas Houston sitting on the set. She gives him a big smile and walks over to take her place in the chair next to him. Once she is seated, Barbara Ellen greets Tom Houston and they shake hands.

"Dr. Houston, what a pleasure it is to see you again."

"Please Barbara Ellen, we've known each other for too long, please call me Tom."

"Well, Tom it's all about to start. Are you ready?"

"I was born ready." Tom says with a smile and she smiles back.

The director yells, Ready on the set, in 5…4…3…2…1."

Barbara Ellen faces that camera as she has done for the past 23 years and reads her lines from the teleprompter to the viewing audience, "Welcome to Newsmakers Now. Tonight, live in our studio, we have a very special guest. He is a true legitimate phenomenon in a world of transient personalities.

He is a recognized scholar and lecturer on many subjects, he's a widely read, bestselling author and a modern-day philosopher and, if that were not enough, he is the head of the largest think tank in America, ACTELECT. Please join me in welcoming Dr. Thomas Houston." The camera that initially focuses on Barbara Ellen goes wide to reveal Tom Houston and after the shot is established, the director cuts to a close up of her guest with graphics of his name and some notable accomplishments.

"Welcome Dr. Houston, I can't tell you how grateful I am to have your first interview since you've declared for the presidential nomination of the Socialist Liberation Party. We truly appreciate the opportunity to speak with you.

"Thank you, Barbara Ellen, the pleasure is all mine."

"I've received so many letters and emails when we first announced your appearance on my program. The correspondence is overwhelmingly from women and the most frequently asked question is, is there a special woman in your life?"

Tom Houston laughs out loud, "Well, let me say this right up front; all the women in my life are special. From my grandmother and mother to the bright and beautiful ladies I date, I consider myself as being lucky just to have known them."

Barbara Ellen follows up, "Is marriage on the horizon for you?"

Tom smiles, "I am sure it is and when I meet that very special person, I will consider my life complete. Oh, and I'll be sure to let you know first."

It's Barbara Ellen's turn to laugh, "Promise?"

"Promise! Oh, by the way you made one slight error in your introduction." Dr. Tom Houston says in a serious tone.

Barbara Ellen, who is known for her meticulous research, appears to be a bit chagrined, "An error? What might that be Dr. Houston?"

"ACTELECT is the largest think tank in the *world*." This made both Barbara Ellen and Tom laugh and she continues the interview.

"Point taken; I'll be sure to remember." Barbara Ellen continues with her interview. "Your boundless energy is well known; how do you find the time and energy to do all you do? Aren't you simply exhausted at the end of every day given your hectic schedule?"

"Actually, Barbara Ellen what I do invigorates me. I thrive on a full schedule and there is so much to learn and understand and so many folks to meet, I only wish there were more hours in the day."

"How much sleep do you get each night?"

"Oh, about 4 hours on average."

"*Four hours!!!*" Barbara Ellen gives the comment added emphasis and Dr. Thomas smiles at this.

"I am one of the lucky people who don't need a great deal of sleep, much to the annoyance of my staff." He smiles and off camera you could hear Barbara Ellen chuckle.

Tom Houston continues, "I use my time to read and to write. I confer with staff as there are always many important issues to deal with. I am fortunate enough to have met with so many leaders, both foreign and domestic who have given me many insights into the matters they confront every day. I also meet with many of the unsung heroes in our country, those people who have given up so much to help others; the downtrodden, the poor workers and those other people who try to survive in an economic system that believes they are superfluous."

"Superfluous, what do you mean when you say they are considered superfluous?" Barbara Ellen appears to viewers to be genuinely interested in his answer, but she lobbed him the softball so he could knock it out of the park.

Dr. Houston leans forward and answers, "What I mean Barbara Ellen is that in our capitalistic society, people are considered commodities. Use them, abuse them and discard them. When they have outlived their use-fulness, they are simply unnecessary, ergo superfluous." He leans back in his chair having made his point.

"Why do you think that these capitalists are doing what you say they are doing?" Another softball and Barbara Ellen hopes for another homerun.

"Why, I'll tell you why, because profits always come before people and that's the way it's always worked. It is only money that rules and it is only money that is coveted by certain powerful capitalists. If someone can't handle the job, if they get sick or if they need to stay home for their family or if they don't have the strength to continue, they are out. Fortunately for these capitalists, there's always someone in line to take over the job and the cycle begins again." At this point Tom Houston recognizes that he sounds more like he's teaching a class on the canons of communism or socialism than as a candidate for President of the United States so he tempers his comments.

"Listen Barbara Ellen, I think it is important for everyone in your audience to understand that I do not condemn capitalism. I am one of its fortunate sons, but I do condemn capitalists that expect hardworking and poor Americans forced to function under the circumstances that allow the rich to accumulate wealth through a worker's labor. All the while these men and women are given little or nothing in return. We have so much in our great country so all I am saying is that maybe they should share a little more of what the rich folks have with others. Come to think of it that's about as American as you can get."

Barbara Ellen seems relieved at his reply, but she knows that she will need to get one of the major negatives out of the way so she continues, "Dr. Houston, you have made some very controversial remarks about what you call and I quote 'The false premise of God and the neutrality of man's role in the universe.' Many in the religious community have condemned your statements as blasphemous and ignorant. One minister even said that he would pray for your soul as you are already damned to an eternity in hell. Would you care to comment on this to our viewers?"

"Thank you for the opportunity to clarify my position. First, I'd like to thank that minister for praying for my soul. I consider it like chicken soup…it can't hurt." At this Barbara Ellen Comstock suppresses the urge to laugh out loud.

Dr. Thomas Houston smiles having noticed her off-camera reaction to his response and he makes his reply. "Whether you want to accept it or not, God is a concept. No one has ever seen God and many consider Him a creation of man's imagination. It was only a few men that wrote the Bible, the Torah, the Koran and other religious manuscripts and we have only their declaration that it is the word of God. I believe that these holy men of all faiths originally wrote these tracts so that they could control the people; control their behavior and in turn what did they promise the faithful? They promise them the reward of heaven or the damnation of hell. So here is what is at issue, early believers having to choose the bounty of heaven or the torments of hell and I ask you Barbara, what do you expect they would choose; what would you choose if given this option?"

Barbara Ellen at first doesn't know if she should answer so she simply keeps silent and waits for Tom Houston to continue.

"No need to answer Barbara Ellen. Of course, you would choose heaven, and what is the path to Heaven? It is whatever was written by the self-proclaimed holy men in the Bible, Torah, Koran or whatever and that is the control I speak of. You must believe that I have no quarrel with the faithful who accept as true the concept of a Supreme Being, whether He is called God or Allah or Jehovah. It is good and proper for them to have that means of spiritual support and I applaud their faith even if I do not accept it for myself. What I am at odds with is that people manipulate this belief in God as justification to commit crimes against humanity, all in His name. Here in America more than 3,000 of our fellow citizens have suffered at the hands of radical Islamists who use manmade disasters to kill and maim the innocent all in the name of Allah, or whatever name He is given. What kind of Allah would allow this to happen and what kind of people would do such a horrendous thing in Allah's name? I don't believe in God because I don't believe that any entity, spiritual or otherwise, would allow such a disaster to happen."

"You make a compelling argument, but I want to address one comment. You say the various religious texts were written by a few men to control the behavior of all. Doesn't society set laws to control behavior?"

"You are correct Barbara Ellen, but there is one important distinction. A few men who wrote those texts said it is God's word and you have to obey or else. Society adapts laws at the will of the people and their duly elected representatives and that is the difference. Consider societies ruled by religious sects and look at the way people are treated. Women are abused in the name of tradition and treated as chattel, societies that condone genital mutilations, children sold into slavery; car bombs that indiscriminately kill thousands for no reason other than the victims are of a different religious sect. These horrors have become more commonplace than we could ever have imagined. Go ahead and read the justification for all this in those holy texts I mentioned. Now consider how a democratic society, a representative republic guided by the rule of law and the principles of freedom chooses to operate. I believe that America is that kind of place, but I also need to acknowledge that we have lost our way and I intend to change it to the type of society people want."

Barbara Ellen considers avoiding the natural follow up questions, but she thinks better of it as Dr. Houston seems to be handling the prior questions well, so she asks, "Didn't our founders believe that the rights are God given?"

As they continue to speak, the interview is interrupted by a special news bulletin. The broadcast of the program breaks away to an anchorman sitting behind the ACN news desk with a somber face as he speaks to the camera,

"ACN News interrupts our regularly scheduled programming to bring you this important news bulletin. Sources close to ACN have learned that police bureau's from around the country are reporting on a series of criminal acts including murder, stabbings, shootings and bombings that have killed and wounded more than 1,490 people including 687 children in the last few days."

The news anchor pauses so the full effect of his words can penetrate, "Reliable sources say that all these acts are of an especially violent nature and they all have one thing in common; the use of the phrase "Lamb of God." Initial inquiries into the crime have not shown the victims of these incidents are connected in any way except for the use of "Lamb of God." That is all the information we have available at the moment. ACN News will continue to report on this rapidly breaking story as it unfolds; now we return you to Barbara Ellen Comstock's exclusive interview with Dr. Thomas Houston."

The direction is given to cut back to the studio set. Barbara Ellen Comstock and Dr. Thomas Houston are sitting in silence for an uncomfortable few seconds until she speaks up,

"What an unspeakable tragedy." Visibly shaken, she is about to continue speaking when a member of the crew hands Barbara Ellen a sheet of paper. She reads it and her face turns pale, "Ladies and gentlemen I have just been handed an important update. It appears that crimes similar to those that are happening throughout the country are also occurring in other countries around the world, all with the common theme, "Lamb of God." All I can say is our thoughts and prayers go out to the victims of these tragedies and their families. I am at a loss for words to describe the horror of it all. Would you like to make a comment on this breaking news Dr. Houston?" Barbara Ellen Comstock appears genuinely shocked by this event.

"Thank you for the opportunity, Barbara Ellen. I want to extend my personal condolences to the families of the victims of these horrific acts." Thomas Houston is at a cross-road, he could stop now or he could continue to speak. He weighs the consequences of speaking his mind or shutting his mouth. It is a great risk. If he continues to speak, he could possibly alienate any large number of the viewers and possibly stall his campaign before it even starts or he could just leave his expression of sympathy to stand. He chooses to continue.

"I also want your viewers to ask themselves this; what kind of Supreme Being, God or any other name you might call Him, could ever allow such a thing to happen. Each of the poor victims and their families have been torn apart by the awful events that have taken place' events so tragic that the terror will stay in their minds and hearts as long as they live. These acts appear to have been committed by some type of religious cult, not unlike the radical Islamists that flew planes into the World Trade Center."

Dr. Houston takes a pregnant pause and continues, "These murderers use God, Christ if you will, as the excuse for killing fellow human beings. The 'Lamb of God' is a reference to Christ and as the story goes God the Father sacrificed His Son for the forgiveness of man's sins. Now we have religious cults using innocent victims in a sacrifice of blood in the name of a god."

Dr. Tom Houston is in the zone and tells himself that he needs to exhibit passion in order for his words to resound to the views. "Barbara Ellen, what kind of a god could justify this insanity? I ask all your viewers, what kind of a god could justify this insanity."

Barbara Ellen seems to regain her legendary self-control and asks, "What makes you so sure it is a cult?"

"I am speculating on this, but the common element to all these unrelated crimes is the words, 'Lamb of God' and that does seem compelling enough to assume a certain association among the victims. Again, it is speculation on my part, not having any possession of the facts. I am sure that the authorities will perform a thorough investigation and ascertain the truth behind what individuals or groups, if any, are involved in the committing of such heinous acts."

The interview goes on for nearly an hour. In it they discuss many topics and Tom Houston is able to give his views on each subject that comes up in the interview. Even though he projects a thoughtful and somber tone and demeanor, Tom Houston speaks with clarity and strength of his convictions. He is witty and erudite when he needs to be, and sympathetic and humble when he is supposed to be. The hour is nearly up when Barbara Ellen begins to wind down the interview,

"Dr. Houston, our hour is nearly up, but I would like to close our program with one last question. Why do you want to be President of the United States?"

"Barbara Ellen, first I would like to thank you and ACN for giving me the opportunity to be interviewed and to give your viewers a chance to see me, hear my views and to understand the kind of man I hope they could vote for. I come from humble beginnings, raised to be the best man I could be and I am fortunate to live the American Dream. I also have the good fortune to have met many of the people that make this country great and I am humbled by the strength they show in all they do; all they are and how they lead their lives. I have also seen many instances where the struggles of many of these people sap the strength they once had. I've seen their once promising lives become a never-ending cycle of hopelessness as they are plowed under by a society that gives them little or no reason to hope. I intend to change all that as President of the United States. For the benefit of each and every American I will create a strong central government, a government that works for all and works well. I will use the peoples hard earned money they pay in taxes wisely so all Americans will have someplace to turn to when they need help. It is through this vision I will provide the leadership that will allow each and every citizen the opportunity to do what they want, to provide for their families, to get the support they need and to finally have the hope they deserve. There is no greater calling I can think of than to have the power to do all that for America. With America as the world leader, we can bring our message to all and become the shining example of how we can change for the better and give hope to everyone."

Dr. Thomas Houston turns away from Barbara Ellen and faces the camera as he speaks directly to all Americans watching him right now.

"Today we have heard news of terrible tragedies from all over the country and beyond to nations around the world. We will mourn for their families and share in the grief of their loss, but it will not end there. As a nation we will rise to confront this darkness that exists in the hearts of men and purge it from our society with hope for a better land and a better life. Together we will look beyond ourselves and embrace all humanity and declare we are the best hope for peace, justice and prosperity in our lifetime. I thank you and pledge you a new beginning for America and a new, better beginning for the world."

Barbara Ellen Comstock smiles and she shakes hands with Dr. Thomas Houston and closes the interview by saying,

"Goodnight to all in our viewing audience and to the families of the victims of the "Lamb of God" murders; you are in our thoughts and prayers."

The interview ends and Barbara Ellen says her goodbyes to Dr. Tom Houston. "Again, Tom I want to thank you so much for kindly agreeing to be our guest. I am sorry that our interview had to pause and focus on this terrible tragedy." Barbara Ellen holds out her hand to shake Tom's.

Tom Houston takes her hand and holds it in both of his. "Barbara Ellen, these events are so much greater in the impact they have on us than anything you can ever imagine. When you compare the life and death of people on a scale like we have been told of today, and in the past, you have to consider how unimportant everything else appears to be. I acknowledge that, at first, it may not seem like that, but I truly believe I was sent here to do something important. I believe it is my duty to impose a sense of strong leadership so Americans can stop fearing that these types of tragedies will become commonplace. It should be me that thanks you for giving me the powerful forum of your wonderful show to pass along that hope to your viewers, and who I hope will be my voters."

Barbara Ellen wants to embrace Tom Houston; she wants to tell him how wonderful he is and how she will be sure to do everything she can to get him elected. This is what she wants to do, but she can't; after all journalists are supposed to be objective. She puts her other hand over his in a warm and friendly handshake,

"I wish you good luck and God speed…oh, I mean good luck," They both laugh and say their farewells.

When he leaves the studio Tom Houston exits through an entrance at the rear of the building. He wants to avoid the waiting crowds of admirers and the press who have assembled outside the front entrance. As he opens the door of his limousine Tom smiles at who is there to greet him. She is young and beautiful and she is his reward. Her long blond hair cascades over her shoulders, and her form fitting dress accentuates every curve on her perfect body. He gets into his waiting Maybach stretch limousine for the drive back to his Garden City mansion. Tom sits back in the plush leather seat and he doesn't need to say a word. The woman reaches for the bar, adds ice to a Waterford crystal tumbler and pours her boss a measure of Oban 14 single malt scotch. She knows his habits well and reaches for the remote to tune to ACN Late News. Dr. Houston is interested in hearing the updates on the 'Lamb of God' murders. Barbara Ellen called them the 'Lamb of God' murders and he likes the tone it communicates and he knows it will stick.

A good portion of the late news is devoted to the murders and the violent ways which they are being committed, but he already knows most of what is said and nothing interesting is added to the reports. The next feature is of far more interest to him, and he turns up the volume so he won't miss a word. The first image is that of the anchorman, but the next image was a full screen shot of his photo along with the graphic "Dr. Thomas Houston, Noted Author, Lecturer and President of ACTELECT." He smiles in approval and has to concede to himself that he looks downright handsome.

The network's anchor begins the feature by saying, "Our next news item is ACN's own Barbara Ellen Comstock's exclusive interview with Dr. Thomas Houston. Initial indications are that it was watched by well over 18,000,000 households making it one of the most viewed news programs of the past 24 months."

ACN cameras cut away from the anchorman to a clip from the interview where Barbara Ellen asks him about some of the fringe groups that he seems to attract to his rallies and his reply,

"Barbara Ellen, these fringe groups as you call them are no different from the many other American collectives who meet because of a common bond, a goal they share. Perhaps some are called fringe because their causes are out, even way out, of the majority of thinking or current popular culture, but they form these groups because they have no voice on their own and nowhere else to go. These groups of people need to be heard in spite of how unusual their views may be and once they understand that they have a voice, they can assimilate into the mainstream of America's dialogue and become part of the system."

The director cuts back to the anchor who continues to read news relating to the interview. "After the Barbara Ellen Comstock interview, ACN took a phone survey of viewers to determine the favorability rating of Dr. Thomas Houston's appearance. The survey uses a cross-section of 1,500 registered voters and the poll finds Dr. Thomas Houston has an overall approval rating of 63%, nearly 3 points higher than the previous high..." The anchor goes on, but that is all Tom needs to hear.

Tom Houston knew that ACN was taking a poll; he was told in advance by the powers at the network and he had hoped for this result. He smiles to himself as it looks like the great gamble he's taken has paid off.

The limo picks up speed after it leaves Manhattan and cruises along the Northern State Parkway heading for the Garden City exit. The woman moves to the space in the seat next to him and she put her hands on his leg. She begins to rub the upper part of his thigh and she smiles when she hears him moan. The beautiful woman uses the button to raise the blacked-out window that separates the rear of the limo from the driver's compartment. Tom Houston likes to see her naked so she obliges him and removes her dress and lets it drop to the floor of the auto. She knows why she is here and she knows what is required of her.

Tom closes his eyes and the tension he feels from the day's events melt away as she strokes him until he gets hard. They have sex in the rear of an $800,000 Mercedes-Maybach Pullman custom stretch limousine and when he comes all he can think of is, isn't the American Dream a wonderful thing.

He will be home in about 30 minutes so he says to himself, "What the heck" and has her pour him another measure of Oban14. He drinks it slowly and savors the spirit.

CHAPTER 11

I walk into the restaurant and up to the table where Uncle Al is sitting. I now channel Robert Duvall and I do my best, "I love the smell of Rosa's Pizza in the morning!", but rather than applauding he says, "Sit down, Chris, you're embarrassing me."

"Well now you know how I feel when you tell one of your jokes."

"Believe me when I tell you that your imitation of Robert Duvall is so bad it can get you arrested in some countries."

The kidding is over, we embrace and I sit down at the table. It's lunchtime so Rosa's is packed, but Uncle Al always manages to get a table. I think he always gets a table when he shows his badge and frightens the high school freshmen that eat there instead of the school's cafeteria. Anyway, it works for me.

"Where's Fr. Aiden?" I ask, looking around.

Uncle Al laments, "He should be here any minute; he's probably stuck in traffic. The traffic situation seems to get worse every year."

I try to soft peddle one my uncle's major gripes and tell him, "Well that's the price we pay for living in paradise."

We catch up a bit, but Uncle Al looks awful and he seems very troubled and I think I know why. Just as I am going to ask him about the headlines plastered all over the web, TV and newspapers, Fr. Langford walks into Rosa's and heads directly for our table.

"Spartaco! What a joy it is to see you again!" and they embrace. He then turns to me, "…and Christopher, it has been too long since we've last broken bread. You look wonderful, unlike your uncle who appears to have lost weight, sleep and his razor." Father Langford has refined the fine art of the initial greeting.

I turn to Uncle Al and in mock anger I protest, "Hey? How come he gets to call you Spartaco? I'm a blood relative, so how come I can't call you Spartaco?"

Uncle Al turns to me in all seriousness, "There are three reasons you can't call me Spartaco, first, I don't want you to, second if you want to keep your blood as in blood relative you won't ever call me Spartaco and third, Aiden has a direct link to God and when I die, I'm going to use his name. Comprendere?"

I refuse to answer him because I pretend, I'm pissed off.

Fr. Aiden expresses sympathy, "Ah, Christopher you must realize that rank does have its privileges and I outrank you even though Spartaco and I do not share the familial bonds you do. At any rate we are, at last, together in the best pizza establishment I know."

We all nod in agreement with Fr. Aiden's critique, but Rosa's doesn't have wait service so you need to go to the counter and order what you want. I volunteer to stand in line and get slices for all.

"Okay, I'll go and get our food. I'm having the eggplant parmigiana slice. What do you want Uncle Al?"

Without hesitation he says, "The eggplant parmigiana slice and a bottle of Snapple Diet Ice Tea."

Father Aiden makes it unanimous, "I wholeheartedly concur; I too shall have an eggplant parmigiana slice and a Snapple Diet Ice Tea seems the perfect accompaniment. It is my understanding that the pizza is the best on planet Earth!"

Well, that's a hat trick so I walk to the counter and wait in line for my turn.

Father Aiden is very concerned with Uncle Al's appearance as he speaks to his friend. "Spartaco, I did not mean to make light of your appearance, but in all candor, you look dreadful and I am greatly troubled about your health."

"Aiden, I suppose you've read the headlines. Seven of the "Lamb of God" victims; that's seven victims, are Suffolk County residents and the way in which they died was more brutal than you can ever imagine."

Fr. Aiden is at a loss for words, "I listened to the interview with Dr. Thomas Houston yesterday and heard about the horror on the special news break. I've since read reports in the press and it appears these events are more dreadful than anyone can comprehend."

"Young kids and their parents, an old man, a woman who attempted to murder a police officer and more victims by the day. I am at a loss to explain this and there is no rationale for these crimes, nothing. We've checked with other police departments around the country and they are expressing the same shock at the violent nature of the crimes. Aiden, it's happening all over the world." Uncle Al lowers his head in anticipation of another headache he knows is coming.

Fr. Aiden asks, "Do you or your fellow officers in law enforcement have any idea as to the "why" behind it all?"

"No, and that's what's so frightening. We cannot seem to find any connection between any of the people who have committed these crimes. The only commonality is the reference to 'Lamb of God' which is often written in the victims' blood beside their bodies. How can this happen?"

"Spartaco, what I find most distressing is that there appears to be a concerted, perhaps covert effort to somehow make our Lord, the Lamb of God, an accomplice to these crimes. You can read it in the news stories about these horrendous acts. It is almost as if the perpetrators want to negate all of the good works done is in our Lords name." Fr. Langford appears greatly saddened by his own words.

By now I return to the table and place the food in front of Fr. Aiden and Uncle Al and they just sit there and stare at their slices and ice tea.

I am puzzled, "What's going on guys? I thought you were starving?"

Uncle Al speaks first, "Aiden and I are just talking about the so-called Lamb of God murders and I guess we lost our appetites."

Knowing Uncle Al and Fr. Langford's sadness at this horror, I am at a loss about what I should say but I tell them, "I read about them online today. It's really unbelievable…come to think of it; you kind of predicted something like this was going to happen."

Father Aiden makes a quick head turn with a puzzled look on his face, "Spartaco, what does Christopher speak of?"

Uncle Al takes a deep breath before he answers a question that he doesn't want to, "I have been having some really bad thoughts lately, I don't know what you'd call them, premonitions of sorts, I guess. They seem to have started after the holidays as the crime rate appeared to be rising and not in the normal pattern we've seen in the past. However, that's not what I am worried about; I seem to see it as a prelude to something bigger… cops' intuition that sort of thing. I tried to shrug it off, but now it appears my worst fears have been realized."

I turn to Fr. Aiden, "Father, I detected a shift in his mood a couple of days ago and I am worried about Uncle Al, he never acts like this." I express my genuine concern for his wellbeing.

Uncle Al says, somewhat embarrassed and annoyed by my comment. "Stop it Chris, you don't have to worry about me."

Fr. Aiden lovingly chastises his friend, "Spartaco, you are indeed a fortunate man to have someone who cares for you to the degree that Christopher does. I would like to add my name to the ranks of those who care for your welfare."

Fr. Aiden then continues, "Now let us consider the source of your anxiety, you say it is this sort of sixth sense that you've developed over your years in law enforcement. There does appear to be an element that goes beyond logic as exemplified in your premonition of recent events. The use of the phrase 'Lamb of God', and its religious implications, does present itself as an indication of some sort of deeper theological connotation. I, as you are aware, have some experience in matters of a theological nature and I would like to delve into the possible connection, playing the role of an amateur detective of sorts, like G. K. Chesterton's beloved Father Brown if you will. Are you agreeable, Spartaco?"

Uncle Al smiles at the reference to the fictional English priest who solves mysteries, but he turns serious as he speaks, "Aiden, right now I can use all the help I can get, but I would appreciate it if we keep this conversation to ourselves for now, you know that separation of church and state thing." Uncle Al says this in a lighthearted way and they exchange a knowing smile.

"Of course, my dear Spartaco, of course! I shall keep this between us and inform you of any thoughts I have on the subject at hand and I will do this surreptitiously." Fr. Aiden winks at his friend and they both laugh.

Uncle Al and Father Aiden continue their conversation. A few minutes later Father Aiden looks down at the plate before him and says, "I suggest that we now indulge in the delicious fare that is before us, but alas the food is cold. Christopher, would you mind asking the counter-person to reheat our delicious eggplant parmigiana slices and perhaps provide us with cups of ice to chill the Snapple which I assume is warm by now."

I load our food onto the tray "No problem, I'll be back in a flash."

Uncle Al seems to be a little less anxious, "Thanks Aiden, I don't know how this can help, but maybe we can get some insights into the motivation behind the crimes and a possible connection."

"Spartaco, I am glad for this moment alone. I am extremely fond of Christopher but our close friendship requires that I speak to you in confidence. I would appreciate if you would wait to comment before passing judgment on my words. Are you agreeable?"

"Of course, Aiden, anything you say to me will be held in complete confidence."

Fr. Aiden takes a deep breath and begins to communicate his hypothesis, "That is very kind of you. In my journey through the priesthood, I've delved into the mysteries of God, of life and death, of heaven and hell and all that is implied. I have learned many things, but what I have found to be of overarching commonality through it all is that He works in mysterious ways. You cannot discount the spirituality that could underlie the events of the past few days. Spartaco, there is evil in this world and there is evil among us right now, and while you may have to deal in the physical realm, I do not. I conduct my inquiry with the objective eliminating the possibilities that there is some other worldly reason for these crimes, I caution you, however, that you must be of an open mind to confront the possibility that there are dark forces beyond the realm of the corporeal that could be at play here."

Chief Detective Spartaco "Al" Barese looks at Fr. Aiden Langford before he gives his reply. It is almost on the tip of his tongue to tell Aiden of Chris' special gift and of his nephew's relationship with the Sainted, but he knows he can't. "Aiden that is the reason I wanted to meet you for lunch. I am at a loss as to how I should deal with this. At first it was the feeling of impending doom that has morphed into a series of horrible murders. I have to concede that given the extent of the crimes throughout the world, there must be another reason and it may have to do with your special area of knowledge. If there is evil at work here…real or otherworldly, I want to know about it and I want to understand how we can stop it and I am thankful for your help with all this"

In his relief, Fr. Aiden says, "I am truly gratified that you are willing to consider the possibility of otherworldly evil being behind these terrifying transgressions. I will begin my research immediately and keep you informed of any possible breakthrough."

"You know, Aiden, as all this is happening, I keep thinking of something from my high school lit class."

"Ah! Something wicked this way comes! A classic bit of prose from Great Britain's gift to the world, William Shakespeare himself. It does seem appropriate to our discussion does it not?"

Uncle Al looks at his friend in amazement, "Of all the works we've studied in English Lit, how the hell did you know I was thinking of exactly that quote?"

Aiden jokingly confides, "Ah Spartaco, I do love to try and second guess you!"

"Well, how come you didn't second guess say 'Double, double toil and trouble' huh? How come, huh?"

"Elementary my dear Spartaco, the answer is simple, first, every high school student studies Shakespeare; at least I hope they still do. Second, you are a good man and you are very worried about all forms of evil, real or otherwise, that will wreak more havoc yet to come. Third, Macbeth has an abundance of evil associated with it. Fourth, I always go for the more obscure lines like 'something wicked this way comes' as opposed to 'double, double toil and trouble' which, in my estimation, is the more popular quote from Macbeth. All this brilliant bit of reasoning took was a bit of deduction and, you must admit, that quote seems more appropriate to the situation."

Uncle Al just shakes his head and tells Aiden, "You are one of a kind old buddy."

Aiden laughs, "Thank you for remembering!"

A cloud of despair crosses Uncle Al's face. "Aiden, I need to tell you something else."

Fr. Langford sees the change in his friend's face and expresses concern. "Why are you so troubled? What is it that you need to tell me?"

"The crimes happening worldwide; they are far more extensive that you can ever imagine."

Father Aiden seems to gasp at what he has just been told. "Spartaco, what has happened?"

"We have received reports from both the FBI and the State Department that are confirming all sorts of the vilest crimes; murder, theft, rape and arson. There are even horrors of people imprisoning and starving children. These kids are so emaciated that they die the moment they are touched. You name it and these abominations are being committed in huge numbers both here and abroad. The authorities are trying to keep the scale of these crimes under wraps until we can determine the cause and connection, but you know that won't last."

Fr. Aiden is shocked and saddened by this news.

"Aiden, there's more bad news. These crimes have one thing in common and I think you know what that is."

Uncle Al doesn't have to complete his thought as Fr. Aiden whispers to himself, Lamb of God."

Uncle Al and Frt. Aiden just sit there in somber contemplation until Uncle Al speaks "That's right Aiden, it doesn't seem to matter what faith the victims or the perpetrators are, it's all the same thing they have in common, Lamb of God."

When I return to the table and I find them involved in what seems to be a very serious discussion, I interrupt and ask, "What's all this serious talk? Hey, don't tell me you lost your appetite because I am not standing on line again to reheat this food."

Aiden quickly changes his demeanor beams up at me and says, "On the contrary my dear Christopher. I am famished. Please set the tray down so I may begin to devour the feast I have been so looking forward to."

Uncle Al, not to be outdone, says, "Put it down before I bite your hand."

"Okay! Okay, calm down big guy!"

I put the tray down but before we all grab our plates and eat with gusto, Fr. Aiden says, "I believe it would be appropriate to say grace." We bow our head as the priest leads us in prayer. "In the name of the Father and the Son and the Holy Spirit; dear Lord, thank you for the bounty you have given us, thank you for your strength in times of need and thank you for the friends we are so fortunate to have. Amen.

Fr. Aiden looks up and no one says another word about the murders or any of the criminal acts occurring throughout the world. Though the events hang in the air like a poisonous cloud, I try to get our conversation more lighthearted so I ask Fr. Aiden, "By the way Father, my girlfriend, Beth would love to meet you. I've told her about you and she would be thrilled to have the opportunity to say hello and speak with you."

Fr. Aiden lights up like a Christmas tree! "My dearest Christopher, what an honor it would be to meet your girlfriend. She must be a very lovely young lady to have captured your heart."

Uncle Al jumps in, "Aiden, you'll love her! Beth Della Russo is truly a beautiful person. She is the nurse that took care of me when I was in the hospital recuperating from the gunshot wound that was, in great measure, instigated by my brain-dead nephew."

I make a wimpy protest, "I resent being called brain-dead."

Uncle Al fires back, "Well if the shoe fits…"

Fr. Aiden feels he must mediate, "Now, now gentlemen let us not dwell on the past. I would be delighted to meet with Beth Della Russo. By the by, is she in any way related to Paul and Catherine Della Russo?"

I jump in to say, "Yeah, she is. They are her parents and they live up on the Neck."

"I know them well. Their generosity is much needed and greatly appreciated by all at the seminary. I would consider it an honor to meet your young lady. Just provide me with a time and place and I will be there." Fr. Aiden pauses and says, "Wait, I have a proposal which you both may enjoy, a personally guided tour of the seminary and its beautiful grounds and lunch, hosted by yours truly, in our cafeteria. We can use the solitude and beauty as a backdrop to our conversation. Are you amenable?"

I love the idea, "That sounds fabulous, I am sure we would both love it!"

Father Aiden is genuinely thrilled by the prospect of showing off his beautiful residence and its surroundings. "Splendid, then it's settled! Please notify me of a convenient time for you both and I will make myself available."

"I will let you know and thanks for your kind offer." I smile knowing that Beth would really enjoy Fr. Aiden's suggestion.

We finish our lunch and leave Rosa's. Uncle Al and Father Aiden are parked in different directions and I have a short walk back to my shop so we say our goodbyes and each of us walk away with our thoughts. I, with the thought of visiting with Fr. Aiden and Beth, Fr. Aiden with thoughts of the research he would begin and Uncle Al with the greater tragedies that he is sure will follow.

CHAPTER 12

The man named John walks the shores that border the island of Patmos. He welcomes the silence as he stares at the rocky cliffs that meet the sandy beach below. He's is in exile; sent to work the mines of Patmos each day, but before the start of his labors he is permitted to wander the island alone, with only his thoughts as company.

John should have perished in the cauldron of boiling oil, but that was not to be his fate. The miracle that God has allowed to happen saved him for what is to be a greater calling. The emperor Domitian is fearful for his loss of influence after his attempt to execute John had failed. It was at the insistence of Julianus that the emperor decrees John should be banished to the island of Patmos as punishment for his beliefs, his prophecies and the miracle that saved his life. The emperor has no knowledge of where these divinations came from, he assumes they are sorcery, some evil spirit prognostications of events to come, but it is not that at all. In truth it is not evil spirits that Domitian should fear, it is the word of God he should accept. John knows there is no use in telling Domitian where this foresight comes from for the emperor would not believe him anyway.

John the Evangelist, as he has become known, would not consider his fate a punishment. Being confined to this place and the shelter of his grotto will provide him with the solitude to pray, write and to try and understand *prophesies of that which will come. To John, the images are vivid and complete in what they predict and he will share them with the faithful.*

The sun is getting higher in the sky and John's thoughts change to the challenge that he needs to face this night. It came about when John first set foot on the island. He was resolute about making the acquaintance of the pagan men and women that populate this place and the condemned, such as himself, that share his fate. For John it would become a mission, a sacred undertaking to preach God's word and to shine the light of truth where there is nothing but darkness.

As he fears, the task will not be easy as old customs and fears of the unknown have many cowering before a malevolent sorcerer, they call Kynops. Kynops is threatened by this man who is new to the island; the island and its people are his and his alone. The sorcerer Kynops often confronts John as he understands that his evil powers, the powers to hold sway over the people of Patmos, are in serious jeopardy.

As John is walking toward the grotto near the shoes of Patmos, Kynops blocks the road and will not let him pass. Angrily the evil one shrieks at the holy man, "I will not allow you to continue!"

John looks knowingly at Kynops and says, "Why is it you will not let me pass? Have I done you some harm or done anything to offend you?"

"Your mere presence is what offends me."

"Ah, my mere presence offends you, well then, let me pass and when I am out of your sight, I will offend you no longer."

Now Kynops knows he is being mocked by John so he bellows, "You will not mock me! I hereby lay forth a challenge, your pitiful God against the forces at my command!"

John the Evangelist continues to be provoked by the wicked Kynops so he accepts the challenge. It is to be a dual of faiths; one that would pit the evil wizard against John's faith in God the Father and His Son. For the next two nights St. John prays for the strength to face the challenge and the confidence to see it through to the end. It is agreed that both will meet by the shoreline of the only small village on the shores of Patmos. Many of the island's population are gathered to see the battle take place for they know the power of the wizard and expect that John will die in the confrontation.

Kynops walks towards John who is standing, waist deep in the waters of the village's small harbor. A thin smile purses Kynops lips as he wades into the waters and stands next to the Apostle John.

"Are you prepared to die for your faith? You are fortunate today for I will show you mercy. I will allow you a coward's way out if you choose to take it. You can run and hide and I will not kill you, but you will be forbidden to speak to anyone and you will be banned from stepping foot into this village." Kynops' belligerence betrays his fear.

"I reject your false pride. You cannot give mercy because you have none to give. I am prepared to meet my Lord and Savior, my God. Are you prepared to meet yours?" John knows the answer to his question is simple.

Kynops face becomes twisted with rage and he shrieks, "Death now awaits you!"

It is then that both John and Kynops wade further into the waters. A fog settles over the harbor and it becomes so thick that the people on the shoreline could no longer see the sorcerer or the saint.

After a long while low whispers can be heard spoken by those among the crowd. They question what has happening to the men. It is now assumed by those present that in a clash no one has witnessed no one could still be alive and with that the assemblages of the natives begin to disperse. As they turn away from the harbor, the villagers hear a splash of water and a lone figure emerges from the depths and walks into the shallows. The townspeople stand still where they are, frozen in fear and bewilderment. How could this be? How could this man, this John the Evangelist, survive so long under the water? How can this man defeat the evil that is the wizard Kynops?

"Good people of Patmos do not fear the power of the Lord our God. Many have thought themselves above Him and many have been struck down. It is false pride and an all-consuming hate that condemned Kynops." John speaks this as the villagers watch and listen. One brave soul among those assembled asks John,

"Where is the evil wizard, good John, what has become of him?"

"The evil wizard will hold sway no more. The Lord our God has seen what is in his heart and has turned him into stone. He lies at the bottom of the harbor, a danger to all ships that are near and he will be there for eternity.

The waters surrounding the impediment will turn noxious and any fish caught there can no longer be eaten. People of Patmos, heed the calling of God and His Son Jesus and no longer fear the evil that has troubled you for so long. For all days peace and mercy will be with those who believe."

At first the people stand in fear, but once John the Evangelist speaks many understand what has happened. One by one they walk toward the man, the one who is prophet and ask to be renewed in the light of John's God and His Son, now their God and Savior.

One by one John of Patmos blesses them in the name of the Lord and when he is done John speaks to the crowd, "May the Lord bless you and yours for the rest of your days, in this world and in the next" and the holy man turns and walks away.

John is sapped of strength, more so than he has ever been at any time in his life. He slowly makes his way back to the grotto where he would sleep and wait for his strength to return. The tiny embers of the fire he lit before leaving his den have nearly burned out. John kneels on the ground and fans the embers so that he is able to build the small flame into a fire that will grow to warm his body and give him light.

John lies on the ground of the grotto waiting for sleep to come, but it does not come for behind him there comes a great voice.

CHAPTER 13

Fr. Aiden Langford has very troubling thoughts as he leaves the pizeria and walks to his car. It is a short ride to Immaculate Conception Seminary, but it is long enough for him to begin to conceive a framework for his research.

Fr. Aiden imagines that it will start with the origins, meanings and implications behind the use of the phrase 'Lamb of God' throughout the centuries. He hopes it will lead to some other avenues of investigation that could help him make some sense of this horror. He worries about his friend, but he has to admit to himself, he will be doing something he truly appreciates and welcomes, delving into the mysteries of his faith and the written word that brings these words to life.

Fr. Aiden silently prays the proclamation of John the Baptist, "Behold the Lamb of God who takes away the sins of the world" and mutters the closing phrase to the Agnus Dei "…have mercy on us." It is with both reverence and familiarity that he ponders the words and considers their meaning. God so loves the people of the world that He gave his only begotten Son to suffer and die for our sins. What could the possible connection to these murders have with the "Lamb of God?" The priest continues to dwell on the derivations of the word lamb as referenced in the Book of Revelations. Could these teachings hold a meaning that provides some sort of insight? Fr. Aiden recites the first words from Revelations Chapter 4 out loud in the car, to no one, "The revelation of Jesus Christ, which God gave Him to show His servants what, must soon take place. He made it known by sending an angel to His servant John."

The priest knows that the Book of Revelations has more than 29 references to the lamb as being slain, but still standing, other references speak of the Seven Spirits of God, but what is the relationship to the events of the past few days. Father Aiden Langford is pondering all this as he turns into the driveway that leads to the main building. He parks the car in his usual spot and gets out and begins to walk to the front entrance.

He is still deep in thought as he opens the front door and walks into the lobby. The association of the word lamb, as personified in Christ, becomes an image that brings to mind one of the journeys he made to Ireland. While there Aiden made a pilgrimage to St. Patrick's Cathedral and prayed in St. Peter's Chapel under the beautiful stained glass Jellett Window depicting the Lamb of God. The light shows though the window and gives a mysterious animation to the beautifully cut colored glass portrayal and he has never forgotten the experience. He also is able to recall his favorite, but most disturbing image of "Agnus Dei" by Francisco de Zurbaran painted in 1638. The exquisite painting depicts the Lamb of God as being bound at the feet, without horns but with the glow of a halo. Father Aiden recalls how beautiful all the paintings, woodcuts, drawings and sculptures of the Lamb are and the images give him both strength and solace, but still no answers.

The scholar priest walks down the familiar halls towards his room. He is looking forward to taking a restful nap; he needs it because he wants to go to the library late at night when all in the seminary are asleep so that he can continue his research in peaceful quiet. Father Aiden would stay up all night if he has to. He makes a resolution to do something and that something is to find the connection and help his friend.

At 12 Midnight sharp, Father Aiden's alarm goes off. He rubs his eyes and gets out of bed feeling rested and anxious to start on his work. The library takes up a good portion of the fourth floor of the seminary and is a short walk from his quarters. The library is usually kept locked during the overnight hours, but because of his status as a scholar and his ongoing research into all things theological, the priest is given his own key. The doors to the library are plain, but they are made of stained and polished mahogany as if to provide a fitting entrance to the treasures within. He turns the knob and enters this sanctum of knowledge.

Father Aiden devises a simple approach to his research and that is to start with familiar references to the Lamb of God and follow up with the more obscure notations as well as their origins and contexts. He begins by rereading references in the Book of Revelations and allows his research study to expand from there. Revelations, the final book of the New Testament, contains many teachings central to Christian theology including those describing the end of days. Fr. Aiden contemplates that this reference could mean an individual's last days or it could mean the end of days for all mankind and the nature of the Kingdom of God. St. John of Patmos was told by an angel to write what he sees and hears and it was this angelic command that became the Book of Revelations and Father Langford loves reading these texts. St. John, one of the twelve Apostles, was someone so close to Jesus that he was chosen to care for Christ's Blessed Mother Mary until her death.

The priest reads each word with care and reverence for he hopes that the teachings may provide some insight into the nature of the hideous crimes being committed in the name of the Lamb of God. As he reads through the text, he wonders at the use of the number "seven", an ancient symbol of perfection, in the Book of Revelations. There are references to Seven Churches, Seven Bowls, Seven Spirits, Seven Stars, Seven Trumpets, Seven Angels and Seven Seals. Each of these articles reveals lessons and prophecies inspired by the Divine and written by a man for the sake of all men. Each of the items in the articles has meanings far beyond the written word for they instruct the faithful on salvation and warn of sins that would deny them eternal life. The Book of Revelations both praises and admonishes all to do good works and repent for any evil that the faithful may have done. Revelations are lessons in life and the afterlife and Aiden never tires of reading them all.

Hours pass and there seems to be so much to grasp that Fr. Aiden's task becomes daunting. He takes copious notes as he reads and rereads the texts trying to isolate anything that would help make a connection, any connection to the events taking place. At one point Fr. Aiden comes on a passage, written by John and it says,

> *"Dear friends, do not believe every spirit, but test the spirits to see whether they are from God, because many false prophets have gone out into the world. This is how you can recognize the Spirit of God: Every spirit that acknowledges that Jesus Christ has come in the flesh is from God, but every spirit that does not acknowledge Jesus, that spirit is not from God. This is the spirit of the antichrist, which you have heard is coming and even now is already in the world"*

Of all that he reads, why does he stop at this passage? Why does it seem so noteworthy? It could be significant, but Father Aiden doesn't know why and what the significance could be so he makes note of it. The actual words, "Lamb of God", are nowhere in the text, however there are references to Jesus, but not in a way that would constitute a connection with the horrors happening around the world. Revelations does reference the antichrist, but they seem to be too vague. While Fr. Aiden ponders that there are many unanswered questions, there does seems to be a mystery unfolding and this reenergizes Father Aiden as he continues his work. In the dark quiet of the library, the priest reads page after page trying to piece together the words of St. John, but nothing seems to fit.

Fr. Aiden is deep in thought when he hears a sound echoing from the other end of the library. It seems to be the sound of someone or something walking along the floor. It is only for a few seconds and it is more of a clicking sound, so he looks up and calls out, "Hello? Is anyone here?" Father Aiden listens intently, but there is no answer. A full moon has come out this night and its light shines through the windows of the library. The light casts eerie shadows over the shelves, but Aiden knows the spirits here are friendly and they all reside in books. Recognizing that it must be some innocent noise, Aiden attempts to go back to work by continuing to read Revelations.

It is a short while later that another sound is heard coming from the other end of the library. The sound seems to be coming from near the Bonaventure Room. The Bonaventure Room is a special section that houses an extraordinary collection of approximately 4,000 old and rare books. Aiden has spent many happy hours among these writings and the thought that someone may be vandalizing or stealing these books makes him angry. Aiden calls out, louder this time, "Hello, who is here?", but he gets no answer. His instincts tell him that the sounds are probably coming from one of the pipes in this older part of the seminary building so he considers going back to his studies. Even though his instincts have served him well, Aiden realizes that he must get up to see what is going on or he will never be able to continue his work.

He mumbles to himself, "Aiden don't be the lazy lout. Get off your duff and determine what is making that noise."

Now Fr. Aiden gets out of his chair and begins to walk down the corridor toward the Bonaventure Room. It is dark, but he knows the library's layout so he walks with confidence. As he gets closer to the rear of the library, he starts to chuckle when he thinks of the traditional Scottish Prayer,

From ghoulies and ghosties
And long-leggedy beasties
And things that go bump in the night
Good Lord, deliver us

The priest finds himself at the entrance to the Bonaventure Room and he reaches for the door knob. To his surprise he finds the door is open. Fr. Aiden knows that because of the valuable items contained in this collection, the room is always kept locked and even he doesn't have a key. The priest is no longer smiling as he quietly enters the room. He looks along a dark hallway with long rows of shelves that contain these rare texts, but he sees nothing suspicious. Fr. Aiden thinks about turning on the light, but he does not want to startle the intruder. Perhaps, he thinks, he can persuade the would-be thief to exit on his own as opposed to being seated in the rear of a police car as long as nothing has been damaged.

Silently Fr. Aiden tip-toes down each of the aisles looking left and right, but he sees nothing amiss. All seems to be in place and when he reaches the end of the Bonaventure Room, he acknowledges that there is no one to be found. Aiden relaxes a bit knowing that at least it seems, given his cursory examination, nothing appears to be stolen or damaged. The priest begins to walk back to the door, thinking that he would tell the head of the library about the open door, when he looks down one of the aisles. At the end of each aisle there are tables used by scholars and students for study. On this particular table, however, there is an opened book and Aiden could swear that it was not there before.

Slowly Father Aiden walks toward the table and the open book. He does not know what to make of all this, but he does not want to admit the possibility of anything other-worldly. The book appears to be the Bible, a very old Bible, perhaps the oldest in the seminary's collection. The book is open to a page in the New Testament and to his surprise it is a page from the Book of Revelations.

Aiden picks up the Bible and stares down at the open page. He immediately recognizes the written word and he looks up from the text in amazement; it is Revelation 6, the Seven Seals. He stares back down and even though he has read the Seven Seals many times, Fr. Aiden seems to be cognizant of them for the first time. "And I saw that the Lamb had opened one of the seven seals…"

He reads each of the seven seals aloud, to himself; the first four are of the horsemen who wreak horror and death on all and the last three speak of God's admonition to the martyrs and the prediction of the Apocalypse to come.

Fr. Aiden lifts his head from the book he has been reading and stares into the surrounding darkness of the library. He knows of The Four Horsemen of the Apocalypse that are described by St. John in the Book of Revelations. The chapter tells of a book or scroll in God's right hand that is closed with seven seals. The Lamb of God, Jesus, The Lion of Judah opens the first four of the seven seals, which summons four beings that ride out on white, red, black, and pale horses. Fr. Aiden knows that the four riders symbolize Conquest, War, Famine, and Death. In his studies of the Christian apocalyptic, Father Aiden Langford also knows that the four horsemen are to set into motion to foretell of the apocalypse upon the world, and as a prediction of the Last Judgment to come.

With Fr. Aiden's mind racing, many of his theological studies come back to mind and he seems to recall one point made by the Reverend Billy Graham regarding the Four Horseman. It had to do with the rider on the white horse with a bow and crown bound on conquest. Many, including the Reverend Graham, believe that this rider is the antichrist and Father Aiden Langford agrees.

Could it be? Could Jesus Christ be opening one of the seven seals? Could all this be the first sign pointing to the end of days, the Apocalypse? Fr. Aiden couldn't conceive the possibility, the reality of this; the most final of cataclysms. The priest lays the book back on the table and lifts his head trying to contemplate the unthinkable when a wind blows through the room. It is a warm wind, but Fr. Aiden sees that no windows are open in the Bonaventure Room. The wind catches the pages of the book and they flutter and stop. When the priest looks down at the book it has turned to a page featuring a verse from Matthew 24, the Olivet Discourse;

> *"At that time many will turn away from the faith and will betray and hate each other, and many false prophets will appear and deceive many people. Because of the increase of wickedness, the love of most will grow cold, but he who stands firm to the end will be saved. . .For false Christs and false prophets will appear and perform great signs and miracles to deceive even the elect — if that were possible. See, I have told you ahead of time"*

Father Aiden Langford is more confounded than ever. All of what he has been shown…all of his study…all of his instincts…all of his faith now tells him that the Lord sends us many signs. His signs of love, His signs of forgiveness, His signs of miracles, but this is the sign of the impending apocalypse. He thinks to himself. "This cannot be true; this cannot be happening. But what if it is happening and what if the first seal has been opened and the antichrist is walking among us? What if the tragedies occurring around the world are foretelling of the final days and the final judgment of God on all men and women?"

The priest closes the old Bible and sets it back on the shelf in its special place of honor. He slowly walks to the door and exits the Bonaventure Room. It is early in the morning so Aiden decides to stop his research and he walks back to his quarters. He should be tired, but he's not as his mind is racing, trying to contemplate the entirety of all he has read…all he has been shown.

CHAPTER 14

The camera crews gather at the main entrance of the hospital to await his coming.

Dr. Houston's public relations people have let it be known that he will be visiting the critically injured police officer at Huntington Hospital. Officer Nicholas Josephs was one of the first persons on the scene of the Lamb of God murder at the mall and Tom Houston's staff knows it would be an important forum for him to expound on the issues brought to bear by these events. The news crews and reporters have already set up for the impromptu press conference and all they need is the man of the hour to arrive. It was decided beforehand that Tom Houston would answer only a few questions prior to visiting the wounded officer.

Prior to alerting the news media, the PR staff met with their boss. They want to discuss what he should and shouldn't say because they know what could happen if a wrong answer is given. Dr. Thomas Houston appears to listen to their advice in earnest, but in reality, he never takes the advice of these people. They are paid to make him look good, but they are more concerned with him not taking any chances and taking chances has gotten him to where he is today. Tom Houston is very smart; he is very astute and he knows what to say and what not to say. Up to this point, he has made all the right decisions and his ratings in the polls made him the man to watch and among the possible front runners in securing the Socialist Liberation Party nomination for President.

Dr. Houston's limousine pulls in front of the hospital's entrance. It is decided that he would use his less ostentatious, brand new, classic black Lincoln stretch because his staff feels that the custom Maybach stretch is a bit over the top. When the reporters see the car, they immediately jockey for the best place to be called on and for the best position to film this charismatic man and potential leader of the free world.

The limo arrives, stops in front of the hospital's entrance and the driver comes around to open the door for Dr. Thomas Houston. As soon as his feet hit the ground, the horde of reporters and cameramen immediately surround Dr. Houston and they begin bombarding him with questions.

"Dr. Houston, Dr. Houston!" screams one reporter, but his voice is drowned out by others in the crowd.

"What is your position on abortion and illegal immigration!" yells another reporter who kept trying to talk above the rest of the throng.

In hopes of quelling the group, Dr. Houston tries to give some order to the mass confusion that seems to be taking over. "Please, please ladies and gentlemen I will be happy to answer your questions, but I think we need to have some semblance of order. Why don't we start with Sally Hinderwood? Good morning, Sally."

"Good morning, Dr. Houston. Can you tell us why you are here and what you hope to achieve?"

"Sally, I am here as a Long Islander that is deeply concerned about the critical condition of Officer Nicholas Josephs. He's a family man, a 12-year veteran of the force and he risked his life to save others. I'm not here to achieve anything except to give whatever comfort I can to his family. Next question…Charlie Sessions what's your question?"

"Dr. Houston, we continue to get reports from around the country and all over the world of the murders taking place and the use of the phrase "Lamb of God. What do you make of these horrific crimes?"

"I can only speculate Charlie, but it seems that given there are no apparent associations between any of the individual events, there has to be a connection that transcends race, culture, language, education and gender.

How can this be? What possible motivation can an innocent phrase like Lamb of God provide what seems to be hundreds if not thousands of these perpetrators and possibly even their victims? If we have the courage to face the truth then we must see that some far-out religious zealotry could be at the bottom of it all. You have heard me expound on the radical Islamist terrorists. If you believe these people, they tell you that their sole motivation is the elimination of all non-believers, their jihad so to speak. Take that simple premise and extend it to all other faiths; Christians, Roman Catholics, Jews, Hindus, Buddhists, Eastern Orthodox and all other organized religions and add to it the fringe radical followers who are capable of the same maniacal actions of terrorists and you have what we are witnessing now; atrocities committed in the name of the Lamb of God."

Tom Houston gives a quick glance over to where his public relations staff is standing and he sees them go pale and he has to smile to himself.

"Brian Thompson, you're next."

"So, you seem to be saying that it could be crazy fringe groups from different faiths, religious zealots if you will, that are committing these murders in the name of Christ, the Lamb of God."

Tom Houston put his hand to his chin, looking up thoughtfully as he begins to speak, "Well let me see? The Islamist terrorists kill 3,000 people and they proclaim that it is in the name of Allah. What possible explanation can there be for murders that are being committed around the world based on a religious phrase Lamb of God other than a fanaticism born of religious fervor. Wasn't it Jim Jones, whose mother believed he was the messiah by the way, who was responsible for the Jonestown Massacre of 909 people, 303 of them children? Wasn't he the religious extremist who formed a cult-following using the pulpit of The People's Temple of the Disciples of Christ? Think of radical terrorist groups that exist today such as Hamas, ISIS, Boko Haram and Al Qaida and try to ponder what they have done and why they have done it. I can go on and on, but I think you get my point."

Dr. Houston takes a breath because he needs to get his point across, "God, Jehovah, Allah are all concepts used by people to control the actions of other people. It is a perversion of the first order; otherwise, how can you explain why people have committed such unimaginable acts. Just look at what has happened to Officer Josephs. I believe that perversion of the radical kind is what we have seen in the past and that perversion is what we are seeing now, acts of violence, by radical zealots in the name of Allah…Jehovah…God." Dr. Houston's pauses for a moment to allow his word to sink into the minds of the news people who are present.

WOLFE Media reporter Maggie Truman jumps in before any other reporter can get their question out. "I would like to clarify what you are saying. First, there is really no God, no heaven, no hell or anything spiritual to guide us as human beings. In other words, we are when we're alive and we are not when we're dead. Second, that these beliefs and places are fantasies created to control peoples' behavior. Third, in reality all that exists is good and evil and both these conditions emanate from the human condition. Did I get it right?"

After Maggie Truman stops speaking, the reporters and crew jam their mics and cameras as close to Tom Houston's face as they can get. They are waiting for an answer to the question and he will not disappoint them.

"I think that your summary of my statement is true, but you leave out a very important factor. Good and evil exist in the hearts of men, women and even children everywhere, but what stops people from doing anything they want? What stops evil from prevailing? What stops the chaos that would ensue once organized religions lose the control they have; it is the fear of being caught, the fear of the forces of government. It is the fear of the good and kind people that surround the forces of evil and it is the fear that policemen like Officer Nick Josephs will rise and do what is right and honorable to protect their fellow citizens. You can never eliminate or even under-estimate the true spirit that guides our actions, the basic goodness that exists in the hearts of men and women everywhere."

The reporters and camera crew go silent.

Dr. Houston breaks the silence, "I realize that what I am presenting here is very difficult for many to accept. So many people, generation after generation, have long held beliefs and traditions that reside in the institutions I've mentioned. I am not saying the there is no good that can come from people who hold firmly to their long held religious beliefs; of course, there is. What I am saying however is that this belief in a god, I personally believe does not exist, is being perverted by a number of extremists for their own ends and horrific acts are being committed in this so-called god's name."

Dr. Thomas Houston looks around at the press gathering and ends by saying, "Thank you for allowing me the time to comment on the tragic events that have taken place and my notion of what may have caused them to happen. I have to reiterate; this is only speculation on my part but my opinion is built on a logical thesis. Now if you will excuse me, I would like to see Officer Josephs to express my sincere wishes for his speedy recovery and express my sympathies to his wife, children and parents."

Dr. Thomas Houston takes a step towards the door and as he does the news crews part ways to let him through. His staff trails behind him not daring to look at the reporters for fear that they would ask them to further explain what their boss has just proclaimed. But something happens to surprise everyone, but Tom Houston. Slowly but surely the sound of hands clapping begins as he walks toward the hospital's entrance until more than half of the news reporters and crew are taking part in a spontaneous tribute.

It is a good start to the day and Dr. Thomas Houston feels it will only get better.

CHAPTER 15

I leave Rosa's and begin to walk back to the shop. Thoughts of the conversation that we had over lunch and the heinous crimes that have been committed are all I can think about. I keep thinking about the poor victims and the pressure that Uncle Al must be feeling at needing to solve the crimes.

The shop is only four blocks away and the cold air feels good so I take my time. As I reach the corner of Main and Wall Street, the traffic stops, people freeze in place and as in the past I am transported, this time back to a stark and desolate place overlooking the cold waters of Lough Derg.

The men stand at the entrance to the cave. One of the men is surrounded by an all-enveloping glow so bright that His features are obscured. Kneeling next to the glowing vision is another man who is supplicating in prayer saying;

"…Christ shield me this day, Christ be with me, Christ within me, Christ with me, Christ before me, Christ behind me, Christ beside me…"

The holy man continues to pray as Jesus Christ places his hand on the shoulders of St. Patrick who ends his prayer and says,

"Christ in the heart of every person who thinks of me, Christ in every eye that sees me, Christ in the ear that hears me."

St. Patrick looks up at his Savior and is told by Christ to stand beside Him as he asks,

"Do you know what place this is?"

"No, my Lord."

"This earthly place is the gateway."

"Gateway? Lord, gateway to where?"

"It is the gateway to Purgatory and beyond. Follow me and it shall be revealed to you."

As St. Patrick follows Christ into the entrance of the cave, I am allowed to follow. Normally I only observe parts of my vision from afar, but this time I seem to know that I am meant to be inside the cave. I do not need to take a step as I find myself in a corner of a niche in the cave. The entrance is very narrow, 2 feet wide and 3 feet high. Once inside there is a short descent of about six steps where the cave is divided into two parts: the first is about 9 feet long with banked sides only high enough to kneel in. Further in is a sharp turn that contains another niche about 5 feet long.

Both men stand in the cave's far niche and stare into the darkness. Christ looks at St. Patrick and says,

"Beyond the darkness there is a place, a state, temporary punishment for those souls who having died in the state of grace, but are not entirely free from the venial sins that plague mankind. These souls have not yet fully paid the satisfaction due

to their transgressions. It is not a state of positive growth in goodness and in merit, but of purification effected by suffering."

"I know of Purgatory Lord. It is the last hope for so many to be at one with God the Father and His Son in the everlasting triumph of Heaven."

As I stare in wonderment, sadness comes to Christ's face and He sheds tears. At the sight of this, St. Patrick becomes distressed,

"Lord, why do You weep? Lord, are you sad because of the suffering of your children? These souls suffer for their sins but it is You who have decreed they will be redeemed through indulgence and the prayers of the faithful."

"It is not only for the souls who suffer in Purgatory that I weep."

"Then for whom do you weep, Lord please let me know, for whom do you weep?"

"Follow me and it shall further be revealed to you."

St. Patrick follows Christ farther and farther into the cave and I am taken along in their journey. The only illumination from the darkness is the glow that surrounds Jesus and in what seems like a short while, we find ourselves standing on the edge of a deep, deep pit. As I stare over the edge, I see a flaming sea and in it are the souls of sinners in torment. These souls atoning through temporal punishments for the transgressions they have committed during their lives.

Christ stares into the chasm and speaks, "Witness a purification that frees one from the temporal punishment of sin, a punishment that must not be conceived of as a kind of vengeance inflicted by God from without, but as following from the very nature of sin itself."

St. Patrick is intent as he looks down into Purgatory; this well of sorrow, but Christ is not done; "Now you must look beyond to the fire further below, past the sinners who are repenting, into the next level and you will see what it is that makes me weep."

St. Patrick looks down into the pit where he is allowed to see what the Lord wants him to see. His eyes go wide over the vast expanse, the lakes of fire, the demon tormentors and the souls of the damned. St. Patrick is permitted to see Hell itself. He looks in revulsion at those condemned to eternal suffering and starts to step away from this horror. But Christ does not want him to turn away and He places his hand on the Saint's shoulder and guides him back to the edge of the precipice.

"Do not turn away; you must see the suffering of the damned in Hell. It is only through these visions that the faithful can know and seek repentance, forgiveness and their rewards in Heaven."

The blessed saint knows in his heart that the suffering in Purgatory is for those who have sinned and can be redeemed, but there is no redemption for the damned as they are destined to spend an eternity in hell and this now saddens St. Patrick greatly.

Christ understands the distress of his Sainted and turns to St. Patrick to speak, "As Mathew hath written, in Hell there is no liberation and in Heaven nothing imperfect can enter therein. Sin is not forgiven when a soul reaches its final destination because in heaven there is no need for forgiveness of sin and in hell the choice to go there is already made."

St. Patrick continues to stare into the depths and he hears the screams and torments of the souls. He can no longer bear the cries and he cover his ears. There is no consolation for St. Patrick for Christ knows the endless suffering of the damned and He also knows of the evil that causes this pain. He says "I know that you cannot bear to hear the lamentations, but you must. You must because there are places of suffering in Hell you cannot ever imagine. There are endless fires in Hell that have been set aside for many more souls."

"What can I do Lord? What can your humble servant do to stop this wickedness that exacts this punishment? Please let me know."

Christ looks to the Heavens and turns to St Patrick and says words that can only be heard by the two. Christ becomes surrounded by the seven Archangels as their spirits dissolve into the glow of Heaven.

In an instant I am standing outside the cave. I look out at the dark waters lapping the shoreline of the lake in Northern Ireland. It is here, in this desolate place that St Patrick appears beside me and speaks.

"The Lord allows his servant to see into the depths of the pit. He allows me to be witness to the suffering of sinners, but He also allows me to see the torment of those who have no remedy, no chance for remorse… those who have no hope."

"But isn't this the punishment that is predicted in the Bible? Aren't Purgatory and Hell where you can expect to go if you have committed sins, venial or mortal, that remain unforgiven?" My observation is simple, but it is what I had learned in religious instruction and what I had read in various religious texts.

"That is true, but I am most troubled by what the Lord has foretold of things that may be coming to plague mankind."

"What do you mean 'may be coming'?" What had Christ implied in this vision of Purgatory and Hell? I am looking at St. Patrick hoping for an answer when his vison begins to disappear. I yell out to him,

"Please don't leave me. I need to know what it is Christ means with this vision."

Before St. Patrick disappears into the heavenly light, I hear him say, "To understand you must look at the world around you. Heed the signs of evil, of temptations and stand bravely as your faith is tried" and then St. Patrick is gone.

I return to the reality of my life and I find myself standing on the corner of Wall Street and Main in the center of town. People are walking, talking, shopping, driving much in the same way they do each and every day and I follow their lead and walk back to the shop.

CHAPTER 16

The automatic doors to the hospital swing open and Tom Houston enters the lobby. The lobby is a pleasant place with couches and tables. There is even a grand piano that plays beautiful music on its own. A number of the staff, many of them women, are assembled in the lobby to greet the luminary and the applause continues as he passes through their ranks.

Dr. Harold McMasters, president of the hospital is first to greet Dr. Houston. "Welcome to Huntington Hospital, Dr. Houston, it is a pleasure to meet you. We know you are here to visit Office Nicholas Josephs, but a number of our staff want to have the chance to see you in person, I hope you don't mind."

Tom smiles and says, "Please call me Tom. I am honored that so many have taken time from their busy schedules to come and say hello. I only wish I had more time to talk with each and every person here, but I would like to say something to the group if that's alright?"

"Of course, Dr. Houston, I mean Tom, I am sure that all present would be thrilled to hear you speak." Then Dr. McMasters turns over the floor to Tom Houston.

Tom Houston takes the opportunity to say a few words. "What a wonderful welcome you have given me here. I have had the honor of meeting so many wonderful medical professionals in my travels and I am truly in awe of what you do each and every day. As a Long Islander I have known of the great works accomplished here at Huntington Hospital and I think that you should give yourselves the applause." Dr. Houston starts to clap his hands and smiles as he looks around the lobby at all that are gathered. There are many who smile back and begin returning the applause as he continues speaking.

"As you may know, I am here to see Officer Nicholas Josephs that brave public servant who was nearly killed by a religious zealot who tried to justify her action in the name of the Lamb of God. While the officer's family worries about the devastation caused by the savage attacks on their loved one, I know that there can be no better place to see that he recovers than right here at Huntington Hospital."

Tom stops speaking, and pauses, as this needs to be timed just right, to allow for a new round of applause, this time taking longer and louder. "In closing I do want to say that I wish I was able to greet each and every one of you personally, but I must visit Officer Josephs and then back on the campaign trail."

Now the crowd starts to chant, "Dr. Tom…Dr. Tom…" and Dr. Houston smiles, raises his hand and waves goodbye to all. His staff now surrounds him as they navigate through the lobby to the North Elevator and the short trip to the 4th floor. The elevator door opens to the ward where Officer Josephs is being cared for and one of the nurses at the station sees Dr. Houston get off. She excitedly let's all within earshot know that he's arrived.

Nancy McGrath, a senior member of Tom Houston's staff walks up to the nurse who is working at the station and smiles as she looks at her nurses' badge, "Good morning, Nurse Breuer, may I call you Diane?"

The nurse smiles back, "Sure."

"Diane, I'm Nancy McGrath and I'm on Dr. Thomas Houston's staff. We are here to visit Officer Nicholas Josephs. We've already notified Dr. McMasters and I believe he has notified you of our arrival."

"Yes, Ms. McGrath we were notified and we are all awaiting your arrival. Our head nurse, Beth Della Russo is with the patient now and she will be out soon to greet you and direct you to Officer Josephs' room. It should just be a short wait and perhaps, if you have no objections, there are a few nurses who would love to say hello to Dr. Houston."

Ms. McGrath seems a bit annoyed and says, "I don't think that it is proper to…" but she is interrupted by Dr. Tom who responds, "Come on Nancy, these women provide the best of care to all of the patients that cross their way. I would be honored to say hello and speak with them." Nancy doesn't betray her annoyance; she is used to being countermanded by her boss so she relents and tells Nurse Breuer that Dr. Tom would enjoy meeting the nursing staff in the ward.

Excitedly Diane calls all the nurses who are gathered at the desk just waiting to get a glimpse of the handsome visitor. Most of them are waiting for this moment and they eagerly hurry to surround Dr. Houston as he stands in the hallway. Tom is getting used to working the crowds, both large and intimate, and this small group seems elated to be in his presence.

"Ladies, first I want to thank you for doing the splendid work you do each and every day. I am sure it is, for you all, a labor of love and just seeing someone come in sick or injured and leave cured must be a reward that can never be matched. I am truly in admiration of your dedication." Dr. Tom is working the crowd and the women love every minute.

"My name is Kimberly; can I ask you a question?" A young nurse named Kimberly Hastings asks before anyone else has a chance.

"Of course." Dr. Houston beams.

"I think you are just about the most beautiful man I have ever seen." At this point the other nurses start to laugh and Dr. Houston laughs along with them and responds, "That's not a question Kimberly" and there is more laughter.

"I know. I want to ask you what type of girl you like. I mean what type of girl would you like to go out with?" Now that is a question all the single and perhaps some married nurses want to ask and they are glad that Kimberly beat them to it.

Tom pretends he is thinking about the question but he has a stock answer that he uses whenever the subject comes up. "Well Kim, can I call you Kim or do you prefer Kimberly?"

"Kim is fine, everyone calls me Kim."

"Well Kim I love beauty, and I do mean both inside and out. The women I date are thoughtful, kind, smart and are not consumed by the superficial, but live their lives knowing that true happiness and fulfillment lies in the company of family and friends. In terms of career, she is fulfilled by what she can hope to accomplish on her own, but knows that it takes a partnership, a team like you have here, that will make her truly successful."

The nurses stand in rapt attention watching and listening to Dr. Tom. They seem captivated by his every word, his charm and his ability to see into their own hearts. Kimberly Hastings stares with her mouth half opened. She listens to every word and thinks to herself, "that's me…Dr. Thomas Houston is describing me!"

"I hope I've answered your question, Kim."

Kim is trying to think how to respond and all she can say is, "Would you like to go out for a drink?"

Now the entire group, both hospital and Tom Houston's campaign staff burst out in laughter, but that is soon broken off as an angry Beth comes storming out of Officer Joseph's patient's room.

"What is going on here? Don't you know there are some very sick and injured people who are trying to get rest? All of you please get back to your assigned duties now." Nurse Della Russo commands the respect of her staff and she always gets it. They all quietly say goodbye to Tom Houston, quickly disband and walk back to their posts.

Nancy McGrath, who reads Beth's nametag, is the first to apologize. "Nurse Della Russo, please accept our apologies. We wanted to be cordial to your staff and perhaps things did get a bit loud. It is certainly not our intention to create a disturbance and we will be sure that it doesn't happen again."

While Beth is speaking with Nancy McGrath, Tom Houston, standing on the side, is staring at Beth. He seems captivated by her demeanor, beauty and apparent strength of character. He interrupts the conversation to speak with Beth while Nancy takes her cue and walks away. Beth turns to face Tom who tries to smooth over what appears to be a bad situation in the ward, "Nurse Della Russo, I'm Thomas Houston and I want to add my personal apology to Ms. McGrath's. It was never our intention to disturb the tranquility of the ward and I hope you will forgive our boisterous behavior and breach of etiquette."

By now Beth has calmed down and says, "Well, I'm glad you see the error of your ways. As it's very seldom that I get to yell at a big shot like you, so you're forgiven." Beth manages a smile and Tom Houston smiles back as he reaches out to shake Beth's hand. Their hands touch for a bit longer than what would pass as a standard handshake, and Beth seems taken aback and reluctantly pulls away.

Tom senses he's made a connection and says to Beth, "I appreciate your absolution. I believe you know I'm here to see Officer Josephs, do you think it would be alright if I visit him and his family now?"

Beth tells him, "He is being given a test at the moment, but it should be only a minute or two. His family is there with him and he is mostly unconsciousness, but it is important not to disturb the patient even in this condition, understood?"

"Of course, In light of his condition, I will be very respectful."

Beth continues to let Tom know, "I will ask the family's permission and if they agree I will escort you to Officer Joseph's room. Do you understand?"

"Yes, of course. I will be the only one of my group to visit the wounded officer. If I may ask, what is his condition?"

"I can only say he continues to be in critical condition and we will not know his chances of recovery for a few days."

"I see…" There is a lull in the conversation so Tom changes the subject, "How long have you been with Huntington Hospital?"

"I've been here since I graduated from nursing school, about 8 years."

Tom estimates she's about 29 or 30 years old, very bright and strikingly beautiful. "You must be very good at your job or they wouldn't have given you so much responsibility."

"Well, you know what they say, do something you love and you'll never work a day in your life."

Tom smiles and not to let any grass grow he asks Beth, "This may sound forward to you and please don't take this as anything, but an innocent query on the part of a lonely bachelor to a beautiful nurse, but would you like to have dinner with me some evening?"

Now Beth blushes a bit, but she regains her composure, "Well what should I tell my boyfriend?"

Tom pretends a quizzical look and says, "How strange, you have a boyfriend?"

She smiles, "Yes, if you can believe it."

"What's the lucky guy's name?"

"Chris…Chris Pella."

Now Tom's smile broadens, "I'll tell you what I am having a big rally at Madison Square Garden on Saturday February 21st. Boyd Somerfield, Fabiano and others celebs will be headlining the event; I want to invite you and Chris as my personal guests. There will be plenty of food and wine, famous people and I am sure you and your boyfriend will enjoy it immensely. What do you say?"

Beth is both flattered and excited at the invitation. "Wow, sounds great, but I'll have to ask Chris."

Tom smiles, "Okay, no problem. I will have Nancy send you an invitation and I hope to see you there."

Beth looks at Tom Houston and says, "You are quite a charmer, aren't you? I'll ask my boyfriend and let you know if we can make it."

Tom smiles knowing she'll be there and says, "That works for me."

Beth and Tom Houston continue to make small talk when the technician, Corrine Johnson, interrupts them. "Beth, I've finished the test, he's resting now, but if you want to send in the visitor, now's as good a time as any."

"Thanks Corrine." Beth tells Tom that she will ask the family and let him know if they are seeing visitors.

She returns moments later and says, "Dr. Houston I am sure that you will handle the situation with the utmost compassion and respect, but please remember that because of his condition he is not responsive and the family is extremely distraught, as you can imagine. Now please follow me to his room."

They walk down the hall and stop at the door to Officer Josephs' room. Before Tom enters Beth says, "Here we are, try to make the visit as short as possible and just leave when you are ready or you can ring and one of the nurses will escort you out."

"Thanks Beth I appreciate your work on his behalf and I do hope we will meet again." Beth shakes Tom's hand and walks away. Tom watches her as she heads for the nurses' station, but he is there on business so he turns away and opens the door.

CHAPTER 17

Tom Houston opens the door and enters Nick Josephs' room. The hospital room is about as cheerful as you might expect a hospital room to be. It is filled with flowers, get well cards and crayon drawings with the words "We miss you Daddy." All is being done to make the room as cheery as possible, but there is no cheer.

Immediately the family members sitting by Nick's bedside look up and recognize the famous visitor and rise from their chairs to greet him. An attractive young woman rises from her seat and tries to smile as she holds out her hand. "Thank you so much for coming. We really appreciate you taking the time to visit Nick. I'm Theresa Josephs, Nick's wife."

"Good morning, I'm Tom Houston and it should be me thanking you on behalf of all of Long Island for your husband's bravery and sacrifice. I know he is receiving the best of care here at Huntington Hospital and I can only hope that he is recovering from his wounds."

"Thank you for your kind concern. Nick is getting wonderful care, but the doctors are very concerned. He continues to go in and out of consciousness, but he mostly is unconscious and when he awakes, he isn't able to speak to us." Theresa Josephs tries to surpass her tears, but she can't hold her emotions in check as she falls into Tom Houston's arms, sobbing uncontrollably.

Tom puts his arms around Theresa, but he's looking beyond her at the other family members in the room. An older man, care worn and tanned from the sun, walks over to Theresa and places his hand on her shoulders. She turns and faces him and continues to breakdown and cry in his arms. Tom Houston stays silent as the emotions of the moment subside and he introduces himself to the man now comforting Officer Josephs' wife.

"I'm Tom Houston and my heart goes out to your family."

The man smiles up at Tom and says, "Hi, I'm Marty Josephs', Nick's father and we appreciate you coming here to visit with us. Theresa and our family have been by Nick's side since this happened and emotions are running very high. We've all had very little sleep and our concerns for Nick's health have left us exhausted."

"I completely understand, please sit down with Theresa. I appreciate your allowing me to be part of your vigil as I can only guess how terrible it must be to have to bear the effects of this tragedy. Tell me, do Theresa and Nick have any children?"

Theresa, who has calmed down a bit, answers, "Yes, we have two beautiful girls, Melanie who is 5 and Ashley who is 3 and they are the joys in our life. Nick is a wonderful father and he adores his beauties as he calls them."

A woman is sitting next to Theresa and Marty and Tom looks in her direction. The woman seems to have a scowl that comes across her face, she is angry as she stares up at Tom. She ignores Tom and turns away to look back at her son lying in the bed. Tom notices the anger, but he feels the need to reach out to her so he says, "My name is Tom Houston, I am sorry to disturb your family's sorrow." There is no answer, only silence as she doesn't return his greeting.

"Please excuse her, that's my wife Karen, Nick's mom and she is very upset and angry at what happened to our son." Karen shoots a look back at her husband as if to say, why are you apologizing for me.

Tom says to Marty, "Please, I am the one imposing on your time of grief and I will be leaving soon. Would it be alright if I stood beside Nick's bedside for a moment? I have heard so many good things about him and his service as a policeman that I would consider it an honor to spend a quiet moment with him."

Theresa and Marty look at each other and feel deep gratitude in their hearts. They both are honored by Dr. Tom Houston's compassionate gesture and they both nod and say that it would be fine. Marty feels that he needs to make Tom aware of Nick's condition, "I must warn you, Nick will not be able to talk or respond to you in any way."

"I am aware of his condition, but it would still be my honor to spend this quiet moment with Nick" and with that Dr. Thomas Houston walks over to the bed where Nick is lying. The headrest is slightly elevated and the white sheets are wrapped around Nick tightly as if to make sure he stays warm; wrapped in the love everyone feels for him.

Tom stands by the bed guard with his back to the family and looks directly down at the face of Nick Josephs. A slightly crooked smile comes across Tom's lips and he reaches down and holds Nick's limp hand in his own and when he does there appears to be a slight flicker of the comatose policeman's eyelids.

Nick tries to open his mouth and speak, but he can't speak. Actually, an inner voice tells him that there is no need to talk, he can speak and Dr. Tom Houston will be able to hear him and answer.

"Hello Nick, things aren't looking too well, are they?"

Nick's eyes are flickering madly now, "How…how can I hear you? Who are you? Where am I? Why can't I move?"

"Ah Nick, so many questions and so little time to answer them all, suffice it to say you are in pretty bad shape."

"I KNOW I AM! My wife, my parents, my beauties what about them, I know they are very worried about me."

In a conversation that no one can hear, Tom answers, "Yes they are. It's kind of interesting what a ten-inch knife could do to a chest isn't it, Nick. It sort of turns the lives of so many people around, just like it did to you. When you least expect it, all that love and emotion cut up by a metal blade that ripped and tore through your chest. Did you like my play on words, 'cut up', 'ten-inch blade'…get it!?"

Nick's eyes stop flickering and they slowly open. Nick's face is hidden to the family as Tom blocks their view. The reality and remembrance of the events that took place come rushing back into Nick's mind.

"Now I remember, I…I was…I was stabbed. I was stabbed by a woman who went crazy at the mall."

"Ah, it is all returning to you now Nick, very good, very good indeed. A woman gone crazy and you are the unfortunate recipient of her act of madness. Oh, by the way you will be happy to learn that she is dead, shot by your partner I believe, so you can revel in the reality that justice is served!"

Nick is well past confused. He cannot understand what is happening to him. He longs for his family, to hold his wife, to hug his daughters, to tell his mom and dad that he is going to be fine. He wants all these things, but he can't have them. His eyeballs move in their socket as he looks up at Tom and says, "Why can't I wake up?"

"Well Nick, I'm not that kind of doctor, but I believe that you are in a coma brought on by the wound you received. What a pity." Tom takes a dramatic pause, for effect, and looks at Nick and tells him, "Oh, I can tell you this however, you are going to die. Death is very, very sad, but a fact that we mortals will need to confront at one point or another."

Nick doesn't seem to have the strength to keep his eyes opened, but he continues with his unconscious speak, "Die? Die? I can't die. I have 2 babies to raise, my wife and I have just bought a house and we are planning a vacation to Disney World next year. I can't die."

"Oh Nick, you know what they say; shit, or is it life, I can never remember which, happens when you are busy making other plans. Anyway, it is a pleasure meeting you and I hope to see you on the other side."

Tom is having trouble containing his pleasure, but he knows he must face the family before he leaves. He turns to face Nick's family, "I have never had such an emotional experience in my whole life." Tom said this as a tear rolls from his eye down his cheek. "I held his hand and there was no response, but for some reason I feel that Nick knows you are all here. He never opened his eyes, but I know he sees the love you have for him." Marty and Theresa stand up and walk over to where Tom is standing. The three hug each other in shared grief. It is only Karen that doesn't get up; she just sits in her chair and stares at her son lying in the bed.

Tom says the obligatory, "If there is anything I can ever do…" as he says his final goodbyes to all including Karen. Karen takes the opportunity to look up at Tom and stares directly into his eyes.

"Mrs. Josephs, I can't express how sorry I am for what happened to your son. Please accept my best wishes for his speedy recovery." Tom says this with a half-smile on his lips. She is just about to tell him to stay the fuck away from her and her family, but she stops. There is something wrong about him and before she has a chance to speak Karen feels a shiver go up her spine.

Tom Houston exits from the hospital room and walks down the hall to the waiting entourage. He passes the desk where Beth is working and he takes the opportunity to say goodbye.

"Beth, I want to thank you and your staff for doing such good work. It was a very emotional visit for me and I only hope Officer Josephs' will recover."

"Thank you, Dr. Houston…we are all praying for his recovery."

"I am sure caring concern is a comfort to his family. Oh, don't forget about the rally at Madison Square Garden. I'll be sure to have the invitation sent to you and your boyfriend. Marvin, Harry, Serge, what was his name?"

Beth smiles knowing she's being teased, "Christopher Pella."

"That's right, Christopher Pella. I'll be sure to remember his name." Tom smiles and shakes Beth's hand. He turns towards his chief of staff, Nancy McGrath, and they walk toward the elevator.

An aide pushes the button for the elevator, but as he does an alarm goes off. A nurse comes running down the hall yelling, "Call Dr. Carlton, Officer Josephs is in cardiac arrest and vitals are dropping rapidly. We should have the crash cart ready." Nurse Breuer wastes no time as she rushes to the phone and uses the intercom to page the doctor.

Tom and his entourage get off the elevator and wait to find out what is going on.

There is frenzied activity as nurses and aides are running in and out of Nick Josephs' room and through the hallways. Beth runs into the patient's room where the family is in near hysterics. She checks the monitor and sees all of his vital signs have flat lined. If something is not done soon Beth knows that death will be imminent and she is not prepared to lose this patient. Beth escorts the family out of the room and asks them to wait in the outside hall. In less than a minute Dr. Carlton enter the room and begins the lifesaving procedures needed to try and save the young officers life. The medical team tries to resuscitate Nick time and time again but each time his vital signs show no indication that Nick Josephs is able to recover. After five minutes of doing all that was possible, an exhausted Dr. Carlton opens the door and gives Nick's family the heartbreaking news,

A crestfallen Dr. Carlton has to break the awful news to the family, "We've tried everything that we could, but there was nothing that could be done. I don't know what to say except the entire staff of Huntington Hospital mourns your loss. Your husband and son are the bravest of the brave and he will be remembered always. You have our deepest sympathies." Dr. Carlton tries to suppress his own tears.

All the family, Beth and members of the nursing staff are crying at the bedside of Officer Josephs, except for Karen. She rises from her chair and walks through the door of her son's room and down the hall, past the nursing station where other staff is crying in stunned disbelief. She arrives at the elevator to find Tom Houston and his staff waiting for the doors to the elevator to close for the trip to the lobby. Karen looks inside the elevator to see Dr. Thomas Houston standing in the center, surrounded by his staff. Nancy McGrath puts her hand out to stop the door from closing.

"Mrs. Josephs please accept our deepest sympathies…"

Karen looks at the chief of staff and says, "Shut up!" Nancy is taken back by the outburst and she stops speaking. Karen turns to Tom and her visceral revulsion is apparent to all. The entire staff is doing whatever they can to avoid looking at the women, except for Dr. Houston. He is looking at her straight in the eye and he smiles as Nancy lets the doors to the elevator close.

The elevator goes down and when it stops the doors open to the lobby. Dr. Tom Houston exits into the vestibule to find a large group of people mulling around. An announcement was made just a minute earlier for all off-duty and clerical staff and volunteers to assemble in the lobby. There is a crowd already gathered as the president of Huntington Hospital, Dr. Harold McMasters has asked. He is circulating among the staff and visitors who are speaking in hushed tones. Among those present are many of the news crews that were present at Tom Houston's press conference outside the hospital earlier.

Dr. McMasters stands by the reception desk and tries to speak above all the conversations that are taking place.

"May I please have your attention…please everyone can I have your attention for an important announcement." Slowly the voices become quiet murmurs and in a short while the entire lobby is silent.

"I have some very sad news for you all. I just received word from Dr. Carlton that Officer Nicholas Josephs has died from the wounds he received in the line of duty." There is a collective gasp from the crowd and Dr. McMasters' voice starts to crack, but he continues.

"Our thoughts and prayers go out the family of Officer Josephs at this truly saddest of times. From what we have learned, he was a wonderful man, a devoted husband and father and a brave and courageous police officer and I want to share this sad news with all of you who have prayed for his recovery."

Before the news has a chance to penetrate the consciousness of most of the people gathered in the lobby, a newsman screams out, "Can you confirm the actual cause of death?"

Dr. McMasters seems puzzled at the question, but he tries to answer, "Initial indications are that his death was due to cardiac arrest stemming from the wounds he received, however we will not know for sure until the autopsy is performed."

Some other reporter yells, "When will that be?"

Dr. McMasters still seems confounded by these questions. "I do not have a schedule yet; Officer Josephs has literally just died minutes ago and the arrangements for post-mortem have yet to be decided."

More and more reporters are now yelling out questions to the doctor who is not sure of how he should handle what is turning into a free-for-all press conference. In the past Dr. McMasters has had many such discussions, conferences and interviews with the press, but this frenzy by the press is far beyond any experience he's had, and he is not accustomed to this kind of commotion.

Before he speaks another word, a voice whispers in his ear, "Dr. McMasters would you like me to help stop this turmoil, I will be glad to assist in any way I can." Dr. Harold McMasters turns and he is facing Tom Houston and he feels a sense of relief that someone sees what he is seeing.

"Thank you for your kind offer Tom, but it is my responsibility and I don't want to put you into a position of having to speak for me."

Tom listens, but he knows that McMasters would like nothing better than to put all this in the hands of someone who is used to such an uproar from the media. Tom is keenly aware of this so he suggests, "I may have a solution; let me act as sort of a press secretary and I will defer all medical questions to you. I am far more practiced at handling the theatrics behind what so many of these dances with the press are. I assure you that this will be over in far shorter a timeframe."

Dr. Harold McMasters stares at Tom Houston. "I appreciate the gesture, Tom. As you can see, I am not accustomed to the havoc this tragedy has caused. I would like to make a statement and then make it more of a joint conference if that works for you?" Tom smiles and says "That's a great idea."

Tom Houston and Dr. Harold McMasters shake hands and turn to face the gathering of all assembled. Dr. McMasters begins by telling the crowd, "I know that there are many questions you have that relate to this tragedy, but you must understand that Officer Josephs' death has just taken place and we will need to approach the post-mortem in a practiced and measured manner. I was just speaking with Dr. Thomas Houston who had been paying a visit to Officer Josephs at the time of his death and I know that he would like to say a few words, Dr. Houston."

Dr. Harold McMasters steps aside and Tom Houston begins to speak. "Dr. McMasters, thank you for giving me this opportunity to speak. First, I would like to say that I have never seen a more devoted staff than here at Huntington Hospital. I have witnessed, first hand, the heroic efforts that were made to save the life of this brave young man by Dr. Joseph Carlton,

Head Nurse Beth Della Russo and the entire nursing staff. In the midst of this tragedy, I continue to be astonished at the selflessness and dedication of these fine professionals; ladies and gentlemen it is a privilege to be here among the best of the best." Dr. McMasters is looking at Tom Houston. He is grateful for the praise, but even more grateful for the reprieve from the madness that would have ensued.

Tom has the people present in the lobby area in rapt attention as he continues, "This man, Officer Nick Josephs, has made the ultimate sacrifice for all of us and his death has left the family and his fellow officers devastated. I think it is important for us to leave the medical professionals and the police to do their work." Tom turns to the side appearing to end his speech, but knowing the press will not listen.

A young reporter shouts to be heard above the other newsmen and women in the crowd. "You have made no attempt to hide the fact that you think there is some religious connection to all the murders, including that of Officer Josephs. Can you expand on that?"

Tom turns to face the young man. "It appears that Officer Josephs died from the actions of a religious zealot that used the Lamb of God as rationalization to commit this monstrous act. I don't know what was in her mind when she killed the unfortunate gentleman sitting in the mall and the police officer responding to the call, but I know what she said and what she wrote had obvious religious associations. As citizens in a nation governed by the rule of law, how can we make any excuses for these types of acts, acts so heinous that we are all forced to face the perversions that urge this type of insanity?"

Another reporter screams, "Are you equating religion with perversion and insanity?"

Tom pretends to be getting annoyed, "What kind of question is that? Of course, I am not equating religion with perversion or insanity. What I am saying is that these acts are driven by insane religious zealotry and it must end. Islam, Judaism, Christianity what does it matter in what name people die, the fact is they die. As a lawful society we must maintain order and these acts must stop."

Another voice calls from the floor, "How do you propose we stop these acts?"

Tom considers the answer to this question as he knows that it is important to his base as well as a potential headline in newspapers, broadcast news and online banners. "That's a question that would take far more consideration and time to answer. What I will say however is that there needs to be a concerted effort to identify the people who are susceptible to this type of religious indoctrination and to be sure they are given the kind of mental health treatment necessary for assimilation back into and ordered, lawful society." Tom turns back to Dr. McMasters and says, "I do not want to take up any more time as I am sure that your staff must get back to their important work."

Dr. McMasters smiles and shakes Tom Houston's hand. He then turns to address the crowd. "Thank you, Dr. Houston, for your time and for the kind words you've said regarding our staff. I will say this in closing; we must give time for the Josephs' family to grieve in their own way and for the postmortem process to do its work. Our communications director, Doreen Belvedere, will be releasing information to the authorities and to the family and, as appropriate, the information will be released to the media. Please keep Officer Josephs and his family in your thoughts and prayers."

The press continues to yell questions, but for all intents and purposes the conference is over. Dr. McMasters thanks Dr. Houston again and they shake hands and part ways. Tom Houston's entourage cuts a path through the crowd and they make their way outside to the waiting limo. There are more meetings scheduled for him today and he has an interview with the Parnell Group, a media conglomerate, later in the afternoon and Tom smiles.

The door of the limousine is opened by one of the staff and Tom sits comfortably in his seat next to a different young and beautiful woman. She is dressed in very fashionable business attire and sits demurely in the seat across from Tom. He knows what rewards await him on the ride back to his Garden City mansion. The chauffer starts the engine and closes the glass panel between them so his boss can have some privacy.

His beautiful companion reaches for the scotch, but Tom stops her. "No, no scotch yet, just pour me a glass of sparkling water." She does as she is told and slides next to him and hands him the tumbler. Tom Houston looks into the eyes of this beauty as she unzips his pants. Tom reaches for her breasts and she smiles.

CHAPTER 18

I unlock the door to the shop and decide I need to do some work as a distraction from the vision. I figure I need time to absorb the meanings that Jesus Christ and St. Patrick were trying to convey and of what I'm being asked to do. I turn on the radio to my favorite classic rock station and a few minutes later there is a break for a special news bulletin.

"We interrupt this program for a special announcement; our newsroom has just received this bulletin; Suffolk County police officer Nicholas Josephs has just died as a result of the wounds he received while trying to apprehend a woman who had committed murder at the Shops of the World Mall. Dr. Harold McMasters, president of Huntington Hospital, released this information at a spur-of-the-moment news conference held in the lobby of the hospital. No more information is available at this time, but we will update this important story as details are released."

I listen in sadness at the news and it then occurs to me that Beth is heading the nursing staff in charge of care for the wounded officer. I know that she will be extremely upset by the policemen's death so I reach for the phone and dial the hospital. I try but all I get is a busy signal. I continue to try again and again, but still all I get is a busy signal and all the while I'm worried about Beth and how she is taking the news.

I want to speak with Beth so I call her mobile number hoping that she will answer. Her phone rings, but my call goes into voice mail so I leave a message. Even though I don't know Nick Josephs it seems that every Long Islander feels close to the man. I just need to speak with someone so I try calling Uncle Al on his mobile.

"Chief Barese here."

"Uncle Al, I just heard the news about Officer Josephs. What can I say? All of this seems so surreal. We were just speaking of this tragedy and now you have to face the death of a fellow cop. I am so sorry Uncle Al."

"I know you are Chris. All I keep thinking about is his family. As a cop you are part of a close group, kind of like a family too, so when someone dies in the line of duty it's like you've lost a brother or sister. I can't tell you how sad we all are."

He didn't have to tell me of his sadness, I could hear it in his voice. I am silent because I don't know what to say or how to react. I suppose that police need to face the very real potential of dying in the line of duty every day, but when it actually happens the reality can be overwhelming. "Uncle Al, I…" My voice trails off because I just can't find the words to say how I feel, of what I could say or do to help him through this, but I know that there is nothing I can do.

Uncle Al says, "I know Chris. I appreciate your concern, I really do. I need to get off now as I have a number of calls to make before I get back to my office. We'll talk later."

"Okay, I love you."

"I love you too." He hangs up and the phone goes silent.

I am tempted to call Beth again, but before I have a chance my phone rings and I see its Beth name on the display. "Beth, I tried to call you when I heard the news, but I couldn't get through."

"I know I got your message Chris…" then she starts to cry. Her pain is evident as she shed tears for the dead policeman. I know Beth and I know the love she has for her own family so I know she is mourning for Nick Joseph's wife, children and his parents as if they were her family too.

"Beth, I don't have the words to help you through this, but I want you to know how sorry I am. From what I know and what you told me about Officer Josephs, he was a really good man." Chris stops speaking to give Beth a chance to try and calm herself.

A few seconds later Beth's weeping stops and in a low voice she says, "Thank you Chris. I can't tell you how sad all this makes me. I don't know why? I didn't know Nick or his family well at all. He was in a coma from the time he was admitted and, as I nurse, I often face dying and death, but this is as sad a situation as I have ever known."

"You are a kind, loving and caring person. The fact that you are so upset should not surprise you. That's one of the reasons I love you so much."

Beth stays silent for a short while and says, "Thank you for that Chris, I love you too. I only wish you were here to hold me."

"Would you like me to come over? I can be there in a few minutes."

"No Chris thanks, but we are all overwhelmed with work and with the repercussions of Nick's death. I'll be okay; it's just that I always feel better when we're together."

Chris wants to see Beth and be with her. He asks, "I miss you too, would you like to have dinner this evening when you get off from work. We can go to Frank and Maria's new place, Mabella's to have something to eat and we can talk. But I understand if you just want to relax after the day you've had."

"No, Chris, I'd love to see you too."

"Okay, how about I pick you up at your home at 7PM and I'll make reservations for 7:30PM?"

"That sounds wonderful. Thanks for being there Chris…I'll see you tonight. I love you."

"See you later, I love you too."

I hang up the phone and call my friend Frank at the restaurant. I make reservations and tell him about Officer Josephs' death and that Beth and I would like a table out of the way so we can talk. Frank, who is always accommodating, assures me that we will have a quiet corner where we can be left alone to speak in private. I thank him and say that Beth and I will be there at 7:30PM. I start feeling better knowing that I will see Beth this evening and I try to go back into the work I started earlier.

As I've said before, I never know when a vision is about to come, and this one came in waves as I watched.

The Sainted fell into what appears to be a trance-like state. He is near death from the ninth hour of the day to cock-crow. It is while in this state St. Fursey receives the first of his ecstatic visions. In this vision are revealed to him both the state of man in sin and the beauty of virtue. In rapture he heard the angelic choirs singing, "The saints shall go from virtue to virtue, the God of Gods will appear in Sion."

Two angels then appear and the command is given to him by the messengers of God, who restore St. Fursey's body to health. They beseech him to become an evangelist for the Lord.

As always, I am confused by these visions or in this case visions within a vision. I know that eventually I will have answers to my questions or at least try to know what questions to ask. In an instance it is three nights later, and the ecstasy is renewed.

He is now taken to the heavens by three angels who contend six times with demons for St. Fursey's soul. He sees the fires of hell, the strife of demons, and then hears the angel hosts sing in four choirs "Holy, holy, holy, Lord God of hosts."

Among the spirits of those just made perfect he recognizes Saints Meldan and Beoan. His abbot teachers were sent from heaven to provide him with spiritual instruction,

"Take heed and know of the duties regarding all ecclesiastics and monks. Be vigilant and watch for the dreadful effects of pride and disobedience and the heinousness of spiritual and internal sins."

The Sainted tell their student of many calamities and predict famine and pestilence brought on by the evil from the pit. As he returns through the fire, the demon hurls a tortured sinner at St. Fursey, burning him; and the angel of the Lord said to him, "Because thou didst receive the mantle of this man when dying in his sin, the fire consuming him hath scarred thy body also." St. Fursey's body bore the mark from that day forward.

The confines of this earthly realm have no hold on The Sainted or on their visions. I am in awe and anxious at once by what this and previous visions reveal. It is then that St. Fursey steps out of the vision and stands before me.

He speaks, "You need to be mindful of all the warnings of what you have seen and to prepare for what lies ahead."

I am as confused and dismayed as I have ever been. "What? What are the warnings? What lies ahead?"

The Sainted tells me, "Heed the message of the angels and of what God has ordained for all faithful and for all sinners. Evil is about and it is resolute, you are told to be a catalyst for good and for this you must also be strong. There is much to fear and much to come in the days ahead."

I am dumbfounded, for one of the only times in my years knowing The Sainted, I ask of him, "Why me? I am a sinner; I don't know if I can continue to be strong in the face of such evil."

St. Fursey looks at me and appears very troubled, "If you lose trust, if you cannot be counted among the faithful then all is lost for so many. The forces of evil are always watchful and you must be vigilant even if they are not, and always remember that you have God, Christ and the Holy Spirit as your strength and all The Sainted praying for you. You need no more than that, but without faith even God and all the powers of Heaven will be of no avail."

St. Fursey melts into the light and he is gone.

I am exhausted and worried about what this could all mean. I have faced evil before and I have been blessed to have survived. It seems with the horrors of hell that have been shown to me, I am told that I will face a far greater challenge to my faith than I have ever had to confront. I try to understand more of what I've seen from all my recent visions, but it is no use. I try to put his latest vision aside for the moment; I have a date with Beth and I don't want anything to get in the way.

I close the shop at 5PM and take the short drive home to my condo. I shower and shave and get dressed for dinner. It is 6PM by the time I finish and I have a few minutes to spare before I have to leave to pick up Beth. I go to my living room and turn on the TV to the early news and sit down to watch. The lead story is about the death of Officer Josephs and the impact it is having on many Long Islanders.

The news anchor reads the lead story that capsulizes the background of the man and the circumstances under which Officer Josephs was wounded and ultimately died. He continues, "At the time of Officer Josephs' death he was being visited by a very famous person, Dr. Thomas Houston. Dr. Houston, a native Long Islander and recently announced candidate for the Socialist Liberation Party nomination for President, spent time with the family only minutes before Officer Josephs' death."

The screen cuts from the anchor to Dr. Houston speaking to the camera, "Religious zealotry may or may not be the reason for Officer Josephs' death, but we cannot discount the possibility. Right now, however, we need to let the family of this brave man and his fellow officers mourn their loss."

The anchor is back on screen telling the viewers that the family also received condolences from all over the state including the governor, senators and congressmen from Long Island as well as other dignitaries, all expressing sadness over the officer's death.

I feel a slight pang of jealousy when I see the video of Tom Houston. I think of Beth and wonder if she got to meet him when he was at the hospital. I decide that I will ask her as I get up to turn off the TV. Beth lives only 20 minutes from me so I get into my car and take the scenic drive to her townhouse. I park my car in her driveway figuring that we would leave soon and I ring her doorbell.

The door opens almost immediately and before I could say "Hi Beth" she rushes into my arms and holds me tightly as she begins to sob.

I wrap my arms around her, "Oh Beth, I am so sorry."

Beth doesn't answer, but she still is hugging me tightly as her sobs begin to diminish. I never have trouble finding the words to say with anyone except Beth so I just keep quiet and continue to hold her in my arms. A minute or so passes and she looks up at me and smiles. "Thanks for being here; I just need to have you hold me and for your understanding."

I smile back and say, "I'm always here for you."

Beth continues to smile and says, "Let's go to eat. I haven't eaten all day and I'm starving. We can talk at the restaurant."

"Okay" and we walk to the car for our short ride to Mabella's. When we arrive, we are greeted by Maria, who's married to Frank. She embraces Beth the moment she sees her,

"I cannot tell you how sad we all are at Nick's death. He came to eat here with his family all the time. I just keep thinking of his beautiful girls and I don't know what to say." Maria's eyes start to fill with tears and Beth hugs her and thanks her, "Thank you Maria. It seems like we all feel the same about Nick."

Maria guides us to our table, gives Beth a kiss on her cheek and leaves us alone to talk. Frank is next and he comes to the table to give his condolences, "I just want to tell you how sorry we all are for this tragic loss. He was a good man and came from a wonderful family and it breaks our hearts just thinking about the kids."

Beth tells him, "We know Frank, I am sure that the family knows how we all feel."

Frank hands us the menu, "I'll leave you alone and send Rich to take your order. Let me know if you need anything."

"Thanks, Frank."

Our favorite waiter, Rich comes to our table, "Hi Beth, hi Chris what can I get you to drink?" I order a bottle of wine and he leaves to get it for us. Since MaBella opened, it is always crowded. The food is wonderfully prepared and the restaurant has a growing group of loyal customers. It can get crowded, but our table is tucked away in a quiet corner so we are able to talk without too many distractions from conversations going on around us.

"Thanks again for taking me out for dinner. I just need to talk to someone about all this and, like it or not, you're the go to guy."

I smile at Beth, "I'm glad to be your go to guy anytime, anywhere."

Beth starts to talk; she needs to unload all of her thoughts and feelings about what's happened and I just want to be there to listen. "Chris, I was in the room when Dr. Carlton tried to save Nick and he tried and tried, but it was useless, everything we did was useless. The worst part is that I had to face the family as the doctor told them the news of Nick's death. When I stepped into the hall outside the room and all the nurses were crying, I can't explain why I feel this way, but I do."

Beth stops speaking as Rich comes to the table with our wine. He sets down the bottle, opens it and pours a small amount for me to taste. I know it's a ritual to taste if the wine has turned, but so far, I haven't had a bad bottle. I tell Rich the wine is fine and he pours us two glasses. We tell him that we will order later and he leaves us to continue our conversation.

I know she still needs to speak so I tell Beth, "Go on Beth, tell me everything that's on your mind. I think it's good that you can speak about this to me."

Beth reaches over the table to hold my hand, "Thanks Chris I know I can always count on you. I just keep thinking about Nick's family. He has two of the most adorable little girls that he called his beauties and now he's dead. He'll never go to parents-teachers' nights, he'll never see them play soccer or go to a dance recital or whatever. He'll never watch them graduate high school or college or walk them down the aisle when they get married…" Tears roll down her cheek, but Beth doesn't wipe them away, it's as if she wants to remember this moment and the life of the man and the family he leaves behind.

We sit continuing to talk about Nick Josephs and other things. A short time later there is a lull in our conversation as Beth tries to collect her thoughts. She looks up at me and says, "You know, we had a special visitor at the hospital today."

I know who the visitor is, but I pretend not to know, "Really, who came to the hospital today?"

She smiles at me and said, "Our very special visitor was Dr. Thomas Houston, candidate for his party's nomination for President."

"You mean that ugly guy who never found a camera he didn't like, you know just like our esteemed senator what-his-name." I smile back at her remembering our conversation at the Huntington Pub House. I know she is on the verge of breaking my balls so I say, "President of what?"

"Of the United States silly." She changes her demeanor to appear surprised. "Don't tell me you're still jealous, Chris?"

"Of course, I'm jealous. I suppose he was there to visit Nick. How did that go?"

"He was there for a few minutes before Nick died. He had his whole entourage with him at the time and they stood by the elevator when Nick's vitals began to drop."

"Wow that must have been a crazy time."

"It really was. We were all scrambling to bring in the crash cart and to have everything ready for Dr. Carlton. After it was declared that Nick had died, we were all grieving then something strange happened."

"Strange? What do you mean strange?"

"Well, I went over to Nick's wife, Theresa, and his parents Marty and Karen', to express my condolences and try to console them. Terri and Marty were so very upset and we hug and cry together, but Karen just stood there for a moment, no crying and no screaming just a look of anger. Then she opens the door of Nick's room and turns to walk to the elevator. I didn't give it a thought, but later I'm speaking with Diane Breuer, you know the nurse who likes to kid you all the time. Well, she tells me something that I don't quite understand."

I don't know why, but suddenly I feel fearful for Beth, "Go on, what don't you understand?"

"Well, Diane said that Karen Josephs walked to the elevator and just stood looking through the open door at Tom Houston. She said something to Tom's chief of staff, Nancy McGrath and then the door closed. Karen came back to the room and the family stayed with Nick for a while before they left. Diane wouldn't think of questioning Karen so she never knew what it was all about, but the entire incident seemed very strange to both of us."

Beth and I sit in silence, trying to let the events of the day sink in, hoping to come up with answers, but knowing that there are no answers, at least none we could come up with. Rich sees that we stopped speaking so he comes over and we both order the special house salad and Beth orders pasta primavera and I order the penne arrabiata. Rich refills our glasses and leaves to put in our order.

Our conversation slowly turns to the more mundane aspects of our daily lives when I remember my conversation with Fr. Aiden.

"Beth, when I had lunch with Father Langford, I told him about you and asked if he would be available for us to visit. He is genuinely happy to do it and suggests that we meet at Immaculate Conception Seminary where he will give us a tour and we could have lunch in their dining room. What do you say?"

"That's sounds great. I'll check my work schedule and give you some dates that I have off. We can see if they work for Father Langford. By the way I have some exciting news for you."

"I could use some exciting news…I mean good exciting, not bad exciting."

"Well, I hope you think this is good exciting. Dr. Thomas Houston, possibly the next President of the United States, has invited us to Madison Square Garden for his huge fundraiser…don't worry you don't have to give him a dime. Fabiano and Boyd Somerfield will be headlining and we'll be his personal guests for the event."

I am dumbfounded, "You're kidding me, right?"

"No!" Beth says with a shit eating grin on her face, "We'll be mingling with the rich and famous. Free food and free drinks, what do you say?" Now she starts singing the chorus from one of Fabiano's hits, but I stop her.

"How the hell did this happen?"

"Well, when Tom, I mean Dr. Houston came to the hospital we got to talking and after I told him that I wouldn't go out with him, that I already have a boyfriend, he invited us to the event."

I am now getting very pissed off. "What the hell? This piece of shit asked you out!"

"Chris, come on, after all he didn't know I have a boyfriend, and it was all done with the utmost innocence." Now Beth puts on her flirty look and tries to soothe my bruised ego, "After all I am kind of cute and adorable."

"Utmost innocence, oh that changes it all? Does that mean he only grabbed your ass and not your tits?" I am getting more aggravated as we continue talking.

"Chris, listen he was a perfect gentleman and I told him you are my boyfriend. As soon as I did, he changed his tone and graciously offered us the invitation. Not "me", "us.""

There's something about Beth that can immediately mollify an argument or the potential for one, but I feel I shouldn't just lie down and roll-over. "There's something about this guy, I can't put my finger on it, but I really don't like this guy." I stammer and go quiet.

"Listen Chris, we will be there together. I won't leave your side and you'll have a chance to see if your opinion of him is right or wrong. Come on, what do you say? Don't you want to take me to this concert or fund-raiser or whatever?" Now she reaches over and touches my cheek, "Come on Christopher, for me, pleeeease?"

Shit, I hate it when she says pleeeease, but I grumble "Okay."

Beth is smiling from ear-to-ear, "That's the boyfriend I love."

"I said okay, but I'm not happy."

Beth leans forward and takes hold of my hand and smiles as she looks into my eyes, "Oh, and what will make you happy?"

Shit, there she goes again…

CHAPTER 19

He always enjoys coming home to his Garden City mansion.

He needed to buy three surrounding homes and properties so that he could have enough room to build his house and enough privacy for when he has time alone. He loves everything about the 14,500 square foot home and guest wing. The 18 rooms, the 8 bedrooms, the 10 bathrooms, library, a home theatre that sits 14 guests comfortably, indoor pool and outdoor pool and cabana, the game room, oh and yes, the fireplaces…all 10 of them.

Dr. Thomas Houston had taken time out of his very hectic schedule to help design the classic brick and stone Georgian Manor style home and spared no expense. From the custom coffered ceilings and intricate paneling, spectacular mantels, columns, archways and detailed moldings, his home is among the most beautiful on Long Island and has been featured in numerous design and architectural publications. The New York Times even did a four-page spread on the mansion which pleased him immensely. When he entertains, Dr. Thomas Houston loves to give tours of the mansion and point to all the special, finer aspects that went into the design and construction. For him, and he imagines everyone who sees this place, his home is exceptional. Even the underground basement level was truly special with a large den, game room, indoor lap pool, hot tub and steam shower along with a wine cellar that stores 5,000 bottles of some of the finest vintages in the world.

There is one place, however, that does not appear on the home's original plans. The space was put in earlier…much earlier…and it is unknown to all but Dr. Thomas Houston for a very good reason; it doesn't really exist, at least not on this earthly plain.

He touches a loose board on one of the wine racks and the rack dissolves revealing a vast, cavernous hollow. An unnatural light seems to surround this place and casts long dark shadows over the interior. The enormous boulders that are scattered all over have sharp, blade like edges that could cut a person in two if ever anyone were unfortunate enough to fall on them, but no one ever would. Tom acknowledges to himself that for anyone entering the cave it would become a frightening experience beyond anything that could be imagined.

Tom has done this many times before and he has no fear because things are going very well, very well indeed. This is a special place; a place of worship, a place of unimaginable power, a place where hopefulness dies and hopelessness lives, but never for Tom. He confidently navigates through the cavern to the place he has been commanded to be. When he gets there, he kneels on the cold damp ground and bows in supplication.

"Master, come forth and reveal yourself to your humble servant."

The ground and surrounding walls of the cavern shake for a moment and the cave fills with the heat and glow of fire. Tom Houston remains kneeling, head down in complete supplication to the Master of his soul.

A voice quakes and the silence of the cave is broken. "Is all going according to the plan?" Satan already knows the answer, but he wants Tom to say it out loud.

Tom Houston continues to remain in the same position, head bowed to the ground as he answers, "Yes, master all is going as planned."

"What have you done so far to sow the seeds of dissonance?"

"I have done as you have commanded. Consciousness is rising to the possibility that the cursed Lamb of God is to blame for all the terror being wrought throughout the world. The possibility has been planted in the minds of many and it has taken root."

"Good, I have placed my dark angels, my princes and their demon hoards around the cursed plain and they will continue to wreak havoc as like none before."

"Master, we have many souls that we must corrupt before evil can triumph. What must we do to assure this victory for you?"

Tom Houston, still on his knees, head bowed, could not see the smile crossing Satan's lips as he answers, "My dark angels are very busy these days, very busy indeed."

"How, my lord? What is it that they are doing to fulfill their unholy pledge to you?"

Satan smiles as his eyes become wide with excitement for, he takes pleasure in listing the eminence of his plan for Thomas Houston to hear. "Leviathan is triumphing in the tasks I ordain. He makes substantial movement among the atheistic sacrilege and there are now many more converts each day. I will find such great pleasure when their disbelief turns into the awakening that they must face, an awakening horror of truth." Now Satan bellows with laughter, "The truth and the torment I will deliver to each and every heathen as their souls will be mine for time without end!"

Satan is taking more pleasure as he tells his slave the plans he continues to put into effect. "Ah! And there are Berith and Sonneillon; my princes Berith and Sonneillon! One needs to look no further than the carnage that is extant in the middle-eastern parts of Adamina, what do they call it, the Holy Land?" Satan stops speaking just long enough for another deafening laugh and continues.

"There will be the beast of the earth to guide the destruction and lead the souls to me and their own damnation. I must say that the Islamic tribes do make our task far easier than I am sure they wish, even those they seek to kill do little to protest. My demons have set upon a task that will cause such destruction as to make the world's peoples scream in terror. These creators of chaos and rage kill each other with wanton abandon in the name of Allah and I am pleased beyond measure. I will be sure to find a special place for them in my world of the damned."

Satan seems to pause for effect.

"Who is it my Lord? Who is the false prophet?" Tom still lays prostrate, his face to the ground.

"You will soon find out." Satan is dismissive of the question.

Now Tom senses a feeling of nausea taking over and tries to suppress the urge to vomit.

Sarcastically, Satan pretends to be concerned as he declares, "It is the Christians that we are finding to be more troublesome than I would have expected. For these souls I have sent Asmodeus and Gressil. The bastard faithful pray on Sunday and debauch all other days and these dark angels will tempt them into such wantonness even their day of rest will become as all others. When they are witness to the carnage and find there is no refuse in their God, they will come screaming to me and I will greet them with the many terrors they will confront for all time to come."

Satan revels as he reveals his blueprint for the end of days and the outcome, he assures the groveling human will happen. He speaks of other peoples and beliefs; Buddhists, Hindus, Taoists and he assures Tom Houston that these so-called people of faith and the beliefs that guide them will crumble and many if not all souls. They will soon be enduring the punishments of the damned. Satan's enthusiasm continues as he pronounces, "It has started, but there is so much more to come; war, disease, drought and pandemic and when the prayers of the faithful go unanswered they will turn against God and to me. I will have my revenge; I will have my victory and I will have the souls of the damned for eternity."

Tom Houston is silent, he does not know what to say, but Satan speaks, "There is one more task that you are to do."

Tom is frightened, but he answers, "What is your command my Master?

"There is someone, a pathetic soul that I want more than any other. It is one that you must acquire for me and I will not tolerate failure."

Tom is now both frightened and puzzled. "Who is this soul my lord?"

Satan is no longer smiling; he is beginning to grow larger and larger as the anger rises in him. "His name is Christopher Pella."

Tom seems disbelieving and says to Satan, "But my lord, I know of this man. He appears to be a pitiful human that you could ruin in mere moments. Why give this mortal a second thought?"

Satan grows in size and screeches at Tom, "What gives you the impudence to tell me what I should do? You pitiful human! What do you know of this man? Do you know anything of this creature? Do you have any understanding of his power?" Tom holds his ears as the screams of Satan deafen him and shake him to the core.

"I am sorry Master; I did not mean to…" but he is silenced by Satan.

"Quiet you fool. Do you know who protects this man? Do you know with whom he communicates? DO YOU?"

Tom is at a loss for words. His fear of Satan, of saying the wrong thing has paralyzed him, but he stammers an answer, "No…no my lord?"

Satan looks up from the cowering man on the ground and stares at the walls of the cave. The demon is in such a state of anger and hatred that he practically spits out the answer, "He is protected by The Sainted."

Thomas Houston is puzzled. He reasons that Satan is looking to confront the powers of Heaven and of God the Father, but why is he so concerned that The Sainted is protecting this nobody, Christopher Pella?

"I know of what you think; you have eyes yet you are blind. The Sainted are far more powerful that you can ever imagine." Satan thought of the battle with St. Agnes in the cave on Pit Island and his anger grows as does his size. "You are to find his weakness and you are to do whatever is required bringing his soul to damnation. When this is complete, I will have my revenge."

At this time Tom Houston summons the courage to rise. He has seen this ultimate evil before, but each time is like the first; the hideousness of the beast nearly takes his breath away. Satan knows that Tom is both repulsed and petrified and he laughs out loud and mockingly says, "What is this? You do not appreciate the face of evil?"

"No, my master, I mean yes…I mean…" and Tom goes silent.

Satan laughs again, this time harder than before and he says to his servant, "Do not fear me. If you succeed in your task and fulfill your vows unfathomable wealth and eternal pleasures will be your reward as you take your place among my most important generals."

It is then that the smile leaves Satan's face as he bends far down and stares into Tom Houston's soul as he says,

"But fail me and you will experience the true meaning of retribution. It will not be a punishment meted out and allowed to wane, it will be of such agonizing torment that your screams will resound over the pit and your agony will last for all eternity."

Dr. Thomas Houston can no longer contain his fear. He falls to the ground, a groveling mass of humanity and implores his master, "Please, I will do as you command, I will obey and you will have your victory over Christopher Pella and all the souls on earth", but there is no answer to his entreaty.

Tom looks up and he is all alone in the cave.

CHAPTER 20

*J*ohn of Patmos hears behind him a great voice, as that of a trumpet.

The angel of God says to him, "What thou seest, write in a book and send to the seven churches which are in Asia, to Ephesus, and to Smyrna, and to Pergamus, and to Thyatira, and to Sardis, and to Philadelphia, and to Laodicea."

John turns to see the image that is revealed to be the Son of Man. In the vision he sees seven golden candlesticks. In the midst of the seven golden candlesticks the Son is clothed with a garment down to his feet, and He is belted about the chest with a golden sash. His head and His hair are white, as white as snow, and His eyes are as a flame of fire.

John hears His voice as the sound of many waters. He looks at the Son and sees that He holds in His right hand seven stars. From His mouth comes out a sharp two-edged sword and His face shines as the sun in His power.

Upon seeing this vision John falls to the ground at the feet of Christ. At first, he does not understand what the meaning of this vision is. John lay there in supplication to the Lord of Lords when Christ lays His right hand upon The Saint, saying,

"Fear not. I am the First and the Last, and alive, and was dead, and behold I am living forever and ever, and have the keys of death and of hell. Write therefore the things which thou hast seen and which are and which must be done hereafter; the mystery of the seven stars, which thou sawest in my right *hand, and the seven golden candlesticks. The seven stars are the angels of the seven churches. And the seven candlesticks are the seven churches."*

As his vision fades John becomes anxious over the burden he must bear. What is the message to be revealed in these visions, how will he make known their meaning to all as he was commanded? John could not yet know of the prophesies of Whore of Babylon, the Beasts of the sea and Earth and of the second coming of Jesus Christ for that will come later.

As time passes, the seven churches welcome many faithful. The messages and their meanings would become clearer to John as he seeks to write them in his epistles and deliver them to the Seven Churches,

"Grace is unto you and peace from Him that is and that was and that is to come and from the seven spirits which are before his throne and from Jesus Christ, who is the faithful witness. The first begotten of the dead and the prince of the kings of the earth who hath loved us and washed us from our sins in His own blood, He hath made us a kingdom, and priests to God and His Father, to Him be glory and empire forever and ever, Amen. Behold, He cometh with the clouds, and every eye shall see Him, and also that pierced Him. All the tribes of the earth shall bewail themselves because of him. Even so, Amen."

John needs to counsel the faithful in all things and at all times with the words of the Lord, "I am Alpha and Omega, the beginning and the end, saith the Lord God, who is, and who was, and who is to come, the Almighty."

The day is filled with dark clouds and rain as the messenger approaches. The messenger has travelled many weeks to deliver the communication and the Apostle knows it carries news of persecutions of the faithful from the Seven Churches and beyond.

John sits near the entrance to his home. He opens the letter and reads the contents with sorrow.

John knows what he must do and it becomes an imperative. He understands that the Revelations are not simply written words containing mystical metaphors. Revelations must deal with suffering endured by the faithful and bring them hope in these trying times. The Roman persecutions of Christians are so severe as to tempt man to deny his faith. John implores the Seven Churches to remain steadfast in their belief knowing God will ultimately be victorious over enemies of His church.

In the months and years to follow, John travels near and far and continues to exhort the faithful to remain steadfast in their belief in God and His ultimate victory over evil. Even as the persecutions continue, John remains unfaltering and he urges his followers to do the same for he knows it is a message for now and for all times.

From the confines of his grotto on Patmos, John seeks to understand all that is revealed to him. It is, however, not until Revelation 6 that John comes to know of the Seven Seals, the coming Apocalypse and Final Judgment of man. Each of the seals reveals terrifying events that will end in the Apocalypse.

It is of the first Seal he writes,

"And I saw that the Lamb had opened one of the seven seals,
And I heard one of the four living creatures,
As it were the voice of thunder, saying:
Come, and see. And I saw: and behold a white horse,
And he that sat on him had a bow, and there was a crown given him,
And he went forth conquering that he might conquer.

John knows the words and their meaning are revealed through Divine providence and their true meaning is made evident to him. John knows the word of God is the word of the way, the truth and light. He will need to make this known to all for in the final Revelation it is written in the battle of good and evil and the coming of the antichrist,

These will wage war against the Lamb,
And the Lamb will overcome them,
Because He is Lord of lords and King of kings,
And those who are with Him are
The called and chosen and faithful.

As John ponders the visions as revealed to him, he becomes much aggrieved as he writes in Revelation 13:1, "And I stood upon the sand of the sea, and saw a beast rise up out of the sea, having seven heads and ten horns, and upon his horns ten crowns, and upon his heads the name of blasphemy."

His vision continues and he writes, "Then I saw another beast that rose out of the earth; it had two horns like a lamb and it spoke like a dragon. It exercises all the authority of the first beast on its behalf, and it makes the earth and its inhabitants worship the first beast, whose mortal wound had been healed. It performs great signs, even making fire come down from heaven to earth in the sight of all."

The holy man pauses to take in the full meaning of the words he has written. Who is this beast of the earth, a lamb with the voice of a dragon, he knows of the first beast, but what does this message portend? John takes special note and vows to bring this warning to the faithful…a warning of the coming dread.

CHAPTER 21

It takes a few days, but I get some dates when Beth is off from work and call Father Langford to see when he would be available. "Good morning, Father, this is Chris, Chris Pella. How are you?"

"I am fine and fit as a fiddle. How are you dear boy, it is good to hear from you! I am hoping above hope that you are calling to set up a rendez-vous at ICS with that lovely young lady of yours!"

I smile at his greeting as I enjoy listening to Father Langford make you, or anyone he speaks to, feel special. He has such a vibrancy and love of life and living it that it's contagious.

"You must be psychic, that's exactly why I am calling. I spoke with Beth and she is very excited to meet you. She gave me a few dates and hopefully you'll be free at one of those times." I give him the dates and we decide on the day and time to meet. As luck would have it, we agree to meet on Valentine's Day and it seems to be preordained that this is the day we choose to meet.

"You know, that is the day we commemorate the life and times of St. Valentine, a truly remarkable individual. I daresay it is also the day that those in love look to each other for some measure of that love." Father Aiden says this with the utmost seriousness.

"I know it is Father and I want to thank you very much; I know how busy you are and I really appreciate you taking the time…"

Father Aiden stops me in mid-sentence and with a smile in his voice says, "Nonsense dear Christopher, nonsense! It is I who should be thanking you for giving me the opportunity to show off this beautiful place in which I live and to have your company for what usually is a very tasty meal. I am looking forward to our time together with eager anticipation!"

I thank Father Langford and we say our goodbyes. After I hang up, I immediately resolve that I will call Beth and give her the date and time, but I stop. I can't seem to help it; I'm still angry…read jealous…about Tom Houston's invitation to Beth for the fundraiser and I am having a tough time getting over it. I figure that I will call her later on so I go back to work appraising a collection of US coins that I recently purchased. When you buy small private collections, you usually have to take the good with the bad so I begin to sort through the coins. I first come across an 1800 "Draped Bust" half-cent in really lousy condition that isn't worth much, but I hope things would get better. As luck would have it the next coin, I pick up is an 1865 silver 3$¢$ piece and I estimate that it is in fine condition and could bring over $300 from a collector. I make a note of this and go to pick up my next coin when another vision appears before my eyes. I am taken to the servant quarters of a palace in Portugal in the 13th century.

The young servant of the queen, Erico stands in the shadows and stares in jealousy at Aurelio. His jealousy turns to hatred for his counterpart, also a servant to the queen. Aurelio seems to gain more and more favor these days. Erico murmurs to himself, "What can be done to rid the palace of this usurper, this man who seeks to gain the favor of the queen and seize my place in the royal household?"

Erico thinks and thinks and then it comes to him. All in the palace know of the King's debauchery and of his illegitimate children. He will use his sovereign's weaknesses to his advantage. The King is known to rage in anger at many things and Erico will somehow plant the seeds of jealousy in his mind. Erico will tell the King of the disloyal servant and of how he witnessed Aurelio seducing the Queen, his Elizabeth. This false accusation will be viewed as an act of treason and this would surely incur the wrath of the King. If all goes according to plan the king will sentence the young page to death and Erico's place among the royal staff would be assured. Now Erico smiles at the possibility of it all and he vows to speak with the King this very night.

The vision changes and I am transported to a large chamber. In the chamber King Dinis is seated in a large chair and Erico kneels at the feet of his King.

"My Lord, it is with great distress that I must tell you of an act of disloyalty, so vile I fear to even make mention of it."

"What is it you have to tell me? Do not waste my time, tell me now!" The King seems to remain calm, but his face betrays an anger that seems to be building.

Now even Erico becomes frightened, but it is too late to re-consider so he speaks, "My Lord, I regret having to tell you, but I fear that the Queen is being seduced by her man-servant Aurelio Gouveia. I know for I have seen him enter her chambers in the dark of night when you are not at court. I am loyal to you my Lord, please command me and I will do anything that you wish."

King Dinis remains silent for a short while and then tells the servant to rise. "You are to tell this Aurelio of Gouveia that, on my order, he is to go to the lime-burner. Do not let him know of the true reason for my command. Once there he will be cast into the flames; punishment for such treachery is demanded!"

*The servant bows and walks to the chamber door as he leaves
the room and as he leaves, I see a smile come across his face.*

Again, the vision changes and I find myself in the chamber of St. Elizabeth of Portugal who is kneeling in prayer.

*The queen suffers greatly. She kneels at the base of a small
pedestal where a cross that bears the image of Christ stands.
She prays and she begs the Lord to make pious the King, her
husband, who has taken to adultery and abuse.*

The saint leaves her earthly self and walks towards me. I am very concerned for poor Aurelio, but then St. Elizabeth calms my fears.

"Aurelio is always loyal to both his King and Queen, but my husband is too blinded by jealousy to see the truth.

"What happened to Aurelio?

"Aurelio was always a pious man. He would attend mass each day and pray to God for mercy and guidance. It is his custom and on the day that he was to die nothing changed. What did change however is that he was late in arriving and the mass had started and Aurelio decided to wait for the next mass to begin.

I am becoming very curious so I ask, "Please, tell me what happened next?"

St. Elizabeth tells me that the King waited a number of hours and sent Erico to check with the lime-burner that his orders were obeyed and that Aurelio has died. I didn't need St. Elizabeth to finish when I whisper an answer to my own question, "The lime-burner throws Erico into the fire."

St. Elizabeth nods and continues, "When my husband found out that Erico had perished, he saw it as a sign from God. He came to know Erico lied and that Erico, not Aurelio, was the guilty one and true justice was served. From that moment on my husband was a changed man. Dinis made an apology to me in full view of all his people; this was a truly hard thing for a man with such pride to admit his adulterous and abusive ways, but he did and from that day on he was faithful.

"I think I know why you are here."

St. Elizabeth smiles at me and asks, "Why do you think I am here and why you were allowed to see this vision?

I couldn't look St. Elizabeth in the face so I lower my head and say, "I have been consumed by the same jealousy that your husband had; maybe not to the same degree, but jealousy just the same."

The saint put her hand under my chin and makes me face her as she says, "Christopher, it is true that jealousy can make you believe in things that are not true. It can also change you in ways so profound that you cannot recognize dangers to you that jealousy expresses."

I am puzzled and disturbed and I ask St. Elizabeth, "Dangers? What dangers?

Now St. Elizabeth's smile fades, "Christopher, the dangers of which I speak should be of great concern to you, of those you love and for all mankind. There are crises to come that will require all your strength and faith. You must not let any pettiness prevail or you will not recognize or understand the nature of the dangers. If this comes to pass, you will fail in the tasks to come and all will be lost."

Before I could utter another word, the vision disappears and I am back in my shop. For a minute I just sit at my desk and try to take in what I have been told and the meaning behind the vision. I realize how my jealousy could corrupt my relationship with Beth and I vow to call her, but before I could pick up the phone, it rings.

"Hello, St. Aloysius Gonzaga Coins and Currency, how may I help you?"

"Hi Chris, it's me." It figures that Beth would call me before I have a chance to call her.

"I'm so glad you called; I was just picking up the phone to call you."

I heard a gulp at the other end of the line, "Chris, I just want to call to tell you that we don't have to go to the fundraiser. I know you don't like Dr. Houston and I don't want to force you to do something you don't want to do."

"Listen Beth, I realize that I'm acting like a jerk and making a big deal out of nothing and I apologize for being jealous. Let's go to the concert fundraiser or whatever, I really mean it." At this point I start to sing the chorus from one of Boyd Somerfield's hits and Beth starts to laugh and says,

"You really have a lousy voice and you're a goofy, but I think I'll keep you. Are you sure you're okay with going?"

"Of course, I am. I promise we'll have a great time and I'll be at my best behavior." I now go back to singing another one of Somerfield's hits.

She's laughing and says, "Listen, you can sing to yourself 'because I've got to go, duty calls, but let's talk later."

"Great, I'll call you later at home." She hangs up and I feel much better now that there isn't an unspoken word between us. The minor concern that I had with Beth is over now I still need to consider what St. Elizabeth means by danger to all mankind.

"All mankind?" The vision of St. Elizabeth comes back in full force and I say the words aloud, to myself. What could it possibly mean? I didn't know or understand, but I fear that I soon would.

CHAPTER 22

It is one of those beautiful mid-winter days on Long Island and it just happens to be the day that we set for our visit with Father Aiden at Immaculate Conception Seminary.

I pick Beth up at her townhouse and we take a leisurely drive to the seminary. We drive through the large Iron Gate that marks the entrance to the grounds. I park the car in an area set aside for visitors and Beth and I get out and begin walking towards the front door. Before we get there, the door swings open and Father Langford rushes out to greet us.

"My dear Christopher what a joy it is to see you so soon after our luncheon!"

"Same here Father." We embrace and shake hands and before I can introduce Beth, Fr. Aiden turns to look at her and says,

"Ah and let me guess, you must be Elizabeth Della Russo. Christopher and Spartaco mentioned how lovely you are and I dare say they did not exaggerate. Welcome my dear, welcome!" Fr. Aiden extends his hand to shakes Beth's.

Beth shakes his hand and gives Fr. Aiden a big smile and says, "Thank you very much Father Langford, I have been looking forward to this visit and please call me Beth."

Fr. Aiden smiles back, "Then you must call me Aiden as friends, new and old, should never stand on ceremony. By the way I understand you are the daughter of Paul and Catherine Della Russo."

"I am and they both asked me to convey their warmest regards. It seems that they are very big fans of yours."

"Please return the kindness and send them my best wishes. Your parents are most benevolent benefactors of ICS and their generosity is most appreciated by all who study and teach here."

Fr. Aiden looks quizzically at Beth and asks, "Can I trust you to keep a secret?" Beth can't imagine what secret the priest would confide so soon after they just met, but her curiosity usually has no bounds and she responds, "Of course!"

Father Aiden is very pleased and excitedly proclaims "I knew I could trust your discretion! It seems that the board of directors plans to rename the eastern wing of the Seminary in honor of your parents and their continuing support. It will become the Paul and Catherine Della Russo Study Center. We will be unveiling a bronze plaque commemorating their generosity. The date of the event plans and the formal announcement still need to be finalized, but the Bishop will preside over a special mass and there will be the induction ceremony and a wonderful dinner and dance with many dignitaries present. Of course, you and Christopher will be invited. We on the Board are most delighted!"

Beth stares back in amazement. "Father, I mean Aiden, I don't know what to say."

"Ah, my dear, say nothing, but that you will come to the event to honor your parents whom I know you love deeply."

I detect a tear coming down Beth's cheek which she rubs away. She hugs Fr. Aiden and kisses his cheek, "Thank you so much, I know it will mean the world to them and I wouldn't miss it for the world."

Fr. Aiden claps his hands together and happily says, "Splendid! I am so pleased. Now let us begin your personally guided tour of these beautiful grounds and the imposing edifice that I call home." With that Fr. Aiden begins our excursion. Our small group takes the path Fr, Aiden usually walks and we bask in the bright sunshine, surprisingly warm February temperatures and clear blue skies. The day and the company make our tour all the more enjoyable.

Fr. Aiden takes us to the water's edge where we have a wonderful view of the harbor. Most of the boats have been stored for the winter so we have an unobstructed view. He points out the area on the seminary grounds where he loves to sit and meditate while enjoying the peace and tranquility of the surroundings.

Father Aiden tells us, "You may not be familiar with St. John of the Cross, but I use him as my inspiration when I contemplate."

I have been fortunate to have had a vision of St. John of the Cross and I spoke with him of many things. His life was a genuine example of why The Sainted is revered to this day. Born in Spain, his father was cast aside by his noble family when he married a poor weaver's daughter. At 14 years of age St. John worked in hospitals caring for the people who suffer from incurable diseases and those who are driven to madness. In the midst of all this suffering John learned to meditate to find the meaning of beauty and contentment in his love of God.

I chimed in, "Yeah, he was an amazing man. Hey, Beth, this guy was locked up in prison and beaten three times a week." I had actually seen him being beaten by other members of his Carmelite order over his belief in religious reforms that were needed. My memory of St. John of the Cross is vivid as I continue to tell bits and pieces of his life. "In his tiny prison cell St. John was able to perfect this contemplative state and he seemed to find his greatest joy in just having the blessing and mercy of God with him at all times. He even found a way to escape his captors and continue his journey. I guess he could have become a cynic, given what life had thrown at him and his family, but he didn't. Instead, he became a compassionate mystic. He lived by the philosophy that tells us 'Where there is no love, put love and you will find love.' Great message for Valentine's Day don't you both agree?"

Father Aiden looks at me; slack jawed, and says, "I cannot believe my ears. Why Christopher this is a revelation!"

I laugh at Fr. Aiden's incredulity, "Don't be so impressed, I've taken up reading about Saints as kind of a hobby. I've been doing it since I was a kid."

Fr. Aiden seems very pleased, "Do not sell your knowledge short; it is a benediction that you are so inspired by the lives of the saints."

For the entire morning we spoke of many things including love and its meaning and consequences. "Well Christopher, I assume you have read about the life of St. Valentine, but if you have not it may be instructive as he exemplifies the true meaning of love. Not in the corporeal sense, but in the transcendent importance of the word." Father Aiden tells us how much he admires St. Valentine and I just smile thinking of my vision of the man and the gift I would give Beth later today.

You may think that I want to impress the priest; some may even think it is false pride on my part, but I really am caught up in the moment. "I think St. Valentine is just about the most kind and brave man I ever met."

Now Fr. Aiden laughs, "Ah Christopher, you met this man? I am most anxious to hear which St. Valentine you met. Was it the St. Valentine that was a Roman priest or perhaps St. Valentine, the priest from Viterbo or the bishop by the same name from Raetia or maybe even the St. Valentine who was a fifth-century priest and hermit?" Father Aiden has the reputation of being kind of a jokester and we all start to laugh.

I got the joke and figure I'd give it right back, "You got it wrong, I met, I mean, I read about St. Valentine, the saint we celebrate today. He's the one who was martyred and buried in Via Flaminia."

Now Fr. Aiden turned serious, "My, my Christopher, that is very astute of you. I had no idea you possess such knowledge of the Sainted and their remarkable lives. I remain quite impressed."

We continue discussing some pretty heady stuff and our talk makes the day seem important just being able to talk about such things. Our small group walks up and down paths that lead through gardens and areas where plantings are maintained. Fr. Aiden tells Beth and I how beautiful the grounds of the seminary are in spring and he invites us back to see the flowers and plantings in bloom. After we exit the gardens, we find ourselves back at the main entrance to the seminary building and Fr. Aiden suggests that we take a quick tour of the interior before we sit down to lunch.

You could see the immense pride that Fr. Langford takes in showing us the classrooms, study areas, lounges and the beautiful chapel for daily prayer and devotions. He also takes us past the offices of the president and other senior staff and we stop at a door with his name. "I would love to show you my office, however, I fear you will think that I am rather an untidy lout, but no matter, I am sure you will not embarrass me by acknowledging my one and only shortcoming." Fr. Aiden makes the sign of the cross and opens the door.

I guess it is about what you would expect the office of a scholar priest to look like; large, dark wooden desk, shelves crammed with books piled in such a way that Fr. Aiden is more than likely the only person who could find anything. There is a large stack of papers on the floor, framed degrees, awards and photos decorating the walls as well as other mementos of a life spent in devotion to theological studies scattered over all flat surfaces. Altogether it looks like a very comfortable place to work and Beth and I take it all in.

I break the silence and tell him, "Wait until I tell Uncle Al about this! His great friend is a closet slob."

"Alas your Uncle Spartaco has been here many times and he has kept my slovenly nature a secret these many years and I expect that you and Beth will do the same."

As I am about to speak Beth puts her hand over my mouth and smiles saying, "Your secret is safe with us."

"I spend many hours here in this environ and I love the comfort it affords me. To be surrounded by such knowledge and to have the ability to read, ponder and write my thoughts down is truly a blessing in my life." Father Aiden is speaking to us, but he seems to be talking to himself.

"Well enough with my den of delight, let us take leave for I would like to escort you to my favorite of all places; in this my favorite of all places, the library!" We walk up the stairway to the fourth floor where the library is located. As we enter, we see a number of students and teachers deep in thought as they sit at the tables working on computers or reading one of the many books available for study. We also see a number of other people, both religious and laymen, and I ask Fr. Aiden who they are.

"Our library is open to all and we welcome visitors, local scholars, retreatants, parish ministers and others who come here to study and learn.

There are many services that the library provides and the staff is among the most dedicated you will ever hope to find." We walk down the main aisle flanked with rows and rows of books on both sides and when we reach the end we come to a large bronze door.

I am curious so I ask, "What's behind this door Father?"

A thoughtful Fr. Aiden looks at the door and says to us, "This is the Bonaventure Room and its use is restricted to all, but a select few. I consider this a very special place as it contains many old and rare texts with special access reserved for scholars and such. I have lost myself many times in the books contained herein." A faraway look comes over Fr. Aiden face and, at first, he doesn't answer me when I ask if he is okay. Beth and I look each other and back at Fr. Aiden who seems somewhat puzzled and I ask again, "Are you alright Father?"

Fr. Aiden snaps out of his trance and with a broad smile says, "Of course I am in fine form and fine spirits, but I believe that lunch awaits us so let us retreat to the dining room for what I am sure will be a culinary delight!"

We walk back down the stairs and along a hallway to the dining room. It is 12:30PM and the tables are already more than half taken. We make our way through the room to a table with a small standing placard written with the word "Reserved."

Bet and I look at it and then Beth jokes, "Hey, we can get into big trouble if we take this table, I'm sure it is meant for somebody very important."

As usual Fr. Aiden comes back with an appropriate retort. "Ah, you may be correct. Perhaps we should hide the sign and when the actual special guests arrive, we can plead innocence. What say you two?"

Beth says, "Works for me, I'm starving!"

Lunch is served cafeteria style so we find our way to the end of the line and pick up our trays and silverware. Making our way down the line, we are treated to a selection of main dishes; chicken, fish and beef as well as potatoes, vegetables and salads and a delicious array of breads. The deserts look wonderful featuring pies and cakes and Fr. Aiden tells us that the kitchen does some of the baking, but they have a standing order with the best bakery in Huntington for everything else. With our trays loaded, we make our way back to the table and sit down to a wonderful lunch.

"You are right, this is delicious." I say as I shovel food into my mouth.

Fr. Aiden "I am so pleased you are enjoying this. The chef and the staff of our kitchen take enormous pride in taking care of us. I must confess I do have trouble keeping my weight down and actually look forward to fasting during the Lenten season."

For some reason Beth starts to laugh. "You know Aiden, I hated Lent because as a child we were taught that it was important to resolve to fast, not to eat meat on Friday and give up desert once or twice a week. Anyway, when I knew that I couldn't have desert on any given day I would stuff my mouth the day before with two sometimes three deserts."

I look at Beth in mock surprise and say, "You never told me that story."

"Well, if the truth be told, it's not really a story; it's more a confession and being here with Father Aiden Langford I want to get his absolution. What do you say, Father?"

Fr. Aiden smiles as he blesses Beth and says, "Ego te absolve, I absolve you. For your penance say the Lord's Prayer five times. Now go in peace to love and serve the Lord."

I change the subject, "Fr. Aiden, can I ask you something?"

He looks up, "Of course you can."

"When we were standing by the Bonaventure Room you seem to pause and a kind of faraway look came over you. I'm just curious to know why, but you don't have to answer if you don't want to."

Beth gives me a dirty look, "Chris, do you have to be so nosy? Father, I mean Aiden, just ignore him, I do."

Fr. Aiden looks at me as if he is thinking about how to answer my question. "Beth, please do not scold Christopher. His curiosity is not un-like mine and his candor is also similar to mine so let me tell you what came over me. I must warn you that what I have to say may appear to be surreal, but I assure you it did happen." Now Beth and I are way beyond curious, we are positively rapt. We both look at Fr. Aiden to hear what he has to say, but he looks around in a conspiratorial manner before he begins.

"It is in my nature to spend hours at the library and I often study late into the night as I enjoy the solitude. While engrossed in my work I hear a noise coming from the other end of the library. I am usually not given to wild concoctions of the mind so fearlessly I go to investigate the sounds. When I arrive at the place from where I had deduced the sounds emanated, there is nothing to be found, but there is a curiosity!"

Beth and I look at each other and back at Fr. Aiden and say in unison, "Curiosity? What curiosity?"

Father Aiden realizes his audience is hooked so he continues, "The door to the Bonaventure Room is unlocked. You must understand that this room is always locked as it contains a number of old and rare texts and to all who have held them, they are priceless. I also assume, however, that these books also are of some monetary value to a thief, so I am determined that no one would steal or damage any of these treasures. I stealthy tread down the main aisle looking to the left and to the right hoping to startle the intruder into making a hasty exit. To my surprise, however I find no one. Everything is in perfect order and there is no intruder to be found."

I'm puzzled, "No one? You found no one? What about the noise?"

Fr. Aiden thought for a moment as his eyes dart from me to Beth and back, as he piques our interest by saying, "I found no one inside the Bonaventure Room, but I did find something."

Beth and I can't take the suspense so we say, practically in unison, "What did you find? Come on don't leave us hanging, what did you find?"

"When first I walk through the room's main aisle, I look left and right and I observe that everything is in its proper place. No book left open; no chair left askew; everything is in its proper place. Once satisfied that there is no one in the room, I turn to walk back to the entrance. By chance I look down one of the rows and there it is, the oldest Bible in our collection, laying open, on one of the tables at the end of the row."

"Really? Are you sure? You might have missed it."

"I have been asking myself the same question. I may have been remiss and I could have missed the open book on my first walk through, however I truly believe I did not."

"You said the bible was opened. Well, if you did miss the open bible, what's the big deal? An opened book in a library seems to be something you'd expect."

"Ah, that is true, but there is something even more curious. When I was in the main section of the library, I was studying the Book of Revelations and the writings of St. John of Patmos, the words of our Lord and lessons that are taught and learned over a lifetime. I must admit that much of the reason for my study is hastened by the horrific events brought on using the Lamb of God."

Fr. Aiden continues with his account of the night's event. "The Bible is opened to the same page in the Book of Revelations that I was studying and I am mystified by the coincidence. When I put down the Bible to contemplate this mystery a warm wind blows, though there are no open windows or vents close to where I am standing, and the pages turn to another chapter in Revelations that I also studied that very night. It has confounded me ever since. Nonetheless, I am not prone to flights of fancy or fantasy or things that go bump in the night, but the experience enthralled me even so."

Beth is deep in thought as she looks up and asks Fr. Aiden, "Do you believe that it could be a sign? Is it possible that maybe it's some kind of sign from God or the Holy Spirit or from Heaven?"

"My dear Beth, of course it could be a sign or it could be happenstance that a wind from one of the far-off vents blew open the page of the Bible I was reading. I am far too unworthy to assume that the powers of Heaven would choose me to be shown a sign such as this. So, if there is a message, it is beyond my comprehension to understand."

The first thought that jumps into my head is; how can a man of God like Father Aiden think he is unworthy. "You know Fr. Aiden, one thing that all the Sainted seem to have in common is that before they became saints, they all thought they were unworthy." Father Aiden takes a moment to consider this and doesn't comment.

I communicate directly with the Sainted and I can't fathom why they think they are unworthy, after all if anyone is unworthy it's me and I am not even close to being a saint. We sit talking for a long while when I notice the time is 2:30PM. I stand up and say, "Beth, it's getting kind of late and we should leave Fr. Aiden to his work." We all get up from the table and I hold out my hand to shake Father Aiden's, "I can't thank you enough for all the time you've spent and the kindness you've shown."

In all sincerity Fr. Aiden says, "Ah, unfortunately our time together has come to an end, but I daresay it is I who should be thanking both of you for the splendid company. Let me walk you to your car."

As we walk to the car Beth turns to the priest, "Aiden, I can't thank you enough. It is about the most pleasant day I have ever spent. Your wonderful stories and your wonderful spirit are what are most appreciated. I also want you to know how much I appreciate the regard you've shown my parents, they will be overwhelmed when they hear that you will be honoring them. Until then it's our secret."

Fr. Aiden smiles and shakes my hand and gives Beth a hug and kiss on the cheek. As we turn onto the road bordering the Seminary, we wave goodbye and leave the grounds.

Beth and I talk nonstop on the drive back to her house and she invites me in for a coffee. She goes ahead to make it while I park the car in a section reserved for visitors. I think this would be the perfect time to give Beth her Valentine's Day gift so I go to the trunk of my car and get the package. I'd had the note from St. Valentine put in kind of a shadowbox frame and had it wrapped up as a gift for her.

Beth leaves the front door open for me and when I go inside her home, she is standing in the living room holding a big box and shouting "Happy Valentine's Day!" I start to laugh thinking about Beth and Christmas and now Valentine's Day and have to acknowledge that she must be a holiday junkie.

Beth sees that I have a gift in my hand so she says, "Hurry up and open your gift so I can open mine."

"How do you know this gift is for you?" I say in all seriousness. She answers in all seriousness, "It better be for me or you're going to leave this house singing in a voice that's five octaves higher. Got it?"

I say, "So much for surprises" and I take Beth's gift and start to open it. The box has a lot of packing in it and I dig and dig, but I can't find anything. As I reach the bottom of the box, I feel something smooth and lift it out. It is wrapped in paper with hearts all over so I rip it off and see it is a book. I turn it over and it is entitled simply "My Life." I open the first page and there is a photo of me from when I was a baby, maybe six months old. Underneath the photo is a caption that says "Eat, Sleep and Shit, that's all I ever do!" I turn page after page and there are photos, letters, cards, even a DVD and each image has a special caption or thought that brings memories flooding back. I look up at Beth and smile and ask her, "How in the world did you get all this stuff? It's amazing."

"It took a few months and I had your Uncle Al help me. Remember when he asked to borrow your photo album so he could make copies of family pictures? Well, here are the copies. I was able to get in touch with a number of your friends that still live in Huntington and they gave me the names of other friends and they all had photos or something to say; I hope you like vulgarity and crudeness because there's a lot of that in here." Beth smiles as I look down and continue to thumb through the book and laughing aloud at some of what people wrote and remembered.

Beth did tell me something that seemed strange to her. "There was one very weird conversation I had with one of your friends, I believe an old high-school girlfriend, who laughed and said you should read her comment in private. Of course, I read it, but I don't get it."

I know it must be something written by Joanie so I look through the book until I find the page. Pasted above her caption is a photo of me and Joanie smiling and standing in front of my 1975 Buick Skylark convertible. I read what she wrote aloud so that Beth can hear it again, "My little dedication to you is a quote from George Costanza and I think it is appropriate, 'The jerk store called and they're running out of you.' I hope things have gotten better in the last 17 years Love, Joanie.

I am now convulsing with laughter and tears are rolling down my eyes. Beth is looking at me like I'm crazy and I have to stop and catch my breath so I can give her some insight into what the message means. I wipe my eyes and tell Beth the story, omitting any talk of The Sainted. "You see, it was prom night and Joanie was my steady girl at the time. After the dance and party, we went to the beach to make out and I figured that I would get laid that night." Now Beth is smiling and I continue, "We were practically naked when I thought I heard something outside the car and from that moment on it went from bad to worse. I was looking out the window thinking that there were police looking at us and Joanie was starting to think I lost my mind. I went on like that for a while until she got so pissed off that she put on her clothes, left me and she walked home." Now Beth is laughing and she says "Good going Romeo."

"That's exactly what Uncle Al said to me when I told him." Now we are both laughing. "Beth, I have to say that this is the most terrific Valentines gift you could have given me. I am going to enjoy reading every page. I know how much effort you put into this, thanks so much. I love you." Beth smiles and gives me a kiss and we let the moment pass as Beth is eagerly looking at the gift in my hand. "Okay, now it's your turn, Happy Valentine's Day."

I hand her the gift and sit back while she opens it. As she is pulling at the ribbon and tearing off the paper she says to me, "Valentine's Day is my second favorite holiday."

"Oh, are there any holiday's you don't like?"

Beth stops unwrapping her gift; she thinks for a moment and emphatically says, "No."

When she is done, she lifts the framed note and looks at me puzzled. "Thanks Chris but what is it?"

"Well, it's a note, written in Latin 'Ex tua Valentine' and it means 'From your Valentine.' It's very old and it was given to me by someone I met who knows a lot about Valentine's Day, as a matter of fact he is a leading authority. He told me that it was written almost 1800 years ago."

Beth stares at me incredulously, "You're kidding? 1800 years ago? Wait, you've got to be kidding how could they have known about Valentine's Day way back then?"

I smile at her, "Well there's more to the story about this note. This Valentine's Day authority told me that it was written around the same time that the real St. Valentine was alive and intimated that it could have been written by the man himself."

Now Beth is staring back at me and then down at the note, back at me and down at the note. I know that she's no fool and she is suspicious about the whole story. "Who is this Valentine's Day authority, huh? I think he sold you a bill of goods, how can this be written 1800 years ago by a saint and all of a sudden it turns up in Huntington Long Island?"

I know it would be hard for Beth to accept, but I had no way of telling her the truth. After all St. Valentine is my authority and I can't let Beth know about my sainted companions, maybe someday, but not now. "Beth, you don't know this expert, but he is a wonderful man, a genuine St, Valentine scholar and a real holy person. He gave me the note to give to someone I love and that someone is you."

Beth looks at me and she touches my cheek, "You are the sweetest for giving this to me. I'm sorry that I gave you a hard time. I'm sure it came from the heart and that's all that matters. I love you. Hey, I just realized, if this was really written by St. Valentine it's kind of a relic, right?"

"Yes, it could be. By the way did you know, aside from being the patron saint of lovers, he's also the patron saint of bee keepers and people who have epilepsy and that when you see a painting or some representation of him, he is surrounded by birds and roses."

"Wow, you're like a walking encyclopedia of saints, but I hope St. Valentine's not looking now." Beth slides over by my side and climbs onto my lap. She is breathing hot on my neck and her lips are soft as she kisses me. I am holding her tightly, my hands running over her body when we hear a little tap at the window.

Unfortunately, we stop what we're doing and turn to the window. On the sill there is a cardinal and in its beak is a red rose…in the middle of winter, a red rose. The cardinal is staring right at the both of us as we sit perfectly still. The cardinal then places the rose gently onto the sill and for a moment continues to look at us before it flies away.

For more than a minute Beth says nothing, but eventually she says, "That just didn't happen, did it?"

I am now smiling at her, "Or maybe St. Valentine sends us his best wishes."

Beth just stares at the rose laying on the window sill and she is uncharacteristically at a loss for words.

CHAPTER 23

The priest's phone rings with the familiar AC/DC ringtone, but he doesn't smile as he usually does when he hears 'Highway to Hell'. He looks at the screen and hits the button to answer.

"Greetings Spartaco, I am so glad you called."

Uncle Al always smiles when Aiden calls him Spartaco. "Hi Aiden, I just want to call and thank you for the day you spent with Beth and Chris, they said they had a wonderful time."

"It was a true pleasure for me. We conversed on some weighty topics and your nephew is far more spiritual that I ever imagined."

Uncle Al smiles and says, "Well, he could have fooled me. How are you, Aiden?"

"If the truth be told Spartaco I am much troubled." Fr. Aiden says this in all seriousness and Uncle Al becomes very concerned. "Please allow me a moment while I find a place to speak in confidence."

With that the priest walks into a quiet corner of an area used as a lounge by the staff at ICS. "Ah, this is better; we can now speak without fear of being overheard."

Uncle Al says, "Whoa, Aiden, I wasn't expecting that answer. What's up? Are you okay?"

Fr. Aiden goes silent for a moment so he might collect his thoughts before he speaks. "Spartaco, as promised, I have begun my research to determine if there is any spiritual connection between the unspeakable horrors taking place around the world and the use of the phrase Lamb of God." Again, Fr. Aiden takes a moment to pause and gather his thoughts. "In my search for an answer I may have been shown a possible relevant connection, but I must warn you even I cannot fathom this possibility."

Uncle Al cuts off the priest and sits up at his desk, "You're kidding? You may have found a connection?"

"Spartaco please let me finish as I am still in somewhat of a state of bewilderment at the possibility of what may have been revealed to me. Please allow me to provide you with an abridgment of what I've experienced and what could be an illumination of the matters at hand."

Father Aiden tells Al of his research, he begins with his knowledge of Lamb of God by virtue of his studies and travels. He then tells his friend of his late-night visit to the library, the many texts he consulted and his determination to find any possible connection, in scripture, to the crimes committed. The priest continues to go on relating to Al what his research has disclosed until he stops to gather his thoughts.

"I have been reading from Revelations and came across certain passages that relates to the seven seals. These passages speak of many things, including the Apocalypse. Revelations are the writings of St. John of Patmos to the faithful who were being persecuted by the Romans in the years after Christ's death. Without getting into exhaustive discussions as to the various truths revealed in the Book of Revelations, these writings have been interpreted in many ways and a number of theologians and biblical scholars believe that words contained are meant as metaphors to guide the spiritual and corporeal lives of man. The Apocalypse as referenced in Revelations can mean a 'lifting of the veil' so that all will be revealed or it can be interpreted as the cataclysm marking the 'end of days' and the return of Christ; a call to judgment for all mankind. No matter what side of the interpretation you fall on, there is a profound truth that lies in the teachings and writings of St. John."

Fr. Aiden takes another pause. He needs to communicate what has happened in the Bonaventure Room and how it could relate to the events taking place worldwide. "Spartaco, what I am about to tell you next is part existential and part conjecture in that I believe I have experienced my own particular revelation. At first, I was inclined to believe that these musings were a product of my over-active imagination, but after careful consideration I am no longer predisposed to believe that." For about ten minutes the priest scholar tells the Suffolk County Chief of Detectives about his late-night studies, his experience in the library's Bonaventure Room, the mysterious appearance of the Bible, the wind blowing open the exact pages of the book he had been studying pointing out the passage in Revelations and that had repeatedly been shown to him.

Fr. Aiden concludes by saying, "What I cannot deny is that all the mystifying occurrences seem to culminate in the coming of the antichrist who obtains his powers from the dragon."

Chief Al Barese listens to his friend speak, but as a detective he has cultivated what you might call a healthy skepticism and he feels the need to probe beyond what the priest may or may not have experienced. "Aiden, I promised you that I would be open to anything even that these events are being orchestrated by the forces of evil so let me get this straight, you say that these events could be tied into the coming of the antichrist?"

There is both sorrow and exhaustion in Aiden's voice as he admits to his friend, "Spartaco, I completely understand your incredulity. I too am dumbfounded at the prospect of the possibility it may be true."

"Aiden, I am not questioning your belief or even your sanity in what you've experienced, but I need to try to better understand the connection between this revelation of yours and the horrors happening around us. Do you really think that the passages you've read point to a message from God or Christ or the angels or saints or whatever?"

"I don't know? It is beyond my comprehension to believe that such a possibility would be revealed to me, but in all honesty, I cannot deny the possibility. If you were there, in the library, with me you might also be questioning this prospect."

"Okay, point taken, but who is this antichrist; man, thing or whatever? Could it be a woman? Either way this thing would need to have some immense power to do what is being done throughout the world."

Fr. Aiden took a deep breath, "References in Revelations refer to the antichrist as an 'it', but it is widely assumed that it is a man, a powerful man. Spartaco, you must understand that this is power beyond anything that has existed or cultivated by mankind alone. In a literal sense there are no men or women in this equation, the antichrist, acting as an agent of Satan, can muster the forces of evil to have them execute these dreadful offenses against the laws of God and humanity. It is a prelude to the ultimate battle; the forces of Heaven against the forces of Hell."

The two men remain silent for a short while. There is so much to absorb so much to consider and they have nothing to go on but a notion which may or may not be valid. Chief Barese is the first to break the silence. "Aiden, how do we know who the antichrist might be? How can we fight against this kind of evil? What do Revelations say comes next?" The questions come pouring out of Al's mouth in what seems like a stream of consciousness.

Fr. Aiden tries to come up with something in the way of answers to these questions, but how do you explain such things. "I am at a loss to answer your questions, but I may be able to offer some background information that you may want to consider. There are varied opinions on the antichrist, the nature of the person and how he may manifest himself as he is thought to be the agent of the Beast. Most references to this being state that he holds great power and sway over millions. This person may be a military leader or politician or captain of industry even a movie star. He is greatly admired and has a great following of those seduced by his false promises. He also causes men to cower in fear and, in the end; he assures that all mankind will worship Lucifer. I may appear to be rambling on, but there is no adequate description other than that which is I've interpreted in the Book of Revelations and that, unfortunately, is woefully inadequate."

Chief Barese takes a moment to absorb what Fr. Aiden says and asks, "So this guy could be some big shot who gets his power from Satan and then gets to corrupt all mankind, how is that possible?"

"I know it sounds impossible, but you need to view this in the context of the writings and teaching in the Bible. If Revelations are a metaphor as many believe them to be, the antichrist could be conjecture referencing the temptations mankind confronts every day. It is nothing less than the eternal conflict between good and evil."

"Well, if that's the case, what do Revelations say happens next?"

Father Aiden considers how he should answer, so he looks to try and make his friend understand the references and framework of the seals. "Spartaco, to answer that would require the need to understand the seven seals, each opened by Christ and revealed to St. John as a prelude of things to come. The first four seals are exemplified in the "Four Horsemen of the Apocalypse"; the first seal describes the rider on a white horse that many believe is the antichrist. The second seal opens to reveal a rider on a red horse to foment war. The third seal opens showing a rider on a black horse visiting famine on all of mankind. When the fourth seal is opened it tells of a pale horse and a rider that will bring death and the forces of hell follow him. The fifth seal opens to reveal the martyrs who are persecuted and die for their faith and who gain the promise of life eternal. The sixth seal speaks of the terror that follows the great cataclysm that destroys the earth and call all to the final judgment."

Al looks at Aiden and asks, "What about the seventh seal?"

Father Aiden pauses for a moment to take a breath before he continues, "The seventh seal tells of silence in heaven for about half an hour. Then seven angels are given seven trumpets."

"Silence? Trumpets? What do you mean by silence and trumpets?" Uncle Al is beyond puzzled.

"That is the subject of some debate. Certain scholars suggest that it is the end of all things and a new beginning, but St. John does not reveal what will happen next. Other scholars believe it is to prepare for the resumption of something more. What that is I cannot say. The fact is that, according to Revelations, the silence is broken by blasts of seven trumpets by the seven angels. Spartaco, please try to understand that these are passages written nearly two thousand years ago and they have been interpreted in many ways over the ages."

Al considers what Aiden has just said and asks, "What do you think this all means in the context of the crimes and horror I've seen so far."

"I can only say this; all of what I have read points to the possibility of some other-worldly force influencing global events at play. If what I suggest is true, our ability to confront this evil and defeat it depends on some divine intervention and that it is well beyond our collective abilities to make happen."

"Thanks Aiden, I'd like to take some time to mull this over in my mind. When I do, can I call you back with any questions?"

"Of course, you can and I shall return the favor and call you with any additional information or thoughts I can summon." With that, both men say their goodbyes and hang up.

Uncle Al's mind begins to race, he thinks…Beyond our collective abilities? Maybe we have some collective abilities that we can call on. With that Al picks up the phone.

CHAPTER 24

"Hello, St. Aloysius Gonzaga Coins and Currency, how may I help you?" Uncle Al didn't even wait to say hello, he just jumps right in. "Chris, I just got off the phone with Aiden."

"Hope you told him that Beth and I had such a great day. I've got to tell you he really is a great guy. We talked…" but Uncle Al stops me.

"Chris this is something very serious, I just got word of eight more major crimes in Suffolk County today alone. These crimes are so unprecedented that no one here has ever seen anything like them. I'm talking about animal mutilations, kidnapping and murder; some guy actually commits suicide by jumping off the top of a power station onto a live electric cable, another person sets fire to a nursing home killing 12 seniors."

"My God!" Is all that I could think of saying.

"Guess what they all have in common."

"What? No, wait…Lamb of God?"

"That's right, Lamb of God. We are examining every part of the lives of each of the criminals and victims, but there is absolutely no connection as far as we can see, none whatsoever. Even in the Middle East, Asia and India where there are no significant Christian populations, there appears one message that is repeated over and over, Lamb of God."

"What does this all-mean Uncle Al?"

Uncle Al just sighs into the phone, "I don't know; I only wish I did. I've got to tell you something. When we met with Aiden for lunch and you were on line to get the food, he and I had a talk."

I am puzzled, "Talk? What kind of talk?"

Uncle Al explains, "I told Aiden I was at my wits end about all that's happening. When I confide in him, he suggests that there may be some kind of connection between these crimes and a kind of spiritual force, an all-encompassing evil controlling the whole thing. It is part desperation and part hopefulness so I asked him for help. I asked him to look into a possible spiritual connection to these horrors and the 'Lamb of God' in the scriptures, bible and other places like that. I don't know why, I guess I am hoping to find something to connect all these horrific crimes, anything that would help us in our investigation."

I can't help but agree that it sounds like desperation on Uncle Al's part, but I say, "Hey, it's a long shot, but what the heck, it can't hurt and if anyone can find a spiritual angle in all this mess its Father Aiden."

"Chris," Uncle Al takes time to pause, "When I spoke with Aiden today, he told me he may have found a possible connection."

"What!"

"You heard me, a possible connection between the devastation that is occurring and some kind of evil force working its way around the world."

"You've got to be kidding, a real connection to these happenings… around the world? What is this possible connection?" I am at a total loss for what to do or say next.

"Listen Chris, Fr. Aiden is a renowned scholar when it comes to matters concerning theological studies, the Bible and all that other stuff, but even he is unable to wrap his head around this." Uncle Al goes on to tell me about their phone conversation about the passages in the Book of Revelations, the silence and then angels with trumpets signaling the end of the world. My uncle even tells me about the strange occurrence in the Bonaventure Room and its impact on the priest.

"You know, Uncle Al, Fr. Aiden mentioned what he experienced in the Bonaventure Room to Beth and I, but he seemed to dismiss it as a coincidence, kind of by chance."

"Well, he may have had a sudden awakening, actually a Revelation, because he is now accepting that a spiritual connection could be a real possibility."

I am dumfounded, "What could possibly have changed his mind? What did he find out that could have made him change his mind?"

Uncle Al sighs again, "The antichrist."

"WHAT!!!"

"You heard me, the antichrist. Fr. Aiden calls him the agent of Satan or some such name and I get the impression that Aiden thinks the antichrist is here and he's not alone. This guy has power and the forces of evil, you know the devil and hell, behind him and when it's all over it ain't gonna be pretty. Get the point?"

I am confounded, "Uncle Al, Fr. Aiden can't be serious. The antichrist, that's like end of the world stuff."

"Exactly, and Aiden doesn't seem to discount that possibility. He quotes passages from Revelation and tries to explain the meaning of them in the context of scripture and the connection between the Lamb of God, the seven seals and the antichrist. I've got to say that a lot of it is way over my head, but I need to ask you something."

"Uh, oh." I must be psychic because I know what Uncle Al is going to say.

"Chris, I wouldn't ask if it wasn't this important, I need to ask you for help, you know, from your friends." Uncle Al is still uncomfortable saying "saints" because he is afraid of being overheard.

"Uncle Al, please listen, I have no power to get the saints to appear, let alone ask for help. I never know when they will come, they just come; I mean the visions just come."

"Chris, if I didn't believe you when you told me you are communicating with the, you know..." and he whispers, "saints, I would think that Aiden is out of his mind, but I do believe you and because I believe you, I believe him. Aiden thinks we need some kind of divine intervention and that because of the possible connections to Revelations, we can't do this on our own. Don't you think that your friends know this evil is here among us and what this antichrist is capable of doing? Chris, good must confront evil, they can't be blind to all this, and if they don't help us, we are all in for a big heap of trouble."

I thought for a moment about my vision of St. Elizabeth and I confide in Uncle Al, "I have been getting a number of visions lately and they are very disturbing."

Uncle Al practically jumps through the phone and he says, "Disturbing? What do you mean disturbing?"

"Just before you called, I had this vision. It was of St. Elizabeth and she warned me of dangers to come."

"What dangers? When? When do these dangers come, Chris what does it all mean?" Uncle Al is as perplexed as I am.

"St. Elizabeth says that the dangers she spoke of are to all mankind not just me and the people I love, but to everyone. Uncle Al, there's one more thing, The Sainted don't ever exaggerate, ever, and she told me that I would need to prepare myself for what, I couldn't tell you, but it won't be good." As I say this to my uncle, I come to the realization that I am heading for another confrontation with Julian or Satan or Lucifer or whatever name he goes by and now I need to worry about his surrogate, the antichrist.

"Chris, do you think the vision of St. Elizabeth might mean that the antichrist is real and is here on earth? Could he and the evil he brings be the danger?"

"I really don't know, but now I believe that Fr. Aiden could be right to consider the possibility." I then have a disturbing thought, "Uncle Al, you didn't mention my visions to Father Aiden, did you?"

Uncle Al answers immediately, "No, no of course not. That will always be our secret."

I am relieved and say, "Thanks, I know you will keep it secret, but I just need to be sure. I don't think it would be wise for anyone else to know about my visions and of the messages that are part of these visions. Sometimes these messages are simple to understand, but some are very puzzling and I need time to come to a better understanding of what they mean."

"Chris, when you spoke to St. Elizabeth she mentioned danger, like you were meant to confront danger. The last time this happened you nearly got killed, how can they think you can confront this evil alone?"

"I ask myself the same thing. Listen, if that is what I'm supposed to do, you know, face this alone then so be it. But I am really never by myself, the saints always have my back, they had my back in the pit and they will have my back now, I just know it."

"Chris, it sounds to me like this could be far worse than anything we can ever imagine. What do you think the next move should be?"

"Well, if Fr. Aiden's fears are correct and the antichrist is here among us now, then the Sainted will know and I'll need to receive some guidance from them. If we are to confront this kind of evil it seems we could use all the help we can get."

I hear a knock on Uncle Al's office door and a brief greeting, he now comes back on the phone and says, "Amen to that. Listen Dan just came into the office and I need to meet with him. I'll call you later. I love you." Uncle Al hangs up the phone.

I sit at my desk in the shop and stare out the window. It's close to dusk and I am alone listening to the wind blow down Main Street. There are clouds in the sky and a few pedestrians walking the street. I am trying to think of all that we talked about and all of the possibilities. What if the antichrist is real and he's here? Who is he? What will happen to all the peoples on earth? What can I do to battle such evil?

I think of my confrontation with Julian on Pit Island and for some reason I realize that this was child's play by comparison to the war that will be fought between Heaven and Hell for the souls of mankind.

CHAPTER 25

The streets surrounding Madison Square Garden are packed with mobile studios from all the major news and entertainment networks. They have their top talent ready to report on all the dignitaries, billionaire businessmen, politicians and other notables from the world of entertainment and music who are here to support the man of the hour, Dr. Tom Houston.

The atmosphere for this invitation only event seems charged as thousands of onlookers, fans of Dr. Houston and celebrity hounds, have turned the occasion into a raucous celebration of their man. ACN sent their top star reporter and closet supporter of Dr. Tom Houston, Barbara Ellen Comstock, for her unique commentary on all that is happening and she seems to be caught up in the festivity herself. The camera frames a medium close up of Barbara Ellen in the foreground and the cheering crowds of onlookers in the background. She raises her mic and speaks into the camera.

"Good evening, America. I'm here in fabulous New York City on Seventh Avenue, near the entrance to historic Madison Square Garden. Thousands of people are lining the street in anticipation of catching a glimpse of the one person who they hope will become the next president of the United States. The man, Dr. Thomas Houston, has electrified his supporters throughout America and even throughout the world by way of his think tank, ACTELECT. Dr. Houston has engendered fervent devotion among his supporters as he champions their causes and helps to bring their ideas into the mainstream of American consciousness. I have breaking news to report this evening, according to a new ACN poll, Dr. Thomas Houston is in a virtual tie for the lead in capturing the Socialist Liberation Party nomination for president. A poll of registered Socialist Liberation Party voters, taken just yesterday, shows frontrunner, former Secretary of Health and Human Services and US Congresswoman, Helen De Witt favored by 46.7% and Dr. Thomas Houston coming in a strong second with 45.2%. The poll has a margin of error of 3 percentage points, so ladies and gentlemen it seems like we have a dead heat here. ACN will be sure to update this breaking news story as more information becomes available."

The police assigned to crowd control, and security for the event, have made a barricade in front of the Garden to allow for limousines to drive near the entrance and let their passengers out. The line of cars is long and Barbara Ellen is in perfect position to greet each and every notable upon their arriving. First to open the door is multi-billionaire Jerome Stellos and Barbara Ellen thrusts the mic in his face for a comment.

"Mr. Stellos…Mr. Stellos can I get a comment from you about Dr. Houston and our new poll showing the race in a virtual dead heat?"

Jerome Stellos speaks with a thick accent, but it never stops him from speaking his mind. "Good evening, Barbara Ellen. I am most gratified to hear that Tom has closed the gap in the polls. His election will signify a new dawning for America, a place where the fascists who run our government will be driven out and we can finally have a country free of the shackles of capitalism, imperialism and greed." There is no smile as he turns to go to his private box in the upper level surrounding the Garden floor.

"Thank you, Mr. Stellos." Barbara Ellen turns to the camera and says "That was Jerome Stellos, self-made billionaire and a giant in the financial world. He is also one of the largest donors to the campaign of Dr. Tom Houston. Jerome Stellos funds many advocates of leftist leaning, socialist policies including the 'Truth Here and Now' news organization. He's never at a loss for words and he didn't disappoint us tonight."

Limousine after limousine pulls up in front of Madison Square Garden and each dignitary stops by to say hello. There are politicians including a former president, former cabinet members from previous Socialist Liberation Party administrations, congressmen and women, New York's leftist mayor, even one of the US Senators from New York, Carl Shellman stops to say hello.

"Barbara Ellen, so good to see you again."

"It's very good to see you again senator. Tell me Senator Shellman, is your being here a formal endorsement of Tom Houston?"

The senator laughs, "No, I make it a policy not to endorse any contender at this stage in the primaries, but Dr. Tom Houston certainly makes an attractive candidate and he's a fellow New Yorker." Senator Shellman winks at Barbara Ellen and continues, "I am here in support of electing the most attractive and capable Socialist Liberation Party candidate to lead this country. I am also going to attend a fundraiser for Congresswoman De Witt next week; you know I can't show any favoritism." He winks at Barbara Ellen again and makes his way into the arena. One after another the limousines stop to let out their passengers and each person poses for the press and the crowd is eating it up.

There is a great cheer from the people herding in the space behind the news crew. Barbara Ellen pauses for a moment as the camera scans the crowd of those waiting for a glimpse of someone…anyone famous. Barbara Ellen knows they will be coming and the fans won't be disappointed. She continues, "The crowds of onlookers are here in hopes of seeing celebrities from the world of film, TV and music that are coming to this event in a strong show of support for Dr. Houston.

With her back to the camera Barbara Ellen hears a roar from the crowd and the screams of young girls as the group Fabiano crawls out of their Prius stretch limousine. They are all smiling and waving at the crowd and they immediately step up to the mic. Their charismatic and handsome lead singer, Gabriel Fabiano is the designated spokesman for the group.

He smiles for the camera in an attempt to show off his gleaming white teeth and says, "Hey, Barbara Ellen, you look stunning!"

Barbara Ellen knows bullshit when she hears it, but she smiles anyway. "Flattery will get you everywhere." Ladies and gentlemen, I am speaking with the lead singer of Fabiano, Gabriel Fabiano or as he is known to his friends, Gabby. So, Gabriel what do you have to tell to your fans across America?"

"Come on Barbara Ellen, call me Gabby. To all my fans and to all of those listening tonight we have an historic chance to make America great by electing Dr. Thomas Houston. Why not vote for no more wars, no more poverty and no more laws that suppress African-Americans, Gay Americans, Transgender Americans, Hispanic Americans, Asian Americans, Undocumented Alien Americans, Native Americans and all the rest. No more useless laws controlling the sale of marijuana and most important no more police over-reaching their authority. That's what Tom stands for and that's why we're here tonight? By the way, we've written a new song especially for this occasion and all the profits from its sale will go to the campaign fund to elect Dr. Tom Houston."

Barbara Ellen is thrilled to be the first to report his and she asks, "That's wonderful, what's the title of the song?"

Gabby smiles and says, "It's called 'Houston, We Have a Problem'."

Barbara Ellen practically chokes with laughter and Gabby and the group just stand there and smile. She regains her composure and tells them that she is sure it will be a big hit and she can't wait to hear the band perform their song this evening. Gabby bends over and gives Barbara Ellen a kiss on the cheek and the group waves to the screaming crowd and Fabiano rushes in to the arena.

She follows them up the stairs and says to the camera, "Well, I feel like a groupie. That was Fabiano and look to download their new song which I'm sure will be coming out very soon." Barbara Ellen starts to speak when she hears a loud cheer from the people surrounding the entrance to the Garden. Immediately she recognizes who it is and tells her TV audience, "But now look who's coming out of his limo, the one, the only, Boyd Somerfield." The stretch limo door opens and out comes the iconic singer whose career spans more than 30 years. The crowd is in a euphoric state at the mere presence of their idol.

Barbara Ellen tries to yell over the crowd, "Boyd! Boyd! Can I have a word with you? Boyd?" He pretends not to hear her plea, but eventually he acquiesces to look in her direction and he smiles and waves to her. "Barbara

Ellen, how great it is to see you again. I want to say how grateful I am for the wonderful feature you did of me and the band on your show." Barbara Ellen did a puff piece on Boyd about a year ago and she's glad he liked it.

The reporter smiles at the star and says, "You're welcome. Boyd, tell us, why you are here tonight."

"I am here for the little guy; you know the men or women who have to work four jobs just to make ends meet. I'm here because of the fact that so many need healthcare and government should provide it for everyone and if you can't pay, some other fortunate Americans should chip in. I'm here in support of the soldiers who fight in unjust wars and come home as broken men and women. I'm here because of the starvation being experienced in countries around the world and America needs to do more. I'm here for open borders. I'm here because the government needs to tax those who can afford it and give it to those who can't do for themselves. I'm here because…"

But Barbara Ellen stops him, "Whoa Boyd take a breath; you might miss the fundraiser if you keep that up. Seriously, maybe you should run for president!" Now Boyd and Barbara Ellen laugh.

"Sorry for rambling on, but I am passionate about these things and I need to let people know what Tom Houston represents. He represents solutions to everything that I stand for and I'm here to help him become the next President of the United States." The crowd behind him is hanging on every word and when he finishes there is a tremendous roar of approval from the crowd of adoring fans. He ends the interview by waving to the crowd and finding his way up the stairs and into Madison Square Garden.

The limos with the famous and wealthy eventually stop arriving and Barbara Ellen goes back to the ACN Mobile Unit to freshen up. She has been invited to the private party being held in the corporate boxes lining at the upper levels of Madison Square Garden. Barbara Ellen is thrilled with the turnout and a few of the surprise attendees that have decided to support Dr. Thomas Houston. She sees this event as a great opportunity to have access to an inordinately large number of luminaries all in one place. She is hoping that she can get them to give her some usable quotes to include in her reporting, maybe even talk some of the most renown into appearing on her show, Newsmakers Now. At any rate Barbara Ellen is looking forward to what should be a great evening and a great party.

She leads her cameraman, director and another crew member and they walk into the front entrance and make their way up the corporate boxes that line the upper deck of the arena. The luxury suites are reserved for special guests and major contributors and the doors to the suites are left open to allow the celebrities attending the event to mingle. Barbara Ellen Comstock finds a corner of the upper level with a wonderful backdrop showing the many sports legends that have played in this historic venue. The cameraman sets up his equipment and both he and the director discuss the placement and the framing for many of the guests that will be enticed by Barbra Ellen to appear on camera.

She hopes to get a word with Tom Houston before he is scheduled to make his speech to the crowd, but his handlers apologize and tell her that he needs to use the time to prepare for his appearance. She is disappointed, but she says that she understands and she finds her way back to the place where the camera is set up. Barbara Ellen is never one to let an opportunity go to waste, so she trolls for other dignitaries to get their comments and thoughts on Dr. Thomas Houston. As she is looking around, she spots someone that looks familiar, but she can't put her hand on it. She grabs the mic and motions for the man to come over and speak with her. He smiles and walks over and faces her standing in front of the camera.

She seems taken with his commanding presence, charisma and hand-some features and says, "Hello, I'm Barbara Ellen Comstock. Have we ever met?"

The man answers, "Unfortunately no, but it is truly a pleasure to meet you. I am a very great fan of your show."

"Well, thank you I'm glad to meet you too. I'd like to get a quick interview with you, if that's okay?" Barbara Ellen doesn't give the man a chance to think about it as she thrusts the mic in his face.

He smiles and Barbara Ellen can't believe how attractive he is and he says to her, "How very flattering, of course I would be thrilled to speak with such an accomplished newsperson as you, fire away!"

"Thank you" Barbara Ellen turns to the camera and makes her introduction. "We are inside the arena awaiting the speech to be given by the man who so many have come out to support, Tom Houston. There are many rich and famous people here and while I look to bring you their comments, I spot this good-looking gentleman. I've asked him if he would speak to me and he has kindly consented to a short interview. Welcome!"

The man smiles at the camera and says, "Thank you Barbara Ellen."

Barbara Ellen quips with her guest, "By the away, are you rich and famous?"

He laughs and responds, "Well I am fortunate in many ways and I am well known in some circles."

"Ah, 'well know' very intriguing, what circles might those be?

The guest thinks for a moment "Confidentiality precludes me from providing you with more exact information, but you might say that I am an advisor to those who seek validation and to those who require admonishment for actions they've taken."

"My, that is about the most mysterious description I have ever heard and I must admit you have piqued my curiosity. Validation? Admonishment? What form might those actions take?"

"Oh, I'm afraid I may disappoint you as those interactions are of a caring nature. To my clients, the validations are most welcome and the admonishments are most benign, I assure you, most benign." The handsome guest smiles warmly to Barbara Ellen.

Barbara Ellen is enthralled and she smiles back and says, "You must be a lawyer or a psychologist then!"

Her mysterious guest laughs, "Ah, good guess, but I am neither an attorney nor a psychologist, but I have met a number of them over the course of my work." ACN's star reporter is captivated by this strange discourse and she wants to know more. "Are you here to validate or admonish Dr. Tom Houston?"

Now the handsome stranger burst out into a hearty laugh again, "No, no neither of those things."

"Well then why are you here?"

There is no hesitation in his voice as he answers the question, "I am here for one reason only, to see that Dr. Thomas Houston is elected the president of the United States. By virtue of his education, his philosophy and his temperament he is the most qualified candidate that Socialist Liberation Party can offer the people of America and of the world. Listen to him speak, read what he has written, delve deep into his beliefs, they are strong, they are honest and they are heartfelt. That is why I am here and that is why I hope everyone who can, will vote for Dr. Thomas Houston for President."

Barbara Ellen is already thinking how she will edit this interview and include it in her feature on Newsmakers Now's 'What's News' segment. "I want to thank you for your time and graciousness in speaking to our audience."

He says, "You are more than welcome; it was a true delight for me."

Barbara Ellen turns back to the camera as she tells her audience, "That was a very interesting and candid interview with…" she pauses, "I can't believe I forgot to ask you what your name is?"

"Please call me Julian."

CHAPTER 26

Beth and I decide that it would be much easier to take the Long Island Railroad to Madison Square Garden for two reasons; first, the Garden is right upstairs from Penn Station and second, it is better than trying to navigate through the pandemonium and a lot cheaper than parking and if you've ever parked in Manhattan, you know what I mean.

Beth is looking especially beautiful this evening. She's wearing a black cocktail dress that starts above her knee and accentuates her curves. The dress is covered with sequins along the upper part and a flowing silky black material on the lower part. She is wearing diamond stud earrings and the gold pendant and chain I gave her for Christmas. I am wearing a dark grey pinstripe suit with a white shirt and red and gold tie. As I'm thinking of this, I wonder why it takes three sentences to describe what Beth is wearing and only one to describe what I'm wearing.

Beth and I go in the main entrance and walk into the lobby. The place is packed and noisy and the line for security clearance is long. When Beth and I finally get to the front of the line the uniformed security person looks at our invitation and says, "I'm so sorry that you had to wait on this line. You could have gone through the 'Special Guest' entrance" and she points to an elegant entryway surrounded by heavy drapery, an elaborate table decorated with large vases filled with beautiful arrangements of fragrant flowers. Women in long evening gowns and men in tuxedos are there to greet all those fortunate enough to be special so Beth and I look at each other and stick our noses in the air as we walk over to the table.

Beth speaks to the woman and says, "Hello, my name is Elizabeth Della Russo and this is Christopher Pella. We have been invited to the fundraiser and we were told our invitations would be waiting at table by the entry."

The young woman smiles at Beth as she begins to leaf though the piles of envelops on her desk. When she locates our invitations, she immediately stares at us in what could only be a look of surprise.

She rises from her chair and says, "Oh Ms. Della Russo, we are so pleased that you could make the event, I am sorry that you had to wait so long. Dr. Houston has asked that we welcome you as his personal guests and provide any assistance you may need. Please let me know if you or Mr. Pella requires anything at all."

I say, "Great, can I have a new Fiat and a certified check for $9,815,387 dollars?" Beth slams her elbow into my side, practically knocking the wind out of me and says to the young lady, "Don't listen to him, he just graduated the 5th grade for the twelfth time." The woman at the desk smiles and ushers us through to the elevator. She steps in the elevator and presses the button to the top floor and then steps out.

We are the only passengers and Beth looks at me as if to say, what the heck is going on? I look around, but all I can do is look around and say, "Top a' the world Ma!"

The elevator comes to a stop and the doors open onto the hallway that circumnavigates the private suites located on the uppermost floor. The floor is jammed, in both directions with so many famous people that I just want to find a corner and gawk at all the prominent persons in sight. Beth is also totally mesmerized by all the celebrities from business, entertainment, politics and pop culture.

Our eyes go wide and Beth nudges me saying, "Look! There's Tim Hanger speaking with Miriam Sepper and Myna Ellison hugging Freddie Wyle and Harvey Traynor with Leticia Hopping…" She's rattling off names that appear all the time in the press and on entertainment news programs. I am just as caught up in the moment as Beth is when I spot a real celebrity, the phenomenally wealthy retail mogul, Harold Lieberman who, among other businesses, is Founder and CEO of Harry's Place department stores. He owns one of the world's most valuable coin collections and he's a leading authority on American coins and currency. I am trying to appear unimpressed by all of this when I spot Wally Newton, only the fourth richest man in the world. He's surrounded by a group of men and women who are hanging onto his every word. I think about going over and eavesdropping on their conversation. Maybe he's giving them advice on investments or telling them about the next big thing to watch but then I think better of it. Except for my business, what the hell do I have to invest?

All in all, we are reveling in the moment and looking to see what we can see next and even I have to admit that I'm glad we came. We go to the bar and order our drinks; Beth gets a glass of Pinot Noir and I order vodka on the rocks with a twist.

Beth doesn't want to leave, but she hands me her glass and says she needs to freshen up. She asks if I'll be okay until she gets back, "Okay? Are you kidding did you see the buffet! I'll be more than okay, oh but don't do much freshening up, you look beautiful tonight." Beth's smile is radiant and she kisses my cheek and walks to the lady's room.

I love food and I make no excuses for the fact that I enjoy eating. I work my way over to the table piled high with some of the best-looking food I've ever seen and I'm no slouch so I gaze before I graze. There are trays piled high with jumbo shrimp so big they should be their own species, clams and oysters on the half-shell, Swedish meatballs in a rich, dark brown sauce, platters with at least nine different cheeses, roasted red peppers, grilled vegetables including eggplant, zucchini, onions and tomatoes. There are platters with fresh fruit and silver chafing dishes filled with all kinds of pasta plus beef stroganoff, skewers with both Thai chicken and Thai beef. So much food it made me doubly glad I came.

A short time later I find a table where chefs are carving prime ribs of beef, and serving certain dishes exotic enough that you need to read the placard next to the chafing dish to know what you're eating. There is a Brazilian dish featuring salmon with a spicy orange crust, medallions of pork with lemon, ginger and citronelle, an African dish of baked pumpkin with rosemary, a wonderful looking Bream with pomegranate prepared from an Israeli recipe, a dish called Dutch liver with wine sauce and smoked Kaiser and much more.

Beth comes out of the lady's room and I hand her the wine glass. She sees me scrutinizing the food and she reaches out and grabs my hand, "Before you stick your face into the chopped liver let's walk around and look into the suites to see who else might be here." Reluctantly I agree and we saunter off as if we belong. As we walk, I notice that every 30 feet or so there is another set of tables featuring the same selections of food so I feel better knowing I won't starve.

We try to be nonchalant, but there are dozens of notables standing and chatting as we walk along. On the hallway walls there are a number of campaign posters all with the image of Dr. Tom Houston. Each poster features a different topic that trumpets Tom's positions on everything from illegal aliens, to poverty, to energy, to war, to abortion and on and on. As Beth and I walk we look into the suites we pass and see so many different people and they all seem to be having a good time. Beth notices one suite that looks as if it were completely empty and she turns to me and asks, "What missing big shot do you think has this suite?"

"Come on, let's sneak inside and see what it looks like."

"Chris, you can't do that, it would be very uncouth."

I put my arms around her waist and hold her close and say, "Hey baby, look up the word 'uncouth' in the dictionary and you'll see my picture."

Beth pushes me away, "I believe you. Now let's get out of here before we are caught."

Playfully I say to Beth, "What's the matter? You're scared? Don't be a sissy we'll just go in and take a peek. What's the worst that could happen?" I take her hand and I pull her into the suite and she very reluctantly follows. We get past the foyer and turn to come face to face with Dr. Thomas Houston.

"Beth! I am so glad you came." He reaches over and gives Beth a kiss on her cheek and says, "I've been waiting for you. I hope you are enjoying yourself."

Beth is totally stunned, "Thank you, yes we are having a wonderful time. We didn't mean to intrude; Chris and I are just looking around; I hope you don't mind."

Tom smiles broadly, "Mind? Of course, I don't mind, this is your suite anyway. I personally reserved it for you and…" he turns to me, "you must be Christopher Pella. May I call you Chris?" Tom Houston holds out his hand and I shake it.

"Sure." I say realizing that Tom Houston said 'your suite', but Beth beats me to the punch.

"Dr. Houston, this is our suite? We cannot possibly accept this special treatment. You would be much better off giving this beautiful space to one of the many famous people who are here to support you."

"Nonsense Beth, I want to be sure that you are given the royal treatment for the great work you do every day. I want to show some small measure of appreciation for the way you and your staff tried to help poor Officer Josephs." Dr. Houston seems sincere when he said this, but for some reason, probably a jealous streak, I think he sounds phony.

Beth seems to stammer, "But…I…this is, I really think that this is too much."

"Beth, you deserve some small token; besides I wouldn't worry about the celebs here. They are being very well taken care of I assure you. In the meantime, I want you and Chris to enjoy the event. I need to give a speech to the attendees, but afterwards I'll be back and introduce you to some of my friends. What do you say?"

"Dr. Houston, I don't know what to say. You are being more than generous and Chris and I are truly appreciative of your kindness."

"Good then it's settled. You can sit in your private seats overlooking the arena and hear what I have to say. Chris, I don't know where you fall on the political spectrum, but wherever you do, I hope you will find my speech interesting." Tom smiles and I smile back; after all I haven't eaten yet.

Tom turns to Beth, "I hope you have a wonderful evening and I want to thank you again for coming." One of Dr. Houston's aides comes into the room. He is carrying a small stack of papers and says, "Dr. Houston, we made the changes you requested and you have 10 minutes before you will be speaking. "Sorry, duty calls, but I'll see you when I'm finished" with that Dr. Houston turns and leaves our suite.

I am a bit taken aback by all this attention he is giving to Beth and I say something that I shouldn't have, "Beth, I think this guy wants to get in your pants."

Beth faces me with as angry a look as I've ever seen. "What a horrible thing to say. Dr. Houston invites us here as his guest and I can't believe that you would assume his kindness is nothing more than an attempt to get in my pants. By the way if I want to be seduced, he wouldn't have to work so hard." Still fuming she turns away and folds here arms in front of her.

"Hey Beth, I was just making a joke" I lied. "I didn't mean to get you so upset. I know you like the guy and he has been very gracious and I apologize for my pissy comment. Forgive me?"

Beth turns back to me and there is no smile on her face. "Okay, I'll forgive you. I want this to be a really special evening and I don't want you to ruin it. If you feel like you can't be around Dr. Houston then you can go home, but if you stay try to be more civil to him and nicer to me."

I know when I've been duly chastised so I put my tail between my legs and my mouth in check and say, "Okay, I'll remember." I know I'm in the doghouse and I don't know how to get out of it. I feel I need to leave Beth alone so she has time to cool off, so I walk to our private box that overlooks the arena floor. From the box I can see there are thousands of people and they all seem to be speaking at the same time. They are all here to see and hear their man speak and I look around at the signs they are waving and the mood is like one of a party celebrating victory rather than a fundraiser and I'm taking it all in.

A few minutes later the door to the box seats open and I turn and Beth is there with a look on her face that seems a lot friendlier than her last scowl. "Okay, you've been punished enough, I guess we can go and have something to eat." Now she's smiling knowing that the way to my heart is…well you know.

"Thanks for letting me off the hook. I really am sorry" and Beth continues to smile and takes my hand as we walk back out to the hallway in search for one of the food stations. We see the line has grown shorter, so we both stand behind someone who looks familiar to me, but I can't place the name. Beth, ever the pop-culture guru, excitedly whispers in my ear, "That's Hamilton Cargill! I can't believe that we are standing right behind Hamilton Cargill!"

Trying to show that I am cool enough to recognize him, I tell Beth, "Yeah, doesn't he star in Andromeda Signal."

Beth looks at me with a certain amount of disdain and says, "He stars in 'Love Will Find a Way' with Callie Henning, I really need to get you to the movies more often."

Beth and I finally get to the front of the line and we begin to fill our plates with all sorts of the great food that is elaborately displayed on the table. When we finish Beth has one plate and I have two, after all I don't know how long the speech will be. Beth suggests we make our way back to the suite and get seated so we can see and hear Tom Houston's speech. We work our way through the crowd and back to the suite where we lay down our plates on a tray specially built into the box seat.

We finish our drink and I ask Beth if she wants another glass of wine and she immediately says "Yes." I walk back into the suite and I see that the bar in our space has been fully stocked so I figure that it beats waiting at the hallway bar and I pour us both a drink. I'm back in a flash and Beth seems surprised. "How did you manage to get the drinks so fast?" I tell her that there is a bar in the suite and it's fully stocked and I say, "I'm taking you to Vegas!" Then I realize that I might have made another mistake, but Beth is just laughing.

As we are sitting in our seats, we see Boyd Somerfield on stage finishing a performance of one of his many hits. He stops singing as the lights in the cavernous arena are turned halfway down and a spotlight shines on the Garden's center stage. Other than a few murmuring conversations, the audience stops speaking to cheer Boyd.

He begins to address the throngs of supporters, "Wow, what a great crowd we have here tonight!"

The gathering roars in approval. "I think I know why you are here… you want to hear me speak right?" The audience now laughs and begins to shout, Boyd! Boyd! Boyd! "Well, I thank you for that, but I kinda know why you're really here; you're here for the same reason that I am here. You are here to support Dr. Thomas Houston for the Socialist Liberation Party nomination for President of the United States!" The crowd screams their approval and Boyd raises his arms to try and quiet those on the floor.

"Before I introduce you to Dr. Tom Houston…" the crowd goes crazy at the mention of his name and Boyd stops to acknowledge enthusiastic reaction. Boyd smiles and continues, "Before I introduce Dr. Tom, I want to sing the chorus from my song Timeline." The crowd screams again at the mention of one of Boyd's most popular songs. He plays a six-string acoustic guitar and sings the chorus, "*The time is right for miracles, a time for hearts talk, the time is right for all of us, a time to run not walk*, ladies and gentlemen, the next President of the United States, Dr. Thomas Houston."

Pandemonium rules as the entire arena rises in overjoyed reaction at the mere mention of their man. Beth and I are looking at all the people, both on the floor and in the box seats outside their suites, standing and clapping in thunderous applause. It is truly a remarkable sight, nothing canned, nothing rehearsed, just a spontaneous eruption of overwhelming devotion.

Dr. Tom Houston walks out on stage and the crescendo increases to the highest decibel levels that would rival crowds at the Super Bowl and World Series. Tom goes to the center of the stage and embraces Boyd who hugs him back. They shake hands and Tom turns to the audience and waves to the adoring crowd. He has learned that it is impossible to quiet a crowd that is so enthralled so he basks in the moment. After what seems like a long time, Tom Houston holds up his hands and asks for quiet. "I cannot thank you enough for your amazing greeting and incredible show of support." The crowd roars back their appreciation for Tom Houston and Beth and I have a fabulous view of it all. We both stare wide-eyed at the rich and famous as well as people who are mesmerized by their champion and we find ourselves caught up in the euphoria of the people in the arena.

"Before I begin, I want to take the time to recognize a very special person. I have known many people who are tireless in their efforts to help others and she is among the best and brightest America has to offer. I have seen firsthand how she and her staff performed heroic measures to save the life of a man who was wounded and ultimately died in the line of duty." Beth now turns to me in panic and I am in a state of bewilderment.

"I have asked her to come to our event and she has graciously accepted the invitation and I would like to introduce her to you now. Ladies and gentlemen would you please give a warm welcome to a person who makes us all proud, a person of great beauty and poise under amazingly difficult circumstances, an American we can all be proud of, Ms. Elizabeth Della Russo."

Tom is looking for the suite and spots Beth, "Beth, Beth!" He yells, "Please stand up and let us see you, Beth, please let us say thanks." Beth is totally flummoxed and seems glued to her seat. She cannot believe that this is happening and I am sitting there ready to begin drinking…heavily.

Smiling at Beth, Tom says, "By the way, did I mention that she is beautiful?" Now the crowd starts to whistle and there are cat calls. "Beth, come on please stand and let us say thanks!" Beth is in still in the state of panic and looks over to me with pleading eyes not knowing what to do next. I whisper, "I know this guy…" I really want to say jerk, "blindsided you so you better get up and let the moment pass." I get up and offer my hand to Beth and she takes it and slowly lifts herself out of the seat. As she stands up, she feels frightened, embarrassed and distraught all at once, but she forces a smile as waves to the crowds. Tom is smiling and applauding and the crowd loves every moment adding to the applause. For Beth it must seem an eternity, but in less than a minute she waves to Tom and the crowd and collapses back into her seat.

Beth is staring blankly into space as the crowd quiets to allow Tom Houston to continue with his speech. I know how upset she is, so I wait until she is able to calm herself. I reach out for her hand and hold it and she turns to me with a look of total incomprehension. "Listen Beth, I'm sure he had good intentions, but I think he should have let you know what he was going to say and do."

"Chris, why did he do that? There are so many other people who played a bigger part than me in taking care of Nick. They should have been acknowledged. They should have been given the applause. How can I face them?"

I know what she means, but I need to try and make her feel better and recognize her contribution. "Listen Beth, he did mention your staff and their efforts. You are the symbol of the caring that was given to Nick and you deserve praise, I mean it, you are a really kind and caring person and now the world knows it."

"My God, this is going to be on TV and on the news. What am I going to do, how can I live this down?"

"Beth, there is nothing to live down. You need to accept the praise with your typical graciousness and when asked by whomever asks, you can tell them that you are part of the best team in the business and Huntington Hospital is the best place to work."

Beth looks at me as if she understands. "You are right. I need to accept it for what it is and just let everyone know that it is a team effort and I am just part of the team." She squeezes my hand and gives me a kiss on the cheek. "I need to go to the ladies room." And she gets up and walks back into the suite. As you can imagine I am very upset for her, but I can't show it so I turn to listen to Tom Houston continuing his speech.

"…And there are so many other problems in America that it will take the courage of a leader, the kind of courage I know I can bring to the job of president!" The crowd begins to chant 'Dr. Tom" and Tom Houston is smiling as he waves back.

Dr. Tom continues his speech, "I want to look at each and everyone in the crowd as I say this." He looks slowly from left to right, along the floor and up at those in the box seats. "I am about the toughest person you will ever confront. I will fight for everything I want, for everything that is in the collective best interest of all Americans and all citizens of the world."

It all seems like the typical political rhetoric you hear from every politician, but something happens next as I look and listen. The resounding cheers and raucous noise in the arena all of a sudden disappear; it is if I have gone completely deaf and I am in a panic as I look around for the reason. Then I hear a voice, a familiar voice and I become terrified.

"Oh Christopher? Ah, there you are! How have you been? It has been much to long since we last, um, got together. I hope you are enjoying the rarefied air among all the useful idiots who attend these things."

"Julian?" I merely thought his name, but I can hear myself speak."

"Yes, yes! Johnny, give the man what's behind door number two!"

The arena goes dark and I am standing in the center of a plain, an enormous plain. The plain extends to the horizon in all directions and I take a few steps to the left then to the right. The ground beneath my feet feels like nothing I've ever walked on and I shout, "Where am I? What is this place?"

Julian's voice reverberates, "You will soon find out what this place is."

There is a low rumbling in the far distance and dark clouds begin to come in from all directions until the entire plain is shrouded in darkness. In an instant I am back in the box overlooking the arena and my body feels paralyzed. Beth is sitting by my side looking at me with worry,

"Chris? Chris? Are you alright? Chris, please speak to me, are you alright?"

I try to snap out of my state of paralysis, but my hands are gripping the arm rests of our box seats so tightly that my knuckles turn white. I look at Beth and there is dread in my eyes and Beth becomes very frightened.

"Chris what's wrong. Please speak to me Chris, please." She pats me gently on the cheek hoping to snap me out of my state.

I slowly come out of my stupor and look at Beth. "I...I, I am sorry Beth. I don't' know what happened, but I seem to have blanked out." I am still shaking from the vison I can't even describe but I can't tell Beth what really happened.

"Chris, I am so worried. Has this ever happened before?" She said this as she begins to take my pulse and feel my head for a fever.

"No, not ever, I don't know what it could be that made me react that way. It might have been my skipping lunch and then eating like a pig now, maybe, I can't say for sure." I try to regain my composure but I'm still somewhat shaky. I don't want her to worry so I tell Beth, "I really am starting to feel much better, honest."

Beth always has her nurse's hat on and she seems somewhat reluctant to accept my explanation. "That could be what happened, but you had such a frightened look on your face that I got frightened myself. Your pulse rate is off the charts. It seems like it is a much stronger reaction than you should have had drinking on an empty stomach." I can see that Beth is still skeptical as she says, "Alright there's not much I can do now, but you have to promise me that you will see Dr. McCreary tomorrow. I'll make the appointment, okay?"

I promise Beth I would go to the doctor and she hugs me, which is the best medicine I could ask for. We turn back to the arena as Tom Houston's speech concludes and the crowd turns the fundraiser into a party complete with entertainment from Fabiano, who is singing "Houston, We've Got a Problem" and the crowd dances to the music.

I then realize something and say, "Beth, I forgot to ask you how you're feeling?"

"Well, it seems that you are the best medicine, I simply forgot about me when I saw you looking as if you met the devil himself."

My face must look ashen and I ask her, "Beth, would you mind if we go back into the suite, the noise is giving me a headache." She smiles and says, "I think that's a great idea. You still look very pale." So, we both walk into the suite and sit down on one of the three couches. I am feeling better and I say, "I'd like a drink, but for now I think I'll just have water, do you want something?"

"You sit down and relax; I'll get you a bottle of water." Beth gets up and walks to the bar and as she does the door to the suite opens and Dr. Tom enters with his entourage and a group of people that look like the index of reporters for the latest edition of AP, Google or Yahoo News and the rest.

Tom is in a terrific mood as he walks into the suite smiling and laughing. Once inside he sees Beth and excuses himself from the group. Tom puts on a serious face as he walks over to Beth and says in a contrite way, "You must be very angry with me."

Beth gives him the dirtiest look I've seen one person give to another, even dirtier that the one she gave me. "How could you do something like that and not let me know in advance? How could you do that?"

Tom answers, "If I'd have let you know in advance you wouldn't have come."

Beth is incredulous, "That's right, I wouldn't have come. You made it seem like I deserve all the credit when you know the entire staff was there for Nick. I'm only one person of many who tried to help."

"Beth, that's not true. I held you up as the example to show the dedication of the staff and hospital for all the great work they do every day. I know I should have said something to you, but I really want to point out your dedication and when I say 'your' I truly mean everyone who does what you do. You can be angry with me, but it was a heartfelt message and I didn't mean any harm. Please forgive me."

Beth looks into Tom's eyes and she determines that he is being sincere. "I suppose that you did this for the right reasons, but you made it seem like it was my efforts and my efforts alone."

"Beth honestly that was not my intention, I meant to include all members of the staff and hospital using you as the symbol of their heroism, but if I fell short, I sincerely apologize."

Beth still will not be appeased, "It's not me who should get the apology; I think you should apologize to the doctors, staff and administrators of Huntington Hospital. They are the ones you insulted."

I am still sitting on the couch watching all this going on, but not hearing a word. I see Tom put his hand on Beth's arm and smile, "I will make it a point to let everyone know how appreciative of their work I am. I want to do the right thing, is that satisfactory?"

I didn't hear what Beth and Tom were talking about, but I could see Beth's mood change. She manages a smile and Tom looks delighted. They continue to speak a little longer when Tom and Beth walk over to the couch.

He appears humbled when he says, "Chris, I've been duly chastised and I want to apologize to you too."

I remark, "Well, join the club." But ever the skeptic, I ask him, "Apologize to me, what for?"

"Well, first for blindsiding Beth the way I did. My tribute was done with the best of intentions, but you know what they say about the road to hell. Second, I understand that it was you who calmed Beth enough for her to stand up and acknowledge the praise, and for that I am grateful."

Beth is looking at me with pleading eyes, hoping that I won't take a punch at Tom but ever the gentleman, I hold out my hand and Tom takes it, gratefully, I think. "No harm done but I think that the folks at Huntington Hospital may have some different thoughts."

Tom holds up his hand as if to surrender, "I know, I know…I'll be sure to straighten that out as soon as possible. Listen, I have a number of people that I would like you both to meet. They are here as supporters, but you may recognize a few and it might be fun to mingle."

I look at Beth, "That might be fun. What do you think, Beth?"

Beth looks around and turns to Tom and excitedly asks, "Is that Hamilton Cargill?"

"Who?" Tom turns to look around and he turns to Beth and smiles, "Who, Hammy? It sure is, are you a fan?"

Beth continues to look at Hamilton Cargill and immediately says, "I am."

"Well, would you like to meet him?"

Beth acts demure as she says, "Oh, no I wouldn't want to bother him after all he's a big star."

"Are you kidding, he would be thrilled to meet you; beautiful women are a hobby with Hammy and you certainly fit the criteria."

Tom turns to me and says, "Chris would you mind if I introduce Beth to Hammy? I'll be right back, and when I get back there is someone I would like to introduce to you. Are you okay with that?"

I shrug my shoulders and say, "Sure, I'll wait here."

Tom takes Beth by the hand and walks her over to Hamilton Cargill. He's talking to a beautiful blond woman, but he stops when he feels a hand on his shoulder. Hamilton turns around and he embraces Tom and looks over at Beth. He immediately smiles and they begin talking.

"Hammy, I mean Hamilton; I'd like to introduce you to Elizabeth Della Russo. Beth is the young woman that I spoke of earlier. She is a dedicated nurse and a big fan of yours and she asked me to make an introduction."

Hammy lifts Beth's hand to his lips and kisses it, "My dear, this is truly a delight to meet you."

Beth blushes and says, "It is truly and honor to meet you Mr. Cargill."

"Mr. Cargill? Please call me Hammy, may I call you Beth?"

Beth is totally enthralled standing there speaking with one of the most popular actors in the entire world. "Of course, but I don't know if I have the nerve to call you Hammy."

"Hamilton Cargill laughs out loud, "Well then how about Hamilton? That is, after all, my name."

Beth laughs back and she says, "Okay, Hamilton."

Tom takes his leave of Beth and Hamilton and as he walks across the room, he stops numerous times to say hello to one rich and famous supporter after another. Finally, he is back at the couch where he sits beside me. He wears a weary smile as looks around, "I suppose I've got to do these things but, believe it or not, it grows stale especially after the number of times I've done them."

Ever the sympathizer I say, "You're breaking my heart."

Tom now cracks up. "I suppose I had that coming."

Waxing philosophical I say, "You know, it's very hard for us in the huddled mass to sympathize or even understand you in the elite strata of society. You get to make and spend millions, you get to associate with other people who are famous and can help you in many ways, you get to live in mansions, travel the world, and stay in the finest places, eat in the best restaurants, buy whatever you want and get treated like gods or goddesses, oh sorry, like kings or queens. It seems strange why you haven't put a bullet in your brain."

Tom now convulses with laughter and a few people standing close by politely smile not knowing or understanding what we are talking about.

"Chris, that is about the most succinct description I've heard defining the haves from the have nots."

I consider how I should react, but I say what's on my mind anyway. "Tom, I don't consider myself a have not, I really don't. I consider myself a working man who tries to do the best he can. I try to grow my business; live in a home I own and buy what I can afford. I try to live my life in a way that would make my parents proud and I understand I need to work hard to secure my future and the future of my family when that time comes. What I don't like is to have what I make, what I save and what I accumulate taken by a government so they can redistribute it to those who chose not to work. Not the truly needy, they should always be helped and we as a nation should do whatever we can to take care of those people. Who I am speaking of are those who live on the government dole, who scam the system and bleed us suckers dry. Oh, by the way I believe in God and His Son, Jesus Christ in case you want to know."

Tom looks at me with a certain amount of astonishment and smiles, "Come on Chris, tell us what you really think."

Now it's my turn to laugh. "I know I probably should keep my mouth shut, but sometimes speaking your mind is better than a session at the shrink, don't you think?"

Tom looks at me for an uncomfortably long time, but he brightens and says, "I promised you I would introduce you to someone that I am sure you will enjoy. Come on, I see him over there."

We get up and walk across the room. Tom stops a few times to shake hands and hug friends, but we finally stop next to Harold Lieberman and I am in awe. This is the man who has one of the finest, if not the finest, American coin and currency collection in the world and I am about to meet him.

Tom touches his arm and asks, "Harry, do you have a moment?"

"Of course, I do Tom."

"Harry, I'd like you to meet a fellow coin collecting enthusiast, Chris Pella." Beth must have told him that I own a coin and currency business.

"Ah, Mr. Pella I am delighted to meet a fellow numismatist, someone who shares my passion. How long have you been collecting?"

I am tongue tied. "Mr. Lieberman, it is truly a pleasure to meet you. I have read your books on collecting American coins and currency and have studied your amazing collection."

Harry Lieberman is genuinely grateful for the compliment and says, "Well that is very kind of you Mr. Pella."

"Oh, please call me Chris."

"Then you must call me Harry. Tom tells me you are a collector."

"Actually, I own a coin shop in my home town of Huntington, Long Island. My father loved collecting and he passed on that love to me. I started collecting when I was very young and turned it into a business."

"How nice it is to hear that; it is nice to share that with your father. Actually, that is how I started; my father and I spent many happy hours looking over his collection and he passed that passion onto me. Tell me does your father still collect?"

"Unfortunately, my father passed away a number of years ago."

"I am very sorry for your loss, but it seems he's left you with the same passion and I hope you never lose it."

I am like a baseball fan speaking to his favorite player. I have this opportunity to ask Harry a question, so I take it, "Would you mind if I ask you a question?"

Harry is very gracious, "Of course, what is the question."

"How on earth did you ever acquire that 1804 Draped Bust Silver Dollar? I think it is one of the most beautiful coins in your collection."

You could see that Harry's eyes go wide as he becomes animated and he speaks to me. "There were only 15 minted and I am fortunate to own the PF-68. It is one of the most valuable coins in the world I daresay, and it is the cornerstone of my collection. If the truth be told the coin was in a private collection that was being liquidated. I purchased the Draped Bust at an auction and the owner at that time was thrilled that I had won the bid. I suppose it was a bittersweet moment for him. On the one hand he had to sell his prized possession on the other hand he knew I am a devoted numismatist, and his cherished coin would have an honored place in my collection. I paid a king's ransom for it, but I have not regretted it a single day, not a single day."

Tom is politely listening, but his attention is needed somewhere else and he excuses himself and leaves Harry and I alone to talk shop. I am too engrossed in my conversation to notice Tom walking over to where Beth is still talking with Hamilton Cargill.

Tom seems pleased, "Well, I see you two are getting along well."

Hammy is effusive with praise for Beth, "Tom, Beth is so intelligent and beautiful that I am thinking of making this young woman my fourth wife." Hammy then turns to Beth and takes her hand saying, "Dearest, would you do me the honor of becoming my fourth wife?" He then puts his hand on his chin and looks up, "Hummm, maybe we can save each other the trouble; I'll just buy you a house with a pool and we'll call it a day!"

Tom and Beth laugh and she turns to Tom and says, "Hamilton Cargill is certainly a charmer. He must have taken lessons from you."

Tom smiles, "Believe me when I tell you that Hammy doesn't need any lessons", and their small group continues to laugh.

"Hammy, do you mind if I steal Beth away, I'd like her to meet Dr. Spencer Price." Hamilton Cargill seems crushed, "Tom, what will I do without Beth to save me from the slings and arrows of your outrageous supporters?"

"I think you'll manage." With that, Tom guides Beth away from Hammy, but not before he shouts to Beth, "Return to me soon, oh lovely one. I shall be distraught until you are in my sphere once more!"

Beth is laughing, but she turns to Tom and says, "Dr. Spencer Price! Oh my God, his work in cancer research is renowned. He is a hero of mine."

Tom seems to know he's hit a homerun. "Dr. Price is a friend and supporter. His work in DNA sequencing is being used to identify metamorphoses at the root of cancerous tumors. He and his team hope to find a guide to the genetic evolution of cancer so they can find effective ways to treat patients and make it personal to each patient. He believes that all the answers can be found by using different ways to treat cancers in different people."

Beth is impressed that Tom is so familiar with the work of Dr. Price. He senses this and tells her, "I have confidence in the work he is doing and I wouldn't accept his support unless I checked it out. I should warn you even though Spencer is a worldwide renowned authority he is quite a character. Come on let's go meet the man himself."

Tom Houston walks Beth over to where Dr. Price is talking to Nancy McGrath, the Chief of Staff to Tom. "Good evening, Spencer, I trust you are enjoying yourself tonight."

The elderly Dr. Price looks at Tom with a frown and says, "Humph! Damn waste of time these things. Why don't they just elect you and get it over with?"

"Now Spencer, you know how important these events are. It gives us a chance to get the message of our campaign out so we can convince the voters that we have solutions to the problems facing America."

"Solutions? Solutions? The solutions are plain as the nose on your face. Want to cure cancer? Spend more money and give me what I need, that's the solution."

Tom is smiling having had this conversation with Dr. Price before. "I agree Spencer and that time will come; I assure you. By the way, I would like to introduce you to this lovely young lady, Elizabeth Della Russo. She is a longtime admirer of you and your work. Beth, I'd like you to meet Dr. Spencer Price."

Dr. Price turns and faces Beth and holds out his hand. "Please excuse me Ms. Della Russo. I am known to speak my mind without fear of repercussion, after all at my age there is only one repercussion that matters." He ends by warmly smiling at Beth as she reaches out with her hand to shake his.

"Dr. Price, I can't tell you what an honor it is to meet you. Tom is correct when he says that I am a great admirer of yours and all you have done."

"Well, that is very kind of you. I seem to recall that Tom introduced you during his speech and that you are a nurse."

"Yes, I am head nurse in the critical care unit of Huntington Hospital. I've read about your work during nursing school and the doctors in our oncology department hold you in very high esteem."

"Well please let them know that I appreciate their confidence." Dr. Price turns to Tom and Nancy as he takes Beth's arm, "I am taking this lovely young lady for a walk to talk shop. You two can mingle with the rest of these…"

Tom chimes in, "Now Spencer!"

Grudgingly Spence says, "…the rest of these supporters of yours."

Tom turns to Beth and whispers, "Good luck" and he and Nancy walk and merge into a group discussion headed by Wally Newton.

The evening goes on and everyone seems to be enjoying themselves immensely including Beth and me. It is after midnight when I look up the LIRR train schedule on my phone and see that a train leaves at 12:48AM with the next train not leaving until after 2AM. I see Beth has ended her conversation with an older man. She seems to be looking for someone and when she sees me, she smiles and walks over.

"Have I got something great to tell you!" I am practically bursting to tell her my good news.

Beth, never to be outdone, says, "Well it looks like we both hit the jackpot, have I got something great to tell you too!"

"Listen before we regale each other with our stories, I thought you should know we've got two choices, stay and party or catch the 12:48AM to Huntington. It's your call."

Beth says, "To tell you the truth, I wish we could stay longer, but I have the PM shift. By the time I get home it will be after 2AM and I need to get some sleep so I think we should head out. We can talk on the train."

I agree and we go to look for Tom to thank him for the invitation. We spot him speaking with Nancy and we walk over. "Tom, it's getting late and Chris and I must be going, but we both want to thank you for the wonderful evening."

Tom protests, "It's far too early please stay a bit longer."

"Thanks so much for asking, but we both have to work tomorrow and as it is we won't be getting home until after 2AM."

"Nonsense!" Tom turns to Nancy and asks, "Can we arrange to have a limo take Beth and Chris home?"

Through her pasted-on smile, Nancy says, "Of course we can, and I'll make the arrangements now."

Tom seems delighted, "Good, that's settled so let's have one last drink together with Celia and Rev. Malcolm Aldridge." Celia L'Seun is the hottest clothing designer in the world today and Rev. Aldridge heads the not-for-profit group, C.O.P.E.T., Committee to Organize the Peoples of Earth for Tomorrow.

Beth is getting used to being manipulated by Tom Houston and she knows it. "That's very kind of you Tom, but just one drink."

Tom looks a bit sullen, but he agrees, "Okay, just one drink" and we walk over to meet Ms. L'Seun and Rev. Aldridge. Tom, Beth and I get to where they are standing and both celebrities greet us with broad smiles.

"Celia, Malcolm, I'd like you to meet two friends of mine. This lovely woman is Ms. Elizabeth Della Russo and her escort, Mr. Christopher Pella. You might remember I paid tribute to Beth and her staff during my speech and I was duly chastised for not giving her advanced warning."

Celia is the first to speak, "How dreadful Tom, you should be ashamed of yourself." Celia places her arms around Beth, "It is a pleasure to meet you my dear and you are quite lovely have you ever modelled?"

Beth practically spits out the wine she is sipping and laughs, "Coming from you Ms. L'Seun, that is really a compliment, but no, I have never modelled."

Ms. L'Seun sees the humor in Beth's reaction and laughs herself. "It was meant as a compliment, however, I can see why you thought it funny. The young women who model today are better suited for posters to feed the starving in Ethiopia or some such place."

Rev. Malcolm Aldridge appears to become angry. "Celia, how can you be so callous in speaking of starving people in Ethiopia." It seems odd coming from someone who is as rotund as the reverend.

"Oh, please Malcolm, you know I didn't mean it the way you made it sound. I give more money to your C.O.P.E.T. thing than practically anyone so get off your high-horse."

Tom believes he needs to intercede and he says, "Now, now let's not fuss over this. Malcolm, you know Celia to be a very generous person and Celia, you know Malcolm is tireless in his efforts to help those in need so let's just kiss and make up." Both Celia and Malcolm laugh and hug each other which I actually think is very magnanimous of both of them.

I figure at this point that I'd stir up some controversy so I ask Reverend Aldridge, "Reverend, it seems odd to me that a Christian minister would be a big supporter Tom Houston who is an acknowledged atheist." I try to see Beth's reaction from the corner of my eye and it looks like a cringe to me.

Now Tom and Malcolm look at each other and laugh and Tom defers to Malcolm, "Why don't you answer Chris, Malcolm."

"With pleasure!" Malcolm addresses his comment directly to me. "Well, it's really simple. I've kind of made Tom my white whale." The entire group now laughs. "You see I made it my quest to bring Tom over from the dark side and my being here as a supporter will bring me into his confidence, so now I can work my magic. So far though, I'm having a pretty tough time with him." He looks back at Tom and Tom smiles and says, "Well Malcolm, I guess you're going to have to work harder." Tom embraces the Reverend and they both laugh. Beth looks relieved and our little group continues to talk. The event appears to be in full swing with the famous, the rich, and the beautiful walking in and out of the suite and the party going full-blast on the floor of the Garden.

Nearly an hour passes and Beth keeps looking at her watch. She seems to be getting tired so I ask her, "What do you think, would you like to go home?"

Beth forces a weak smile, "Yeah, I think I'm fading fast. Let's say our goodbyes and get going." I happily agree and we grab our coats and get ready to leave.

We shake hands with the group and turn to Tom. Beth says, "Tom I want to thank you again for a wonderful evening and for the limo to take us home."

"Well, I'm truly sorry you have to leave so soon, but I understand. I want to thank you and Chris for coming tonight, you've made it very special for me. Nancy will show you to your car and, again, I want to thank you for being so gracious." Tom looks at Beth and I think they share a moment as he reaches over to give her a kiss on the cheek.

Tom now turns to me and says, "Well its back to the salt mines for me, I hope you can appreciate the sacrifices I make." I smile, remembering our conversation, and reply, "I'm sure we are all grateful for the extreme lengths you go through on your own behalf." Tom now burst out in laughter and says, "That's a pretty good response. Mind if I use it from time to time?"

I smile at him, "Of course, my pleasure." I'm trying hard not to like this guy, but I'm beginning to and we both laugh and shake hands. Beth looks back and forth at each of us with a puzzled look on her face. Nancy is waiting for us to finish our goodbyes and she tells us that our car is waiting and that she will escort us out.

The hallway that encircles the suites is still nearly full and people are still in the mood to party. Beth and I wait with Nancy at the elevator for our ride to the lobby. We walk out to the street in front of the Garden to find our car is waiting. The driver opens the door, but before we get in, Beth and I thank Nancy for her efforts and for all she did to make the evening a success.

Nancy smiles, "No need to thank me, Tom wanted to be sure that you both had a wonderful time and I hope you did." We both assure her that the evening was wonderful and that we enjoyed ourselves immensely. We shake hands with Nancy and get into the car.

Beth is seated on the far side of the back seat and she is looking at me with what might be called a scowl. "What? Why are you staring at me like that? What did I do?"

"I can't believe that you would confront Tom and Malcolm with that whole thing about atheism. You must be born under a lucky star to have them both be so…I don't know…offhand about the whole question. You know that you were this close" and she show a small space between her thumb and finger, "from becoming a permanent resident in the dog house." Beth folds her arms and looks out the window of the limo so she won't have to look at me.

I am more relieved that I can say, but I say something anyway. "Well, I am a very pleasant fellow and the boys seem to delight in their repartee so who am I to prevent them from enjoying themselves. Speaking of delight, why don't you come and sit over here?" Beth just ignores me and continues to looks out the window as the limo cruises through the streets of New York City on the way to the Midtown Tunnel.

I am getting a bit playful and pat the space in the seat beside me, "Come on Beth, you can't be angry with me twice in the same evening. I am a real sweetheart and I want to tell you a secret." Beth continues to look away, but I detect a smile on her face.

"You're gonna love this secret! I promise, you're gonna be glad I told you this secret!" Now Beth has a full-fledged smile on her face, but she still won't look at me so I slowly slide beside her. I brush her long hair to the side to reveal her neck and ear. I kiss her neck and Beth says, "What do you think you're doing?"

"I'm trying to tell you a secret." I'm still kissing her neck and letting my hands roam over her body. Her eyes are closed and her breathing is getting heavy, but she stops me.

Beth says, "Have you considered that we are not alone?" Now she is looking at me and turning her head towards the driver. I look at the man behind the wheel and tell Beth, "I think he's seen this before, anyway tell him to get his own girl." She pushes me away and asks, "What's this big secret you want to tell me before your libido took over?"

I look Beth straight in the eye and say, "You know all those beautiful women we saw tonight?"

Beth smirks at me and says, "What about them?"

I proudly proclaim, "Well you are the most beautiful of them all!"

Beth looks at me with some disdain having heard my complements before, "Huh, some secret."

"Well, that's not all."

Beth is not one to let me off the hook so easy. "Oh yeah, well what's the other part of the secret?"

I am practically standing on the backseat of the limo as I tell her, "Beth you won't believe this, but Harry Lieberman, the Harry of 'Harry's Place', invited me to see his entire coin collection, in person! We had an amazing discussion about coins and he told me that his father started him on collecting just like my dad. Now here's the best part, he also offers to consign a number of coins from his collection to my company for sale! Can you believe it! That could be a fortune in commissions!"

Beth's jaw drops, "You're kidding?"

"Nope, not kidding. It really is the opportunity of a lifetime and I can't believe that it's all because of you."

Beth seems genuinely happy and she kisses me. I hold her in my arms and I never want to let her go. Then I remember that she has something to tell me so I ask her, "You told me that you have something special to tell so what gives?"

Beth becomes animated, "Well it's been quite an evening! I met Hamilton Cargill and he asked me to become his fourth wife." I know better than to do anything but laugh, so that's what I did.

Beth continues, "And you won't believe this! I met Dr. Spencer Price; can you believe it Dr. Spencer Price!"

I look at her questioningly, "Who?"

Beth just shakes her head, "You are a Neanderthal…Dr. Spencer Price! He's only the genius who's working on the cure for cancer!"

I immediately come back with, "Oh you mean Dr. Spencer Price! I thought you said Dr. Spicy Rice."

Beth is now laughing and all she can manage in response is, "I take Neanderthal back, you are a Cro-Magnon. By the way don't plan anything for vacation because he invited us to visit his lab. He's going to give us a private tour! Can you believe it? A private tour of the Price Clinic for Cancer Research in Miami Florida!"

Beth and I share a moment of silence and after a while Beth turns to me and asks, "Chris, can you believe this is actually happening to us. It is like something out of a movie."

I consider what she said, "You're right and it's unreal. Are you trying to be my fairy godmother? If you are, you can't have the job that belongs to Angelica Grometti."

"Seriously, things like this don't just happen to people like us. Don't get me wrong, I'm glad they did happen, but it all seems so unreal."

In our minds that just about sums up how we are feeling at this moment…unreal. Silence breaks out again as sleep overcomes the both of us. Beth puts her head on my shoulder and she is out like a light. Its 1:30AM as the limo passes Exit 40 on the LIE and I close my eyes and join her.

CHAPTER 27

The apostle sits at a small table in the small stone cottage near Ephesus. He writes all that he sees, all that he is told, and he makes a vow to fulfill the sacred command given to him by the Lord.

St. John writes by the low light of a single candle. The parchment proclaims "The revelation of Jesus Christ, which God gave Him to show His servants what must soon take place." The words are made known to John by the Lord and the words of God are what John must pass on to the faithful of the Seven Churches.

John has spoken and written much over the years. The words as contained in the Book of Life. "Behold the Lamb of God which taketh away the sins of the world". In years past, John spoke these words as he knelt in profound reverence at the feet of Jesus. He whispers these words again for he truly believes that Jesus is the Son of God, and the revelation given to him just confirms what he already believes. John, like the rest of the disciples, has great faith. He gave up everything to follow Jesus and that became his undying commitment and his life's work.

John's hand starts to shake as he writes the words which are to become a passage from the Book of Revelations,

"Then I saw another beast that rose out of the earth; it had two horns like a lamb and it spoke like a dragon. It exercises

all the authority of the first beast on its behalf, and it makes the earth and its inhabitants worship the first beast, whose mortal wound had been healed. It performs great signs, even making fire come down from heaven to earth in the sight of all; and by the signs that it is allowed to perform on behalf of the beast, it deceives the inhabitants of earth, telling them to make an image for the beast that had been wounded by the sword and yet lived; and it was allowed to give breath to the image of the beast so that the image of the beast could even speak and cause those who would not worship the image of the beast to be killed. Also, it causes all, both small and great, both rich and poor, both free and slave, to be marked on the right hand or the forehead, so that no one can buy or sell who does not have the mark, that is, the name of the beast or the number of its name."

John is fearful. The foretelling of the antichrist has been made, but when or where this blasphemy will come has not been told. To what generation will the beast speak? What will be the manner of men at the unholy coming? Will the faithful remain true or will they be corrupted? The words of Christ must be communicated to all and the prospect of deceit that could lead to their destruction must become a warning to all.

St. John continues with the words told to him and he writes them down, "Who is the liar but the one who denies that Jesus is the Christ? This is the antichrist, the one who denies the Father and the Son."

St. John has been given this ponderous task and he knows that it is a command from God the Father and His Son. He knows that he can write these truths, but will man be willing to accept them? Man is subject to so many whims and corruptions that the perversions cannot be counted, but then man can be held accountable. The apostle of Christ stops writing and places his hands over his eyes. He is weary, but he is also sad. Will these words of warning be enough to save mankind from the temptations of the beast or will be they be forever cast into the lake of fire and sulfur?

CHAPTER 28

A few days pass since attending the fundraiser and Beth has taken a lot of good-natured ribbing from her staff and hospital management about her being singled out for praise.

She protests telling everyone she could that she was blindsided and that she lambasted Tom for his lack of appreciation for all the staff and their caring help, but for a few it is an opportunity to have some good-natured fun. Nurse Diane Breuer is having the most fun of all at Beth's expense, "Hey! Can I have your autograph?"

Beth is exasperated at this point, but she figures that she would have some fun herself as she answers, "Okay, I give up. Do you have a pen?" Now both Beth and Diane are laughing uncontrollably and things get back to what accounts for normal at any hospital.

Just as Beth is about to start her shift, the phone rings at the nurses' station and she picks it up, "Nurse Della Russo, how may I help you?"

On the other end there is the excited voice of Jennifer Archer, administrative assistant to Dr. McMasters. "Beth, you've got to come down here now! You won't believe what's happening!"

Beth can't believe her ears, "What's going on?"

Jen is practically breathless, "Come down and find out for yourself." With that Jen hangs up and Beth quickly makes her way to the elevator and presses the button for the lobby. As the doors open, she hears voices mixed with laughter and excitement coming from the large foyer near the front entrance. Beth makes her way through the hallway leading to the foyer and she is immediately engulfed by many of the hospital staff in what seems to be a party like atmosphere. Beth sees Terry Crenshaw, an orderly who works in the ICU.

"What's going on here Terry?"

Terry turns to Beth and he is smiling from ear to ear. "Hey Beth, Dr. Thomas Houston just came here and he met with Dr. McMasters. The boss is going to make an important announcement and he asked that all the staff not on duty come to the lobby and we all can't wait to hear what it is."

Beth seems more puzzled than ever when she spots Jen. "Jen what's all this about?"

"Beth, you won't believe what's happening, but I don't want to spoil it for you or anyone here. Dr. McMasters is going to make the announcement right about now."

Jen and Beth stop speaking when Dr. McMasters holds the microphone at the reception desk and tells everyone to please quiet down as he has a special announcement to make. It takes about a minute, but everyone quiets down to hear what their boss has to say.

Dr. McMasters seems elated as he begins, "Ladies and gentlemen, staff members and guests I have the most wonderful news to tell you all, but first let me introduce our very special guest. He has come to Huntington Hospital before to visit the hero police officer, Nicholas Josephs at the moment of his untimely passing. Dr. Thomas Houston is a great advocate for Huntington Hospital and all the good work that you do every day and we are always grateful for his kind words. Today, however Dr. Thomas Houston brings more than kind words. Dr. Houston has come here in person for a very special announcement and I would like him to tell you himself, Dr. Houston the floor is all yours."

The assembled staff and others clap loudly and cheer at the mention of his name. Tom is waiting for the applause to subside as he looks over the faces of those here in the lobby. He spots Beth and immediately smiles and waves, but she just stares back fearing the worst. "Thank you, Dr. McMasters, before I begin, I have a few things to clear up. First, I would like to apologize to everyone for an unforgivable mistake I made." The crowd turns to each other in puzzlement, whispering what the mistake could possibly be.

"I gave a speech last week at a fundraiser for my campaign. During the speech I took time to thank Nurse Della Russo and her staff for their tireless effort on behalf of Officer Josephs. She was totally unaware that I was going to mention her name and she was very upset with me. She was not upset for herself, but she was angry that I failed to give proper mention to the doctors and nursing team, the hospital staff and all those that make this a great place to work or come to when you are sick and in need of care. I told this to Dr. McMasters and now I'm telling it to you that it was an unintentional omission…believe me I was duly chastised by Nurse Della Russo."

Beth is turning various shades of crimson as the crowd laughs and turns to her and starts to clap and cheer.

"Okay, enough with my groveling. I am very pleased to make the following announcement. Today I am presenting a check from my foundation, ACTELECT World Visions, to Dr. McMasters made out to Huntington Hospital in the amount of $10,000,000 to be used in whatever manner he and the hospital's board of directors' see fit."

First the crowd listens in disbelief, then a look of amazement can be read on each and every face and that is followed by tumultuous applause and uproarious cheering. Beth stands there, her jaw dropping nearly to the floor, in confusion and incredulity. Dr. McMasters steps away from the podium and works his way through the crowd to stand next to Beth. He is overwhelmed at being given this gift and he seems overcome with emotion as he gives Beth a hug. Beth looks at her boss in utter disbelief and he smiles as he puts his arm on her shoulder and they both continue to listen as Dr. Houston speaks.

Dr. Houston raises his hand and gestures to the gathering, "May I have quiet please?" The crowd dutifully obeys as they face Tom in rapt attention.

"I have also directed the foundation to set up scholarship funds for the daughters of Nick and Theresa Josephs. Nick called them his beauties, what a wonderful and devoted father he must have been." The group goes wild at the news. "The foundation has also arranged for the mortgage on Nick and Theresa's home to be fully paid as well as any taxes that are levied as a result of this gift. We cannot bring Nick back, but we can make sure his family is taken care of. Again, I want to thank you all for what you do every day and in memory of Nicholas Josephs we make this small token to his family for the great sacrifice he has made for us." The people in the lobby burst out in spontaneous applause and cheers at hearing the news of Tom's magnanimous gift to the hospital and his very thoughtful gift to the Josephs' family.

A large group surrounds Dr. Houston; all wanting to shake his hand and thank him. There are even a few asking for his autograph, but he politely refuses trying to work his way through the crowds to where Beth and Dr. McMasters are standing. Finally, after what seems like a long time, Tom is standing next to Beth and smiling at her and Dr. McMasters. Beth is in shock and speechless so Tom breaks the ice,

"Well Harold, how do you think that went?"

"Tom, words can't express the gratitude we all feel at your most generous gift. Saying thank you seems so inadequate, but I do thank you, as a matter of fact, we all thank you for your kindness and for taking the time out of your very busy schedule just to be here with us." Dr. McMasters still appears overwhelmed and Beth is still in the state of shock. There is always a cadre of press that follow Tom Houston and his entourage, but before Tom has a chance to answer, a photographer from Newsday asks to take a photo of their small group. Beth stands between Tom and Harold and Tom puts his arm around Beth and they simply smile for the camera.

"Beth, I hope you are not angry with me. I really want to clear the air and I want to show my true appreciation so don't be mad that I didn't let you in on my surprise."

Beth seems to somewhat snap out of her state, "Dr. Houston I, I can't believe, I mean…" She stops for a moment and takes a breath, "What I want to say is thank you so much for this wonderful gift to Huntington Hospital. You have no idea how much this means to the hospital and all the staff. I don't know how Dr. McMasters will spend such a generous donation, but I do know it will be spent well, to help provide the equipment and services to help the sick and injured and to continue to make this hospital a place where all of Huntington and all Long Island can be proud."

Dr. Harold McMasters wipes a tear from his eye and gives Beth a kiss on the cheek. Tom is smiling at her, "Well, to both of you, you're very welcome. Now if you approve, I'd like to go up to thank your staff in person and to make amends for my faux pas."

Beth doesn't know how to answer so she looks at Dr. McMasters for some kind of sign as to what she should do. He looks at her and says, "Beth, I know you are busy, but do you think it will be alright if Tom, I mean Dr. Houston, spends a few minutes with your staff?"

Beth tries to look stern as she folds her arms and says, "Of course, as long as he doesn't get as rowdy as he did the first time he visited" and she now smiles at both of the men. Tom burst out laughing and Harold seems puzzled at what apparently is an inside joke.

Dr. McMasters put on his sternest professorial face and asks, "Well Tom, do you agree not to get rowdy?" Tom looks at Beth, "It will be very difficult as it seems I have a number of aficionadas in your unit, but I will do my best to keep the decorum you require." Beth, Harold and Tom now all laugh and they all get ready to go to the 4th floor station. Harold decides to join Tom and his staff, along with Beth so he can tell everyone on duty the good news.

The elevator doors open on the 4th floor and there to greet Tom is nearly the entire staff of the critical care unit. Nurse Breuer is the first to speak, "Don't worry Dr. McMasters and Beth, we have a few of the staff who have reluctantly agreed to stay and keep an eye on things while we get to greet Dr. Houston."

Dr. McMasters realizes that the group knows what he is going to say so he makes it brief. "I guess you've all heard the wonderful news, through Dr. Houston's generosity Huntington Hospital has been given a very substantial gift and we will put it to very good use. Tom asked to come and speak with you for a short moment and then it's back to work." A few groans could be heard, but everyone is anxious to hear from their special guest.

"Thank you, Dr. McMasters. Well, I think I should start with an apology to you all. Beth let me have it with both barrels for not giving you all the proper commendation during my speech last week and for that I am sorry. I know how hard you work, I've seen it for myself, and I regret not saying it for all to hear."

Someone in the back of the crowd yells out, "You're forgiven; now how about buying us a drink after work?" All the people now start to laugh, but Tom quiets them down. "Listen, I promised Beth and Harold that I wouldn't allow this group to get too raucous so let's keep it down, okay?" Everyone stops laughing and agrees to keep it quiet. Tom continues, "Well, you know, that suggestion by someone in the back...by the way, who was that?"

Kimberly Hastings, a nurse with the unit, speaks out, "Hi Dr. Houston, it's me, Kim, remember we spoke the last time you were here? I asked if you wanted to go for a drink, remember?"

There is laughter at the comment and Tom says, "Of course I remember and that's why I came to see you all. I know that Dr. McMasters would frown at having alcohol while on duty so I asked him if I could cater a lunch for you all. He happily agreed so, with Beth's permission, I'll ask Nancy and her team to set up something in the nurses' lounge. Please enjoy!" In subdued tones, the entire group smiles at the news and cheers their benefactor. Tom wades his way through the small group of doctors, nurses, technicians and orderlies that are present. He shakes hands with everybody and seems very comfortable talking to each person as if he knows them personally.

Beth is standing with Dr. McMasters who says to her, "Beth, I want to thank you too. Tom told me how upset you were and he said that he wanted to make amends. Can you imagine? Amends! $10,000,000 in amends and it's all because of you! I can't thank you enough..." but Beth stops him. "Please Dr. McMasters; I had nothing to do with this. You must believe me; I am in the same state of shock as you."

At that moment Nurse Diane Breuer slides her arm into Beth's and says to Harold, "Dr. McMasters, you won't mind if I steal Beth for a few moments, do you?"

Dr. McMasters smiles, "Of course not; Beth. Enjoy the lunch and we'll continue our little talk later." He leaves Beth and Nurse Breuer and walks over to a group of doctors that are speaking with Tom.

Diane looks around and checks to see that no one is listening and she knowingly smiles at Beth and says, "Nice going girl, you really hit the jackpot this time. What's going on huh? Come on you can tell me." Beth looks questioningly at her friend. "What do you mean 'what's going on?' Nothing's going on."

Diane just smiles "Come on, I can see the way he looks at you." Diane motions with her head towards Tom Houston. "You can tell me I promise I won't tell another soul…well actually the whole department is coming up with their own ideas about you two."

Beth is now getting embarrassed; she knows she should just ignore this so all she says is "I refuse to dignify your snarky comment with an answer." With that, Beth tries to muster up enough of her own dignity and she slinks back into the crowd to get away from Diane who is just standing there smiling.

Dr. Houston is circulating among the nurses and other personnel thanking each and every one for their service and their caring nature. The staff is enamored by this man and they all are expressing their gratitude for his gift to the hospital. Tom is talking to one of the staff, a woman named Addie Simmons who works in patient services. They seem to be having a pleasant conversation and Tom looks as if he's enjoying himself. Beth is very uncomfortable as she walks over to Tom Houston while he is talking to Addie and interrupts. "Dr. Houston, may I have a word with you?"

"Of course, Beth, Addie it's wonderful speaking with you and I hope to continue our discussion soon." Addie is captivated by Tom's attention and she reluctantly shakes his hand and walks away.

"Beth, I want you to know…" but she stops him in mid-sentence.

"Dr. Houston…"

"Come on Beth, call me Tom."

"Alright, Tom it is. Tom, I can't tell you how much your kindness has overwhelmed us all. You are very generous and the Huntington Hospital staff and management are most grateful, but I'm afraid that it is causing some unexpected consequences for me."

Tom seems genuinely puzzled, "Consequences, what consequences can those be?"

Beth looks in both directions and speaking in a low whisper she tells Tom, "Well, to tell the truth, I am sure they are unintended on your part, but it seems that there is spreading gossip concerning rumors about…" Now Beth is turning flush with embarrassment as she continues to whisper to Tom, "…about us. People seem to think that there is something going on between us, romantically that is."

Tom smiles at Beth and just says, "I should only be so lucky!"

"Please don't make a joke of this. I need to work with these people and I need to be taken seriously, I have a boyfriend that I love and I am not used to being in the spotlight like this."

Tom turns serious, "Listen Beth, I made it no secret that I like you very much. I certainly did not mean to give your staff the impression that there is something romantic going on, although hope does spring eternal. If the people you work with want to make something out of our relationship, then let them. My advice to you is to just ignore them all and it will go away…take it from someone who has this happen to him all the time."

Beth is still anxious, but she becomes somewhat placated. "Okay, I guess I am making too much of this. Thank you for talking to me about all this."

"You're welcome. Oh, by the way, I am having a dinner party at my home in Garden City and I'd love you to come. It's next Friday evening at 7PM."

Beth is now grinding her teeth. Tom notices her reticence and he says, "Listen, it is a very special dinner party I'm throwing for Dr. Spencer Price. I know he would love to have you there; after all you are his biggest fan. Now come to think of it, if there is any romance here, I think you need to be careful around Spencer."

Beth bursts out laughing and Tom seems relieved. "And, you can invite that boyfriend of yours. I know that I've met him, what's his name again? Pasquale, Mustafa, Radcliff? I forget."

Beth smiles at their inside joke, "Its Chris."

"Oh yeah, that's it, Chris. You can invite him even though I will be crest fallen." Tom smiles, however, Beth still cannot shake her feelings of unease because of all that's happening, but she tells Tom that she will go. Now all that's left is to tell Chris and that has her worried.

"That's great both Spencer and I are delighted, now I know I've taken up enough of your and your staff's time so I'll say my goodbyes to all and I'll have Nancy send you the information."

"Okay, thanks for the lunch and the invite and again, thank you so very much for your most generous gift. I really don't know what to say, it seems thank you is not enough."

Tom reaches out to shake Beth's hand, "You're welcome and thanks are enough." With that Tom walks over to where Dr. McMaster is standing and they say their goodbyes to one another. Tom then thanks everyone for their hard work and dedication and that he hopes that they enjoy their lunch.

Once Dr. Houston's entourage leaves the floor everything goes back to normal or what counts as normal around the critical care unit. Beth is still very anxious about all that's happening and she still needs to call Chris so she tells herself, "Well there's no time like the present" and she picks up the phone. Chris' phone rings, but it goes straight into voice mail and, on some level, Beth is relieved. She puts the phone back on its cradle and seems lost in thought when she hears a voice over the intercom at the nurses' station,

"Emergency in Room 418, code red, patient has stopped breathing and will need to be intubated stat!"

All of a sudden Beth's complications seem small as she rushes down the hospital hallway.

CHAPTER 29

The phone rings in the shop and I answer as I usually do, "St. Aloysius Coins and Currency, how can I help you."

The person on the other ends says, "May I speak to Mr. Christopher Pella?"

"This is Chris Pella."

"Good morning Mr. Pella, my name is Natalie Ambrose; I am personal assistant to Mr. Harry Lieberman."

My heart skips not just one, but two beats. "Good morning to you Ms. Ambrose. How may I help you?"

Ms. Ambrose is all business, "Mr. Lieberman asked me to call you to ascertain your availability to travel. He would like to arrange for you to spend a few days with him to appraise the portion of his collection that you and Mr. Lieberman discussed when you met in New York City. It seems that the items in his collection that are going to be set aside for consignment are far more extensive than he initially anticipated and Mr. Lieberman feels you and he will need more time to estimate its worth. He has certain days that are free and I would like to know if you can accommodate his very busy schedule." Ms. Ambrose sounds as if she is giving me no alternative, but I am practically jumping up and down with excitement and I would agree to meet him on New Year's Eve if necessary. I give her the answer I am sure she wants to hear, "I am totally at Mr. Lieberman's disposal, whenever he is available."

I sense Ms. Ambrose is looking at her calendar and she replies, "He has Friday March 21st and Saturday March 22nd available. Mr. Lieberman is leaving on an extended business trip on Sunday March 23rd so that would be most suitable. I can arrange to have you fly back out the same day Mr. Lieberman leaves."

"Let me check." I pretend to look at my schedule and say, "That works for me."

"Splendid, I will make your travel arrangements and have a car pick you up at the airport. Mr. Lieberman would be delighted to welcome you as his guest at his country home or, if you prefer, I can make reservations for you at the St. Regis."

I am floored that I am invited to Harry's home. "That's really kind of him, but I really don't want to put Harry, I mean Mr. Lieberman, out."

Ms. Ambrose says, "Mr. Lieberman made it a point to tell me that he hopes you would stay at his home. It seems you have made a very favorable impression on him so please do not feel you would be a burden of any sort."

I smile, "Then I would be honored. Please thank Mr. Lieberman for his kindness and I am looking forward to our meeting."

"I will be sure to pass on your information and your acceptance of his invitation. I will be forwarding your travel documents so may I have your complete contact information." I give Natalie Ambrose my information and I agree to confirm as soon as I get confirmation of the travel arrangements she is making. We say our goodbyes and I hang up the phone and I just stare into space. What has just happened? In the span of a little more than a week my life is taking a significant turn, for the better…possibly much better. I can't wait to tell Beth so I pick up the phone again.

Her phone rings and goes into voice mail so I leave her a message. "Beth, you're not gonna believe this! I just got a call from Harry Lieberman's personal assistant and she wants me to come to meet with Harry. We're going to discuss the consignment of the coins and currency he wants to give me to sell. Can you believe it! He even invited me to stay at his country home.

He has a country home and I've never stayed at someone's country home. Call me when you get a chance. Love you."

I hang up the phone and that's when the world stands still.

Many people are lined up to see her. Those nuns in the convent beg her to see the faithful, to guide them, to help them achieve holiness to become one with God.

The sisters implore her, "Please see those who wait. They will hear your words in prayer and they will provide gifts to help in our time of need. One after another they enter her quarters; the nun is loved by all and she takes joy in being loved. The nun seems to be taken with all the praise and reverence the faithful accord her. As time goes by, the woman becomes consumed by her worldly existence and she chooses to ignore God.

The vision changes and I am taken to the side of a sick bed. The woman is lying there motionless; she has been this way for more than three years as her illness has caused paralysis. In past visions, I've witnessed these types of sufferings that bring on greater spirituality among the Sainted, but this is not the case for her. It is then I hear her words spoken in whispers.

"Prayer is an act of love, words are not needed. Even if sickness distracts from thoughts, all that is needed is the will to love."

Time seems to speed up and I observe many events in the nun's life. Over the years her face is transformed to reveal the suffering she endures, but her paralysis is gone. In spite of this gift, she had ceased to pray long ago.

"I am no longer worthy; I do not deserve God's mercy or His love. I have been tempted to sin. I have succumbed to flattery, vanity and gossip, all at a cost of prayerful guidance." It is the woman lying there, a nun, who sees herself as a wicked sinner who turns away from God, not deserving of His benediction.

The door to her small room opens and in walks the priest, Gaspar Daza. He sits in a chair and looks directly at her. At first, she turns away, but then she faces the priest and looks into his eyes and begs him to hear her confession. He smiles in a kindly manner but tells her, "I cannot hear your confession, but you must return to prayer for it is the road back to God and it is His plan for you." He kneels on the cold stone floor and asks the nun to kneel with him and pray.

She kneels, but she is afraid as she tells the priest, "I am more anxious for the hour of prayer to be over than I am to remain there. I don't know what heavy penance I would not have gladly undertaken rather than practice prayer." But it is over time that the mystic's visions and thoughtful prayers turn the woman back to God again.

I wait for St. Teresa of Avila as she steps out of her earthly body and stands at my side. I witness her experiencing a true epiphany and how the meaning of prayer becomes the center of her being. She comes to understand spiritual espousals as a mystic and she says to me, "I have been so blessed to have been chosen to know the mystical union of love between God and His children to be raised to the highest degree of contemplation."

I had to admit to Saint Teresa that I did not understand the meaning behind what she has shown me. She looks lovingly at me and says, "Christopher, it is mental prayer that, in my opinion, is nothing else than an intimate sharing between friends; it means taking time frequently to be alone with Him who we know loves us. The important thing is not to think much, but to love much and so do that which best stirs you to love. Love is not great delight, but desire to please God in everything. It is how God reveals Himself." I nod as if I understand, but I am as a clueless as before.

We talk for hours as she tries to make me understand how she among The Sainted evolved in her relationship with God. "I know with all my heart that I am a sinner and I fear that it was delusions that made me think so. I feel I was cursed with the sins of vanity and self-love, but it was Satan who tempted me to believe that these were only sins in my imagination. It is through God's love and mercy that I persevered in prayer and He rewarded me. I have always thought that in my sinfulness, the grace of God would be a torment to me. I know now that I was wrong and that God was always by my side."

I am puzzled as I often am when many of The Sainted tell me of their trials and of the faith that ultimately rewards them with God's love. "Why have you chosen to show me these events? What are you trying to tell me?" It is always a mystery at first and I try to understand what the implications are in my life.

St. Teresa turns very serious and says this, "You are being shown my personal battle with temptation because it is you that will have to confront temptations of your own. What will come will not only test the man's will to overcome evil, but it will test your own faith to assure evil does not triumph. I do not envy your task and know that my prayers and all of the prayers of The Sainted are with you."

"But…" it is all I can say as St. Teresa begins to disappear in a circle of light, but not before I see a tear roll from her eye.

The world goes back to normal; however, the vision lingers in my mind. It is not as disturbing as some of the other visions I've been shown, but it is one of the most enigmatic. Prayer? Temptation? I always know that God is by my side, that The Sainted are my guardians and that prayer is what's gotten me though so many of my troubles. I ask myself what does it all mean.

Suddenly Lamb of God and Fr. Langford's investigation into the possibility of the antichrist walking among us comes flooding back in my mind. What can the possible connection be with the horrors happening around the world and the temptations St. Teresa spoke of? I pick up my phone thinking that I would call Uncle Al and talk it over with him, but I cancel the connection. What could I possibly tell him that would be of value? I need some time to try and figure it out myself, but I am at a loss as where to start?

As I am trying to wrap my head around the situation my phone chimes, I see it's Beth and I hit accept.

"Hi Beth, thanks for calling back."

"Hi Chris, sorry I couldn't call sooner, but we had an emergency."

"Really? How's the patient?"

"Well, it will be touch and go for a while, but we are all hopeful. Say a prayer, won't you?"

"I sure will. By the way there is a reason that I called you!" I am getting excited just thinking about it.

"YES! I know! Congratulations, what a great thing to happen to you. So, tell me, what's the deal?" Beth seems just as excited as I am.

"Well, out of the blue I get this call and Harry's assistant tells me that he wants to fly me to Chicago to look over the part of his collection he wants to consign. I need to be gone for two days and Harry even invited me to stay at his home. Can you imagine me staying at a billionaire's home?!"

Beth laughs, "Well I hope you exercise better table manners than you have when we eat out."

I pretend that I'm insulted. "What do you mean? Are you telling me that I have poor table manners?" I then bring up a belch that I've have been holding onto since last Thanksgiving.

"That's disgusting!" Beth is cracking up and so am I. "Chris, I am so happy for you and this opportunity, I really am. I know that you will do great."

"Thanks, I will do my best. Hey, want to go out and celebrate tonight? I'd love to see you."

"Sure. I get off at 6PM so I can meet you wherever."

"Terrific, let meet at Mabella's."

"Gee, why did I think you were going to suggest that place?"

We continue talking…mostly me…but when there is a lull in the conversation, I suspect that there is something troubling Beth, "What's up Beth? Why so quiet?"

"Well, to tell you the truth, I have some news for you, but you may not be too happy."

Now I become worried, "Whoa, what is it?"

"Well, we had a special visitor at the hospital today."

"Okay, who was it."

Beth cringes and through clenched teeth she tells me, "Dr. Tom Houston." I immediately think that I need to be calm and not overreact.

Now it's my turn to speak through gritted teeth and I say, "Oh isn't that nice."

"Chris, it really was nice, I'm sure it will be all over the news. He came to the hospital and gave us a gift of $10,000,000. He also gave Nick Joseph's children the funds to pay for their college and he paid off the mortgage on their home. It is a wonderful gesture on his part and I think he did it because of my reaction to being singled out at the fundraiser."

I don't know how to react to the news, but realizing that it is a very generous gesture I say, "Beth, that's really wonderful. I guess I need to reevaluate the man."

Beth sighed, "There's something else I need to tell you."

"What, that he bought you one of those Caribbean islands that are still uninhabited?"

"No, we're invited to his home for an event honoring Dr. Spencer Price."

"Really, you're kidding."

"No."

I have to admit to myself that I am getting intrigued by the whole idea of becoming Tom Houston's best friend. I'm sure Beth is somewhere between a rock and a hard place; on one hand she would love to go, but on the other she knows I won't want to go. So, I throw her a curve ball, "I'd love to go; when is this dinner?"

Beth can't believe what she just heard. "You're kidding, really? You want to go?"

"Sure, I'd love to go. When is it?"

"I can't believe it; I was dreading having to call you and you are being so sweet. Hold on, did aliens just take over my boyfriend's brain and body? Wait, he has no brain…just his body."

"Ha, ha very funny, so when's the celebration?"

"Friday, March 21st. Don't worry you won't have to close up early because it doesn't start until 7:30PM and we can drive to…"

I stop her in mid-sentence, "Beth, I can't go."

Beth gasps, "Why, why can't you go?"

"That's the day I flying to Chicago to meet with Harry over the collection." Beth can hear the disappointment in my voice.

"Can't you tell Harry that you need to come a day later and stay?" She is desperate to find a way to have me at the dinner party.

"No, he leaves the next day on a business trip besides I think I would be insulting him if I try to cancel now.

Beth and I stay silent for a while when she says, "I won't go. I'll just tell Tom that I can't go, I'll just make up some excuse."

I smile to myself and realize that I am lucky to have such a great person to love me. "Thanks Beth, I know you are doing that because of me and I appreciate your effort. You really should go, after all he did make that generous gift to the hospital and Dr. Spicy Rice, I mean Dr. Spencer Price, will be there; but you need to promise me one thing."

Beth is anxious to promise me anything so I tell her, "You have to promise to look as ugly as possible. Okay?"

Beth laughs at my joke and says, "I promise, it will be hard, but I promise."

"Okay then, it's settled. I'll see you at 6PM."

Through the phone I can hear Beth's voice start to crack, "Thank you Chris, I love you," and she hangs up.

CHAPTER 30

I am getting depressed. The thought of Beth going to that dinner party hosted by Mr. Perfect is getting me down. When these types of things happen, I do what I usually do and call Uncle Al.

The phone rings and he picks it up, "Chief Barese."

"Hey Uncle Al, how's it going?"

My uncle is able to read me like a book. "What the hell's the matter with you?"

"Oh nothing" and I just sigh into the phone.

"Nothing? Come on, who are you kidding. Something is wrong and you called so you could dump it on me like you always do, right?"

"Yeah, I guess I do."

"Well, give it up."

"Well, you know that I met Harry Lieberman of "Harry's Place" right?"

"Yeah, you only mentioned it about a thousand times."

"Well, he invited me to his country estate to go over his collection. He's flying me out to Chicago, he's invited me to stay at his country estate and we're going to work on evaluating the coins and currency he wants to put up for sale. It might be a lot more than he originally thought and I could make a fortune in commissions."

Uncle Al with all due sympathy says, "You poor bastard, how could that piece of shit do that to you?"

"That's not why I'm upset."

"So, what's the problem then?"

"Well, I'm leaving for Chicago the same night that Beth is invited to a dinner party for Dr. Spencer Price."

"Who?"

"Dr. Spencer Price. I can't believe my uncle doesn't know who Dr. Spencer Price is."

Even sympathetic, Uncle Al says, "Does he do colonoscopies? I must admit that I could use a good colonoscopy."

I stifle the urge to laugh as I try to sound like an authority on the man, so I tell Uncle Al, "No, Dr. Price is only the world-renown doctor who is close to finding a cure for cancer."

Uncle Al sounds pretty impressed, "Wow, sorry for making a joke. That sounds really awesome for Beth so what's the problem?"

"It's being hosted by Tom Houston, you know, Mr. Perfect in everything."

"Oh, now I see the problem, you're jealous. I can't say as I blame you. He certainly is the perfect man, at least compared to you."

"Come on Uncle Al, don't kid around. I really am upset about this. I'm trying to be calm and understanding, even be happy for Beth, but I still have this jealous streak in me that I can't seem to shake."

"Listen Chris, can I tell you a little story?"

I cringe at the prospect because Uncle Al can get a bit off the subject with his stories, but I have no choice and sigh, "Okay."

"I have a good friend of mine, his Hebrew name is Shealtiyel, but everyone calls him Danny. Now Danny is from Israel and if you have ever known anyone from the Middle East you know that they are big on using stories to make a point."

I sigh, "Okay" again.

"Well Danny and I are talking and I'm waxing philosophical about how ethnic looking I am, you know a typical Italian looking guy. Danny, who you wouldn't recognize as anything but Israeli says, 'let me tell you a story.' So, he tells me that when he came to this country from Israel, he had no money so he spent most of his free time watching television.

Well, one Sunday night a long time ago he's home watching TV; Danny is watching '60 Minutes'; you know "60 Minutes?"

I sigh again, "Yeah, I know "60 Minutes."

"It seems that there is a report being given by Mike Wallace, you know Mike Wallace?"

I sigh for a fourth time, "Yeah, I know Mike Wallace."

"Well Mike Wallace is conducting an interview with someone. As this person is being interviewed, the camera goes from Mike to this guy sitting in a chair. Danny says the man literally took his breath away! Danny tells me this man has the face of an angel, the body of an Adonis, crystal clear blue eyes, tall and blond…literally the most handsome man he's ever seen."

"Yeah, so what?"

"Well, Danny tells me that Mike Wallace is interviewing this perfect man about how he just killed his whole family."

For a moment I don't understand, but then I make the connection and know what Uncle Al is trying to tell me. I smile to myself, thankful that I have such a great uncle and friend to count on for advice.

I'm sure Uncle Al is smiling at the other end of the phone when he says, "Get it?"

I am now smiling too, "I get it. Thanks Uncle Al, you always have a way of bringing me back off the ledge."

"You're welcome. Now what have you heard from your friends from up there?" I'm sure he's looking up at the ceiling in his office.

I collect my thoughts and I tell Uncle Al about St. Teresa. "I have to admit that I really am puzzled by her vision. She's saying that I need to fight temptations and that it will get pretty bad. She told me that The Sainted will be praying for me and it sounds like I'll need all the prayers I can get."

Uncle Al becomes very serious, "Chris if all that we know and all that we fear is possible I am really worried for you. How can your friends expect you to face the kind of evil forces that are written about in the Bible? How can you be expected to deal with all that, especially on your own?"

I tell Uncle Al "You know, I never think of myself as being alone. I know it sounds weird, but I have the powers of Heaven with me and I have these amazing saints who guide me and protect me."

"And you've got me backing you up. Don't forget that."

"I never do…I love you."

Uncle Al says goodbye and ends the call as he always does by saying, "Love you too."

I look at the clock and it's nearly 5PM so I put everything of value back in the safe and clear my desk for the next day's work. I have to meet Beth in about an hour and I resolve that I will be as positive as I can. It won't be easy but I'll try.

I lock the door to the shop and start to walk towards where my car is parked and I bump into Fr. Langford. I am genuinely happy to see him, "Hi Father, it's great to see you, how are things."

Fr. Aiden seems delighted to see me too and says, "Christopher, what a wonderful surprise! How are you and how is that lovely girlfriend of yours, Beth?"

"Oh, we're both fine Father. As a matter of fact, I am meeting Beth for dinner. Would you like to join us, she'd love to see you?"

Fr. Langford has packages in both hands and says, "Oh no, I just came to town to do some shopping. It seems that my well-worn shoes, socks and shirts all managed to develop holes in them at the same time, so I am forced to spend some of my valuable time buying new ones. Alas, it is my penance for being a slacker." We both laugh, but I think this might be an opportunity to talk so I ask him.

"Father, do you have a few minutes to talk. I have something on my mind and I'd like to get your thoughts."

"Why Christopher, I would be most happy to provide you with any guidance that I might be able to give."

"Great, why don't we get out of the cold" We walk back to the door to my shop and I welcome Father Aiden inside. I have a small sitting area with a small couch and two chairs where the old guys who come here love to sit down and talk and I offer the priest a seat.

"Well Christopher, you have quite a nice enterprise going. So, to quote a well-worn phrase, how's business?"

"Actually Father, business is very good. I don't do much in the way of sales out of the shop, but I still buy up collections from estates and collectors. I've expanded my online business by using some social media to get the word out and I write a blog which helps to grow sales at my end. All this seems to be developing into a network for fellow collectors so all in all things are going great."

"That is splendid. Now, not to beat around the proverbial bush, what is on that very fertile mind of yours?"

"Well to tell you the truth, this might be sort of a confession, can we do that here?"

Fr. Aiden, "Of course we can."

I make the sign of the cross and say, "In the name of the Father, and of the Son, and of the Holy Spirit. My last confession was 6 months ago."

"What sins do you have to confess?"

I figure that I'd confess my sins, and I did, but I really want to talk about my jealousness. "Father, I am having a tough time getting over being jealous about Beth."

Fr. Aiden asks, "Why is it that you are jealous?"

I go into the whole story and tell Father Langford about Tom Houston, him asking Beth out and my reaction. I tell him about the fundraiser, my stupid comment and Beth's response. I tell him about the dinner party and how I can't go, but it's very difficult getting over my feelings of jealousy at Beth spending time with Tom Houston.

Father Aiden takes a breath before he gives me his thoughts. "Christopher, when one is in the state of jealousy, he or she can conjure up images that can have no basis in fact. These imaginations grow and grow until they are so far removed from reality that they take on a life of their own. Let me ask you a question; has Beth ever given you any indication that she is anything other than committed to your relationship?"

I answer immediately, "No."

"Ah, I was hoping you would say that. Now a second question; do you love her?"

I answer immediately again, "Yes."

"Ah, I knew you would say yes. Question number three; do you believe that Beth loves you?

I am a bit slower to answer this, but I say, "Yeah, I think she does."

"Now the fourth and final question; what has this Dr. Thomas Houston have that you don't?"

I laugh out loud. "Are you kidding? He's about the handsomest man you've ever seen. He is amazingly successful. He is a multi-multi-multi-millionaire; by the way, he just gave $10,000,000 to Huntington Hospital. I can go on, but you get the idea."

Father Aiden smiles, "So you are worried that you are not handsome enough, successful enough and rich or smart enough for Beth."

"No…well, I don't know. I guess I do feel inferior, my lord who wouldn't? Just look at what this guy has done in his life and now look at what I've accomplished." Now that I say this aloud, I'm really feeling sorry for myself.

Father Aiden is no fan of self-pity, "My, my, Christopher you are really a poor excuse for a human being. Let us take the time to evaluate your life in terms of what you have or have not accomplished."

I just sit there with my eyes cast down knowing that I am going to be given a pep-talk by the priest.

Ever wise Father Aiden says, "Ah Christopher, you think I am going to give you a pep-talk, is that it."

I look up, "Yeah, I kinda figure that's coming next."

"Well then, dear lad, you will be sorely disappointed, I am not going to put salve on your bruised ego I am merely going to recount what your blessings are. Let me see, you have family and friends that love and admire you and that should account for something. You may not have the material and professional successes of this Dr. Houston, but success is a relative thing and given your life and circumstances I would say you are very successful, both materially and spiritually. I know you can easily dismiss what I am saying, but if you do you will realize nothing. You will become mired in self-pity, you will be consumed by jealousy and, in the end, you will lose the love of a beautiful woman."

When Father Aiden says that I am risking the love of Beth, his words, St. Elizabeth's and those of Uncle Al, come rushing into my mind. Given that I am consumed by jealousy didn't allow me to see the truth, but now it all seems so clear. "Father, from the heart, thanks so much. I heard the same thing from folks I admire and our talk brings it all home, it really helps."

Father Aiden reminds me, "Christopher, this is more than a talk; it is a confession so for penance say ten 'Our Father's' and ten 'Hail Mary's.' The priest gives me a blessing and says, "May God give you pardon and peace and I absolve you from your sins in the name of the Father, and of the Son, and of the Holy Spirit. Now go in peace to love and serve the Lord" and we both say, "Amen."

Father Aiden and I get up and we embrace. I thank him again and he smiles and tells me that all will be well as long as I follow my heart and use my head. As he leaves the shop, I consider the day and the lessons and I really do feel better. It is 5:30PM by the time I get to my car so I figure that I will go directly to the restaurant, park my car and wait inside. I am early and the place is less than half-full so I have my choice of tables. Rich, our favorite waiter, is on duty so he asks me where I would like to sit and I tell him that I want a quiet table in the corner.

A few moments later Beth walks in and she comes over to the table. I kiss her on the cheek and we sit down. Beth looks nervous and she speaks first, "Chris, I don't know what to say. I really am upset that you can't come to Dr. Price's dinner party."

I think to myself "...you mean Tom Houston's dinner party," but I think better than to make a snarky comment so I say, "I wish I could be there too, but it seems that the gods are conspiring against us" and I smile trying to make Beth feel at ease with the situation.

"Thanks Chris, I want to feel okay about all this, but I think that you are still upset about all the attention Tom, I mean Dr. Houston has given me. I just want you to know that you are all that matters to me and I love you very much."

I hear these words that Beth has spoken and they make me happy. I reach over and hold Beth's hand, "I know that and I love you too. I have gotten over my jealousy and I want you to go to the dinner and have a terrible time, I mean it, the worst time you have ever had at any party. Would you do that for me?"

Beth laughs out loud, loud enough for the people sitting at nearby tables to look in our direction. She quickly covers her mouth with one hand and holds mine with the other. When she lowers her hand from her face, she dazzles me with one of her beautiful smiles, and tells me, "I promise I will."

We sit, eat, drink wine and talk for more than two hours. It is one of the most pleasurable times we've ever spent together. I pay the bill and walk Beth to her car. "Thanks for a great evening."

Beth puts her arms around my waist and brings her body close to mine. "You know it's customary for a man to kiss a woman at the end of their time together. He could even cop a feel if the mood's right."

I put my hand to my chin as if I am considering the opportunity. "I must admit the thought of copping a feel does sound very appealing, but in surveying the surroundings I notice that we are parked in front of a Carvel Ice Cream store and it seems that a Girl Scout troop is having some soft serve." Sure enough, there are three girl scouts holding cones and staring wide eyed at Beth and I. Beth turns to see the trio licking their ice cream and she immediately gets very serious and she stands at attention to look me straight in the eye.

Beth, holding three fingers in salute, solemnly swears, "On my honor, I will try to serve God and my country, to help people at all times, and to live by the Girl Scout Law." Beth turns back to the girls at the window and they are all laughing and she laughs back. I touch Beth on the shoulder as she turns to face me and I kiss her and hold her tight for a long time. When we are done, we both look at the girls in the window and they are clapping and laughing at us and we just laugh back.

What a way to end the evening.

CHAPTER 31

always get to the airport early. I guess with all the extra security these days it pays to leave plenty of time.

Natalie Ambrose, Harry Lieberman's administrative assistant made arrangements for a direct flight from Islip MacArthur Airport on Long Island to Chicago. She phoned to apologize that there are no first-class seats on the plane, but it's is a short flight and the plane is only half full so I get to spread out and relax.

I have one piece of luggage that is too big to take onboard, so when I land, I go directly to baggage claim. I have a short wait and after I get my luggage, I'm instructed by Ms. Ambrose to look for a driver holding a placard with my name. As promised, there he is; a driver in a black suit with a white shirt and black tie.

"Good morning Mr. Pella. Here, let me take you bag."

"Thanks, and please call me Chris."

The driver doesn't answer me so I assume I will be Mr. Pella for the remainder of the trip. The car is a new, black Lincoln Town Car that was converted into a stretch limo and the interior is very plush, but in an understated way. I climb into the rear, facing the driver's seat, and as I sit the driver points to the various compartments that make a limousine a limousine.

"I trust you will be comfortable. There is sparkling and still water in the small refrigerator compartment as well as beer if you prefer. There is also scotch, vodka and bourbon in the crystal decanters in the console to your left. If you wish to have something to eat, there are prepackaged snacks in the side compartments or if you are hungry, I can stop at a local establishment for something more substantial. Of course, you can watch television, listen to the radio or if you prefer there is a selection of compact discs that you can play."

I think about a Chicago Deep Dish Pizza, but say, "I'm really not hungry and it's a bit early for alcohol, so I think I'll just stay with the water, but thanks for the offer."

"You're welcome, sir, now please sit back and enjoy the trip. I will close the partition so that you may have some privacy." I didn't have a chance to tell him it isn't necessary, but he closes the interior glass window before I can open my mouth.

Alone and inquisitive, I open all the compartments to be sure that the driver got it straight. I find the refrigerator and I open a bottle of sparkling water, put some ice into a crystal tumbler and take a long sip. I find the compartment with some packages of cheese and crackers so I dig into those. Imagine me, a nice Italian boy from the Bronx being chauffeured to the country home of a billionaire; only in America.

We slowly drive out of the congested area surrounding O'Hare and proceed on the highway going north in what I assume is the direction to Harry's home. As the housing becomes less dense and the surroundings become more countrified, I want to call Beth and tell her of my good fortune.

Her mobile phone rings and she picks up, "Hi! I'm so glad you called. How was the flight?"

"Hi Beth, the flight was uneventful, which is the way I want all flights to be, and I'm now sitting in the back of this Lincoln stretch limo sipping sparkling water from a genuine Waterford crystal tumbler. This is not the same Lincoln we took home from the Garden, oh no indeed! This is a custom stretch limo complete with all the accoutrements one of my status would come to expect."

"Oh, now you're a big shot and probably want to dump this poor Italian girl from Long Island. Well, if that's what you're thinking you've got another thing coming. If you ever want to see your 2014 Mustang again you will follow my instructions very carefully."

"What instructions?"

"They will come in a separate communication; in the meantime, stay close to your phone until further notice."

"Whoa, this is a side of you I've never seen…I kind of like it!"

We laugh and I reassure her that all is fine and that I want her to have a good time at the dinner party and to tell me all about it when we speak again. Beth promises and she says, "Thanks Chris, I love you."

"I love you too" and we hang up.

By the time my call is over we are well out of the Chicago city limits. The houses are fewer and far from each other, and they are enormous, I guess you'd call them mansions. These mansions are set further and further back from the road until all I see are the gated entrances and winding roads that soon disappear behind the trees. I'm curious about how much further we would be driving and I see the intercom so I press the button and ask the driver, "How much longer do we have to drive?"

The partition is still up, but the driver answers, "We should arrive at Mr. Lieberman's estate in approximately 40 minutes."

"Thanks" including the 40 minutes that would make at between 2 to 2 ½ hours for the entire drive, so I continue to sit back in my seat and just enjoy the ride. I had bought a newspaper at Islip MacArthur, but I was too excited on the flight to read it. Now I have the time and I am far more relaxed so I dig into the news of the day or the prior day, I guess. The time goes by quickly when the silence is broken by the driver, who says,

"We will be arriving at Mr. Lieberman's estate shortly."

The car stops and I look out the window and see a nine-foot iron fence that seems to go on and on. There are large iron gates affixed to two large stone columns and I watch the gates silently open to let the car in. We drive up a gravel road that is lined with tall stately oak trees and beautiful long leafed shrubs. We drive what seems to me a long time when the oak trees end and we arrive at a clearing and in the center of the clearing is a mansion, Harry Lieberman's country home. The huge building is constructed in such a way as to downplay its imposing configuration, but you immediately sense that it belongs to someone very important and, I might add, very rich. In the rear to the left is a lighted tennis court and beyond that is a putting green. Set further back and on the other side of his home is an Olympic size pool and pool house that mimics the style of the main house. I can see that there are gardens and paths that make their way around the property and, all in all, it is most impressive for a country home or any home for that matter.

The limo comes to a stop at the imposing front entrance and the door is opened by a person in rather formal attire. He rushes to open the car door and holds his hand out to assist my exit from the car. Being a real man, I refuse the help and get out of the limo glad to stretch my legs.

"Welcome to Tall Oaks Manor. Mr. Lieberman is awaiting your arrival and I will take your belongings to your room. Please follow me."

"What's your name?"

"My name is Jonathan."

"Well Jonathan, thanks and lead the way" and with that we walk into the entry foyer that looks something like a museum. The high ceilings are designed to include intricate octagon shaped coffered panels and amazing moldings. There are alcoves and pedestals where statues are on display and on the walls hang paintings that can only be originals and very old.

I stop to admire a statue that rests on a tall marble pedestal. I ask Jonathan if I could take a minute to look at this beautiful work of art and he dutifully stands to the side while I examine the statue.

A familiar voice from behind me begins to speak, "That is a bust of Marcus Vipsanius Agrippa. He was the Roman statesman, general and architect responsible for the construction of some of the most beautiful buildings in Rome. He was most notably the victor at the Battle of Actium against the forces of Mark Antony and Cleopatra." I turn and I'm facing Harry Lieberman who is smiling as he says, "I am so happy you could come; I am looking forward to the time we will be spending together and sharing our mutual passion."

"Oh, Mr. Lieberman it is really great to see you again. I am so thankful for the opportunity you've given me. I can't tell what an honor this is."

"Nonsense, it is I who am thankful for this welcomed diversion from my normal schedule. However, if we are to get along, you must call me Harry."

I smile and say, "If you insist, Harry." We shake hands and he tells Jonathan that he would escort me from here on. Jonathan takes my suitcase and walks up a flight of stairs to where I assume my room is.

"Well, I trust you had a pleasant flight?"

"I did. It was actually shorter than the ride to your estate. I have to tell you that the grounds and your home are truly beautiful…and the artwork…I can't believe you have such a collection. I mean, it's like a museum."

Harry smiles at me, "I love collecting beautiful things and I have all my life. Art for me is man's closest connection to the divine. It is representation of God in us for this talent must come from Him."

I am in shock, "God? You believe in God?"

Harry stops walking and is somewhat taken aback, "Of course I believe in God, why do you ask?"

"Well, I assume that, given that you are such an avid supporter of Tom Houston, that you're of the same mindset."

"Chris, I have my own set of beliefs and some of them do not mesh with Tom's, but I agree with him more than I disagree and that's why I support much of his progressive agenda."

Almost immediately I am sorry that I made the comment I did and I quickly apologize. "Harry, please forgive my comment. It is driven by the fact that I am a complete idiot."

Harry laughs, "We all have the right to be idiots once in a while. I'll tell you who's a real idiot, that Jerome Stellos. He feeds off the same capitalist notions he condemns and that made him phenomenally wealthy. Anyway, enough talk of politics, let me show you to your room."

We walk up this very elegant circular staircase and down a long hallway on the second floor. There are beautiful paintings and antique furniture decorating the walls and spaces between doors leading to a number of bedrooms. Harry takes the time to tell me of some of the artwork that he is especially fond of. At one point we stop at a door near the end of the hallway and Harry opens the door and tells me to enter. It is a room about half `the size of my entire condo with a king size canopy bed, marble fireplace, mahogany armoire and chest of draws, tiffany lamps, an antique desk and a magnificent oriental rug beneath our feet. There is a wall of closets and a door leading to what I presume is the bathroom.

"Whoa! Do I have to share this with anybody?"

Harry laughs, "No, it's all yours. I believe that your suitcase was brought up and your clothes are put away in the closet and chest of draws over there. You have a private bath and you may want to freshen up before we get down to business."

"I do and thank you so much for your hospitality."

"Think nothing of it. I'll see you in a half-hour in my library. Just go down the main staircase to your right and it's the second door to your left." Harry closes the door and leaves me to my freshening up. The first thing I do, however, is call Beth and let her know what an incredible home Harry has. I dial the phone, but I can't seem to connect so I continue to try and still no connection. I give up and decide to wash up and change my clothes. Harry's home sort of implies that you dress up more than dress down, so I put on a blazer, button down white and blue checked shirt, beige khakis and brown leather loafers.

I walk the long hallway, down the stairs and knock on the door to the library. I hear a voice telling me to come in, but it's not Harry's. When I open the door, I come face to face with one of the most beautiful women I have ever seen. I have this dumbfounded look on my face, but she seems use to this happening and she holds out her hand,

"Hi, I'm Amanda Sellers. Dad, I mean Harry asked me to greet you. He's been called away by some sort of problem on the grounds."

My mouth is still open until I realize that I must look stupid. "Hi, I mean hello, it's a pleasure to meet you. I don't go to the movies much, but I've seen your films and you are great. I mean you act great; I mean…" shit, even I don't know what I mean.

Amanda Sellers is smiling as she thanks me for my kind words and asks me to sit down on one of the twin sofas that face each other flanking a beautiful fireplace with a fabulous hand carved wooden mantle. I am flush with embarrassment at speaking and acting like a jerk, but she makes me feel at ease.

"You are Chris, Chris Pella, right?"

"Yeah, I'm also one of the seven dwarfs, just call me Dopey."

Amanda laughs, "Please don't be embarrassed on my account. Celebrity has its perks but it has its issues."

I half-smile and half-smirk and ask the obvious, "Issues? What issues could you possibly have?"

Amanda says, "Well, for example, I can walk down the street and be mobbed by a bunch of adoring fans which is great, but if I see a cute guy and would like to speak to him, he generally runs away thinking that I am beyond his reach. Well, let me tell you all he would have to do is put out his hand and I'd take it."

This place is full of surprises and I say, "You're kidding right? You would?"

"No, Chris Pella, I'm not kidding, so don't be uptight about this. Just relax and we can talk like normal human beings. Well, you'll be a normal human being and I'll be a goddess, how about that?" Now we both laugh and my initial tenseness seems to melt away.

"You're here to work with Dad on his collection, am I right?"

"Yeah, I consider this the greatest privilege of my life. To work with Harry Lieberman, one of the world's foremost authorities on collecting American coins and currency is like a dream come true."

Amanda is smiling at me, "You sound like a groupie."

"If ever there was a Harry groupie, it would be me. Your father is an amazing man."

"I never understood his passion for collecting coins, but I know it makes him happy and that is what is most important to me."

I smile at her, "It's nice to hear someone speak about a parent in that way."

Amanda turns serious, "I live in LA, but ever since mom died, I've tried to take over being the woman of the house and I know Dad appreciates it. Mom was a wonderful person and we both miss her every day. As a young woman she studied ballet and music and I guess I take my cues from her side."

I hear the sorrow in Amanda's voice and I tell her, "I am sorry to hear about your mother. I lost my parents a number of years ago, but I still miss them every day. They were wonderful people and they taught me how to be an adult. I try to live up to their expectations, but I'm sure they're disappointed because in some ways I'm still a kid."

Amanda smiles back at me and says, "I think that all men and women should have something of the little boy and little girl left inside them. It helps to deal with what is truly serious and what is not."

"I couldn't agree more." Amanda and I sit and talk for a short time when the library door opens and Harry walks in.

"Chris I'm sorry to keep you waiting. Ah! I see you've met Amanda."

"Yes, she has been the perfect hostess. I hope your emergency isn't too serious."

"No, no, all is well. It seems that the grounds keeper noticed a problem with the pool and it will delay the opening, but no worries, it will get fixed and we will get wet. Can I offer you anything to drink, perhaps wine, beer, soda anything?"

I still am intimidated by just being here so I think that proper etiquette would tell me to say, "No thanks Harry, I'm good."

"I'm going to have a glass of wine. Amanda, how about you?"

"Well, I would enjoy a glass of wine, are you sure we can tempt you Chris?"

I think to myself, well if I can't beat them, "Sure, you talked me into it."

Harry picks up the intercom and after a short conversation with the person on the other end, he tells him to bring us a bottle of wine.

Harry muses, "I must tell you in advance that I am a bit of a wine snob. When I was a young man, I was forced to drink the swill some people try to pass off as prime vintage. Now, however, I can afford to indulge my tastes so I've asked Jonathan to bring us the Château La Mission-Haut-Brion

- Pessac-Léognan 2009. It's a young wine born of grapes from the Bordeaux region of France and is a blend of cabernet sauvignon, merlot and cabernet franc. There is a story…"

"Father, enough!"

Harry turns a bit sullen. "Alright, alright it seems my daughter does not share the same enthusiasm as I do for exceptional wines."

Amanda's smiles not wanting to have her father unhappy in any way, so she reaches for his hand and says, "Dad, you must admit that even though I don't appreciate the stories behind the wines you serve, I do enjoy drinking them." We all laugh and agree with the statement. I hear a knock on the door and Jonathan enters with the bottle of wine, uncorked along with three beautiful Baccarat Massena Red wine glasses. As Harry points out beautiful glasses enhance the experience of drinking vintage wines as he ceremoniously takes charge of pouring the wine. He insists that we take time to savor the aroma, gaze at the color as he performs that ritual I've only seen on television. Harry insists that we perform the same wine tasting ritual in the proper manner, you know the one where you swirl the wine in the glass, place your nose near the glasses' rim, and take a small sip etc.

My initial reaction is, "Wow!"

Amanda's reaction is similar to mine, "I believe I should rethink my view of your wine stories!"

Harry just sits back, satisfied that his choice is a good one. "I am happy you both are enjoying the wine. It is young, but it will become a classic I assure you both." The next hour is a pleasant time where we talk of many things and enjoy each other's company while sipping our wine.

Amanda gets up from the couch and excuses herself, "Dad, I am going for my walk and then I'm going to relax a bit before dinner." She bends over and kisses him on the cheek and you can see the love Harry has for his daughter. I get up from the couch and I put my hand out to shake hers, but she places her hands on my shoulders and kisses my cheek. "That's for being Dad's groupie" and Amanda smiles and leaves the room.

I touch my cheek in surprise at Amanda's kiss and we both watch her leave the room. Harry looks questioningly at me, "What was that all about?" and I say, "I don't know, when we were talking before you came in, I told her how much I admire you and that it was the fulfillment of a dream for me to be here."

Harry takes another sip of wine and looks at me smiling and says "Chris, you are a fine young man. You know I had you checked out?"

I am a bit taken back, but not really surprised. I ask, "No, really, how did I do?"

Harry takes a deliberately long sip before he answers. He looks me straight in the eye, "You passed with flying colors; you don't think I would trust just anyone with the treasures from my collection. These treasures of mine represent the work of a lifetime, no two lifetimes and they are something I prize greatly. Do you understand?"

"Of course, si ho comprendere."

Harry looks at me smiling and says, "È meraviglioso, ora consente di andare al lavoro!"

Incredulously I ask, "Tu parli italiano?"

"Sì, ma non è un bene come vorrei."

I am truly impressed, "Well you speak better than I do, but you are right, lets get to work" and for the next three hours Harry lets me have an insiders view into his and his father's life's work. We walk into a large outer room, more like a vault, where he keeps his collection. The door is secured with a special electronic touch pad and Harry carefully punches in the code. Harry tells me the room is constructed using steel and concrete with interior finishes of solid oak. The walls of the room contain pullout shelves, each housing coins organized by type, denomination and grade. There are special holders for colonials, proof and mint sets, territorial and fractional gold coins and so much more. There is a separate section with files that house his collection of paper currency from the earliest of US issues to more contemporary notes. It is an amazing place and I am in my glory.

Harry obviously takes great pride in what his collection represents. "I've taken the time to set aside the coins that I would like to consign. They are mostly doubles and some are of the more common variety, but they are all valuable and in uncirculated or better condition as I am sure you will agree."

"I am sure I will." I look into the corner of the room and ask Harry, "What's behind that door?"

"Ah, that is my inner sanctum. It is where I hold the most precious and valuable coins and currency in my collection. Would you like to see it?"

"If this is a joke I'm waiting for the punchline."

The door is secured with another electronic touch pad that requires a special code to open. Harry carefully blocks my view of the key pad as he puts in the secret code. The door automatically opens and a light goes on. The room is far smaller than the main vault; big enough to accomodate both Harry and I, but not by much. There are small framed display cases mounted on the wall, each containing a single coin or paper currency. In the center of the room is a display case and I am immediately drawn to it. Inside the case is the famed 1804 Draped Bust Silver Dollar. It is in remarkable condition, a PF-68 in numismatic terms, and I'm in awe of its beauty.

I am wide-eyed. "Harry, this is the most remarkable coin I have had the good fortune to view in person."

Harry is also looking at the case, "I know. I never get tired of looking at her. The display is of the obverse, but when you press this button, the display turns so you can see the reverse. I do believe that I am the most fortunate of collectors just to possess her." His reverence for this truly unique coin is apparent as he speaks in solemn tones.

I finally look up from the case and study the other treasures in Harry's inner sanctum. There are 28 in all; among them are the 1797 Liberty Cap Half-Cent with gripped edge, 1870S Liberty Seated Half-Dollar, a 1913 Proof Liberty Head Nickle-Five Cent piece and other rarities that are all in amazing condition. Some of these coins are so rare that they are among the last few, perhaps only two or three in existence and are valued in the millions of dollars. It is hard for many to understand the importance of these coins and to understand the true measure of their beauty and of their true value in an historical sense, but Harry and I do and viewing them is a special moment for me. By the time we finish examining and cataloging just a small part of his collection, it is after 6PM.

"The time seems to fly by when I am looking over my collection, but I think that this is enough for the first day. Tomorrow we will continue to review the rest of the coins in my collection that I wish to put up for sale and work on inventorying the pieces and place a range of value to determine what they may be worth. What do you say Chris?"

I am still in a state of awe over what I have seen, but I manage a simple, "That sounds like a plan."

"Splendid, now let's get ready for dinner, the chef has prepared a special meal and I've selected the wine. I have another tradition that I would like to share with you. We always get dressed in formal attire for dinner when we are at my country home."

I am a bit ashamed to admit it, but I tell Harry, "I am sorry, I didn't know. I didn't bring or even own a tuxedo."

Harry immediately tells me not to worry, "Don't give it another thought, I've asked Jonathan to put out a tuxedo for you to wear. I know what you're going to say; how did you know my size? Let me remind you, I am Harry of Harry's Place and you are a 40 long, 34 waist and 32-inch inseam. Am I right?"

I keep thinking of how this guy is an expert on everything. "Wow, that's right."

Harry smiles, "I keep a few tuxedos on hand for just such emergencies. We usually dine at 7:30PM so you should have enough time to get ready." Harry is sure to lock the inner vault and secure the door to the outer room.

We say our goodbyes and I walk to my room and sit down on the bed. I think to myself, "How did I get here?" but I can't come up with an answer at least not one that makes sense. I take a warm shower and it feels good so I stay longer than I should have. As I dry myself off, I walk to the closet where there it is hanging on the rack, one truly handsome tux. There is a tuxedo shirt and black bowtie, not the clip on, a real genuine bowtie. I get dressed and the last thing I do is try to tie my bowtie. I hadn't done this in a long while, but I finally get it and I think that my efforts turn out well.

I take one last look in the mirror and think that I am presentable, even attractive enough to sit down to eat with a billionaire. I wonder what Beth would say and then I think better. Beth likes to keep me grounded and she would probably laugh and say, "Don't get ahead of yourself buster, you're not that good-looking." Oh well, I open the door to the hallway leads down to the stairway toward the dining room and what I hope will be a memorable dinner. I walk towards the top of the stairway and someone is waiting there.

Amanda says, "Can I take your arm?"

Her beauty dazzles me, but I don't say a thing. I just hold out my arm and we walk down the stairway. She is looking at me and I am lost for words, but she doesn't care. Amanda squeezes my arm and simply says, "This is nice."

CHAPTER 32

The limousines line the road leading to Tom Houston's mansion. One by one the cars reach the circular driveway to the front entrance. There are uniformed men to open the car doors to allow passengers to exit. More than 100 notables from the world of politics, business, entertainment and media are there as guests of Dr. Houston ostensibly to celebrate the life and work of Dr. Spencer Price. The house is brightly lit and the atmosphere is festive as guest after guest walk up the imposing front stairway that leads to the large entrance foyer. Each guest is offered champagne, wine or water as they enter and the doors leading to all the rooms on the first floor. The interior doors have been left open for all the visitors to roam about and mingle with each other.

Dr. Tom Houston takes the time to personally greet each of his guests. He has a remarkable memory for names and he takes delight in saying things like, "Hello John, thank you for coming and this must be your lovely wife, Pauline. Welcome, and please enjoy the evening. I think you know Senator Shellman, well he's over there and I'm sure he would love it if you would go and say hello." It is the same with each of the guests entering Tom's home; he wants them to feel special and they do.

Beth drives alone to the event, but she doesn't want to wait in the long line of limos in her Ford Escape. She finds a spot on the street where a number of cars are parked; she locks the doors and walks up the driveway to Tom's home. Chris had jokingly asked her to look ugly and have a horrible time, but this is a special event and she tries to dress and look as if she belongs in the same rarified circles as the rest. She's wearing a strapless long gown made of a silky gold fabric that accentuates her perfect figure. Beth wears the necklace that Chris gave her as well as gold drop earrings and a diamond and gold bracelet that her father and mother gave her when she graduated nursing school. It is a cool evening so she wears a full-length mink coat that she borrowed from her mother. Beth looks stunning and everyone takes notice as she walks up to the front entrance.

Most of the guests have arrived so the line to greet Tom is short and when he sees Beth he smiles from ear-to-ear. He embraces her and kisses her on the cheek. "Beth, thank you so much for coming, you look absolutely lovely tonight. Where's what's his name?"

Beth smiles at the joke and says, "Chris."

"Oh yeah, Chris, well where's the lucky guy?"

"He's in Chicago with Harry Lieberman. It seems that the introduction you made did wonders for him. Harry is letting Chris broker part of his coin collection and he's there evaluating the pieces for sale."

"Oh, that's terrible, I mean wonderful. Well, terrible that he's not here and wonderful that he has this opportunity." Tom is staring at Beth like the cat that swallowed the canary.

She looks suspiciously at Tom and says, "Did you have anything to do with this?"

Tom looks at Beth in disbelief, "How could you say such a thing? I had nothing to do with this unfortunate turn of events. I can't say that I'm unhappy, but I had nothing to do with his good fortune except the introduction I made at the fundraiser. Don't you believe me?"

Beth is still a little skeptical, but she smiles, "Well, I guess I believe you, for Dr. Prices' sake." They both laugh and Tom takes her by the arm and says, "Let me take you to see Spencer and remember what I told you about your possible romantic entanglement."

Tom and Beth walk arm-in-arm as they make their way through the crowd to see Dr. Price. Inquisitive eyes follow the pair and the crowd parts to let them through. Once they reach Dr. Price, Tom taps him on the shoulder and says, "Spencer, look who's here to help celebrate your life and work."

Dr. Price turns and greets Beth with a warm smile and he embraces her. "My dear, I am honored that you took time to come to this hideous party with all these…"

"Now Spencer!" Tom looks at him in mock anger.

Now Spencer realizing his poor form says, "These guests, and well I guess the party is not that hideous" and the group laughs.

"Dr. Price it is truly my honor to even be invited."

"Nonsense my dear, nonsense, when Tom told me that he would be holding this function I asked him to invite you, but it seems he beat me to the punch and now you are here." Spencer takes Beth in his arms and gives her a fatherly hug.

"Thank you so much Dr. Price."

"No need to thank me, its Tom here we both should thank. Now may I get you a glass of champagne or perhaps something else?"

Beth says, "Thank you; I'd love a glass of champagne."

Dr. Price looks for the waiter and reaches for two glasses as Tom whispers into Beth's ear, "I told you that Spencer has the hots for you" and Beth suppresses the urge to laugh as she holds her hand to her mouth. Spencer Price returns with two glasses and hands one to Beth. Tom looks at him and asks, "Where's mine?"

In all seriousness Dr. Price answers, "Get your own damn champagne, I only serve beautiful women."

"Alright Spencer, I'll remember this when you come looking for more funding for the research center." Spencer now looks thoughtfully at his benefactor and says, "Oh, alright, take my damn champagne" and he hands the glass to Tom. They all laugh again and it is apparent they have affection for one another.

Spencer and Tom ask Beth, at the same time, "Beth, are you hungry?" She finds this funny and answers, "Wow, I am a lucky girl to have two handsome men ask me if I'm hungry. The answer is I'm starving."

The party is going strong by the time their little group has finished their glasses of champagne and they make their way to the buffet table.

The buffet is a wonderful array of seafood in huge piles, carving stations with beef tenderloin and other meats, blocks of different cheeses, carefully arranged platters of roasted vegetables, delicious pasta dishes and much more. Tom, Spencer and Beth eagerly fill their plates and look for a table to rest their feasts so they can continue talking.

"Tom, the food looks delicious."

Spencer adds, "Better than the food they served at that horrid fundraiser you forced me to attend."

Tom smiles at them and says, "Thank you for the accolades, but I cannot take credit. The food was prepared by Wilcoxson and Pratt Premium Catering, a place I've used before. By the way Beth, what Spencer just said is about as close to a real compliment I'll ever get from him."

Spencer smiles, shoves a shrimp in his mouth, and says, "You're damn right!"

Their group is in a wonderful mood as they continue their conversation when Tom interrupts. "I have to make a speech to the crowd, you know typical stuff, but I will return. I assume that's okay with you Spencer?"

"Damn right it's okay! I've been trying to get Beth alone all night!"

Tom leaves and walks towards a small podium that is set up near the buffet table. He steps up to the microphone and taps it gently, "Ladies and gentlemen may I have your attention please." Conversations immediately stop as everyone turns to face Tom at the podium.

"First, I would like to thank you for coming; I am delighted to see you all. I want to say a few words about why we are here. We are here first and foremost to honor a truly great man, Dr. Spencer Price." The guests immediately burst into applause at the mention of his name. When the applause dies down, Tom continues,

"Dr. Price is a recognized leader, a pioneer in the fight against a disease that has affected us all in one way or another, cancer. Dr. Price is tirelessly working on determining the sources of this horrible illness, looking for answers through DNA sequencing research and he is now near to finding a cure that will help so many men, women and children fight their way back to good health and a long life. In my work and lately in my campaign for the nomination, I have come to know and admire Dr. Spencer Price and don't tell Spencer, but I love the man." The crowd laughs and bursts into another round of applause. Beth looks over to Spencer and sees him smiling and gently waving to Tom, it's the most genuine gesture that could come from this brilliant, playful curmudgeon.

"Now, Spencer knows that in order to complete his most important work he needs funding, quite frankly a lot of funding. We at ACTELECT have been active supporters of his work and I am proud to make this donation." Tom looks to the side and one of his staff brings out a two foot by four-foot check and Tom holds it up for all to see.

"This is a check written to the Price Center for Cancer Research in the amount of $5,000,000 dollars." The audience now erupts in applause and they all turn to Dr. Price who appears overwhelmed. Tom has more to say, but the crowd is still cheering.

"Ladies and gentlemen may I have your attention; please may I have your attention." The crowd now quiets down to allow Tom to continue, "Ah, but this check comes with a few strings attached." Now the crowd is intent on hearing about the strings.

"It is set aside as a matching fund and what that means is by the end of the evening, I expect contributions and pledges totaling $5,000,000 for a grand total of $10,000,000. I'm sure if we raise more than $5,000,000 Spencer won't mind if ACTELECT also matches any amount over the initial donation. So, what do you say, let's help Dr. Spencer Price find a cure for cancer once and for all?"

The crowd screams "YES!" and everyone seems to be reaching inside their pockets and pulling out pens and paper, maybe even checks.

Tom thanks everyone, "Thank you for your kind attention and for those who contribute, Spencer and I want to thank you from the bottom of our hearts. Now I've asked our fabulous band to begin the music so put your dancing shoes on and have a wonderful time."

Tom steps from behind the podium to the applause of all. He walks over to the table stopping to shake hands with some of his guests and embraces close friends. There are a number of people surrounding Dr. Price trying to get his attention and congratulating him on his work. Spencer seems a bit confounded and uncomfortable with all the attention so Beth comes to his rescue and takes his arm and they both stand up.

Beth feels it necessary to take charge of the conversation and tell all those in earshot, "Dr. Price is overwhelmed by this show of support and I think that has him at a loss for words, which, I understand, is very rare for Dr. Price." The crowd surrounding Spencer and Beth burst into laughter. "I know that he is very grateful for the accolades, but even more grateful for all the help Tom and you all have given." Tom is standing out of Beth's line of sight, but he is listening intently.

"Now, Spencer is far too gentile to ask for funds to help in his work." Everyone who knows Spencer is laughing again, "…but fortunately he has me as his surrogate. I am a nurse and I have seen the ravages of this disease firsthand as I am sure many of you have. Family, friends, young and old, rich and poor; not one of us are spared from the effects of this plague, but there is hope and it is through the work of Dr. Price that we have this hope. So please give whatever you can and add to Tom Houston's very, very generous donation. Dr. Price thanks you all from the bottom of his heart." The crowd is enthralled with Beth and she gives Spencer a kiss on his cheek and the guests surrounding them smile and applaud the man of the hour.

Tom makes his way back to Spencer and Beth as the crowd parts to let him through. Spencer is still holding onto Beth's hand, but the minute he spots Tom, he reaches over and puts his hands on Tom's shoulder. "Thank you, Tom, thank you from the bottom of my heart" and they embrace. Tom is elated at all excitement being created and confides to Spencer and Beth, "Want to hear a secret?"

Both of them answer in unison, "What's the secret!?"

Tom looks around to be sure no one is listening in. "We have raised at least $30,000,000 dollars for Spencer's research."

Spencer and Beth both say, very loudly, "WHAT?"

"SHHHHH! Calm down. It was kind of in the bag as Joel Connor, the head of Foremost Hedge Funds of America donated $5,000,000 himself. Then a few of my other friends, Ron and Barbara Thomas and Sherry and Tim Goldman donated and additional $10,000,000 so with my matching you've got at least $30,000,000 dollars. I am sure that will grow substantially by the end of the evening." Spencer is in the state of shock and he sits down.

Tom turns to Beth, "Thank you for helping Spencer out of his curious lack of response to his adoring fans."

Beth looks at Spencer trying to be cordial to the crowd around him and she smiles, "I was more than glad to help." Beth looks back at Tom and says, "Tom, what you've done is astounding."

The band begins to play and Tom smiles at Beth, "May I have this dance?" Beth starts to panic. "Tom, I don't think that…"

Tom smiles, "Why not?"

"Tom, what will people say? I have a boyfriend and I don't want people to get the wrong impression. I think…"

"Beth, that's your problem, you think too much. I'm not asking you to marry me I just want to dance with you." With that Tom holds out his hand to escort Beth to the dance floor.

Beth looks like a deer caught in the headlights as she unconsciously holds out her hand for Tom to take. Tom smiles and takes Beth's hand as the crowd parts to let them on the dance floor. He holds Beth in his arms and brings her close to him. She looks into his eyes as they glide across the floor not realizing they are the only one's dancing.

CHAPTER 33

Матвей Орлов likes his surname, Орлов or Orlov, from the Russian meaning 'son of Oryol'; he likes his nickname even better for everyone calls him the 'Eagle'.

Orlov though, hates his life, his bad luck, but he hates something even more, he hates living in Norilsk. This cursed city in the Siberian tundra is his home and it is like a noose around his neck…he is condemned and it is choking him. What good is his position as a Communist Party representative if he must spend his life in this God-forsaken place? Orlov feels his blood pressure rising as he thinks of his fate and of what has become of the Communist Party. End of communism that's what everyone keeps saying, but he knows better. "Ha!" he thought, it has not ended not even slowed down. The money keeps going to the same people only in different ways, but none came to Матвей Орлов and this makes him even madder. He is no fool, there will always be corruption so why couldn't he get a little piece of the pie after all he isn't greedy.

Orlov is in a foul mood as he thinks to himself, "Why didn't they keep this place as the center of the gulag systems in all of Russia?" He is in charge of the Norilsk Prison and at least he could have taken bribes, he could have many slave laborers as servants to do what he wishes and he could even have women and children he could violate in whatever ways he wants. He curses his bad fortune and decides he is too upset to do any work today. There is a bottle of vodka in his desk draw. It is a cheap brand, but they pay him so little it is all

"

he can afford. Orlov enjoys drinking; it helps keep the cold from consuming his every waking hour and he awakened only two hours ago.

After just a few drinks he hears a knock on the door. Orlov has the good sense to exercise some discretion so he hides the bottle back in the draw and summons the person to enter.

"Ah! It is you Юлианский Волков come in, come in Volkov…sit with me and have a drink!"

Volkov smiles, "Is it not a bit early for drinking my friend?"

"It is never too early or too late for that matter, to have a drink with friends. Come sit down and help me to forget my misery."

"Well, I see that you have not taken my advice."

Orlov begins to feel the effects of the alcohol, "What advice is that Юлианский Волков?"

"To be thankful for what you have and that you do not have to work in the freezing cold. It is sound advice and you would do well to heed it."

A glaze is forming over Orlov's eyes. "You are a fool Volkov. Where does it say that I must endure this punishment, this torment of mine? A lowly civil servant condemned to spending life in this city of snow and ice and wretchedness, I ask you where does it say that?"

Volkov nods his head in sympathy with his friend. "I understand what you are saying, but what can be done? It seems preordained for you to be here. How can you find a way out of this existence?"

Orlov sighs, "I do not know my friend, I do not know, but I do know that I would move heaven and hell if there were a way out of this place. Heaven and hell…" His voice trails off as the alcohol takes the desired effect and Orlov falls asleep.

A while later, perhaps six or seven hours, Orlov wakes up. The day has turned into night, night…it is always night in this cursed Siberia city of Norilsk. His head hurts from drinking so much cheap vodka and he is alone. The civil servant remembers his friend Юлианский Волков had been with him, but now he is gone. I suppose he got bored waiting for the alcohol to wear off like it always does. Unfortunately, the drink also leaves behind a blinding headache and Orlov has one of the worse he's ever had to endure.

Orlov sneers when he thinks that no one on his staff would dare wake him when he is in this condition. The head of the prison slowly rises from his desk chair and makes his way to the coat rack to put on the parka he always wears, it is the warmest one that he owns. He opens the door to his office to where the workers are busy at their desks and not one of them looks up as he passes. Orlov knows that if anyone questions him it will be all the worse for them.

Orlov opens the outer door to the administrative center and the cold stings him like a bee would sting and he takes the hood from his parka and bundles it closer to his face. He mumbles all the way to his car "Why me? Why must I suffer this brutal cold?" His car is in a space closest to the center's front door and he gets in, thankful to be out of the bitter cold and wind. He puts the key into the ignition, but all he hears is the click…click…click of a dead battery. Orlov screams in fury and frustration, "This is all I need to end a perfect day."

He jumps out of his car and runs to the front door. The guard at the front desk immediately rises and stands at attention. Orlov yells at the guard, "My cursed car will not start; get me someone to fix it, NOW!" The guard knows better than to say anything so he picks up the line and dials the mechanic shop. The guard's face becomes pale and he prays that someone picks up the phone. The phone rings and rings, but no one picks up and after at least ten rings he returns the phone to the cradle and tells Матвей Орлов,

"Sir, no one picked up the phone, I let it ring, but no one answers."

Orlov's face becomes twisted with rage. He reaches over the desk and grabs the guard by the throat. The guard begins to gag and choke as Orlov's hand squeezes tighter and tighter. Orlov says to the guard in a slow and measured tone, "You will find someone to fix my car and you will do it now." The head of Norilsk Prison releases the guard and the man falls to the floor grabbing his neck, cowering as he rubs the bruises that are already beginning to swell. "Yes sir, yes sir I will find someone immediately."

The guard waits for Orlov to leave before he picks himself off the floor and reaches for the phone. Orlov is furious and he storms back to his office. The staff is still at their desks afraid to make any eye contact with Матвей Орлов because they know what could happen when he is in such a foul mood.

Before Orlov sits down at his desk there is a knock on the door and he yells "Come in!" The door opens and Volkov walks in trailed by another man dressed in a prisoner's uniform. "Orlov, my friend, I hear that you are having trouble with your car."

"Damn cursed weather and damn cursed Russian automobiles. They are as unreliable as the prisoners I have working for me. Who is that behind you?"

"Ah, this is, well I'm sure you don't care who this is. He is a prisoner from cell block 12 and he is skilled in automobile mechanics. I received a call from a very frightened guard who is pleading to me for help. Seeing that your prison mechanics are all gone for the evening I brought him here to fix your car."

"Юлианский Волков, you are a genius! How fortunate am I to have such a good friend in this moment of misery."

"Orlov, do not be so melodramatic this happens all the time."

"I know it does, but it always seems to happen to me."

Volkov smiles and instructs the guard to take the prisoner to the mechanics shop and provide him with whatever he needs to fix the car. The guard and prisoner leave and Volkov takes his usual seat in front of Orlov's desk and says, "Well, Матвей Орлов I'm sure this has put you in an even better mood. Orlov just stares into space and commiserates with his friend, "Volkov, what am I to do?"

Suddenly Volkov sits upright in the chair and excitedly says, "I have an idea!"

Orlov immediately brightens, "You do? You have an idea?"

"Yes, my friend, the end to your torment and the beginning of a new life!"

"Well, tell me, tell me now."

"I will. It will require planning and cunning, but if anyone can do it, it is you Матвей Орлов! First you will plan to have the prisoners' riot and then you will put down the riot and you will become the hero of Norilsk. The Party will be sure to take notice and you will be hailed as a brave and resourceful comrade. The powers that be will want you to head their largest most prestigious prison and you will be assigned there. You will have power, you will have wealth, you will have a dacha near the Black Sea, ah Orlov, you will finally have your place in the sun so to speak and best of all you will be rid of Norilsk. For my brilliant scheme I only ask one thing…take me with you!" Volkov can no longer hold back, he starts to laugh uncontrollably, but Orlov doesn't seem to think it's a joke.

"*Volkov, do you think this will work?*"

"*Матвей Орлов it is a joke; I want to see you laugh. You don't think I'm serious, do you?*'

Orlov stays silent for a while, but brightens up as he says to Volkov, "Of course I know it is a joke and you did make me smile. Thank you, my friend." The two men sit and talk for a short while when the phone rings.

Orlov picks up the receiver, "Yes." A voice on the other end speaks as Orlov listens. "I will be out in a moment" and he hangs up the phone.

"My car is fixed and I can go home now."

"Good, I think you need to relax a bit my friend." Orlov and Volkov get up and embrace. "Thank you Volkov you are a good friend and you make this place a bit more bearable."

Orlov leaves and walks outside. The car is running so it would be warm and the prison head is happy for small miracles. The guard is standing next to the prisoner as they wait to be sure all is in order.

Orlov stands next to the guard as he asks the prisoner his name. "My name is Афонька Лукьяненко." The prisoner did not dare to look up.

Orlov smiles, does this man even know that his name means immortal? Immortal and prison in the same sentence are not a good thing. "What do the prisoners call you?"

"They call me Afon, sir"

"Well, Afon, I want to see you in my office first thing tomorrow." Orlov turns to the guard, "Be sure that it is done" and he climbs into his car allowing the warmth to cover him.

The guard salutes and responds, "Yes, sir."

On the drive to his home Матвей Орлов's mind is racing. He knows Volkov was joking, but the idea has merits, in fact it is brilliant. Can it work? What would he need to do? What are the potential problems? What are the consequences? Who can I trust?" True, there are many questions, but none of the possible answers seems to make the scheme undoable.

Orlov pulls into the parking space in front of his small wretched flat and he thinks that all of this can change if he could execute the plan without, how do the American's call it, a hitch. He puts the key in to open the door to his apartment and turns the lights on. At one time Нонна, his Nonna would have been there, but there is no one to greet him now. How unfortunate for him. She would cook and clean, she wasn't even a bad lay, but now she is gone. Why couldn't the bitch just keep her mouth shut why was she always nagging? Isn't it enough that she got money for food and clothing? No, it's never enough for these women. As hard as he tried nothing ever satisfied Nonna. Even when he was drunk you would think she would just leave him alone, but not Nonna. Nag, nag, nag, well I guess she won't be nagging him anymore; he'd seen to that.

The nights are cold as they always are in Norilsk. Orlov sits in the over-stuffed chair in what you would call his living room and he pours himself another glass of vodka recalling his last night with Nonna. He didn't mean to hit her, but who would blame him anyway. The nagging bitch keeps crying and screaming at him. It was just a tap, nothing that you could call serious, but she fell anyway. She did not move so he checks for a heartbeat, but there is none he can hear. Orlov remembers thinking that a lesser man would have panicked, but he kept his wits about him.

He waits until it is very late as he wraps her battered body in an old blanket. He lifts Nonna's body, walks to his car and puts it in his trunk. The trunk is too small so he has to shove the body in very forcefully. Orlov hears a bone crack as he does this, but he takes solace in the fact that Nonna would feel no pain, no pain at all.

Orlov finds a desolate place where he dumps the body. He is very glad he remembers to take the blanket with him so no one can trace any of this back to him. In the morning and he will call the authorities and report her missing. Матвей Орлов will be sure to weep, express his fear for her safety and beg the police to begin the search. It is a good plan executed in a flawless manner and Orlov is very proud of himself.

When the police find Nonna her body is frozen so stiff the local coroner has to wait three days for her to thaw out before the post-mortem can take place. The autopsy reveals that she died of blunt force trauma and that it is deemed to be a homicide. In his role as prison head, Orlov has a good enough relation-ship with the local police who will try to do all they can to solve the crime, but Orlov knows better. Month after month passes and there is nothing to report. The police are overwhelmed by so many crimes being committed in their city *that Nonna's murder soon becomes nothing more than a statistic and her file becomes part of a pile of unsolved homicides and that is that.*

Orlov finishes his drink; however, he is not looking to get drunk. Vodka always helps him to relax and when he is relaxed, he is able to think clearly. Volkov made a joke of the plan, but as Orlov thinks more and more about the possibilities, it becomes clear that it can work and he will be free of the scourge Norilsk and his life. Once he finishes working out his plan Orlov decides to go to bed, after all he has a lot to do. For the first time in a long time Orlov sleeps like a baby.

Early the next morning Orlov rises from bed like he is a man born anew. He makes coffee while he whistles a popular song that is playing on the radio called "Samaya Samaya" by Egor Kreed. He likes the song because there is whistling in it and he likes to whistle. He thinks that when he is able to buy a dacha, he will have a big party and invite everyone he can think of. He would serve caviar and the best vodka and he might even hire Egor to perform. These thoughts run through his head and they make him very happy as he leaves his apartment and walks to his car.

Orlov arrives at Norilsk Prison at 7:30AM and walks through the front entrance. There is a different guard from the night before on duty who lazily looks up expecting no one important until he sees who it is.

Seeing Orlov, the guard immediately rises at attention and says, "Good morning, sir!"

"Good morning" and he pauses to read the name tag, "Модя Богатырёва, are you any relations to the famous footballer?"

"No sir" the guard stands at attention, but he is incredulous. The head of the prison never comes in this early and he never speaks to him, ever.

"Well, that is bad luck; at least he would have been able to get you tickets to the games eh!"

The guard, still at attention, says, "I suppose so, yes sir."

Orlov laughs and walks towards his office.

The desks in the work area are empty as the staff usually arrives at 8AM. Orlov unlocks the door to his office and decides he would go over his plan again and again to see if it is still viable. The more he goes over the plan the more Orlov is convinced that it will work very well. The head of Norilsk picks up the phone and calls the head guard for cell block 12.

"I have asked that prisoner Афонька Лукьяненко be brought to my office first thing in the morning. Were those instructions passed onto you?" Orlov is about to yell if he is given the wrong answer.

"Yes sir" the guard immediately responds, "I was going to bring him down at 9AM. I was told that is the time you usually arrive."

"Well, I am here now, bring the prisoner to my office!" and Orlov slams down the receiver.

No more than five minutes pass when Orlov hears a knock at the door and he says, "Come in."

The door opens and Афонька Лукьяненко walks in trailed by a prison guard. Orlov looks at the guard and says, "That is all, wait outside the door and I will call you when I am finished with the prisoner."

The guard does not question the command; he does not even look at Orlov, and just turns and leaves the two men alone.

"Ah, Афонька Лукьяненко, welcome, may I call you Afon?"

Afon stares at the floor, he is very nervous and does not know what the proper response should be at least the proper response that won't get his head cracked open. "Yes sir."

"Splendid Afon, I want to personally thank you for the good job you did on my car yesterday it seems to be running so much better. What is it you did to make it run so well?" Orlov seems genuinely interested so Afon replies.

"Sir, the battery cable was badly frayed and I replaced it. The fan belts were also loose so I tightened them and there were some loose connections on the distributor so I fixed that also. It also appears that your air filter had not been replaced in quite a long time so I changed it. I would have done more, but the shop was closed and I knew you were anxious to get to your home."

"My, my Afon that is very industrious of you. Tell me, why are you a resident at our lovely establishment?"

Афонька Лукьяненко lowers his head in shame, "I was caught trying to steal a car for its parts and I know that I did wrong. My sentence is five years and I am paying for my crime. I am ashamed for my family and myself."

"You have a family?"

"Yes sir, my wife and I have a son and a daughter."

"How old are they?"

Afon raises his head to look Orlov in the eyes, "My son is 8 and my daughter is 6."

"Do you miss them?" Orlov seems concerned and sympathetic.

Afon says, "Each and every day sir."

"Ah, I am sure, I am sure. You know Afon children so young should not be without a father. It is very bad that you are not there to give them the guidance they need to grow into good Russian citizens."

There are tears rolling down Afon's cheek and he buries his face in his hands and begins to sob uncontrollably. Orlov waits patiently; he knows that in order to get Afon to do what needs to be done he must let these emotions of the moment be pass. Finally, Afon's chest heaves as he sits in the chair exhausted from the emotional outpouring that has been building for so long.

"I am very sorry sir. I do not know what happened to me and I apologize for this uncalled-for display."

"Afon, you are distraught and I cannot blame you. I am without the love of a good woman and God has denied me the pleasure of children. In my old age I am sure they would be of great comfort as I am sure your children will be of comfort to you. But I have a question, what would you do to be released from Norilsk Prison, Afon?"

The question frightens Afon, "Sir, I swear to you that I would never attempt to escape. I try to do my best at work and never give the guards a reason to believe I am anything but obedient. I will serve my sentence…" but Orlov interrupts him.

"Афонька Лукьяненко, Afon I did not mean to suggest that you would try to escape. That would be a very foolish thing to do; after all a dead father is no good to his children. Am I correct?"

The prisoner looks down, "Yes sir."

"Afon look up at me as I have something to tell you." Afon looks at Orlov and sees that he is smiling. "I may have a way for you to, how shall I put it, shorten you sentence. I mean really shorten it, what would you say to that?"

"Sir, what do you mean, how can I shorten my sentence. I would do anything to be with my family."

"Well, I may have a way, but it will take a little time and you will need to do what I ask and be on your best behavior for me to help move your release along. In the meantime, I am assigning you to the garage. You will work along with the other prison's mechanics; I assure you it will be warmer than where you work now, the food will be better and you will have my protection. How does that sound to you?"

Afon is nearly speechless. He does not know what to make of this turn of events, but he is ecstatic at the possibility of an early release and says, "Sir, I don't know what to say, but I will help you in whatever way I can. Thank you, sir, thank you very much."

"Ah, Afon no need to thank me yet. In a few days I will let you know what you will need to do, but in the meantime go about your new assignment and keep this little discussion between the two of us. Agreed?"

Afon smiles for the first time since he came to prison, "Yes sir, you can count of my discretion.

Orlov rises from his chair and walks around the desk. He puts out his hand to shake Afon's, "Excellent Afon, excellent. We will speak soon." Orlov opens the door and tells the guard to take him back to his cell. He tells one of his staff of Afon's reassignment and goes back into his office satisfied that he has done a good day's work.

The days turn to weeks and Orlov is sure that his plan is in perfect order and that he can begin to execute it. He calls the guard in the mechanics shop and tells him to bring Afon to his office immediately. In a few minutes Orlov hears a knock at his door and he says, "Come in."

The guard opens the door and gestures for Afon to walk in. The prisoner dutifully does as he is told and Orlov tells him to take a seat.

Orlov smiles at the man who will be the key to his future. "So Afon, how are things going in the mechanics shop?"

Afon looks like a different man. He appears healthier and in much better spirits. "Sir, all is going very well. The other mechanics and I are working very well together. I believe that you will see a far greater improvement in our overall work flow and we have been able to improve our quality of work."

"Yes, yes Afon. I have read the reports and I am very pleased that all is going so well and I have you to thank for that."

"Sir, it is the entire mechanics on your staff that are doing the job and I am glad it pleases you." Afon is taking pride at telling this to the prison head.

"That is wonderful Afon, wonderful and I have some more wonderful news for you and the others in the mechanics shop." Orlov smiles and looks to his right and left to pretend no one is listening.

Afon is growing very curious and asks, "Sir, what is this wonderful news?"

"Well, I looked at the records of all who work in the mechanics shop. Most of these men are here on relatively minor non-violent crimes and I do not think that the long sentences for such crimes are warranted. Afon, do you not agree?"

"Sir, the sentences are what they are and I have no say as to the fairness. Of course, I would like mine to be shorter, but I am resigned to this fate."

"I see your point Afon, but listen to me. As you may know, we are very overcrowded. It is a fact that I need to confront every day. There are, however, procedures that come down from the Ministry of Prison Supervision that may hold the key to your, how shall I call it, deliverance." Orlov is now smiling and Afon is getting more and more excited.

"Very well, I shall no longer beat around the bush, Afon. I have called the ministry and I asked them to review the terms of all prisoners in the mechanics shop along with my recommendations and do you know what they said?"

Afon is sitting at attention; his hands are gripping the arms of the chair so tightly that they are turning white. "No sir."

Orlov smiles at Afon allowing the moment to linger knowing what the prisoner is hoping to hear. "Afon, I have secured releases for you and five of the other prisoners in the mechanics shop."

Afon is reeling from the news, but he tries to regain his composure. "Sir, can this be true? Are we to be released? My God, is it true?"

"Yes Afon, yes, it is true. You will be reunited with you family. You will go back to your life before prison. I will arrange for the release to take place in 2 days, but you must promise something to me."

"Promise? Sir, I will promise anything you wish please ask me anything… anything" and Afon's voice trails off.

"You must promise me you will no longer look to commit any crimes because if you are returned to this prison, I will not be able to help you. Is that understood?"

"Sir, I would die before I would commit another crime."

"Good then it's settled. I am going to ask you not to reveal this to anyone, even those in the shop; I want to tell them myself."

"Of course, sir, I will keep this secret until you have spoken to the men."

Orlov seems elated, "Good Afon, good man! Now you will go back to work, but remember do not tell anyone." Orlov does not wait for a reply as he calls the guard back into his office. "Take prisoner Афонька Лукьяненко back to the mechanics shop" and the men leave his office. Orlov is pleased, very pleased, and he looks to prepare for the second phase of his plan.

That evening the head of Norilsk Prison comes home in the best mood he has been in a very long time. He wants to celebrate so he purchases a bottle of the finest vodka available and passable caviar with all the appropriate sides. He always has a few plates chilled for such occasions. He uses a serving dish that Nonna had bought a few years ago and places ice cubes in the large bowl surrounding the smaller bowl that holds the caviar. Orlov then places blinis, as well as crème fraiche, in the chilled plates and he sips the vodka as he hungrily devours the caviar.

Orlov thinks about telling his friend Юлианский Волков of the plan, but Volkov would never understand. He is a bureaucrat; once a bureaucrat always a bureaucrat and Orlov knows that men of such minds cannot think creatively. Orlov drinks half the bottle of vodka and finishes the entire tin of caviar and he feels sated. Sleep is taking hold as Orlov crawls into his bed happier than ever before. He has been sleeping very well for the last few weeks and tonight would be the same. As Orlov sleeps he dreams of dachas and beautiful women.

The next morning, he knows he needs to get everything ready. He loads an AKM, a modernized version of the AK47, which is still in use by the Russian militia and police. Orlov has purchased the weapon from the thriving black market in Norilsk keeping a low profile so as not to be recognized. He loads one of the clips and has another clip loaded and ready just in case, but he is sure he will not need it. He also collects other items that he will need so any investigators of the incident will believe that the prisoners were trying to escape. He hides the rifle and other items under his desk and picks up the phone. He calls the guard post outside the mechanics shop and asks the guard to bring

Afon to his office. A few minutes later Orlov hears a knock and he tells the person to enter.

"Ah, Afon!" The prison head turns to the guard and tells him to wait outside. Orlov is smiling from ear to ear as he tells Afon to sit down.

"Afon, I have splendid news for you, splendid news!"

Afon is beyond excited and in a voice shaking with anticipation says, "Yes sir, what news do you have?"

"Afon, I have heard from the Central Bureau of Prison Affairs and they have given me permission to provide conditional releases for you and the five other mechanics in the shop!"

"Conditional releases, what does that mean sir? What is a conditional release?"

Orlov explains, "Afon, conditional releases are given to prisoners who have not completed their sentences and are released early. In exchange they must sign a document that says if they commit any crime, any crime whatsoever, they will be sentenced for that crime and the balance of their prior sentence will be added to the time, no exceptions. Is that understood and agreed to by you?"

"Can it be true? Can this really be true?" Afon still cannot comprehend his good fortune.

Orlov smiles at Afon, "Yes, my friend, I have prepared the documents listing the terms of the conditional releases for you and each of your coworkers."

"Sir, I am so grateful. I can never repay your kindness, but rest assured that I will be honest and hardworking and do nothing that will ever disappoint you or break the bond I have made."

"Marvelous Afon, I know that you will do what is right. As for the other men tell them I called for a meeting later tonight, but don't tell them why. I would like you to have them wait for me to come to the shop and I will break the good news myself. It is important that you say nothing for if word of the release gets out before we have a chance to manage reactions, there could be a great uproar among the inmates who would like the same consideration for themselves. Do you understand what I mean Afon?"

Afon doesn't want to ask any questions of his benefactor for fear of ruining his chances for release, "Yes sir, I can see that could be a problem."

"Let us meet later, say 9PM. You and the others can have dinner and come back to the shop. I will let the guards know that you are working late. Well once all that is taken care of, you can then pack your belongings and be free of this place first thing in the morning." Orlov is effusive in his praise for Afon and in the prisoner's good fortune. Orlov reminds Afon that he should not say a word to the other men in that he wants to be the one to tell them personally.

"Sir, I don't know what to say."

"Say nothing Afon, just promise me you will hold your children tight the next time you see them."

Afon holds back a tear as he promises, "I will sir, I will."

Orlov now sees it coming together for him. He is nearly busting to tell someone and he thinks of his friend Volkov. He goes to pick up the phone, but puts it back in the cradle. There is no need to tell anyone else, Volkov will hear about this in the morning and by then it will be all over the news. The "Hero of Norilsk Prison" that's what they will call him and that is what will assure his future. Volkov will also be happy as Orlov will recommend him as his replacement. Time drags on for Матвей Орлов who is not normally a patient man. He keeps looking at the clock as the minutes and hours passing seem interminable. At 6PM the staff leaves and all that remains are the guards posted on the night shift.

At 7PM he calls the kitchen and demands that they bring him something to eat. Orlov knows there is prison food and there is his food and he knows that they better not disappoint him. A short while later there is a knock and Orlov opens the door and some prisoner on the kitchen staff enters carrying a tray.

"Set the tray down on the desk and leave." The man only looks down and hurriedly sets the food down and rushes out the door. Orlov smiles for he knows that they all fear him, prisoners and staff alike. The food smells very good and he lifts the covers to see what the cooks have made. There is a bowl of hot Rassolnik, stuffed Kalduny dumplings, red cabbage, an Olivier salad and for dessert, Lymonnyk; all in all, it looks delicious and Orlov wonders how they manage to get all this done in such a short period of time. Ah, the wonders of Russian ingenuity. Orlov takes his time eating for he still has 2 hours before the meeting in the mechanic's shop. He slowly savors the food and finishes the *meal in little more than an hour. He calls the kitchen and tells the worker still on duty to come and take the tray away and in a few minutes, it is done.*

Orlov now surveys all the items he will need for his plan to succeed. He examines each article before he packs them into a large canvas duffle bag; now he is ready. He looks at the clock and it is 8:50PM as he puts on his parka and lifts the duffle bag for his walk to the mechanic's shop. The shop is over in the far eastern corner of the prison and it is the perfect location for an escape. There is only a guard tower and infrequent patrols, but Orlov has seen that for tonight it is manned and patrolled. He also makes sure that the prisoners have a reason to be in the shop so late. They are to be repairing and servicing cars trucks and cars for the staff and they need to get the job done.

How simple it is, a planned escape by six dangerous criminals foiled by the warden of Norilsk Prison. Orlov will tell investigators that he was just walking to his car when he decides to see the progress his mechanics have made and catches them in their attempt to escape. The prisoners try to attack him with hammers and iron crow bars and the AKM, but he is able to wrest the rifle from one of the prisoners and in fear for his life he shoots them all. It is fortunate that he is able to thwart this escape otherwise he would be dead. The investigators would be sure to take the word of a loyal party member and devoted public servant over a few dead miscreants. Матвей Орлов is euphoric. This act of bravery will make him a hero, this act of bravery will assure his future and this act of bravery will get him out of Norilsk for good!

Orlov reaches the door to the mechanics shop and drops the duffle bag. He looks around but sees no one. He calls out, "Afon? Afon? Where are you?" but there is no answer.

Orlov calls again, Afon? Anyone, where are you?"

"Here, I am here" and out from the shadows walks Afon who is so pale as to look like a ghost.

"Afon, why did you not answer? Where are the other men?" but Afon does not answer. Orlov is now becoming very afraid, "Afon, speak to me, Afon."

It is then that a second figure walks out of the shadows and Юлианский Волков stands before Orlov. "Volkov, why, what are you doing here?" Volkov remains silent and just stares at Orlov. Afon drops to the floor cowering in terror afraid to look at either of the men.

Orlov sees his plan falling apart, but he thinks that he still may be able to salvage it. "Volkov, I am giving you an order leave this minute."

Still silent, Volkov smiles as he paces slowly back and forth. Orlov is now in near panic, as he screams for Volkov to leave at once, but Volkov just continues to pace. Orlov does not know what to do next, but he fears to yell for the guards as his plan may be discovered.

Orlov tries another tactic, "Volkov, we are friends, why will you not speak to me? Please tell me why are you here? Where are the other men?"

"Ah, Orlov, that is better. I do not respond well to screams and threats."

"Volkov, why are you here?

"Well, to tell the truth, I am here to help you carry out your plan. Perhaps not in the way you had envisioned, but the results will be the same." Volkov's entire being changes and he appears as the demon he always is, Sonneillon. The terrifying beast lifts Afon off the floor with one hand as the man is crying and screaming. The demon stares at Orlov and slams the prisoner against the wall as his body hangs upside down, impaled by an iron rail protruding from the wall. Sonneillon kicks an old oil pan under the dead man and the blood from his body now drips into the vessel.

Orlov is nearing incoherence bordering on insanity, but there is one more task Sonneillon has for Orlov. "Dip your hand into the blood and write what I tell you."

Orlov is petrified and cannot move, but the demon shrieks, "DO AS I SAY!"

Orlov walks towards the vessel as he continues to stare at the beast before him. Orlov dips his hand into the blood and writes what he is told on the wall next to the dead Afon.

Sonneillon smiles, "Матвей Орлов you have done well, very well."

The demon walks towards Orlov who seems frozen in place. Sonneillon stands three feet above the head of the prison and looks down to say, "I am here to grant your deepest desire Orlov." Orlov does not know what the beast is speaking about nonetheless he soon finds out. Sonneillon thrusts his long, tapering, knife like fingernails into Orlov and in an instant disembowels the man ripping out his insides. For a moment Orlov doesn't understand what is happening to him, but he looks down and realizes he is dead and he realizes his wish to leave his life in Norilsk has been granted.

Sonneillon throws Orlov's guts on the floor and goes over to examine the wall. He is satisfied that all is done and smiles at Orlov's handy work. The demon disappears pleased that the guards will discover the deaths and wonder at the words written in blood; "Lamb of God."

CHAPTER 34

His team is silent as they sit in the Chief's office. Chief Barese's head is pounding. The headache starts as a bit of pressure and is now threatening to crush him. Chief Barese holds his skull in his hands hoping to stop it from exploding.

"Are you okay Chief?" Dan Orello, the chief's right-hand man is genuinely concerned for his friend.

Chief Barese doesn't bother to look up when he asks, "How did it happen? When was it discovered? How many victims are there?" Al assumes that the answers would only make his headache worse.

Det. Christian Oliver speaks up, "We just got back from our initial survey of the crime scene. The coroner was there when we arrived and he estimates that the deaths occurred eight to ten hours ago. So far eighteen bodies have been discovered. I say so far because we found some bodies in one of the outbuildings and another two bodies in a shallow grave on the property. There is a team combing all the surrounding area and they will report back."

"Who are the victims?"

"As far as we can tell they are all part of an organization, Atheists in America and they were gathered there for some kind of a meeting."

"Atheists in America? How did they die?"

There is momentary silence as no one spoke up.

Chief Barese looks up at them and asks again, "Well, how the hell did they die?"

"Chief, the victims died in a number of different ways."

Chief Barese is not known for his patience so he snaps at Det. Oliver, "Well do you want me to guess?"

"No chief, some of them were stabbed to death; one was hanging from a rafter, hands tied behind his back while several died from gunshot wounds, but…" Det. Oliver's voice trailed off.

"What? What are you holding back?"

"Chief, there are some other deaths that were committed in about the most horrific ways I've ever come across."

Al Barese doesn't want to ask the question, but he knows he has to. "How were these people killed?"

Det. Christina Shannon speaks up much to the relief of Det. Oliver. "Christian, I'll take over from here. Chief, some of the victims' bodies were so badly mutilated you couldn't tell what sex they were. Many of the dead have been decapitated and their entrails ripped out of their bodies." The Chief goes back to rubbing his temples and Det. Shannon takes the time to take a deep breath as she continues, "There's more, a number of bodies were found hanging upside down on the wall."

Al looks up, "The same way that the murdered kids were found?"

"Yes, but with some notable exceptions, it appears that these dead were found to be victims to be some kind of ritual killing. The bodies were lined up and each one had a large cross cut into their mid sections. Their heads were cut off and replaced with the head of a ram."

"A what?"

"A ram."

"You mean like a male sheep, ram?"

"Yes, like a male sheep, but that's not all. The horns of the ram were cut off and placed on the floor underneath the hanging bodies."

Chief Barese couldn't even find words to ask the questions he wants to, "What, why?"

Dan Orello speaks up, "Chief, I think that you need to go to the Bible for the answers to questions that I know you want to ask."

"Didn't you tell me that they were there for a meeting of atheists? The Bible, now I need to go to the Bible?"

"Yes, they're all considered to be atheists, but the whole sacrificial thing, except the cross, is the only thing that makes no sense in these murders." Dan is just thinking aloud and Chief Barese knows immediately what to do next, "I think that I may have someone I can ask for help with this whole Bible thing. I'll call him immediately."

Dan interrupts, "Chief, I am just speculating, it may have nothing to do with the Bible."

Det. Avery Michaels remains quiet until now, but she speaks up, "When you call whomever, you might want to tell him that "Lamb of God" is written in what we believe is the victims' blood all over the walls."

The detectives sit there for a moment trying to understand the meaning of it all when the chief's phone rings. He picks it up, "Chief Barese here." Al listens and hangs up the phone. He stares at a blank wall in this offices and mutters to his team, "They found another eleven bodies."

CHAPTER 35

The phone rings in Fr. Langford's office and he picks up, "Aiden Langford here."

"Good morning, Aiden, how are you?"

"Ah Spartaco, I am fine. I'm in the midst of research into those incidents that have so confounded you and me."

"Well Aiden, be prepared to be even more confounded." Chief Barese then begins to tell the priest all that had happened earlier, the ritual slaughter and the cross carved deeply into the chest of the victims, the rams' heads with the horns cut off and placed on the floor. When he finishes Aiden can hear Al expel the breath, he has held for just this moment.

There is complete silence as the priest ponders the description of the killings. Fr. Aiden doesn't know exactly where to begin questioning his friend or even to know the right questions to ask. "This is truly horrific, Spartaco. I am at a loss to explain how so many innocents could have been murdered. Men and women…"

Al interrupts, "…and children, don't forget the kids who were killed in ways I can't even bring myself to say." The sorrow in the chief's voice is palpable.

"You say the victims are part of the group 'Atheists in America' and they seem to have been killed in a ritualistic manner."

"Yes, at least that's what it appears like; there are some victims who were stabbed and some who were shot, but all in the weirdest of ways. That's what we are assuming at this time but the investigation in still ongoing."

Father Aiden continues his questioning, "You also found the words 'Lamb of God" written in the blood of some of these victims. Is this true?"

"Yeah, it's true. Lamb of God is written all over the place in what appears to be the blood of the victims. We won't know for sure until forensics does their analysis, but I'd bet my life it's the blood of the victims."

Father Aiden tells the chief, "I am particularly interested in those of the murdered men, women and children that were found hanging upside down, crosses carved into their chests, decapitated and their heads replaced with those of a ram. This is most curious."

"Curious, yeah I guess you can call it curious."

Father Langford knows his friend is on edge and wants to explain his comment. "I did not mean to be flippant about this tragedy Spartaco. What I am referencing is the way in which these people were sacrificed in what appears to be a biblical context."

"That's what Dan said. He said that the mass murder seems to be connected to something you would find in the Bible."

"Well Dan is precisely correct. The ram, oxen, bulls and other animals as well as references to their horns are replete in biblical literature."

"Really? What do you mean?"

"Well, Spartaco, the cross as an apparent reference to Christ, would seem obvious. As for the rams' horns, the bible and tradition tell us the horns were used by the ancients to carry oil or used as trumpets. Horns are also symbolic of power and ferocity. On the animal, horns are formidable for both defense and offense and the people of the time recognized the horn as a symbol of authority."

"Well that all makes sense except for the fact that the horns of the ram were cut off the head and laid on the floor in front of the bowls filled with the blood of the victims. I guess in a sick perverted way this is power."

Fr. Aiden thinks for a moment. How would he explain to his friend both good and evil in terms of the significance of horns to the people who lived before and during the time of Christ? "In order for you to understand both the good and evil associated with the horn, it may be instructive to hear what the bible and other texts have to say."

"Ok, I'm listening."

"For example, the blood sacrifice of the horned animal is recounted in Leviticus 4:7, *"The priest shall then put some of the blood on the horns of the (Yahweh's) altar of fragrant incense that is before the LORD in the tent of meeting. The rest of the bull's blood he shall pour out at the base of the altar of burnt offering at the entrance to the tent of meeting."* In Exodus, Luke 1:69, the expression "horn of salvation" as it applies to Christ, means a salvation of strength or a strong Savior."

Uncle Al tries to understand what he is being told, "I think I get it; anything else?"

Fr. Aiden says, "Well there are a number of other quotes from scripture I can give you, but there is one reference of 'good' associated with 'horn' and that is from Psalms 148:14 and I think it is particularly appropriate, *"He also exalteth the horn of his people, the praise of all his saints; [even] of the children of Israel, a people near unto him. Praise Ye the LORD."*

"Okay, I get the references on how the horn was sacred, but what about all the dead people and the use of horns in their murders. What sense can you make of all that."

"Spartaco, I cannot make sense of any of these murders, all I can do is try to provide a biblical association to the evidence you have discovered at your crime scene."

"I know Aiden, I'm sorry. All of this has me so baffled that I don't know where to turn next. You're a great help, please go on."

Father Aiden knows of his friend's dilemma, "No need for apologies you are a good man in search of answers that, in my estimation, could possibly be found in other than earthly realms. Now let us consider the horn and its association with evil. Consider that in Psalm 75:10 it is said, *"I will cut off the horns of all the wicked, but the horns of the righteous will be lifted up."* In Revelation 13:11[30], it is also written, *"Then I saw a second beast, coming out of the earth. It had two horns like a lamb, but it spoke like a dragon."*

Uncle Al asks, "Second beast? Isn't that the devil, you know Satan?"

"The second beast, the beast of the earth, as referenced in Revelations is denoted as the false prophet. As it is written in the Apocalypse, the false prophet is the agent of the Beast. He is there to pave the way for the antichrist and he has been sent to deceive the believers and destroy the Christian faith."

"Antichrist, Aiden you've mentioned him to me before and it still seems impossible to comprehend."

"I know Spartaco, but what I am discerning from all this is that the murderous events taking place, the findings of many inquiries, quotes from scripture even your premonitions of something wicked coming are somehow connected in a disparate way. It is now our ponderous task to somehow find the link."

Uncle Al begins to speak to himself, aloud. "Link? Well, we have 'Lamb of God' written in blood by, Muslims, Atheists, Buddhists, Jews and Christians, Sikhs, you name it; we have what seem to be horrific, sacrificial killings being carried out by otherwise ordinary folks. Many of these people don't even believe in Christ as the son of God and we have these 'Lamb of God' murders happening all over the world without any connection. I am at a total loss. Is there anything else you can tell me?"

"Well, actually there are two additional biblical anecdotes; first, it has been written in scriptures by Jerimiah that cutting off the horns of a sacrificial animal invalidates the sacrifice itself and it is considered a desecration of the altar. The fact that the scene of these murders displays this form of profanation is instructive."

"And the second thing?"

"Beelzebub."

"Beelzebub?"

"Correct. He is the horned demon, one of the seven princes of Hell according to the Christian view. If we are to theorize as to a possible connection to all the disparate events, then you might say the Beelzebub could be orchestrating these happenings. It is a farfetched theory, but while you deal in fact, I can look beyond the concrete and consider the ethereal."

Al holds the receiver as he contemplates what Aiden is saying. He cannot fathom the possibility of a hellish demon being behind the murders, but he knows there are The Sainted and he knows there is a Julian and that means the demon Beelzebub and other forces of hell could be at work here.

"Spartaco, are you there?'

"Sorry Aiden, there's a lot to take in and I am trying to make sense of it all."

"You know Spartaco, you may be right."

"Right? What do you think I may be right about?"

"Something wicked this way comes."

Suffolk County Chief of Detectives Barese sits and considers what Fr. Aiden said and concludes that he could be right. Damn it, he could be right.

CHAPTER 36

As we walk down the stairs, I get the nerve to look at Amanda. I find she is smiling at me, but I turn away quickly feeling my heart beating faster.

We reach the bottom of the stairs and Amanda leads me to the right and we walk through a large set of doors into the formal dining room. The room is large enough to accommodate a table that comfortably seats 24 for dinner. The table is flanked by an intricately woven antique tapestry of a unicorn hanging on one wall. On the opposite wall there is a large fireplace surrounded by what appears to be a very old marble mantle. There is a fire burning in the hearth and it gives the room a beautiful glow and emits comforting warmth.

Harry is seated at the head of the table. As we approach, Harry gets up from his chair and smiles at us, "Good evening, Amanda my dear, you are looking especially lovely tonight." Amanda smiles tenderly at her father, kisses him and says, "Well thank you dad, I want to look especially nice for the two handsome men I'm having dinner with."

Harry turns to me to size up my appearance. He puts his hands on my shoulders and runs them down the sleeves of my tuxedo jacket. He adjusts the silk lapel, brushes off the top of the tux and gives me a very discerning look. "My, my Christopher, that tuxedo seems to fit rather well." Harry has a smug look on his face knowing that he is able to know my exact measurements by just looking at me.

I blush, but I don't think either Harry or Amanda notice. "Well, after all you are Harry of Harry's Place."

Harry smiles and says, "That is true, I must admit."

I look around the room and comment, "Harry, I see you must have run out of money when you designed the dining room."

Harry bursts into laughter and begins to walk around the dining room, surveying the décor. "Well let's see. The mahogany table, which previously graced the summer residence of a king, is early18th century and very reasonably priced at $485,000. The chairs are French circa 18th Century Louis XV Period Fauteuil as I'm sure you've noticed; they are rare antiques of course."

I immediately chime in, "Of course."

Harry continues, "…also reasonably priced at $240,000 for the lot. The English Palladian carved marble mantle cost us a mere $175,000, but I had to scrimp somewhere. Ah, here is a bargain basement work of art that I threw against the wall to hide some water stains. The tapestry is said to have been created by someone named Jean Jans in the 17th century, but it could not be absolutely verified so I was able to negotiate a price of only $275,000. Imagine this treasure for only $275,000!"

I am quashing the urge to laugh as I know that Harry is enjoying this immensely. "Well, I guess that's why you're Harry of Harry's Place."

"Astute observation young man, anyway, the rest of the room contains the odd statuary, paintings by artists of some renown I already had laying around, all thrown together to create this vestige of thriftiness and moderation. All in all, I believe the dining room cost me less than three million." Harry stretches out his arms and looks about the room. "Can you imagine, under three million for all this! I am truly a shrewd bargain hunter, wouldn't you agree?"

I put my hand to my chin and carefully look around the room. "I think you overpaid for the Rembrandt."

Harry and Amanda both laugh and I join in. "Seriously Harry, this is an amazing room as is your entire home. I can't thank you enough for having me as a guest in your beautiful home; I am honored."

Harry puts his hand on my shoulder and says, "It is truly my pleasure, now let's sit down and have dinner."

Harry sits at the head of the table and I sit on one side of him while Amanda sits on the other. I hold out the chair for Amanda who smiles at me as she sits down. I take my seat and before I know it, someone is filling my glass with wine.

Harry gets serious and turns to each of us and looks us straight in the eye, "In deference to Amanda's impatience with my penchant to go on about wine, I trust you both will defer to my choices and agree that I have forgotten more about wine than both of you could ever learn in twelve lifetimes."

Amanda and I both laugh and say, in unison, "We agree."

The table is set with all Chinese antique blue and white porcelain plates, antique wine goblets and what looks like gold flatware. Harry sees that I am admiring the dinnerware. "Chris, as you can see, I love beauty in all forms and these are some of them on the table."

He then turns to look at Amanda and says, "Your mother knew that and that is why she gave you to me." With that Amanda reaches for Harry's hand and the love they have for each other is evident in that they don't need to say another word.

The food is served and each course is delicious. Harry tells us that he dined on the menu being served while on a trip to one of his stores in St. Louis. The store management catered a special dinner in his honor and he enjoyed it so much that he asked his chef to make it on special occasions. For the first course we have these wonderful crepes with smoked salmon and dill sour cream. The second course is an olive and tomato tart served on a bed of Greens with marinated goat cheese. As Harry likes to remind us, he usually choses Pinot Grigio to serve with this first two courses and the wine is the perfect accompaniment.

The second course features honeydew melon soup with blackberries and Orange-Flower Crème Fraiche. For the main course we are served grilled tenderloin of beef with wild mushroom vinaigrette paired with an amazing Cabernet Sauvignon. When dessert finally comes, I am stuffed and glad to see it is a simple small platter of fresh fruit and a selection of chesses. Harry pairs the dessert with the most marvelous Port I have ever tasted.

Throughout the meal we engage in light conversation and Harry dominates the discussion. He tells me of his start in business and how he is able to see where the marketplace is going and how he is able to capitalize on it.

Amanda tells me of her career and how Harry helped her get her start. "It is one tough business and they will crush you no sooner than look at you, but I have a guardian angel and it comes in very handy for me. Once I was able to prove myself, I got the opportunity to read for any number of roles and, well, it all worked out, thanks in great measure to dad."

"Nonsense Amanda! You have your mother's talent and her beauty and you deserve everything you have accomplished. I am very proud of you."

"Thanks dad, but I think you are a bit partial."

Harry smiles and turns to Chris. "Well Chris, what are your plans for the future?"

I have to think about the future because I now have the opportunity to prove myself and to make some money. "I always thought that I would grow my business organically, you know, little by little each year. That seems to have changed for me since I've met you and you've given me the opportunity to make my mark. I'll never be a Harry of Harry's' Place but, corny as it is, I'll be happy and content with being the best businessman and best person I can be."

Harry smiles and looks at me, but speaking to Amanda he says, "You know I had this guy checked out?" Amanda stares at me and says to her father, "I wouldn't have expected anything less. What did you find out?"

"Well, according to reports Chris here is a fine young man. He's honest, probably to a fault, very well-liked by friends, acquaintances and many of the people he does business with. He has some good ideas about how to grow his operation, but is woefully under-funded. He comes from a good family; he is seeing a lovely young nurse and he owns his own home and drives a five-year-old Mustang."

Amanda turns to her father, "How many times a day does he go to the bathroom?"

Harry ignores his daughter and keeps looking at me, "His uncle is the Chief of Detectives in Suffolk County and they have a very good relationship. Chris, in an act of bravery or foolishness, was responsible for rescuing a young girl from the clutches of a gang that specializes in drugs and child prostitution. There was, as I understand it, some sort of gun battle where Chris' uncle nearly dies and Chris nearly gets himself killed. By the way, how is your uncle? Spartaco, I believe?"

I carefully lift the glass of Port to my lips before answering. "He is fine, but don't ever call him Spartaco to his face, he has some kind of issue with his name. As a matter of fact, I can't even call him that so I just call him Uncle Al."

"Ah, well everyone is entitled to their preferences and vanities. I understand that his recovery was quite miraculous."

"It was and I thank God every day."

Amanda looks at me with amazement, "Chris is all this true?"

"Well yeah it is true, but Harry's characterization of this act as foolishness is closer to the truth. I nearly got myself and my uncle killed and it is sheer luck that I am alive to be here with you both." I said a short prayer under my breath to thank The Sainted for their part in the whole episode.

Amanda is staring at me in a way she never has before. "Chris that is amazing. How is the young girl, what's her name?"

"Her name is Tina and she is doing well. Her mom and dad were getting a divorce and I guess it had a far greater impact on her life than her parents ever imagined. Her granddad, Fred, is a good friend of mine and I know he's helping to get her life back on track."

Harry has not taken his eyes off me for the entire time we have been discussing his background check. "You know Chris, I consider myself a good judge of character."

I try to lighten things up, "Well you are Harry of Harry's Place."

He ignores my comment and continues, "You are a good person, an honest one and I am pleased that you are going to be handling the sale of part of my collection."

I don't know what to say, "Thank you Harry, coming from you that is about the greatest compliment I have ever had."

"Good, we will continue first thing in the morning. Now I hope you will both excuse me, but I have some work to do before I retire for the evening. Please relax and enjoy yourselves. Amanda, would you perform hostess duties?" Amanda looks me straight in the eye and tells Harry, "Of course I will dad." The she turns to Harry and says, "Please don't work too hard and get a good night's rest."

I got up from my chair and shake Harry's hand and wish him a good night and he leaves the room. Amanda and I are alone in the dining room and we sit in silence for a moment. She is still looking at me and I am feeling uncomfortable, but I find myself getting curiously excited being alone with Amanda. Amanda is beautiful and she knows that her beauty gives her a powerful advantage that she could use whenever it suits her.

"What do you say we take our glasses and go into the library, it much cozier there."

I find myself getting a bit nervous, but I muster up enough courage to say "Okay."

We walk back down the hall to the library where we sat earlier and enjoyed the wine that Harry served. Unlike earlier, however, we sit down and Amanda sits beside me on the same couch. Her body is turned to face me and she is smiling as if to try and make me even more nervous.

"So, you have a girlfriend, I believe dad said she is, and I quote, a lovely young nurse. What's her name?"

I try to avoid looking at Amanda direct so I take a sip of port and tell her. "Her name is Elizabeth Della Russo, but everyone calls her Beth.

Amanda starts to probe, "How long have you two been going out?"

"We've been going out for about 9 months."

Amanda continues the interrogation, "and…"

"And she is the nurse that treated Uncle Al when he was shot."

I am becoming a bit unnerved as Amanda is enjoying my obvious discomfort as she continues, "and…"

"And we met while I was waiting outside the hospital door to visit Tina's granddad, Fred. My face was busted up so she took pity on me."

Now Amanda is in the zone. She knows how embarrassing it is for me to talk about my girlfriend to another woman, especially one as hot as Amanda, but she continues, "AND…"

I want to slug down the port, but decorum is the rule of the day so I take another sip and say, "And I must have made a good enough impression that she said yes when I asked her to go out with me."

Amanda laughs, "Well that was easy, so tell me about you. What do you enjoy doing when you're not at the selling coins or wherever?"

I think about this for a moment. I know I can't tell her about my visions and the time I spend with The Sainted and I don't want to tell her about my time with Beth, then I realize there is not much more to my life. "You know, now that I think about it, there is not much more to my life than what I do every day. My family and friends are very important to me, but it's not like I go to the opera or to Zumba classes or on African safaris. Now that I think about it, my life can seem pretty boring."

I am anxious to change the subject so I ask, "Well enough about me, it's my turn to ask some questions, how about you, are anyone special in your life?"

Amanda smiles at me. "You don't look at the entertainment sites, read the Hollywood blogs or tabloids, do you?"

I am emphatic when I answer, "Nope, never do."

"Well, if you did you would have read that I am sleeping with every Hollywood hunk or hunkette that is considered a rising star. For the record I'm not a lesbian, never have been. I am 100% heterosexual if you are interested, I date, but never anyone in the business."

I am getting curious, "So what do you do to have fun? Who do you date?"

"Well, there is no one special; I'm attracted to men who are really more grounded, you know men who are programmers or micro brewers or teachers or guys who own their own business." She is on the verge of laughing.

I try not to look directly at Amanda as my face goes flush. Amanda sees my face anyway and stifles the urge to laugh out loud as she continues, "I meet a lot of men through the movie studios and Harry's businesses and some of them are very nice. There's a problem though; most of those guys see me as a way to bypass their climb up the ladder of success and go straight to the top. I guess that it's something that I have to cope with, but it's a turnoff, so I just date casually with the hope that I find someone who is better than that."

Amanda is smiling at me and reveling in that fact that I look like a kid who can't get up enough nerve to approach the prettiest girl in class, but I'm not that easily swayed. "You know, you sound like the poor little rich girl who can't find happiness. I think my mom read me the fairy tale."

Amanda laughs, "Hey, that's pretty funny; you're a funny guy."

I smile back and then I think about Tom Houston. "Hey Amanda, I've got a brilliant idea. Why don't you go out with Tom Houston? He's got it all; perfect face, perfect hair, and he looks great in suits. He's very successful so he's already made it to the top, he's got plenty of money so no need for help from Harry, who already likes him; sounds like a perfect match to me, what do you think?"

Amanda gets serious as she thinks about how to answer my question. "Well to tell the truth, he certainly is all the things you say of him, but there is something very strange about the man. I don't know call it feminine intuition, but I don't like him."

I am surprised at her reaction, "Does Harry know how you feel?"

"He does, but he doesn't force his opinions on me and he understands that I have a different point of view."

I consider what I should say and say it anyway, "To tell the truth, I don't particularly care for his views on politics and religion, but I have to admit he makes it very difficult to dislike him. You know Beth and I were invited to the fundraising event at Madison Square Garden and that's where I met Harry."

Amanda seems curious, "Yes dad told me. What was a peasant like you doing on Mt. Olympus?"

I tell Amanda about how Tom tried to pick-up Beth and how she told him about me. "I guess that Tom wanted to make amends, so he invites us to the event." I went on about Beth being blindsided by Tom and how we managed to sort it out and have a good time. "For me, meeting Harry is the highlight of my career and that's about it. Well except for one thing."

Amanda sits up straight on the couch. "Oh, what's the one thing?"

"Well, I think that Tom likes Beth, I mean he really likes her a lot and he invited us to an event he is holding for Dr. Spencer Price at his house. I couldn't go because I need to be here and so she's there alone. I am sort of jealous and it's not a great feeling."

Amanda is just staring at me and it's making me uncomfortable. I try to sip the last of my port just to give me something to concentrate on other than her, but my nervousness is too obvious to conceal. "Listen Chris, there is no need to be nervous with me. I haven't had a discussion like this since, well I can't even remember when. I think it's very sweet that you're jealous."

"Well, that's me, one sweet guy." We talk and talk and after about two hours Amanda looks at the grandfather clock in the library. "Well, it's getting late, what do you say we go to bed?"

I turn bright red, "Huh? Umm…what?"

Amanda bursts into laughter. "You heard me, let's go to bed. As you are our guest, we can do it together or we can go on our own, either way works for me." Now Amanda is getting a real charge out of embarrassing me.

I gulp and all I can think of to say is, "Well, I am getting tired." I get up and take Amanda's hand to help her up off the couch. As she gets up, she moves very close to me. "I had a wonderful evening; I hope you did too."

I start to answer, "I did…" when she kisses me, I mean really kisses me. I am frozen in place and don't know how to react. Amanda stops and she looks at me and says, "Good night, sleep tight" and smiles as she turns to walk out of the den and up the stairs to her room.

I collapse back onto the couch not knowing how to react. I just got a thinly veiled invitation to go to bed with one of the most beautiful actresses in the world and I am at a loss as to how to react. After a few moments I get back up off the couch and walk toward the stairs leading to the second-floor bedrooms. When I reach the top of the stairs, I look down the hall in the direction of Amanda's bedroom. I stand there for a moment and stare while thinking that I could get into a lot of trouble so I put the thought out of my mind and walk to my room. Just as I am about to open the door, I hear a sound coming from the hall. I look towards her door and see Amanda step into the hallway. She is completely naked and I am paralyzed by her beauty. She stands there; no awkwardness, no insecurities, no discomfiture, just an embodiment of beauty and I look at her, but I don't make a move.

Amanda seems to sense my reticence so she just smiles, blows me a kiss, and steps back into her room. She closes her door and I open mine believing that I will get little or no sleep that night.

Surprisingly, I manage to get a good night's sleep, no dreams of beautiful Amanda, just the pleasant unconsciousness of sleep. I awake at 7AM I shave, brush my teeth and I jump into the shower and let the hot water run over my body for a while. I dress and at 7:30AM I leave my room and walk down the hallway only to find Amanda at the top of the stairs.

"Good morning, how did you sleep?"

I smile at her and respond, "A lot better than I ever thought given the unexpected distraction just before I went into my room."

Amanda laughs and says, "I'll bet it was a surprise. I know that I shouldn't have done what I did, but I thought that we had a special moment and you weren't going to make the first move so I thought that I would. I'm sorry and I apologize."

I realize Amanda is being very genuine and I say, "Listen Amanda, that was about the most exciting and flattering thing that has ever happened to me. Please don't apologize. As a matter of fact, when I write my life story that moment is going to be in chapter five. Of course, I'll change the names to protect the innocent and you know who you are."

Amanda laughs again, "How come the encounter is in Chapter Five and not Chapter One?"

"I guess you're just gonna have to read the book to find out." We are both talking and laughing when Harry walks down the hallway.

He looks questioningly, "What are you two laughing about?"

Amanda and I look at each other and she answers, "Well dad it's like this, Chris here tried to have his way with me last night and it took all my courage, stamina and fortitude to make sure he kept his hands off me."

My face turns deadly serious and my face turns from Amanda to Harry and back as I stammer, "I…I…Amanda is, uh, just kidding…I… I swear, I…"

Now Harry bursts into laughter, "Amanda does this to me all the time. She says the same thing after I meet any man she happens to go out with. You know Chris; I'd have to have you killed you if you ever laid hands on Amanda."

I'm close to being in panic mode. "I…I am…can't, would never…I…"

Now Harry and Amanda are laughing hysterically. I become well aware that they relish making a fool out of me and that helps to calm me down. Harry is the first to say, "Chris, we are just kidding you. First and foremost, you are a gentleman; I found that out for myself. Second Amanda is a big girl and can make her own decisions about how she lives her life and third she could do a lot worse than having you as a friend."

I stare at them both, but all I can say is, "You two should take this show on the road."

Now we all laugh and head down the stairs to breakfast. Believe me when I tell you that I could get used to living and eating like a king. Fresh fruit and juices, eggs made to order, choice of breakfast meats, the most delicious home-fries I've ever eaten, home-made brioches and some great coffee. We sit for an hour talking of many things and enjoying each other's company. After a time, Harry sets down his fork and says, "Well Chris, it's time we get down to work. I will have Jonathan bring us more coffee while we look over the collection."

"That works for me. I am very excited to begin, thanks again for all you've done and the opportunity you've given me."

"You're welcome, now to work!"

We say goodbye to Amanda and leave the room to go into the vault. In the center of the outer room there is a large table with light boxes, large and small magnifying glasses, reference books, inventory lists, note pads, pens etc. "I had my secretary, Natalie, lay this out earlier as I want to spend all the time working out the details. So, what say we dig in!" and that's exactly what we did. I had brought my own laptop, but there is another laptop available for research. For hours we review each and every coin and currency that Harry wants to put up for sale, but there are so many rarities that I find myself spending more time than I should admiring each piece.

We first work with the paper currency and there are some fabulous items of great value. One note that I especially like is the 1896 $5 Silver Certificate in Gem Uncirculated condition. I hold it over the light box to be able to see the remarkable detail of the engraving. I tell Harry, "This is extraordinary, I believe that the auction value should be somewhere upwards of $25,000 possibly $30,000 in this condition." When we finish with the initial survey, we estimate the value of the currency to be worth between $2,800,000 and $3,200,000 and we haven't even begun to evaluate the coins which look to be worth far more.

Harry goes over to another one of the draws that line the room. He takes out one of the draws and brings it over to the table. Harry tells me that there are three draws containing the 800 coins he wishes to sell. Most of the coins are uncirculated or above and graded MS61 and higher. I look at each one under the magnifying glass to determine if they are properly evaluated and what in my opinion is the proper grading. I am sure that Harry or the dealers he works with have done their job very well, but I want to impress Harry.

After working on the first of the draws for about two hours I come across a coin that I have always loved. I am enthralled holding the coin as it is very unusual in terms of its design. I jokingly tell Harry, "I know that this is not the rarest of coins in your collection, but I love just looking at it."

Harry asks me which coin am I looking at and I hand it to him. He takes it and smiles, "The 1915-S Panama-Pacific Octagonal MS62 Gold Issued $50 piece. I love this eight-sided beauty. There were a little more than 1,500 minted, but only 645 were sold. Should be worth upwards of $60,000 to $70,000, do you agree?"

"Yes, but why are you selling it?"

"Well, I own the MS64 and it is worth over $100,000, but value is only part of the story. Coins like this one and so many others are treasures and they should be shared with other collectors, ones who love and appreciate their beauty, value and history. That's probably the main reason that I've resolved to sell part of my collection."

I mean it when I say, "That's very selfless and noble of you Harry."

Harry smiles, "Are you mocking me?"

In all sincerity I answer, "No, not at all, as an enthusiast I have the highest admiration for you, after all you are Harry of Harry Place and there are so many collectors that would consider it an honor to own treasures from your collection." I am hoping Harry knows my good-natured teasing is meant as the highest of compliments.

Harry looks at me and says, "It's yours, my gift to you."

I go from staring at Harry to the coin and back, "Harry I could never accept such a gift."

"Why?"

"First of all, it's worth a lot of money and second well I don't have a second except maybe I don't deserve such generosity."

"Listen Chris, I wouldn't have given you the coin if I didn't want to. When someone gives you a gift you should accept it graciously and understand that it comes from the heart."

I listen to Harry and I can't help but have a flashback of my vision of St. Nicholas. "I don't know what to say Harry."

"Just say thank you and we can get on with our work."

"Thank you, Harry, from the bottom of my heart, thank you."

Harry smiles and says "You're welcome" and we continue. For the next five hours we go through each coin. We are having such a good time as Harry and I continue on the coins from the second draw and spend time determining their value. I look at the clock on the wall and its past five o'clock and I expect to continue, but Harry says that we have covered most of what he hoped to accomplish.

"I think we've done enough for one day. You can take the information on the coins and currency we have covered and you can complete you evaluation. Once you've finished you can send me a report with what you estimate the range of value and your ideas for how to realize the highest prices. We can discuss this and I assure you that I will have some ideas as how to proceed and then we can take it to the next step. I will send you the inventory list and descriptions of the coins in the third draw and you can study them at your leisure. What do you say?"

I am busily consulting my laptop and reviewing the inventory spreadsheets trying to let Harry know my estimates. "Sounds like a plan. Harry I've done some rough calculations relating to the value of the coins we have examined and I've come up with a range of value so far from $6,900,000 to $7,400,000! Counting the currency, you should realize at least $10,000,000! This is unbelievable!"

Harry considers that number, "Well, well that is a tidy sum. It's about what I thought, but having you confirm the amount gives me some measure of comfort. What do you say we go and have a cocktail before dinner?"

I respond, "That's a great idea" and we both walk out of his vault and up to the library where Amanda is waiting. "So did you two have fun?"

Harry's first to reply, "Amanda, I get so much pleasure just looking over Pop-Pop's and my collection."

Amanda seems delighted, "I am so happy you get such joy from your collection. Chris, Pop-Pop is my nickname for my grandfather. Unfortunately, he passed away, but he and Dad had a wonderful relationship"

"I kind of figured that by the way Harry speaks of his father. I have to tell you that Harry and I had the most amazing day…another chapter in my book." I give Amanda a big smile and she just laughs. Jonathan comes into the den to ask us what we would like to drink; Amanda has a gin and tonic; I have a vodka gimlet and Harry has a glass of single malt scotch. We all are talking as Jonathan sets our drinks down on the table and leaves.

I am truly grateful for the opportunity Harry has given me and the amazing gift of the $50 gold piece, "Well, I'd like to make a toast if that's okay with both of you." They each nodded and I begin, "To Harry, I cannot begin to express my sincere gratitude for all you have done for me. It is not every day that a man of your accomplishments reaches out to a, what did you call me Amanda? Ah yes, a peasant, and allow me into your life. It is, for me, an honor that I will always consider among my most special moments. I also have to thank Harry for his generous gift and his lesson in learning how to accept it graciously. Thank you so much Harry, you are a very special and unique individual."

Harry smiles and I continue my toast, "Now to Amanda, you have my thanks for being a beautiful and often hilarious diversion from the business of working on Harry's collection. Finally, I'd like to thank your exceptionally capable staff for making me feel so welcome and at home. So, to all, cent'anni di salute e felicità."

Harry smiles and nods at me and we all take a sip of our drinks and Harry replies, "i miei ringraziamenti per quella meravigliosa oast ei sentimenti che conosco che si voleva esprimere."

I smile, "Grazie."

Amanda now chimes in, "I see that dad thanked you for your wonderful toast and the sentiment behind it and so do I."

"You know Italian?"

"If you live in this house you better learn three languages aside from English; Hebrew, Italian and French and I know all three."

I smile at Amanda and say, "Why am I not surprised? My book is getting longer, now I need to write a Chapter Seven."

We talk for a while when Jonathan comes into the library and reminds us that dinner will be served in a half-hour so we all leave to wash up and get changed into our formal attire. I walk to the steps and Amanda is waiting for me to escort her to the dining room. I won't go into the details, but she looks beautiful and the meal is as delicious as the night before with Harry's choice of wines as the perfect accompanyment.

Harry seems very pleased with the way things went. "I am leaving very early tomorrow morning, but I want to thank you for your smart thinking and good work. I will be gone by the time you get up, but I will have a car take you to the airport in plenty of time for your flight, Natalie will arrange it all."

I reply, "Thank you Harry, my flight isn't until early afternoon so I'll have plenty of time…" but Amanda interupts, "Dad, I am going to Chicago for my interview with "O" Magazine and I can drive Chris."

Harry seems happy and says, "Amanda, that's a splendid idea."

I'm feeling trapped, but I put up a mild protest, "Really Amanda, it's too much trouble. I'm sure the traffic will be crazy."

Amanda ignores me, "Then it's settled, just be ready to leave by 10:30AM, but a word of warning, I drive pretty fast." This all seems to be destined so I just reconcile myself to being driven to the airport by Amanda Sellers, the hottest actress in Hollywood. I guess somebody needs to do it.

It's pretty late when we finish dinner so we all say goodnight and head to our bedrooms. I take a little extra time at my door as I look down the hallway looking to see if Amanda surprises me again, but she doesn't. I guess it's all for the best so I open the door and get ready for bed. Sleep comes easy and I am out for the night.

The next morning I get up and shower. I've got my comfortable travelling clothes on and I've packed all my belongings. I carry my luggage and head towards the stairway, but Amanda's not waiting for me as she usually does. I see Jonathan and say "Good morning Jonathan." He replies, "Good morning sir, please let me take that for you. Breakfast is served and Ms. Sellers is in the dining room waiting for you to join her."

I tell him thanks and head for the dining room. Amanda is sitting down sipping her coffee and smiling as I take my ususal seat.

"Good morning sleepy head, I thought you would never wake up."

"Sleepy head? It's 8AM and I've been up for an hour. What time do you get up?"

"Oh I'm usually up by 5:30AM to exercise and then I shower and have breakfast between 7:30 and 8AM."

"Well that's just perfect 'cause I'm hear right on time." Breakfast is served and we talk about her interview at "O" and about her next movie.

"The studio's PR firm arranged for the interview as part of the promotion for my current feature film which is being released next month."

I'm curious, "What's the movie about?"

"Well the movie is a thriller and I play the role of a woman who begins hallucinating. She decides that she needs to gat away so she decides to take the train going out west to some spa ressort. When she gets there she meets this guy and they get to talking and there is an immediate connection, but things begin to happen to both of them that are pretty freaky. I'm sworn to secrecy so I can't say any more, but it is a juicy part for me and I had a great time doing the movie."

"Really, you can't tell me what's going to happen?"

"Nope, I can't tell you so you're just gonna have to pay to see it on the big screen. So, are you all packed?"

"Regrettabley so, Amanda. This was a great experience for me and one I will never forget. Living large is easy to get use to, being waited on hand and foot if you know what I mean, and now it's back to reality."

Amanda smiles knowingly and tells me she has to get ready for her interview and the more than two hour ride to the airport so she excuses herself and leaves the room. I manage to occupy myself and when it's time, Amanda comes down the stairway into the foyer where I'm waiting. She says, "Well, are you ready for the ride of a lifetime? Hopefully it won't be the last ride of your lifetime."

I gulp, "Maybe I should call a cab."

Amanda laughs knowing that she is a very fast driver and says, "Come on, don't be a sissy; after all you only live once."

With that I say goodbye to Jonathan and shake his hand. I ask him to give my regards and thanks to all who've made this a visit to remember. He smiles and tells me that my luggage is in the trunk of Amanda's car. We exit through the front door and I see Amanda's car. It's a 2016 Mercedes-Benz SL65 AMG 6.0L V-12 with a 621hp twin turbo. How do I know? Well, Amanda makes sure she tells me after I get in and we speed off.

Even though it is early spring and the air is still chilly, the top is down, the heat is on and we cruise the back roads until we reach the highway. Once on the highway Amanda opens it up and the car effortlessly climbs from 0 to 60mph in just over three seconds, but we are doing 90mph before I can speak.

I yell, "Whoa, this is awesome!"

Amanda looks over to me and says, "I just love this car. I've got a few others, but this one is my favorite." It's late morning and the highway is not so crowded, but there is enough traffic that Amanda needs to slow down to a comfortable 75 to 80mph. Amanda checks the rear-view mirror and she says, "Oh, oh!"

I think she's talking about the police, "What, did they catch you for trying to set the land speed record?"

"No, it's the paparazzi. They are always following me; they were probably camping out at the country home. They follow me all the time and I usually recognize them."

"Wow, you have your own paparazzi! That's pretty cool." Amanda and I laugh as she accelerates the car while her nemeses try and keep up. "I like to keep them on their toes so I'll play all kinds of tricks on them. Once I was being followed and I thought that I would try and give them the slip. I sped up, maneuvered around some cars and they tried to follow. Little did they know that there was a highway patrol car just ahead; I managed to slow down in time, but they didn't and they got stopped, I live for these moments!"

The two plus hour trip to the airport takes under two hours and we arrive at Chicago's O'Hare in plenty of time for my flight to Long Island's Islip MacArthur Airport. Amanda stops the car in front of the terminal and I get out and retrieve my luggage from the trunk.

Amanda gets out and stands on the curb. I set the luggage down and I tell her, "Thanks so much for everything; you are an amazing person and I intend to get all my friends very jealous by telling them that I met you."

"Is that all you're going to tell them?"

"Why, what do you mean?"

"This is what I mean." Amanda puts her arms around my neck as she stares into my eyes for a brief moment. Her lips are soft and her embrace is warm and she kisses me for a very long time. I am in a state of complete paralysis; I can't move and Amanda just keeps holding me tight in her arms. I come alive when I hear the click of cameras and murmurs of the growing crowd now surrounding us.

When we finally part, we both look around at the paparazzi and adoring fans that are applauding our encounter. I am a very confused, "What was that all about Amanda?" but Amanda just laughs at my chagrin.

"I don't know I just felt like kissing you. Tell that beautiful nurse of yours that she has nothing to worry about, or does she? Have a safe trip home." Amanda smiles and touches my cheek; more clicks more murmurs and she get back into her car and eases away from the curb. I then realize, "Shit, Beth is gonna see this! What am I gonna tell her?" The crowd disperses and I drag my bag through security and to the gate for my flight home.

The flight takes off and I am getting more and more depressed at the prospect of having to explain what happened with Amanda to Beth. The stewardess is coming down the aisle with drinks and that is when everything freezes and the vision appears.

The archangel leads the man and woman from high atop the mountain. The man and woman know of the dangers as the Father has told them. The archangel hopes to help rescue the two from the evils of Satan, but it appears that there is no recourse for them other than what God has commanded.

"Bring them down from the top of the high mountain and take them to the Cave of Treasures" and Selaphiel did as he was told.

The man and woman are without robes or any other garments. They are as they were created, naked and innocent, free of shame. But that is no longer to be. Their pride betrays them and it is Satan that blinded them to the truth and they are ashamed of their nakedness. Their being, their entire existence is born of God's love and His desire for mankind to live in the Paradise He created for them.

The man and woman take measured steps as they know they are to be exiles, outcasts from the Garden, condemned by God to the worldly realm where there are only the labors of life outside of His holy, blessed light.

I look at the Archangel, St. Selaphiel, and I am ashamed. "I was tempted and I feel like I betrayed someone I care for and love. I know the Sainted must be very upset with me."

"It is not for The Sainted to judge, it is for you to decide what is right and what is not; if you judge your actions to be betrayal then that is what they are. Adam and Eve thought only of themselves and not of the admonition of God. They became prideful and embraced the temptations brought on by the serpent and gave into his all-consuming wickedness."

In the vision St. Selaphiel walks toward the cave and as he points to the entrance, Adam and Eve fall to the ground. Adam cries and says to Eve,

> *"Look at this cave that is to be our prison in this world, and a place of punishment! What is it compared with the garden? What is its narrowness compared with the space of the other? What is this rock, by the side of those groves? What is the gloom of this cavern, compared with the light of the garden? What is this overhanging ledge of rock to shelter us, compared with the mercy of the Lord that overshadowed us?"*

> *Eve is prostrate with grief, but she gets up off the ground and lifts her arms toward God, appealing to Him for mercy and pity, and says, "O God, forgive me my sin, the sin which I committed, and don't remember it against me for I caused Your servant to fall from the garden into this condemned land, from light into this darkness and from the house of joy into this prison."*

> *After this Adam does not want to enter the cave, under the overhanging rock nor would he ever want to enter it. But he bows to God's orders and says to himself, "Unless I enter the cave, I shall again be a transgressor."*

I stare at the vision and I speak to St. Selaphiel, "I know that like Adam, I have confronted temptation and I cannot hope for redemption without acknowledging my sins."

St. Selaphiel speaks, "That is true Christopher, but as God the Father admonished Adam and Eve, so all are admonished that do not heed His words."

> *"It was Satan who made the tree appear pleasant in your eyes, until you ate of it, by believing his words. Thus, have you transgressed My commandment and therefore I have brought on you all these sorrows, for I am God the Creator, who, when I created My creatures, did not intend to destroy them."*

"Our creed is simple, heed the word of God and your reward is eternal life, heed the word of Satan and your punishment will be eternal damnation." St. Selaphiel becomes surrounded by the heavenly glow and disappears.

My hands are gripping the armrests of the seat when someone says, "Sir?" I jump up; stunned at the voice and I see it's the stewardess. She says, "Sorry I didn't mean to startle you, would you like something to drink?"

I don't hesitate, "Double vodka on the rocks."

CHAPTER 37

He weeps on hearing of the deaths of his friends, brothers in Christ, Paul and Peter. He knows his mission is to preach to the faithful throughout Asia Minor, but his sadness is all consuming. The holy man's ministry continues as his travels take him to the countryside near and around Ephesus and that is where he settles.

John spreads the word of the Lord in the land where many of the people worship as idolaters. As he preaches in the shadow of the temple, the pagans assemble and there they move against the apostle. They force him into the temple dedicated to Diana and they demand that he do sacrifice to the idol, but he will have none of it.

"If ye believe that the powers of your goddess are so great then I demand you call on her. Implore her to wield her powers to undermine and overthrow the church of Christ. If her powers are so great then these things will come to pass and I shall kneel before your god." The crowd looks back at the holy man as he continues to speak, "In turn, you must allow me to pray to my God through His son Jesus Christ that He overthrows this temple and if it comes to pass then it is you, followers of the false god, who must believe."

The high priest, Aristodemus, sneers from a dark corner of the temple. He remains silent as the assembled crowd voices consent to this pact and await the impending collapse of the church that this fool speaks of; this church of the Jew from Galilee.

John raises his arms toward heaven and prays. He asks that a sign from Heaven be sent and the temple be destroyed so that all may become believers. In a matter of moments there is a terrible rumbling that seems to come from above and below. The people that have gathered become very frightened they look around and see the large stone pillars and granite walls of the temple shake. With great haste the men and women flee the temple and run for safety outside their place of worship. John continues to pray as the temple falls upon itself and the statue of Diana turns to dust.

All those who are witnesses become silent as the holy man arises and looks at the destruction. "Do you now see the power of God? Do you now know there shall be no gods before Him? Do you now believe?"

Aristodemus stares in stunned silence, but he knows that he cannot allow this blasphemy to go unanswered. In desperation he puts forth a challenge to John, "I have another test for your God and if you survive, I will bow down and swear my allegiance."

John looks at the priest and answers, "What is this test you have for me?"

This time Aristodemus smiles, "You will take this cup of poisonous wormwood oil and drink it." He then points to two men who are bound and kneeling on the ground before him and says, "To prove that it is truly poison you will make these two prisoners drink from the cup first and then you will take the cup and drink from it yourself. If you endure then I will acknowledge your God as the one true God above all."

John knows that this is a trial he must face; one that will affirm his faith in the Lord and in the presence of the crowd that bears witness. The men are shaking with fear for they know their fate. John takes the cup to each of the prisoners; he blesses them telling them not to fear. The men have little choice but to drink from the cup of poison and in moments they are dead. Next John takes the cup and drinks all that is left and he drops the vessel to the ground. He kneels over the bodies of the dead men who drank the poison and St. John places hands on them and says a quiet prayer.

Both men open their eyes and look up only to see John praying over them. The prisoners manage to stand and look at each other in disbelief and then back at John. They speak, "How is it that we are still alive?"

There is a loud gasp that comes from many of those in the crowd who witnessed this miracle and John admonishes the prisoners, "You are alive through the blessings and mercy of God the Father and His Son Jesus Christ. Now go in peace and sin no more."

The men, now unbound, are confounded as they walk through the crowd. John stands there staring at Aristodemus who is nearing madness. The pagan priest cannot imagine how all this could transpire: how did John survive? How did the prisoners survive? Can it be that his God is the true God?

Aristodemus wishes to speak, but he has no words for the holy man. As the pagan priest stands there in stunned silence it is John who speaks first, "I know my Lord and Savior, I would gladly die for Him as He has died for us. You can be saved, change my son, change for Jesus for He has sent me to you."

On hearing the words of John, Aristodemus falls to his knees and with a heavy heart begins to weep saying to John, "I now know the truth." The pagan priest begs forgiveness and kisses the hand of the holy man in penance. With this sign of reverence to God the Father and His Son Jesus, John knows the Aristodemus is truly repentant. John then turns to the crowd and preaches from an earlier epistle that was sent to the faithful among the seven churches.

"Dear friends, do not believe every spirit, but test the spirits to see whether they are from God, because many false diviners have gone out into the world. This is how you can recognize the Spirit of God: Every spirit that acknowledges that Jesus Christ has come in the flesh is from God, but every spirit that does not acknowledge Jesus, that spirit is not from God. This is the spirit of the antichrist, which you have heard is coming and even now is already in the world."

John continues to speak to the crowd, "As it has also been prophesized that there will be a false prophet and he will be called the Beast from the earth and he will become an agent of the antichrist within the Church, sent to destroy and deceive the Christian faith. You must reject him or lose your souls to the madness and eternal punishment that is hell."

The crowd stares at John in both wonder and puzzlement. What are the meanings in the words he speaks? How could they know this beast and this antichrist? What must they do to be spared from eternal damnation? The people have no answers as it seems this miracle worker did, but do they have the courage to follow him?

John turns and walks away knowing that more is to be revealed…much more.

CHAPTER 38

Beth and Tom stop dancing when the music ends, but he continues to hold Beth in his arms as they look into each other's eyes. At once Beth seems to snap out of her entranced state and she gently pushes Tom away. Tom smiles and says, "You are a wonderful dancer." Beth doesn't know how she should answer, but finally says, "Thanks, so are you."

The fundraiser for Dr. Price is going great as Tom takes Beth's hand and leads her off the dance floor. Everyone seems to be having a wonderful time and Spencer Price is in his glory. The band is keeping the party mood alive and people are dancing, drinking, laughing and all-in-all it is being called the event of the social season by those who are there.

Time goes by and Beth is enjoying herself immensely. The champagne is flowing as she relishes glass after glass. Eventually Beth and Tom find their way back to Spencer who is smiling broadly as he sees them approach. Spencer is surrounded by a small, but highly renowned group of wealthy individuals and he says, loud enough for all to hear, "Tom, thank you from the bottom of my heart for the wonderful gesture in hosting this fundraiser. I cannot believe the money that you have raised on behalf of the center for its work in cancer research. I want to make you this pledge. All the money that is being contributed will be used for this vital effort and I will labor tirelessly until we find the cure."

The group surrounding Dr. Price, including Beth and Tom, burst into applause and Spencer embraces Tom and they both smile.

"Well, you are more than welcome. I believe this near bit of effusive praise from Spencer calls for a toast." Spencer and the group laugh at Tom's words and as soon as he finishes, a waiter comes over with a tray full of fluted champagne glasses filled to the brim with Taittinger Comtes Blanc de Blancs 2005 and the small group raises their glasses and turn to face the man of the hour, Dr. Spencer Price.

There is silence as Tom speaks, "Spencer, when you tell us that you are committed to finding a cure for cancer no one here, or for that matter in the entire world, would ever doubt that. As a matter of fact, if there is ever hope for a cure it will come from your leadership at the Price Center for Cancer Research and for that the entire world is grateful. Now let's raise our glasses to Spencer, a genius, a trusted friend and a true American original."

In unison the group says, "To Spencer!"

Spencer lifts his glass to his lips and with his patented impish grin looks over the top of the rim of his glass at Tom and announces, "Thank you Tom, truer words were never spoken." And everyone starts to laugh.

For some reason, possibly her uneaten plate of food or too much champagne or both, Beth starts to laugh hysterically. Spencer and Tom look at each other and back at Beth and they start to laugh hysterically too. The laughter becomes contagious and now the whole group joins in. Before the laughter has a chance to die down, Beth takes a step towards Tom and trips and falls into his arms.

He looks at her and says, "Well I see that you're a real light weight."

Beth looks at him and in a serious tone she says, "Oh, not I am!" and she starts laughing again.

Spencer and Tom smile at each other and Tom puts his arm around Beth's waist trying to keep her from collapsing and he says to all, "Ms. Della Russo seems to have had too much champagne and not enough food so I think that we will bring her to someplace where she can rest for a while."

He motions to one of his staff, "Please take Ms. Della Russo to one of the guest bedrooms and see that she is made comfortable." His aide responds, "Of course Dr. Houston" and his aide leads the compliant Beth to the elevator that goes to the second-floor bedrooms. Beth, with help from the aide, opens the door to one of the guest bedrooms and he puts her down on the bed and covers her with a quilt. He turns off the light as he closes the door, but Beth doesn't notice as she has long since passed out.

The party goes strong for the next couple of hours and at 2AM most of the guests have left and those who are still there are putting on their coats and saying their good-byes to Tom and Spencer. The staff and caterers are dutifully cleaning up and Tom is confident that his home would look perfect and there would be little or no remnants left of the party in the morning.

An ebullient Tom looks at Spencer and says, "Well Spencer, looks like the event was a resounding success."

An exhausted, but happy Dr. Price says, "Thanks to you, my friend."

"Glad to do it. Now even I need to get some rest so let me show you to your bedroom and we can meet for breakfast tomorrow morning at say 5AM."

"Go to hell, I'm sleeping in" and both men start to laugh.

They take the elevator to the third floor and Tom walks Spencer to his bedroom. "Get a good night's rest Spencer and dream of all the cancer you will be eradicating over the next decade or two."

"I should only live so long, but thanks again Tom for all you have done and all you continue to do." Spencer embraces his benefactor and he opens the door to his bedroom.

Tom's room is on the second floor and he decides to take the stairway down. The house is quiet except for some movement on the floor below as the cleanup continues. He walks down the hallway but walks past the entrance to his bedroom. Tom Houston passes two more closed doors before he stops in front of Beth's bedroom and he opens the door and enters. Once inside he closes the bedroom door and he stands and gazes at the form of Beth sleeping under the quilt, breathing softly. Although the room is shrouded in darkness Tom has no trouble navigating to her bedside.

"Things are going according to your plan." Tom speaks in a low voice to no one in the room.

Beth is still asleep, but her body starts to stir under the quilt.

Tom stares at the beautiful woman and speaks again to no one. "I will not fail. All you have commanded will be done." He gently sits down on the edge of the bed for fear he would wake her up. He brushes back a strand of hair that has fallen across Beth's forehead and her stunning beauty is not lost on Tom.

In an instance Tom snaps his head towards the darkness that envelops the room. He speaks again to no one, "Of course not, I will not let anything get in the way of your plan it's just that…" but Tom's voice trails off. Now a sense of fear seems to overtake Tom as he raises his voice, "Please my lord, please…I am loyal. I will do all you command I will never…" but he stops speaking as if someone or something commanded him to be silent.

Tom detects a movement as Beth's body seems to softly writhe under the quilt. She moans as if she were in a dream of some unknown happening. Her face seems to attract whatever light there is in the room and Tom is mesmerized. He reaches to touch her face and his hands move down her neck and shoulders and he can no longer hold himself back. His face is inches from Beth's and he finally kisses her, first softly then more passionately.

When he lifts his head up to look at Beth, she manages to open her eyes and then realizes that Tom is sitting next to her.

"Where am I?"

Tom smiles, "You are in one of the bedrooms in my house sleeping off what appears to be the effects of too much champagne and not enough food."

Staring beyond the haze of an alcohol induced headache, Beth realizes what has happened and she becomes distressed. "Tom, I can't believe that I got drunk! I must have made such a fool of myself, oh my God, in front of all your guests and Spencer too!"

Tom starts to laugh, but Beth is getting more and more upset. "How can you laugh? This is the most embarrassing thing that has ever happened to me."

Tom says, "Oh Beth, you're still young I'm sure you have a lot more embarrassing moments to come so don't make yourself crazy."

Beth tries to lift herself off the bed, but she immediately collapses back, a result of the blinding headache that seems to be taking hold. "Tom, how can you make fun of me, how can you laugh at what has happened? I've embarrassed myself; I've embarrassed Spencer and I've embarrassed you." Now Beth starts to cry and turns away.

Tom is no longer smiling, "Listen to me Beth, I know that you are embarrassed by what happened, but believe me when I tell you that no one even noticed and even if they did notice, if it's not about them, they really don't care."

Beth stops crying however she refuses to look at Tom. He hands her a handkerchief so she can wipe the tears away. "By the way, while you were sleeping, a few guests had some mishaps that you might want to hear about."

Tom hopes to see the hint of a smile coming to Beth's face, but there is none; however, he takes Beth's silence as a sign to continue. "Well Pauline Carletto, you know the famous TV chef, had an unfortunate wardrobe malfunction as one of her breasts explodes from her dress. If you saw her dress, you would understand that this was inevitable." Tom knows how to engage an audience so when he detects a smile on Beth's face he continues,

"Oh, and Aaron Knowles, the hip-hop mogul; well, he was holding court over a number of the most strait-laced investment banker types you could ever hope to find. It seems that there was a lull in the conversation and that's when Aaron let's go of one of the loudest farts you have ever heard." Now Beth can't hold it back any longer and bursts into laughter.

"Now here is the 'pièce de résistance'! I am sure you are familiar with Romulus Coltrane, the world-renowned concert pianist. He has been known to, shall we say, over-indulge at the buffet troth. Well Romulus was in rare form tonight. He made countless trips to the buffet table and filled his plate with everything in sight. After five or six hours even, Romulus had his fill so he decides that he should dance some of the calories off. He spots Constance Beam, the billionaire widow and heiress to the Beam Fortune, and drags her to the dance floor. Well, the band and singer are playing their version of "Happy" made famous by singer, songwriter Pharrell Williams and Romulus is doing his very best dance moves with prim and proper Constance starting to get into the mood."

Beth is trying her very best not to laugh, but it is futile and Tom knows it so he continues. "Now everyone, but Constance, notices that Romulus' face is turning green. It seems that the combination of fettuccine Alfredo, shrimp scampi, beef wellington, Brussel sprouts with chives and bacon, tempura and, of course, an extra helping of baked Alaska is something to avoid if you are going to dance to Pharrell's "Happy." Beth is now laughing hysterically surmising what will come next.

"Well Romulus now realizes he is no longer in control of his stomach and all his gyrations have increased the noises coming from his mid-section. Constance is still dancing, oblivious to the predicament that Romulus is in, but eventually she deems it fitting that she should look at her dance partner and smile. Unfortunately, she picks the exact moment that Romulus decides to hurl and he vomits all over the poor billionaire heiress."

"Next…" but Beth stops him as she wipes away her tears of laughter, "Tom, I get it and thank you for trying to make me feel better. Did those things really happen?"

"Of course, they did, would I lie to you?"

Beth stays silent for a moment looking into Tom's eyes and whispers, "Yes you would."

Tom answers, "I guess I had that coming. What can I do to get it right with you Beth?"

Beth is staring at Tom "You've done so much for the hospital, for Spencer you don't need to get it right with me, you already have."

Beth is still shaky from the effects of the alcohol when Tom bends down and kisses her. Her eyes close, her lips are warm and welcoming, but she does not understand why she is feeling the way she does. Tom is gentle as his lips move across her cheek and down to her neckline. In an instance, Beth comes to the realization of what is happening and pushes Tom away. "Tom, please we can't do this, it's wrong of me to be here with you like this. I think I need to go home now."

Tom pulls back and he's sitting at the edge of the bed. "Beth, I've made it no secret how much I like you. I don't mean to upset you, but I can't get you out of my mind. It's a feeling that I've never felt before and I just couldn't resist kissing you."

Beth is quiet trying to consider what to say to Tom, but he speaks first, "Listen, you are in no condition to drive. It's nearly 3AM and you could use a good night's sleep. I promise I will leave you alone to get some rest and, in the morning, I will have someone drive you and your car home."

"Tom, I really should…"

"Please Beth, if not for me do it for Spencer. I know he would be heart-broken if you leave without saying goodbye and if you got into an accident, he would never forgive himself. Please stay here and in the morning, things will look much brighter, I promise."

Beth sighs, "Okay, I am so dizzy and the room is spinning so I guess trying to drive is not a good idea."

"Terrific, it's settled and now I wish you a good night." Tom bends over and Beth immediately tenses up, but he kisses her on the forehead much to her relief. Tom walks to the bedroom door and leaves Beth to try and get a good night's sleep.

The next day Beth wakes up and for an instance she doesn't know where she is. In a few moments though, the memories of the night before come flooding back and Beth lays in the bed and tries to make sense of it all. There is a private bath and Beth goes and gets undressed and takes a shower. She looks around and finds that there are plush robes, toiletries and all the many sundry items she needs to freshen up.

After Beth showers and washes her hair, she finds a blow dryer and begins to dry her long, dark hair. She decides to leave it down and goes to put on her formal gown from the night before. It is all she has to wear, but as she begins to dress herself there is a knock on the door.

Knowing it might be Tom she asks from behind the closed door, "Who's there?"

"Good morning, Ms. Della Russo, I'm Lisa Talbot, the head of house-keeping and Dr. Houston asked me to see that you have everything you need."

Beth is relieved and answers, "Yes, thank you it seems that I have everything I need."

"Dr. Houston thought that you might like a change of clothes."

Beth is nonplussed, "How did he…how could he know that I…"

"Lisa explains, "Dr. Houston mentioned that you were staying as his guest and that you might need something to wear as all you have is your formal attire. This morning he asked me to go and pick up something for you to wear and I went to a wonderful local boutique shop and bought these items. If you open the door, I can show them to you."

"This morning? What time is it?" Beth said this at the same time she opens the door.

"It is 12:45PM." Beth gasps at the time as Lisa enters the room with a bundle of clothing. She lays it out on the bed for Beth to see, but Beth is still mystified. "How did you know my size?"

Lisa explains, "Well I came into your bedroom and while you were sleeping and I took a guess as to your size, but I also bought a size smaller and a size larger just in case I was wrong, but I assure you I am seldom wrong when it comes to these things. Now, may I help you get dressed?"

Beth is still tired and decides that she could use some help. "Thanks Lisa, I'm still a little shaky from last night." Lisa smiles and reaches for Dolce and Gabbana beige colored blazer, beautiful Giorgio Armani navy silk lined pants, a form fitting silk blouse by Marc Jacobs, she even thought to bring shoes, undergarments and hosiery.

Beth looks at the clothing Lisa chose and she says, "Wow, you are spot on. These are just beautiful and they are my exact size! Thank you so much for doing this."

Lisa smiles, "You are most welcome. I will remove the tags and you can take these into your dressing room and change. I will take your evening gown and coat along with your shoes and place them into the limousine for your ride home. I hope you had a pleasant stay." Beth gives Lisa her thanks and they say good-bye.

Next Beth finishes drying her hair and finds the clothes that Lisa selected hanging in the dressing room next to the bath. Beth puts on the new clothing and she looks at herself in the mirror and judges that Lisa's choices are the right ones.

Beth takes a deep breath knowing that she must open the door and face Tom again after their encounter last night. As she leaves the room, she looks down the hallway and to her right she sees the stairway leading to the first floor. She is beyond nervous, but overcomes her unease and walks down to the main floor. There at the bottom of the stairway is Tom is talking to someone, but he hears footsteps and he looks up to see Beth walking down.

She looks beautiful and Tom asks, "How did you sleep last night?"

Beth answers, "Fine, I guess, but I'm still a little shaky. By the way, thank you so much for the clothes, they are beautiful and thanks to Lisa they fit perfectly. I will dry clean them when I get home and send them back."

Tom gets serious, "You will need to leave your credit card otherwise take those clothes off now." Beth doesn't want to smile, but she does anyway.

"Tom, sincerely, thanks for your understanding and kindness. Now I think I should get home."

Tom tries to persuade her "Come on Beth; at least have lunch with me. You must be hungry and you should get something in your stomach."

"No, I really want to get home. Can I say goodbye to Spencer before I leave?"

"Spencer did try to wait, but he had to catch a flight to Miami and left here at 11:30AM. He did make me promise to tell you that he is so glad you were at the event and he especially wants to thank you for rescuing him from the onrush of admirers last night."

Beth smiles as she recollects the moment and says, "I am so sorry I missed saying goodbye to him. He has been so nice to me, as you have Tom." When Beth says this, she looks away for fear her emotions will take over.

Tom doesn't press the issue of lunch with Beth and just says he will let Spencer know how sorry she is that she didn't have a chance to say goodbye. He offers his arm to Beth and she takes it as they walk through the foyer out onto the circular drive and to the waiting limo. "Lisa put your belongings in the trunk and Carter will follow the limo and drive your car home. Thank you for being a beautiful addition to the event. I am smitten and I shall reconcile myself to being the victim of unrequited love."

Beth laughs at Tom and says "For some reason I can't imagine that you'll be a victim very long." She moves toward Tom and she gives him a kiss on the check and he holds her tight and kisses her back.

Tom opens the door and Beth gets in the limo. He bends down and tells her "Make sure you say hello to, what's his name, ah yes, Fennimore from me."

Beth tries not to smile at their inside joke, but she can't help it. "I will."

The chauffeur starts the limousine and pulls out of the driveway and away from Tom's mansion, much to Beth's relief. Tom waits until the limo is out of sight and goes back inside his home and closes the front door.

Across the street the two men hiding behind a tall hedge remain still. Man number one asks, "Did you get it?"

Number two smirks, "Did I ever. These photos should go for at least $5,000."

"You think?"

"Yep" and with that, number two packs his Nikon D3S digital camera and telephoto lens. The men sneak through the yard of the home directly across from Tom Houston's mansion to their car with dreams of $5,000 dancing in their heads.

ST. JOHN THE EVANGELIST

Saint John the Divine was the son of Zebedee, and his mother's name was Salome [Matthew 4:21, 27:56; Mark 15:40, 16:1]. They lived on the shores of the sea of Galilee. The brother of Saint John, probably considerably older, was Saint James. The mention of the "hired men" [Mark 1:20], and of Saint John's "home" [John 19:27], implies that the condition of Salome and her children was not one of great poverty.

SS. John and James followed the Baptist when he preached repentance in the wilderness of Jordan. There can be little doubt that the two disciples, whom Saint John does not name (John 1:35), who looked on Jesus "as he walked," when the Baptist exclaimed with prophetic perception, "Behold the Lamb of God!" were Andrew and John. They followed and asked the Lord where he dwelt. He bade them come and see, and they stayed with him all day. Of the subject of conversation that took place in this inter-view no record has come to us, but it was probably the starting-point of the entire devotion of heart and soul which lasted through the life of the Beloved Apostle.

John apparently followed his new Master to Galilee, and was with him at the marriage feast of Cana, journeyed with him to Capernaum, and thenceforth never left him, save when sent on the missionary expedition with another, invested with the power of healing. He, James, and Peter, came within the innermost circle of their Lord's friends, and these three were suffered to remain with Christ when all the rest of the apostles were kept at a distance [Mark 5:37, Matthew 17:1, 26:37]. Peter, James, and John were with Christ in the Garden of Gethsemane. The mother of James and John, knowing our Lord's love for the brethren, made special request for them, that they might sit, one on his right hand, the other on his left, in his kingdom [Matthew 20:21]. There must have been much impetuosity in the character of the brothers, for they obtained the nickname of Boanerges, Sons of Thunder [Mark 3:17, see also Luke 9:54]. It is not necessary to dwell on the familiar history of the Last Supper and the Passion. John was committed by our Lord the highest of privileges, the care of his mother [John 19:27]. John [the "disciple whom Jesus loved"] and Peter were the first to receive the news from the Magdalene of the Resurrection [John 20:2], and they hastened at once to the sepulcher, and there when Peter was restrained by awe, John impetuously "reached the tomb first."

In the interval between the Resurrection and the Ascension, John and Peter were together on the Sea of Galilee [John 21:1], having returned to their old calling, and old familiar haunts.

When Christ appeared on the shore in the dusk of morning, John was the first to recognize him. The last words of the Gospel reveal the attachment which existed between the two apostles. It was not enough for Peter to know his own fate; he must learn also something of the future that awaited his friend. The Acts show them still united, entering together as worshippers into the Temple [Acts 3:1], and protesting together against the threats of the Sanhedrin [Acts 4:13]. They were fellow-workers together in the first step of Church expansion. The apostle whose wrath had been kindled at the unbelief of the Samaritans, was the first to receive these Samaritans as brethren [Luke 9:54, Acts 8:14].

He probably remained at Jerusalem until the death of the Virgin, though tradition of no great antiquity or weight asserts that he took her to Ephesus. When he went to Ephesus is uncertain. He was at Jerusalem fifteen years after Saint Paul's first visit there [Acts 15:6]. There is no trace of his presence there when Saint Paul was at Jerusalem for the last time.

Tradition, more or less trustworthy, completes the history. Irenaeus says that Saint John did not settle at Ephesus until after the death SS. Peter and

Paul, and this is probable. He certainly was not there when Saint Timothy was appointed bishop of that place. Saint Jerome says that he supervised and governed all the Churches of Asia. He probably took up his abode finally in Ephesus in 97. In the persecution of Domitian he was taken to Rome, and was placed in a cauldron of boiling oil, outside the Latin gate, without the boiling fluid doing him any injury. [Eusebius makes no mention of this. The legend of the boiling oil occurs in Tertullian and in Saint Jerome]. He was sent to labor at the mines in Patmos. At the accession of Nerva he was set free, and returned to Ephesus, and there it is thought that he wrote his gospel. Of his zeal and love combined we have examples in Eusebius, who tells, on the authority of Irenaeus, that Saint John once fled out of a bath on hearing that Cerinthus was in it, lest, as he asserted, the roof should fall in, and crush the heretic. On the other hand, he showed the love that was in him. He commended a young man in whom he was interested, to a bishop, and bade him keep his trust well. Some years after he learned that the young man had become a robber. Saint John, though very old, pursued him among the mountain fastnesses, and by his tenderness recovered him.

In his old age, when unable to do more, he was carried into the assembly of the Church at Ephesus, and his sole exhortation was, "Little children, love one another."

The date of his death cannot be fixed with anything like precision, but it is certain that he lived to a very advanced age. He is represented holding a chalice from which issues a dragon, as he is supposed to have been given poison, which was, however, innocuous. Also, his symbol is an eagle.

From The Lives of the Saints by the Rev. S. Baring-Gould, M.A., published in 1914 in Edinburgh.

ACKNOWLEDGEMENTS

I'm sitting at my desk trying to come up with a few short paragraphs about those I would like to acknowledge among The Sainted, their chroniclers and other sources who I've used to help in writing this book. I was able to get a large measure of knowledge of The Sainted, the lives they lived, their insights and through research available online to all, including authors like myself.

Imagine yourself a prisoner or a preacher or a believer in a land of non-believers. Now imagine you are condemned to death and the only sanctuary you have is your belief. It is impossible for me to conceive what so many of The Sainted had to face, but they did. They lived their lives, even faced their own deaths with such deep and abiding faith that one can only contemplate in admiration at the sacrifices of these remarkable men and women.

This is not to say that all saints are martyrs or perfect human beings, far from it. Many of these people were sinners who found their way to God. They were soldiers, priests, teachers, scholars among many other callings. Some saints were kings and queens, converts, poets, slaves and farmers… and, yes, some were even lawyers and politicians. Some were married, some had children, some were very wealthy and some were very poor, but they had a commonality of single-mindedness and that is their belief in God the Father and His Son, Jesus Christ. I think that it would be important to note there is such a diversity of personalities and life experiences that to truly comprehend the worth of The Sainted and their inspiration would require an encyclopedia itself.

As usual, words cannot express true gratitude for allowing me to have access to such information, inspiration and to know how fortunate we are, as a people, for such Sainted to have walked among us.

St. Anthony of Padua

St. Elizabeth of Portugal

St. John of the Cross

St. John the Evangelist

St. George

St. Matthew

Sts. Meldan and Beoan

St. Nicholas

St. Patrick

St. Selaphiel

St. Teresa of Avila

Catholic Online

www.catholic.org

Immaculate Conception Seminary - http://www.icseminary.edu

Rev. S. Baring-Gould

Saints.SQPN.org - http://saints.sqpn.com

Wikipedia - www.wikipedia.org

http://www.jesuswalk.com/lamb/lamb-agnus-dei-artwork.htm

www.biblehub.com

http://www.britannica.com

http://www.sacred-texts.com

http://www.catholicculture.org

http://catholicsaints.info/pictorial-lives-of-the-saints

http://www.bible-history.com

http://www.christianiconography.info

"The Forgotten Books of Eden" (1927) The World Publishing Company. Translated in the late 1800's by Dr. S. C. Malan and Dr. E. Trumpp.
http://www.scborromeo.org/ccc/p2s2c2a4.htm
http://www.beginningcatholic.com/sacrament-of-reconciliation.html
"Handed Down: The Catholic Faith of the Early Christians by James L. Papandrea."
Catholic Answers Press (October 28, 2015)
http://satanicverses.org/
Beatle Copyright (?)
Seinfeld Copyright (?)
The Bible, Old and New Testaments

Excerpt from
The Sainted Trilogy
Book Three "MEGIDDO"

The priest sits in the confessional and waits.

The chapel at the Immaculate Conceptions Seminary is open every Thursday and is reserved for those lay people who wish to partake in the Sacrament of Reconciliation. It is still early and there is no one in the chapel so Fr. Aiden Langford takes the opportunity to read while he waits for his first penitent.

He picks up the book he chose to read, "Handed Down: The Catholic Faith of the Early Christians by James L. Papandrea." The book speaks to the fact that most Protestants believe there is little similarity between modern Catholic orthodoxy and that of Christians in the first centuries. Fr. Aiden finds the book very interesting as it is written by a former Protestant minister who is able to show that modern Catholics and early Christians are in fact staunch in their adherence to the rituals and beliefs of the church. Fr. Aiden is especially interested in the author's claim that pastors, teachers and writers known as the Church Fathers use the gospel to develop doctrines and practices that define the Christian religion. These doctrines continue today, faithfully kept alive in the Catholic Church. Father Langford's interest stems from his own belief that this premise is true.

He has been reading a short time when the curtain to the confessional opens and a person sits down. Both he and the penitent's figures are cloaked in the darkness of the booth and there is only a thin screen and wall that separates them. The priest puts the book on the side of his bench, turns on the confessional's occupied light and speaks,

"Good morning, welcome and let us pray, in the name of the Father, the Son and the Holy Spirit."

There is no answer.

"Do you wish to confess your sins?"

Still no answer...

Fr. Aiden is a bit perplexed, but he assumes that the person is gathering his or her thoughts or is too embarrassed to speak so he asks, "What is troubling you? Do you wish to confess your sins? I am here to help you."

But, as before, there is nothing but silence

"If you do not wish to confess, why are you here?"

"That is a good question, why am I here?"

Father Aiden loves a clandestine penitent for he knows that it will be a benediction for that person if he or she can be forgiven their sins. The priest replies, "Ah, you can speak! This is the first step to helping you to reconcile yourself with God the Father through the blessings of his Son, Jesus Christ. Do not be afraid or embarrassed for I've heard from many who thought they could never be redeemed and they have found their peace through penance and forgiveness and salvation through the love of the Lord."

The man behind the screen answers, "That is most interesting and comforting to hear."

"Well then, let us start, how long has it been since your last confession?" The priest hears a chuckle from behind the screen.

"It has been ages."

"Ages, so I take it that you are lapsed in your faith and in the Holy Church's sacraments."

"Yes, I think lapsed is an appropriate word."

"Well even your absence from the Church of Christ and its sacraments are not enough to separate you from the grace to be found in confessing your sins. That is why we have the sacrament of reconciliation."

"So, you say that God will forgive me my sins. Well, why don't I just go to the top and confess to God."

The priest smiles enjoying the repartee, "God, through his Son Jesus Christ, anointed the Apostles with the power of the Holy Spirit and He said 'whose sins you shall forgive, they are forgiven them; and whose sins you shall retain, they are retained.' As a priest, I am God and Christ's representative on earth and He has given priests the power to hear confession and forgive sins. The power to forgive sins is a part of the power of the priesthood, to be passed on in the sacrament of Holy Orders from generation to generation."

"Sounds like a lot of power."

Fr. Aiden nearly laughs out loud, "It is! Not only that, but God's mercy is infinite and knowing the nature of man and the nature of sin, God will provide a second chance or a third or a fourth or a hundred if necessary for those who might fall victim to the evils of sin. It might be difficult to believe that sin, even the most egregious kind, can be forgiven, but it is true."

"Hmmm, a hundred chances, so if God can forgive a hundred times, He technically can forgive sins a billion times, is that correct?"

Fr. Aiden thinks for a moment, "I suppose God would forgive such a sinner given in that He is infinitely merciful."

"So, that being said, it sounds like a sinner can go about his or her business and commit all the sins they want and come back here and they are forgiven."

"Yes, but that sinner would find himself or herself in a bit of a dilemma."

There seems to be a genuine curiosity of the man in the booth as he says, "Interesting, what is this dilemma you speak of?"

"Well, you will need to figure that the more you sin, the further from God's grace you are and the harder it is to work your way back. Next some of the sins you speak of may be illegal and in that instance the rule of law instituted by governments have their own statutes and punishments which can be severe in and of themselves. Third, because we never know when the Lord may call us home, you may die with a plethora of sins staining your very soul and no one to turn to for forgiveness for it is then too late."

The man speaks to the priest, "And that is when you are condemned to suffer eternal damnation."

The priest responds, "If you die with your soul stained with mortal sins, that is what scripture tells us and that is my understanding."

"Most curious"

Fr. Aiden considers what to say next to the man occupying the confessional. The priest wants all who try to reconcile to leave with hope in promise that they will be forgiven. "No one is beyond forgiveness and punishment given for committing sins, it is simply the way for you satisfy a debt you owe to God and to the authorities as the case may be. This satisfaction can be paid in life with penance, prayer and good works. What the tenets of our faith tell us is that any debt owed to God at the time of our death must be paid in purgatory."

"…or Hell?"

Fr. Aiden is sad when he says, "or Hell."

There is an eerie silence that follows and the priest becomes concerned. "Would you like to take this time to recount your sins, my son?"

"Ah, that would probably take more time than you have."

"Well, let us try anyway. Why not confess your sins for, shall we say the past week?"

"How should I begin?"

"You should begin by saying 'Bless me father for I have sinned" and then recite your sins as best you can remember them."

"Can I reserve using the words 'bless me' until after I tell my sins to you?"

Father Aiden seeks to provide a measure of comfort to the penitent so he says, "If it makes this process easier for you, of course."

"It does…father I have sinned."

The priest continues, "What sins have you committed in the past week?"

The man behind the screen asks, "By the way, are you still obliged not to repeat anything I say in the act of confession?"

"Yes, I, as well as all priests, am bound by the Seal of the Sacrament. The Code of Canon Law states: The sacramental seal is inviolable; therefore, it is absolutely forbidden for a confessor to betray in any way a penitent in words or in any manner and for any reason. The punishment for a violation of this trust is excommunication."

"So, I can tell you anything and you can't say a word to anyone. Is that correct?"

"Yes"

"…and if you reveal what I say you get booted out of the church. Is that correct?"

The priest says, "Yes"

"OK, sounds pretty fair to me so let's continue."

The priest asks again, "What sins have you committed in the past week?"

"Well, to tell the truth they are many and varied in their scope, duration and severity."

"Go on."

"For example, during the past week there was one incident where I murdered 37 people including children. I must admit that it was an enlightening experience, but given that it is sinful in nature I thought I would start there."

It doesn't take, but a few words before Fr. Aiden comes to the realization that the man in the confessional is mentally deranged. Although he has had training in dealing with people who are afflicted with delusions, the priest is in a quandary as to what he should do. Nonetheless he asks, "Why did you murder these people my son?"

"By the way, let's not use the words 'father' or 'son' because you technically can't screw a woman and get her pregnant although, with you priests, I've seen it happen many times before. And let's not have you call me 'son' because if you ever became a father, believe me, you wouldn't want me for a son."

He wants to keep the man talking so Fr, Aiden says, "If that is what you want it is acceptable to me."

"Good, now that it's settled, what's next? Oh yes, why I murdered those people. Well, they were atheists so who cares anyway. As a matter of fact, maybe that's not a sin at all! Maybe God is pleased with me for killing those bastards! What do you think!?"

"My son…sorry, I mean the taking of innocent life can never be condoned least of all by God."

"Then I guess that's a sin. Oh well, onwards and upwards. By the way I have to tell you that I love your British accent." The man in the confessional now tries to speak with a British accent, "Very public school don't you think?"

Fr. Aiden is now getting very nervous as he is anxiously contemplating what to do next. What can he do or say to placate the madness that has overcome this penitent? The priest decides that he would attempt to keep the dialog going so he simply says, "Let us continue, what other sins do you have to confess?"

"Well last week I also was able to assist in the torching of a factory in the city of Dongguan in central Guangdong province. I'm afraid that another 417 people lost their lives. I guess we could have done better, you know taken more lives, but we didn't have the time to plan it properly."

Fr, Aiden asks, "Why did you set fire to the factory?"

"I said I assisted. Someone else actually set the fire."

"But you were there, so why was the fire set at the factory?"

The man thinks for a moment, "I guess you can say we did it for the same reason that Sir Edmond Hillary climbed Mt. Everest…because it was there!"

"So, you're saying that the only reason you assisted burning down a factory and killing 400…"

"417"

The priest corrects himself, "417 people are because they were there?"

"Yes, exactly! It is important for you to understand the nature of this beast. I am a being of infinite needs and if God is infinite in His mercy, I'm hoping He will be gracious enough to bestow His infinite mercy on my infinite needs."

"What about the families of the people you've murdered? Do you expect them to forgive you? What about those in the criminal justice system? Do you expect them to forgive you? God can forgive you and show you His mercy, but you must do penance and your penance will be meted out at the hands of law enforcement."

The man laughs, "Fuck them. Law enforcement, dim witted idiots the whole bunch. What the hell do they know anyway? I can tell you about some of the law enforcement people I've met…"

Fr. Aiden stops the man from speaking, "This is your confession, so let us continue. What other sins do you wish to confess?"

"Good idea priest, why get sidetracked. In the same week…listen, why don't I just tell you that I did a lot of bad stuff, you know beheadings, bombings, murders, rapes, arson, starvation; you know once we starved a group of men, women and children in Africa. Yep, we just shut them in a large room, well more like a cave. They managed to survive for a while, but the first of them died after only 2 days and then the rest just dropped like flies. I once got this guy to embezzle a fortune; unfortunately, the money belonged to some people who really couldn't afford to lose it. Anyway, the good news is that the guy killed himself. I would have done it, but he killed himself before I had the chance."

The man stops speaking, but there is silence from Fr. Aiden.

"Hey, I can see you through this screen, why so quiet?"

"Please continue."

"Like I said, I've committed a lot of sins, got other people to commit them too. It's been a trip I tell you, a real trip. Anyway, I've committed a lot of

what I guess you'd call lesser sins like lying, cheating, stealing, but they don't count right?"

The priest's mind is racing, "All sins, mortal as well as venial, must be confessed before they can be forgiven."

"I've committed many more sins in the past week. The list goes on and on, but I think you get the idea. Remember I said you didn't have enough time to hear them all. Do you believe me now?"

A worried Father Langford says, "I guess I do."

There is a short silence when the man in the confessional says, "How about we discuss something else, say the eternal struggle between good and evil, what do you think?"

"It appears to me that you are in great need of help, the kind of help a doctor can provide. You appear to be undergoing some crises and these crises are manifesting themselves in the delusions you are experiencing. Murder, arson, rape, crimes taking place all over the world, if you truly believe that you have committed these heinous crimes you must try to get the help you need."

The man considers what the priest is saying and responds, "You don't believe I have done these things?"

"Quite frankly, no."

"Why not?"

"Well, I believe that you believe that you have committed these crimes. However, it seems impossible for you to be in so many places around the world and commit so many heinous crimes while your identity remains unknown, especially to the police and other authorities in all those countries."

"What makes you think that my identity is unknown?"

Fr. Aiden is beginning to feel a bit more at ease. He considers that the man in his confessional has not exhibited any violent behavior towards him, at least so far. The priest also considers that in order get the man behind the screen to realize he needs help; he must keep him talking. "I suppose because there would have been reports on the news and you be the focus of a far-reaching manhunt."

"Ah, I see your point, but you are wrong."

"I am?"

"Yes, ever hear of the Lamb of God murders?"

Chills run down Fr. Aiden's spine. "Yes. Are you saying you have something to do with these murders?"

"Yes, and I get by with a little help from my friends." He sings the line from the famous Beatles song.

"Why in God's holy name would you want to say something like that?" Father Aiden Langford is bewildered and stunned that anyone would confess to such horrid crimes.

The man smiles from behind the veil of the screen, "Well, to tell the truth, this is something that's been building up for a long time now. I see it as a way to help redefine the nature of evil in ways that we haven't seen since, well, we've never seen murders quite like these. Of course, I'm not counting the holocaust or the pogroms or the mass exterminations in Germany, Russia, Southeast Asia, the Middle East and China. Those were done by the governments so they are legal and don't count. But in the end, I assure you that the Lamb of God killings will give a whole new meaning to the word genocide."

The priest feels a pain in his chest as his heart is pounding faster.

"Oh, sorry I'd mean to upset you. You've already had a heart attack; I wouldn't want to be responsible for another one."

"What? How…"

"Oh, I know a lot of things. I know that you are considered a biblical scholar so let's have a little discussion. What do you say?"

Fr. Aiden takes a deep breath and reaches for a bottle of water that he has sitting on the shelf next to the seat, "Yes."

"Ah! Glad you are feeling better now where shall we start. Oh, how about Leviticus, who writes, according to scripture, 'Whoever lies with a beast shall surely be put to death.' Sounds pretty extreme to me, after all a goat can be very attractive at times and it's right there in the Bible."

The priest is silent.

"Well come on, tell me what you are thinking?

"God would never have said that, He wound never condone murder."

"So, you say, but let's move on, this one's from scripture according to Exodus, 'Whoever does ANY work on the Sabbath day, he shall surely be put to death.' Sounds pretty extreme to me after all I might want to keep busy, you know an idle mind is the devil's workshop."

"Is it your premise that God would actually condone such a punishment for working on the Sabbath?"

Yep, it's right there in the Bible."

"This is absurd. How can anyone believe that men and women who need to do honest work to provide for their families are removed from the love and mercy of God?"

"Like I said, it's right there in the Bible, but let's continue. It's back to good old Leviticus, 'The adulterer and adulteress shall surely be put to death' sounds like God wants to keep us from having a good time. I like getting laid, don't you? Oh sorry..."

The priest is incredulous, but he knows that if they stop talking the man in the confessional may get violent. He resolves to keep this going until other penitents arrive. "From the beginning of man's knowledge of God, he has been confronted by temptation and, in the hearts of mankind, what he knows to be sinful is sinful in the eyes of God. However, to say that God would put all adulterers to death because they have sinned assumes God is merciless and that is not true in any sense of the word."

"Oh, come on priest let's take a look at what Moses said in Numbers 31: 15-18, 'Have you kept all the women alive? Now therefore kill every male among the little ones; and kill every woman who has known man intimately. But keep alive for yourselves all the young girls...' sounds like Moses was a greedy perv; all the young girls for themselves, and all with God's approval, can you imagine?"

Fr. Aiden is dumbfounded, "What are you suggesting, that God commanded Moses to commit genocide and rape?"

"I'm not suggesting it, the Bible spells it out."

Father Langford hears some movement in the chapel and he feels much safer now that others are around. He takes this opportunity to continue their discussion. "Your selective readings have one commonality, they are from scripture, but they are not of God. They were written by the men at the time, perhaps inspired by Satan, but not of the Lord."

The man chuckles, "Inspired by Satan, not a bad conclusion on your part. I've seen much evil, especially the evil of man and in most instances, I agree with you and I did inspire such sinfulness."

The priest cannot believe what he is hearing, "You? Inspire? What are you saying?"

"Listen priest and listen well, neither God nor His Son can stop the horror I will wreak on mankind; do you understand?"

Fr. Aiden jumps up from the bench and opens the door to the confessional; he throws back the curtain to the penitent's booth to find there is no one there. It is dark, but he detects something scratched in the wall of the wooden enclosure.

He sees the words "Lamb of God" and they are written in blood. The priest grabs his chest and falls to the floor.

AUTHOR MICHAEL MEDICO

Michael Medico was born and grew up in New York City. He attended Power Memorial Academy High School and, on graduation, Mike joined the US Navy and served stateside during the Viet Nam War. After being honorably discharged from the service, Michael attended Pace University and graduated with a degree in Marketing and Advertising.

Michael started his career in advertising and worked at various agencies until in 1980 he founded and ran an agency specializing in direct response marketing for 35 years. Over the years he has written numerous articles published in various trade journals and has been a featured participant on industry panel discussions and workshops.

In 2013 he retired to become a full-time author with "Evil Awaits" being his first novel and Book One in The Sainted Trilogy. He has also written the political satire, "Absolutely, Positively, Genuine, Real Fake News" as well a number of short stories.

Michael and his wife Joan have sons, Anthony and Richard, daughters-in-law, Shannon and Christina and six grandchildren. He and Joan spend time between their homes in Northport, NY and Hallandale Beach, FL.

www.ingramcontent.com/pod-product-compliance
Lightning Source LLC
Chambersburg PA
CBHW070802120726

47910CB00001B/260